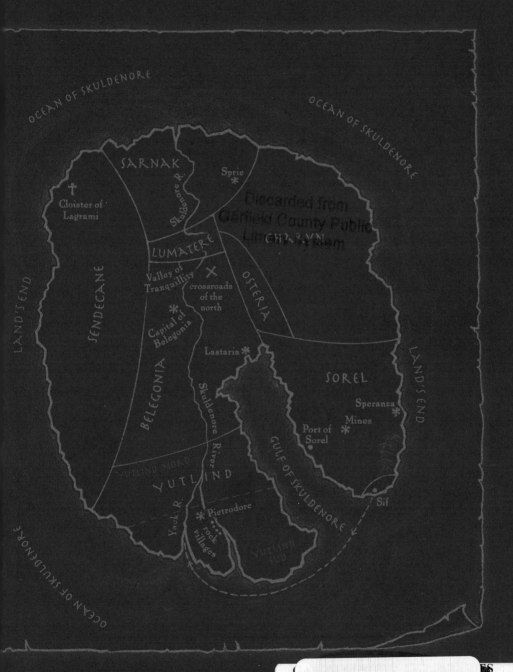

OCEAN OF SKULDENORE

OCEAN OF SKULDENORE

SARNAK

Sprie *

Discarded from
Garfield County Public
Library System

Cloister of
Lagrami †

Skuldenore R.

LUMATERE

LAND'S END

SENDECANE

Valley of
Tranquillity

crossroads
of the
north

OSTERIA

Capital of
Belegonia *

Lastaria *

SOREL

BELEGONIA

Speranza *

Mines
*

Port of
Sorel *

LAND'S END

Skuldenore River

VUTLIND NORD

GULF OF SKULDENORE

VUTLIND

Yack R.

* Pietrodore

rock
villages

Sif

VUTLIND
SUD

OCEAN OF SKULDENORE

# fiNNiKiN
## of the
# ROCK

# fiNNIKiN
## of the
# ROCK

## MELINA MARCHETTA

CANDLEWICK PRESS

Copyright © 2008 by Melina Marchetta
Maps by Cathy Larsen, copyright © 2008 by the Penguin Group (Australia)

First Candlewick Press edition 2010

First published by Viking/Penguin Books (Australia) 2008

Library of Congress Cataloging-in-Publication Data
Marchetta, Melina, date.
Finnikin of the rock / Melina Marchetta. —1st Candlewick Press ed.
p. cm.
Summary: Now on the cusp of manhood, Finnikin, who was a child when the royal family of Lumatere was brutally murdered and replaced by an imposter, reluctantly joins forces with an enigmatic young novice and fellow-exile, who claims that her dark dreams will lead them to a surviving royal child and a way to regain the throne of Lumatere.
ISBN 978-0-7636-4361-4
[1. Fantasy.]   I. Title.
PZ7.M32855Fin 2010
[Fic]—dc22      2009028046

10 11 12 13 14 15 RRC 10 9 8 7 6 5 4 3 2

Printed in Crawfordsville, IN, U.S.A.

This book was typeset in Palatino.

Candlewick Press
99 Dover Street
Somerville, Massachusetts 02144

visit us at www. candlewick.com

*For Marisa and Daniela*
*because I've always loved being a Marchetta sister . . .*

*"If This Is a Man"*

*You who live safe*
*In your warm houses,*
*You who find on returning in the evening,*
*Hot food and friendly faces:*
    *Consider if this is a man*
    *Who works in the mud*
    *Who does not know peace*
    *Who fights for a scrap of bread*
    *Who dies because of a yes or a no.*
    *Consider if this is a woman,*
    *Without hair and without name*
    *With no more strength to remember,*
    *Her eyes empty and her womb cold*
    *Like a frog in winter.*
*Meditate that this came about:*
*I commend these words to you.*
*Carve them in your hearts*
*At home, in the street,*
*Going to bed, rising;*
*Repeat them to your children,*
    *Or may your house fall apart,*
    *May illness impede you,*
    *May your children turn their faces from you.*

—Primo Levi
   Translated by Stuart Woolf

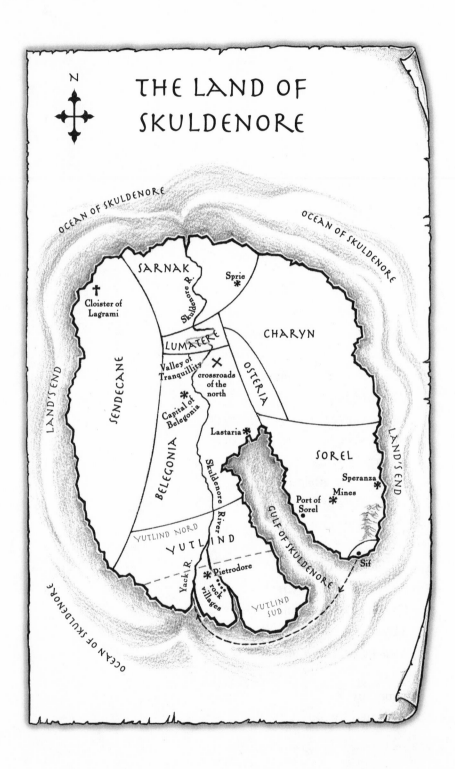

# THE LAND OF SKULDENORE

N

OCEAN OF SKULDENORE

OCEAN OF SKULDENORE

LAND'S END

LAND'S END

OCEAN OF SKULDENORE

SARNAK

Sprie

CHARYN

Cloister of
Lagrami

Skuldenore R.

LUMATERE

Valley of
Tranquillity

crossroads
of the
north

OSTERIA

SENDECANE

Capital of
Belegonia

Lastaria

SOREL

Speranza

Mines

BELEGONIA

Skuldenore River

Port of
Sorel

GULF OF SKULDENORE

YUTLIND NORD

YUTLIND

Yack R.

Pietrodore

rock
villages

Sif

YUTLIND
SUD

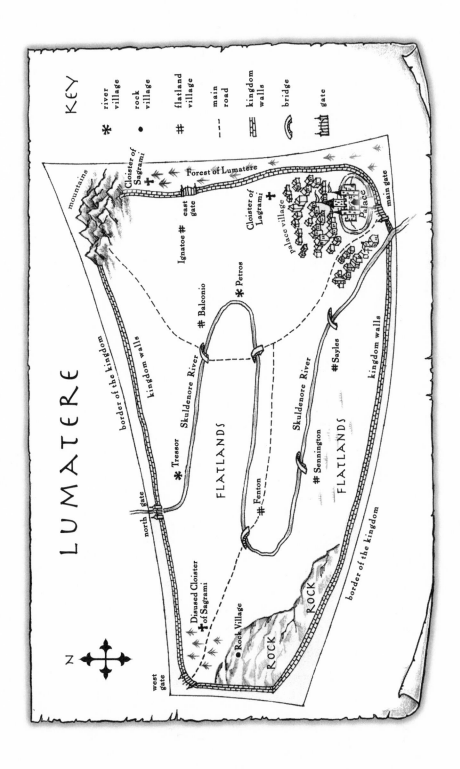

## PROLOGUE

A long time ago, in the spring before the five days of the unspeakable, Finnikin of the Rock dreamed that he was to sacrifice a pound of flesh to save the royal house of Lumatere.

The dream came to him from the gods on the eve of the Harvest Moon Festival, when the whole of the kingdom slept under the stars in the Field of Celebration. It was Finnikin's favorite night of the year, watching his fellow Lumaterans dance and give thanks for a life of peace and plenty. When the dawn broke and the priest-king sang the Song of Lumatere, the joy in people's souls lit up their world. And what a world it was—made up of those hailing from the Flatlands, the Forest, the Rock, the Mountains, and the River. All protected by a beloved king and queen and their five children, said to be descended from the gods themselves.

Finnikin told his friends Prince Balthazar and Lucian of the Monts about the dream the next morning as they spat olive pits into the river. The three boys loved their mornings on the waterfront, watching Finnikin's father, the captain of the King's Guard, as he and his men checked the merchandise on the barges. No one was more formidable than Captain Trevanion when he was protecting the kingdom, and many spoke of his love for the gentle Lady Beatriss of the Flatlands, who would give birth to their child that year, and how she adored Finnikin as if he were her own.

Upon hearing Finnikin's dream that day, Balthazar convinced them that no harm would ever come to Lumatere as long as his father was king. Lucian claimed that if the gods were serious, they would have asked him to protect his royal cousins, for no other reason than that he had turned nine that spring and was a head taller than the others. And so, for a time, the dream was forgotten.

Each afternoon, Finnikin, Balthazar, and Lucian played in the Forest of Lumatere, practicing how they would one day catch the silver wolf. Legend had it that only a true warrior could conquer such a beast, and they were certain that Balthazar, the heir to the throne of Lumatere, would be the one. The three friends spent all summer digging the trap, and when it was finished, they dragged Balthazar's youngest sister, Princess Isaboe, along to be the bait. But the wolf never appeared.

As summer moved into autumn and the days grew shorter, Finnikin began to worry. He would tremble in fear when he remembered his dream. At night he prayed to Lagrami, the goddess of light, to protect his unborn sibling, to keep Balthazar and his four sisters safe, and to watch over the Forest Dwellers, even though they worshipped another goddess and lived outside the kingdom walls. Until one day, finally, he convinced his companions to make a pledge.

And so they climbed the rock of three wonders at the crest of Finnikin's village, and they cut flesh from their bodies and tugged a strand of hair from the weeping Isaboe's head to make a sacrifice to their goddess. Balthazar pledged to die defending his royal house of Lumatere. Finnikin swore to be their protector and guide for as long as he lived. Lucian vowed he would be the light whom they traveled toward in times of need.

That evening, Finnikin and Balthazar sat perched high on the flat *roof of a cottage in the village. As always, they spoke of the silver wolf and the might of a warrior king, and they imagined the years to come when one would rule and one would guard. Finnikin looked down at Princess Isaboe, who slept between them, and although his thigh ached from the pledge wound, he felt peace in his heart that he had done the right thing. They were indeed blessed as no other kingdom in the land.*

*Until the five days of the unspeakable.*

*When the king and queen and their three oldest daughters were slaughtered in the palace and Princess Isaboe was slain in the Forest of Lumatere.*

*When Balthazar's bloody handprints were found splattered on the kingdom walls and the people of Lumatere, seeking someone to blame, turned on one another.*

*When the despised cousin of the dead king entered the kingdom with six hundred of his men and began to burn the Forest Dwellers in their homes.*

*When Captain Trevanion was arrested for treason and sent to a foreign prison and his beloved Lady Beatriss died delivering a stillborn baby in the palace dungeon.*

*When Seranonna, the matriarch of the Forest Dwellers, cried a blood curse as she burned at the stake, a curse that caused the land to shudder and split the earth, that swallowed those who failed to run from the fury of its jaws, that crumbled village homes and shook the palace to its foundations.*

*Those who could escaped to the Valley of Tranquillity, outside the kingdom walls, trampling their neighbors who were left behind. And then the dark forces of the curse entombed the kingdom, dividing the people in two.*

*This is the story, as told to those not born to see such days, recorded in the* Book of Lumatere *so they will never forget.*

*The story of those trapped inside the kingdom, never to be heard from again, and those who escaped but were forced to walk the land in a diaspora of misery.*

*Until ten years later, when Finnikin of Lumatere climbed another rock. . . .*

# part one
## *The Novice*

CHAPTER 1

When it finally appeared in the distance, Finnikin wondered if it was some phantom half-imagined in this soulless kingdom at the end of the world.

There had always been talk that this land had been forsaken by the gods. Yet perched at the top of a rocky outcrop, cloaked in blue-gray mist, was proof to the contrary: the cloister of the goddess Lagrami.

From where they stood, the flat expanse that led to its fortified entrance resembled the softness of sand over a desert. Finnikin could see a trail of pilgrims with their heads bent low, sacks across their shoulders and staffs in their hands. They made a line across the low-lying country like tiny insignificant ants at the mercy of the nothingness surrounding them.

"We must hurry," the king's First Man urged, speaking the Sarnak language. Sir Topher had decided that once they reached this wasteland of Sendecane, they would use the language of the neighboring kingdom to the north. At the inn two nights before, he had made it known that they were pilgrims themselves: holy men who had come to the end of the earth to pay homage at the greatest temple of the blessed goddess Lagrami. To be anything else in this part of the land would raise suspicion and fear, and Finnikin had come to realize that those full of fear were the most dangerous of people.

As they drew closer to the rock, the terrain beneath their feet began to change. What Finnikin had thought was sand turned out to be a thick claylike substance that tested his balance. They were walking on a seabed, and by nightfall the waters would return and there would be no hope of leaving this place until the next low tide.

At the entrance of the rock of Lagrami, they followed the wide stone steps that circled up to the summit, passing the pilgrims kneeling at the shrine of welcome. The leather of Finnikin's boots gave little protection from the cold hard surface, and he found himself looking back to where the pilgrims knelt, knowing that some would make their way up on their knees as a display of devotion to their goddess. He had witnessed the ignorance that came from blind faith time and time again over the years, and he wondered how many of these pilgrims were Lumateran exiles searching for some kind of salvation.

Higher, the steps became stones to climb. Finnikin suspected that sooner or later they would be forced to crawl their way to the top, where the messenger of the High Priestess was surely waiting. Yet not even halfway up, the stones gave way to a smooth cliff face, leaving them nothing to grip except tiny metal bars embedded in the rock. Finnikin stared, confused. He looked down at his oversize feet and wondered how it would be possible to balance them on so narrow a ledge.

"Not for our feet, my boy," Sir Topher said with a sigh. He wiggled his fingers in front of Finnikin's face.

*Mercy.*

"Do not look down," he warned.

4

Sir Topher began to climb, and Finnikin felt a shower of grains from the rocks above as they crumbled under his mentor's weight. One caught him in the eye, and he resisted the urge to wipe it free, preferring to be blinded rather than lose his grip.

"I said, do not look down," Sir Topher grunted, as if reading his thoughts.

"If I look up, I'll lose my dinner," Finnikin gasped.

"And what a pity that would be. All those lovely goose gizzards. All that rabbit pie you insisted on wolfing down despite my warning. All gone to waste."

Finnikin paused, his head spinning and his mouth beginning to taste of a sickly substance. The dull stench of pigeon filled his nostrils and turned the contents of his belly. His hands ached from gripping the metal bars, and he longed to be able to place his feet flat against the rock. Yet this journey up the cliff face had to be worth it. Somehow the High Priestess had located him and Sir Topher in the kingdom of Belegonia. Not an easy feat when most of the time they chose not to be found.

For the past ten years, Sir Topher and Finnikin had worked to improve the conditions of Lumaterans living in overcrowded camps rife with fever, fear, and despair. Former dukes of Lumatere, now employed in foreign courts, had often requested their presence, eager to fund their efforts to bring a reprieve to their people. Less welcome were the approaches from foreign kings and queens, who always seemed to have a price for their goodwill. Often it was information about what was taking place in a neighboring kingdom in exchange for palace protection for the exiles camped along their riverbanks and valleys. While protocol ensured that the king's First Man and his apprentice were granted access to any court in the land, Sir Topher had learned to be cautious when it came to accepting invitations.

But this one had been different. It began with a name

whispered to Finnikin deep in the night as he lay sleeping among
the exiles in Belegonia.

*Balthazar.*

Finnikin had dragged Sir Topher from his sleep in an instant.
He could hardly describe the messenger to his mentor. He could
only remember the voice in his ear and the disappearing robes of
one who spoke of the isolated cloister of Sendecane. The moment
Finnikin had finished speaking, Sir Topher rose from his bedroll
and packed it without a word.

Finnikin reached the summit of the cliff first and stayed draped
over the stone, trying to regain his breath before leaning across to
help Sir Topher, who was wheezing and hungering for air. Hearing
a sound behind them, they turned to where a wizened old novice
stood before an opening in the wall. When she shuffled around
and disappeared into the confines of the cloister, they understood
that they were to follow.

Finnikin's lanky frame meant he was forced to crouch through
the damp tunnel, which led to a set of narrow spiral stairs. When
they reached the top, they followed the old woman along a hall-
way, past rooms where other novices knelt in prayer. They crossed
the cloister and entered a large chamber with high windows that
let in the light. This room interested Finnikin greatly. There were
rows and rows of tables where novices sat, absorbed in their work.
Some were poring over bound manuscripts, copying their contents, while others read. Finnikin had seen a room like this before,
at the palace of Osteria. The manuscripts there held records of
each kingdom of the land: their gods and goddesses, their wars,
their origins, their landscape, their language, their art, their food,
their lives.

As a child in exile, Finnikin had worried that his kingdom
would have no further record of existence, so he began his own

work on the *Book of Lumatere*. He wondered if these scholars felt the same way he did about the scent of parchment and the feel of a quill in their hands. But their faces revealed little, and the old novice's pace began to quicken, leading them into a dimly lit room full of columns. And there, in the middle of the room, stood the High Priestess.

"Blessed Kiria." Sir Topher bowed and kissed her hand.

"You have come a long way, Sir Topher."

Finnikin heard the note of surprise in her voice, almost wonder. Like all priestesses of Lagrami, her hair was worn long, almost to her knees, marking her years of devotion to her goddess. Upon her death, the braid would be cut and offered as a sacrifice, while somewhere else in the land a novice would enter the cloister, her hair shorn and her journey begun.

"The Lumateran pilgrims who have made their way to us over the years have taken courage in the existence of the king's First Man and his young apprentice," she said, looking at them both.

"It is good of you to acknowledge our cursed people, blessed Kiria," Sir Topher said.

She smiled warmly. "We are neighbors, despite the distance. I feel anguish for your beloved priest-king, to have lost his people in such a way, and I am here as a servant to your people as much as to mine. It is the wish of our goddess."

"Do you have the good fortune to know of our priest-king's whereabouts?" Sir Topher asked.

The High Priestess shook her head sadly. Then her expression changed and she walked farther into the room, beckoning them to follow. "You have come for the girl?" she asked.

*Girl.* Finnikin's heart dropped. He had hoped; *stupidly* he had hoped. The fury he felt for harboring such a dream made him sway on his feet.

"We have little time before the tide rises, so I will speak quickly," she said in a low voice. "Two springs past, a girl came to us. Her name, Evanjalin. Unlike many of our Lumateran novices, she was not orphaned during the five days of the unspeakable but belonged to the exiles in Sarnak."

Finnikin flinched and closed his eyes. When he opened them again, he saw that Sir Topher had paled. The High Priestess nodded. "I see that you are well aware of the ill-fated exiles in Sarnak."

"We have petitioned the king of Sarnak to have those responsible for the massacre brought to justice," Sir Topher said.

Finnikin wondered why they had wasted their time. The slaughter of a group of Lumateran exiles, two years past, was of little concern to an apathetic king.

The High Priestess leaned forward to whisper. "The novice Evanjalin has a gift, and I promise you this: in my time I have come across many who claim to have extraordinary gifts, but I know this girl speaks the truth. She professes to have walked through the sleep, not only of your beloved heir, but of your people trapped inside Lumatere."

It was one of the most fanciful stories they had heard to date, and Finnikin bit his tongue to hold back a contemptuous retort.

"It is not that we are surprised by the notion of Prince Balthazar being alive," Sir Topher said carefully, clearing his voice as a warning to Finnikin. "It has always been our hope that there was truth in the tales that the heir survived. But these past ten years, there have been many claims to the Lumateran throne across the land. Each one has proved to be false. You are aware that as a consequence, the ruler of each kingdom of Skuldenore has decreed it treason to make such claims."

"Yet I hear that no Lumateran acknowledges the reign of the

king trapped behind those walls," the High Priestess said. "Is he not referred to as the impostor king?"

"Despite our belief that the one ruling inside Lumatere played a role in the deaths of our beloveds, as far as the leaders of Skuldenore are concerned, he was legitimately crowned the king."

*A hasty decision made by those controlled by fear, who dared to meddle in the affairs of another kingdom,* Finnikin thought bitterly.

"If you are to believe anything, believe this," she said firmly. "The rightful heir to the throne of Lumatere and survivor of that wretched night has spoken to the novice Evanjalin."

"Does the novice have a message from him?" Sir Topher asked.

"Just a name," the High Priestess said, "of a childhood companion of your prince. A trusted friend."

Suddenly every pulse in Finnikin's body pounded. He felt the eyes of both the High Priestess and Sir Topher on him. Then the High Priestess came closer, taking his face between her callused hands.

"Is that what you were to him, Finnikin of the Rock?" she said softly. "For I do believe your king is calling. It has been ten years too long and Balthazar has chosen you, through this girl, to take your people home."

"Who is she to be worthy of the association with our heir?" Finnikin asked stiffly, moving away. "Does she claim to have made his acquaintance?"

"She is a simpleton. She has taken the vow of silence, broken only to tell me of the sleep and that you, Finnikin, would one day come to collect her. I believe she is somehow promised to your heir."

"What makes you believe such a thing, blessed Kiria?" Sir Topher asked.

"At night she whispers his name in her sleep with intimacy and reverence. As if their bond is ordained by the gods."

This time Finnikin failed to hold back the sound of his disbelief.

The High Priestess smiled sadly. "You have lost faith in the gods."

He held her gaze and knew she could read the confirmation in his eyes.

"Do you believe in magic?" she persisted.

"My kingdom has been impenetrable for the past ten years with no logical explanation, so I have no choice but to say I do believe," he admitted ruefully.

"It was indeed a very dark magic used by the matriarch of the Forest Dwellers. Made up mostly of hatred and grief for what Lumaterans had allowed to happen to her people in the days following the deaths of the king and his family. But somehow some kind of good survived, and the novice Evanjalin is the key. You would know by now the meaning of the archaic words spoken by Seranonna that day."

Finnikin had not heard the name Seranonna since his child-hood. He did not want her to be known as anything other than the witch who had cursed Lumatere.

"We were in the square that day," Sir Topher said, "and have spent these past ten summers deciphering the curse, but there are words we are still unsure of. Seranonna used more than one of the ancient languages."

"And those words you do understand?" the High Priestess asked. She stared at Finnikin, waiting for him to speak.

" 'Dark will lead the light, and our *resurdus* will rise.' It's the ancient word for king, is it not? *Resurdus*?"

The High Priestess nodded. "The curse was to condemn

Lumaterans for allowing the slaughter of her people, but it was also to protect the one she claimed to have seen fleeing from the forest that night. The *resurdus*. The heir. The dark and light will lead you to him."

"But where are we supposed to take this . . . child? Evanjalin?" Finnikin asked.

The High Priestess gave a small humorless laugh. "Do you consider yourself a child, Finnikin?"

"Of course not."

"The novice Evanjalin is nearly your age and left her childhood behind far too early."

"Where are we to take her, blessed Kiria?" Sir Topher prompted gently.

The High Priestess hesitated. "She claims that the answers lie in the kingdom of Sorel."

*Mercy.* Finnikin would have preferred to have heard Sarnak or Yutlind. Even Charyn with its barbaric ways. He would have preferred to take her to hell. It would certainly be less dangerous than Sorel.

"And you believe Balthazar will contact us there?" Sir Topher said.

"I do not know what to believe. The goddess has not bestowed the gift of foresight on me. All I can pass on is this girl and the name of the one she claimed would come for her." Once again her eyes were on Finnikin. "Perhaps both chosen by a missing king to be his guide."

There was a sound by the door, and the High Priestess held out her hand as a figure appeared from the shadows.

The girl had the coloring of the Lumateran Mont people, a golden skin tone, much darker than Finnikin's own fair skin. Her hair was shaved, but he imagined that if it were allowed to grow, it would match the darkness of her eyes. Dressed in a gray shift made of coarse fabric, she would easily be passed by without a second glance.

"Sir Topher, Finnikin, I present to you the novice Evanjalin."

She cast her eyes down, and Finnikin watched as her hands shook and then clenched.

"What is it you fear?" he asked in Lumateran.

"Most of her time was spent in Sarnak," the High Priestess explained. "It is the language we have used during the break of silence."

Finnikin could no longer hold back his frustration. He pulled Sir Topher aside. "We know nothing of her," he said in Belegonian to ensure the novice and the High Priestess would not understand. "This is all too strange."

"Enough, Finnikin," Sir Topher said firmly. He turned back to the High Priestess. "Has she spoken since?"

She shook her head. "She has taken the vow of silence. She has suffered much, Sir Topher, and her faith is strong. It's the least we can leave her with."

Sir Topher nodded. "If we are to make the tide, we must leave soon."

Finnikin was stunned at how swiftly Sir Topher had made his decision, but the look in the older man's eyes warned him not to protest. Biting his tongue, Finnikin watched as the High Priestess took the girl's head in her hands and pressed her lips tenderly to her forehead. He saw the girl's eyes close and her mouth tremble, but then her face became impassive again and she walked away from the High Priestess without a backward glance.

The descent was as nauseating as the climb up, made worse for Finnikin by the burden he carried in his heart. Taking this girl halfway across the land had not been part of the plan he and Sir

Topher had worked out in the early days of winter. The uncertainty of their new path did not sit well with him.

When they reached the base of the cliff, they passed the group of kneeling pilgrims. A hand snaked out to grab the cloth of the novice's cloak.

"Your feet," Finnikin said, noticing for the first time that she was barefoot. "We can't afford to be slowed down because you don't have shoes."

But the girl did not respond and continued walking. It was only when they were a good distance from the cloister that she looked back and he saw the raw emotion of loss on her face. By then the waters reached their knees and Finnikin feared they would not make it to safety without being washed away. Here, the tide was said to return at amazing speed and pilgrims had drowned without any warning. He grabbed her arm and pulled her forward, and suddenly her look of vulnerability disappeared and in its place was a flash of triumph.

As if somehow the novice Evanjalin had gotten her way.

## CHAPTER 2

In the days that followed, cold winds gnawed at their bones and a winter that refused to end kept the days short and darkness a constant companion. Sir Topher decided that the best route to Sorel would be to cross into Sarnak and follow the road through Charyn. Although the quickest route was down through Belegonia, Sir Topher argued that they would not return to Sarnak for at least another year and there was a chance they would encounter survivors from the massacre. On this point Finnikin agreed; it was their destination he could not accept.

"We're making a mistake," he said on the third morning, forced now to dress behind a tree. He pulled on his buckskin trousers and then his boots, tucking a tiny dagger next to his calf.

"As you have now mentioned for the tenth time, Finnikin," Sir Topher called out with maddening patience.

Finnikin had come to appreciate Sir Topher's patience over the years, ever since he had been placed in his care by Perri the Savage, his father's second-in-charge. Today, however, there was more irritation than appreciation.

"Sorel," he muttered as he stepped out from behind the tree. "No one goes to Sorel. No exile would set up camp in Sorel. Not even the people of Sorel want to live in Sorel."

"Let's accept our path, Finnikin, and hold our tongue, as the novice does so beautifully," Sir Topher replied.

The girl did little to lessen Finnikin's frustration. At night he watched her toss in her bedroll as though possessed by demons, crying, gritting her teeth, calling out with such despair. As they trekked across the flat treeless earth, sometimes her body would slump as if what she dreamed was weighing down her spirit. Other times there was a spring in her step and a soft dreamy smile on her lips, as if she was remembering a moment so happy that it effortlessly carried her over the cold barren land.

Deep down, Finnikin knew there was something more to his unease than this strange girl traveling with them. The mention of the heir had awoken memories, and with them came a restlessness, a sense of futility about the future. In the past ten years, the pages of the dead in the *Book of Lumatere* had grown. There were those who had been slain in Sarnak, those who had died in a plague village in Charyn, those who had drowned when the floods in Belegonia swept over the river camps. Without their own healers, there were no cures for the ailments that others in the land seemed to easily survive.

When they crossed the border into Sarnak, there was little relief from the weather, but a hot meal was more readily available and Finnikin was glad to be able to leave behind the stale bread and moldy cheese that had been their staple diet for over a week. Trees and shrubs began to appear beside the road, and as they continued east, they found themselves in thick woodland, where they decided to camp.

———

That night, as Sir Topher pored over the map, Finnikin caught the girl staring at the sword that lay by his saddlebag.

"It's my father's," he said gruffly. He pulled it out of its scabbard. The grip was plain, except for a stone—a ruby, rich and bright—embedded in the handle. As a child, Finnikin had imagined it had powers. He believed anything Trevanion touched did. The novice reached out and placed a finger on the stone.

"The ruby is the official stone of Lumatere. Did you know that?" Sir Topher asked, looking up from his map.

In response, the novice dug her hand deep into her pocket and withdrew a ruby ring. She gently traced its contours, then extended her hand as if offering it to Finnikin to take. When he made no attempt to touch it, Sir Topher reached over and examined it instead. Finnikin could see from the warmth in her eyes that the ring held memories much the same as his father's sword did. At the thought of his father, he was suddenly swamped by a wave of grief. Standing abruptly, he grabbed the crossbow and disappeared into the woods.

Later, Finnikin emerged from the forest with two fair-sized hares. With little fuss, the novice took one of the hares and sat by the fire, cutting into the skin and stripping it from the body of the dead animal with ease. As Finnikin watched, she wiped her brow, leaving a streak of blood across her face. Feeling his gaze on her, she looked up, and in the flickering light of the fire, he saw a fierceness in her eyes that no humble dress or pious look could disguise.

Sir Topher was melancholy that night, and the mead they had secured in the border town had loosened his tongue. Finnikin knew that in this state, Sir Topher would drink and talk. Always about the five days of the unspeakable. Finnikin loved this man dearly and knew he would be dead if not for his mentor's kindness, but when Sir Topher spoke of those days, Finnikin wanted to shout at him to stick to facts and plans. Facts and plans had results. The days of the unspeakable were impossible to explain or to solve. Finnikin had learned over the years not to think of anything beyond the practicalities of getting from one point to another. To focus on the achievable. Locating a piece of land for the exiles of Lumatere was achievable. But only if they could find a benevolent host, and he knew in his heart that the kingdom of Belegonia was the place. Most of the time Sir Topher agreed, except when he was drinking mead and succumbing to memory.

The girl showed interest in Sir Topher's story. She put aside the half-skinned hare and kept his words flowing by refilling his cup each time it emptied. Sir Topher relished the opportunity to tell the tale again.

"Does she need to know?" Finnikin asked at one point, not looking up.

"The silence that meets us in every exile camp is a paralysis that has been passed on to the next generation," Sir Topher said reprovingly.

And so Finnikin heard it again. How the enemy had come in the dead of the night. How they were never able to explain how the assassins had managed to get past the guards, for it was only five days later that the kingdom gates became impenetrable, and questions stayed unanswered. Some said the assassins were in Lumatere long before that night, hiding and plotting to sweep through the palace and take the lives of every single inhabitant: the cooks, the guards, the ladies-in-waiting, the pages, the nurse-maids, the groundsmen. Sir Topher had been sent to Belegonia with the ambassador on palace business and had lived with the guilt of surviving ever since.

It was Trevanion, captain of the King's Guard and Finnikin's father, who made the gruesome discovery. At the second change of guard, he returned and found the first man dead at the palace entrance. A path of bodies led to the grand hall where the king, queen, and three older princesses were found slain. A desperate search for Balthazar and Isaboe followed. Balthazar alive meant the survival of Lumatere. It meant that no stranger would dare enter the kingdom and claim it as theirs. The King's Guard searched every house in the palace village, every square inch of the Flatlands, crossed the mountains, searched the Rock Village, and scoured the caves. Finally, they left the confines of the kingdom walls and there they saw it, in the cold light of the rising sun. A small bloody handprint on the outside wall of their fortress. As if Balthazar had been hammering all night long to reenter a world that had already ceased to be.

Sir Topher stopped speaking, and Finnikin looked up. As always, there were tears on the face of the king's First Man as he relived the horror of what they found in the Forest of Lumatere that day. Limbs and flesh, clumps of hair, and finally the blood-soaked clothing of the youngest princess, Isaboe.

The novice Evanjalin barely seemed to breathe. Her hands were clasped under her chin as if in prayer, but unlike Finnikin, who could not bear to hear more, her eyes begged Sir Topher to continue.

"In the Forest of Lumatere lived the worshippers of Sagrami, the goddess of night," Sir Topher said, composing himself. "In centuries past they were persecuted and forced to live outside the kingdom walls. Many were healers, mystics, and empaths, with gifts that could not be explained, but over the years, they had begun to work and live among their fellow Lumaterans again.

"The matriarch of the Forest Dwellers was a powerful woman named Seranonna. She was once the wet nurse to the queen, and there was a bond between them that the king honored for the love of his wife.

"But on the morning after the slaughter, Seranonna was found with her hands and clothes soaked with blood. Grief-stricken Lumaterans said it belonged to the youngest princess, that somehow the Forest Dwellers were involved in a sacrifice using the blood of the royal children. The Forest Dwellers claimed that at least two of their people had seen Balthazar running through the forest that night, and that in her search for him, Seranonna had found the remains of Isaboe and tried to gather up the pieces. It was for this reason, they swore, that Seranonna had the blood of the child stained in the lifelines on the palms of her hands.

"But the villagers would not listen. Their king was dead. A king directly descended from the gods. His beloved queen of the Mont people dead. His beautiful daughters raped, slaughtered. His youngest daughter torn to shreds. His son, the heir, missing. His palace guards and people slain. And so the Lumateran people rounded up all those who worshipped Sagrami within the kingdom walls and burned down their homes, forcing them out into the Forest of Lumatere with the rest of their people. Neighbors fought neighbors. Cattle were slaughtered. Crops were burned. It was a world gone mad."

Finnikin had watched it all from the Rock Village, clutched in the arms of his great-aunt Celestina. "It's the end of the world, Finnikin," she had chanted. "The end of the world."

"On the second day, the king's cousin rode into Lumatere with six hundred men, most of them Charynites," Sir Topher continued. "He had been serving in the Charyn court for almost ten years. With the blessing of the remaining rulers of Skuldenore, who were desperate to keep peace in the region, he was appointed the new king of Lumatere.

"The impostor's first decree? Any worshipper of the goddess Sagrami was to be put to death for treason. Those known for practicing dark magic were to be burned at the stake. The Lumateran people were horrified. There was a difference between running the worshippers of Sagrami out of their homes and killing them. But they stood and watched what they had started. One by one over the next three days, men, women, and children were slaughtered, burned in their homes in the Forest of Lumatere. Until the people of Lumatere dreamed crimson dreams and could not walk out of their own homes for the stench of death that blew over their kingdom."

The novice closed her eyes, even covered her ears for a moment. Finnikin knew there were parts of this story she may never have heard before. No one spoke of those days in any of the exile camps he and Sir Topher visited. Their guilt and despair kept them silent.

"Lumaterans began to leave in droves," Sir Topher went on. "The Monts, the queen's people, had already left, gathering every one of their kin and moving them to the safety of the Valley of Tranquillity, outside the kingdom walls, to wait. The noblemen and women of the Flatlands joined them, fearing they would be next on the impostor's list. Some convinced those in their villages to travel with them. The elders of the Rock Village forbade their people to leave. Strategically, they were the safest, perched high, overlooking the whole kingdom. Many of the River clans followed their Flatland neighbors, while others traveled up the river to Sarnak to seek refuge there until the trouble subsided. By the end of the third day, more than half of Lumatere could be found outside the kingdom walls, either in the Valley of Tranquillity or in Sarnak.

"The next day, the captain of the King's Guard was called forward to swear allegiance to the new king. In Lumatere, tradition dictated that all should kneel in the presence of the king. Except for the King's Guard. Since the time the gods walked the earth, the King's Guard of Lumatere would lie prostrate at the feet of their leader when first in his presence.

"That day, Captain Trevanion refused. It was his belief that the impostor's hands were soaked with the blood of the innocent. And in revenge for the disrespect shown by the captain, the impostor king's men arrested Lady Beatriss, accusing her of treason aided by Trevanion. You see, on the night of the royal murders, the only palace dweller to survive was Beatriss, lady-in-waiting to the princesses. How did she survive such carnage? the impostor king asked. How did the assassins enter a guarded palace if not through the captain of the King's Guard? Of course, deep down, the people of Lumatere did not believe that Beatriss and Trevanion had had anything to do with the murders, but by then everything was in turmoil.

"In front of Trevanion," Sir Topher said, "they tortured her. I heard her screams. They tortured her until Trevanion confessed to treason, confessed to anything, for he knew they would come for his son next."

Finnikin clenched his fist, his fingernails digging into his palms. He watched the novice flinch as if she felt the impact of his nails herself.

"Beatriss was sentenced to death, Trevanion exiled. Some say the king of neighboring Belegonia intervened to save Trevanion's life. But others had a different theory. They thought the impostor king feared an uprising by Trevanion's men. He knew that while their captain was still alive, they would not act."

Finnikin busied himself with cleaning the crossbow. He tried not to think of what took place after his father was taken away. At times it felt like a blur, while other times he remembered it with complete clarity.

"On the fifth day, they dragged Seranonna into the town

square. She was the last of the Forest Dwellers to be put to death, and there was talk that Lady Beatriss would be hanged next. Seranonna's clothes and hands were soaked with blood. Some believed it belonged to the dead child she had delivered of Lady Beatriss in the palace dungeon. Others said it was still Isaboe's blood.

"I was there in the crowd," Sir Topher told the girl. "My king always believed we should not turn our backs on our people as they suffered. I don't think anyone understood the rage Seranonna felt for what had been done to her people. Nor did they understand the extent of her grief for the queen and the royal children."

Finnikin remembered how they dragged Seranonna into the square and she screamed with fury. Screamed the words, *"Beatriss the Beloved is dead!"* And the wails rose around him while Finnikin shook with fear at the sound of her voice. He had heard that voice before. She had spoken to him as he played with Isaboe in the Forest of Lumatere. Spoken words that had haunted him for most of his life.

"And then from her mouth came a curse so fierce that it split the earth," Sir Topher said. "People were screaming, and those not even an arm's length from me disappeared into the crack before it shuddered closed once more. Others ran for the path that led to the main gate. Cottages that were built high over the main road collapsed on top of those fleeing. I saw the blacksmith's entire family disappear beneath the rubble of bricks and mud. Many were trampled trying to reach the gate."

Finnikin shuddered. He remembered the Flatlander who had been holding the rope to keep the gate open, urging his terrified family through. As the gate began to shut, the rope tore at the farmer's hands, and his wife and son were forced to let go. But the man's daughter would not leave him, and Finnikin's last image of Lumatere, as he slid beneath the jaws of the iron gate, was of a family separated. Then nothing. No sounds from the other side. And then a black mist appearing above the kingdom.

Finnikin felt Evanjalin's eyes on him as Sir Topher put his head in his hands.

"Cursed land. Cursed people."

Slowly Evanjalin picked up the hare again and resumed removing the skin, her hands shaking.

*Speak,* Finnikin wanted to shout at her. *Lay blame. Shout. Rage. Rage!*

"I think I may have frightened her," Sir Topher murmured in Belegonian.

"You frightened me," said Finnikin.

The fire crackled. Beyond it, the novice Evanjalin continued with her task.

"This year will be our last traveling, Finnikin. If he is alive, Balthazar will have come of age these past two years. If he hasn't appeared by now, he never will."

"You've never believed that he survived," Finnikin said. "She's lying."

"For what reason?"

"A Charyn spy? A vengeful Forest Dweller? Perhaps she believes we will lead her to the heir, so she can kill him out of revenge for her people."

Sir Topher placed a finger to his lips. Their tone was too obvious and they knew little of this girl. "She looks too much like a Mont," he said, switching to Osterian. "The Forest Dwellers were as fair as you, Finnikin. Perhaps she just wants to get home to her people and knows that the only way to survive such a journey is under our protection."

Finnikin felt his agitation rise. "This is a mistake, Sir Topher. We've never trusted anyone to travel with us. *Never.*"

"Yet your eyes stray to her frequently, my boy."

"Out of fury," Finnikin argued. "We could be doing something of worth. We were summoned to the cloister believing there was *someone* of worth."

*Like Balthazar,* he wanted to say. Unlike Sir Topher, he had allowed himself to believe that the messenger would lead them to his beloved friend. And now here they were, burdened with this insignificant girl. Finnikin's resentment toward her clawed at him.

"I thought you liked them fragile," Sir Topher said, smiling. "I saw how you flirted with Lord Tascan's daughter, Lady Zarah."

"I prefer them sweet, not simple, and I like to hear their voices," Finnikin corrected. "And a little refinement would be nice."

He looked sideways at the novice. She was removing the entrails of the hare, her tongue resting between her teeth in her deep concentration. *A simpleton indeed,* Finnikin thought bitterly.

They ate dinner in silence. Later, the girl sat with her arms around her knees, shivering. Perhaps Sir Topher was right and the story she had been told would plague her sleep. In that way they were the same, Finnikin mused, for lately his sleep no longer seemed to belong to him. Usually his dreams were of the river, of traveling down it in a barge with his father. Other times he dreamed of Lady Beatriss and her soft lulling voice and the love he had seen between her and Trevanion. But from the moment the messenger had arrived to summon them to the cloister in Sendecane, Finnikin's dreams had been filled with carnage. And tonight he was consumed with images of the novice Evanjalin, her hands soaked with the blood of the hare, screaming as she was burned alive. Screaming the name that had escaped her lips each night this past week.

*Balthazar.*

## CHaPteR 3

T he town of Sprie in Sarnak reeked of rotten berries and boiled cabbage. Filth was embedded between the cobblestones beneath their feet and grime seemed to invade their skin. It was the last town before the Charyn border, and Sir Topher and Finnikin agreed that it was safer to buy provisions here than to stop in any Charyn town. Nevertheless, Finnikin sensed malevolence around him. Apart from Lumatere, Sarnak had suffered the most in the past ten years, and the fury of its people toward Lumateran exiles was boundless. Once, the Skuldenore River had flowed through Lumatere into Belegonia and Yutlind, and each day, the best of Sarnak produce was sent down the busy waterway into the rest of the land. Sarnak's climate was perfect for growing almost anything, from succulent mangoes to sweet plump grapes. Their fresh river trout had graced the tables of kings and queens.

But without a trade route, such produce meant little. After the five days of the unspeakable, the river through Lumatere had disappeared into a whirl of fog, and the only passage now from Sarnak to the rest of the land was west into Sendecane or east into

Charyn: one a wasteland, the other an enemy. Outside the exile camps, the poverty in Sarnak was the worst in the land, and two years past, armed Sarnak civilians had unleashed their wrath on Lumaterans camped on their southern border, a slaughter the king of Sarnak refused to acknowledge or condemn. And why would he, Finnikin thought, when there was no one to demand it except the First Man of a slain king and his apprentice from a kingdom that no longer existed?

On their first night in Sarnak, Sir Topher chose a place to set up camp deep in the woods. They would use it merely as a resting point to collect provisions and then move on. There would be no fire to keep them warm. Nothing to draw attention to themselves. Nothing to make them prey to a desperate people who needed someone to blame for their suffering.

Sir Topher and Finnikin made careful plans. They were not like the exiles who huddled in camps, waiting for someone to return them to Lumatere or for the captain of the King's Guard to escape and save the day. Finnikin knew that if they wanted their people to survive, they needed strategies that would push them forward. Despite their detour into Sendecane and the presence of the novice and her extraordinary claim, he and Sir Topher were on a mission to find a piece of land for the exiles. And they always had a plan. Never a dream.

Sir Topher decided that Finnikin would go to the marketplace to purchase enough food to see them through to Sorel.

"Take the girl," Sir Topher said. "They worship Lagrami here. They're less likely to bother a novice and her companion. But don't let her out of your sight."

The town was a labyrinth of stalls and alleyways. More than once the novice seemed to become disoriented and wander in the wrong direction.

"Listen," Finnikin said firmly. "Stay close and do not lose sight of me. Do you understand? Nod if you understand."

She nodded, but he wasn't satisfied.

"This whistle, I want you to listen for it in case we do get lost." He whistled a birdlike tune. Twice. Just to be sure she understood. He watched her for a reaction, but there was none.

"I don't expect you to learn it. But listen for it."

She nodded again.

The sun was beginning to disappear, and vendors were packing up their wares. Finnikin walked over to purchase their supplies. A few moments later, he heard a furious cry and turned to see a young boy disappear into one of the alleyways. As he turned back to the vendor, he saw the novice stumble to her feet in a daze, but before he could call out to her, she was off in pursuit of the youth.

*Stupid, stupid girl.* In a moment's frustration, he hesitated. It was a perfect opportunity to leave her behind so he and Sir Topher could continue on their way as planned. His mentor had promised him they would go searching for Trevanion's men this autumn. This was his chance to go south, where a group of exiles had once reported seeing the Guard. But Lumatere had lost enough of its people to Sarnak, and before he could stop himself, he threw down his coins and raced after her.

Within a short distance, the alleyway branched out into a cluster of five others, each already seeped in darkness, indistinguishable from one another. Using instinct, Finnikin took the middle one, a mistake he realized too late when he found himself turning into yet another, which seemed to fork out into more and then more—never-ending high stone walls that seemed to conquer the light of the moon, forcing him to turn back until he lost track of where he had begun.

"Evanjalin!"

He caught sight of a flicker of her robe as she disappeared around a bend. He had smelled her fear when they arrived, had sensed the memory of her family's death in Sarnak in every tremble of her body.

The light was disappearing fast. He called out her name as he ran after her, but there was desperation in her movements as she disappeared again and again. Finally she was brought to a stop by a dead end. But there was someone in the shadows, and before Finnikin could reach her, she was flung to the ground. Her assailant looked no more than fourteen or fifteen. Finnikin pulled Trevanion's sword from its scabbard in an attempt to scare the boy rather than wound him.

Suddenly he felt the cold sharp tip of steel pressed against his neck. He felt little fear. From the moment he was born, Trevanion had taught him to fight, a skill Sir Topher made sure he continued to develop as they traveled from kingdom to kingdom. But when he turned, he could see four of them. Sensing that Evanjalin was no threat, the thieves had made Finnikin their target.

"Drop it!"

*Not likely,* he thought. He looked to where Evanjalin lay. When she raised herself onto her hands and knees, the youth shoved her and she fell again, whimpering. The young thief hammered her across the temple while holding her to the ground. Then he straddled her and began to search through the folds of her clothing, as if looking for something else of worth. This was why Sir Topher preferred they travel alone. No one to fear for. No one to protect. The girl would be their weak point until they left her in Sorel.

"Drop it!" The order came again.

Without taking his eyes off the novice, Finnikin reluctantly placed his sword on the ground and kicked it across the cobblestones. It stopped a few meters short of the girl's feet, and he felt impotent rage as he watched the boy continue to fumble under her shift.

"Pockets first!"

"We have nothing. . . ."

The sword at his neck moved to his cheek. He felt it pierce his skin, and a trickle of blood make its way down his face. But he tried to keep his eyes on what was taking place with Evanjalin and saw the boy leap up and disappear into the night.

Evanjalin screamed the moment she saw his bloody face. Finnikin knew the odds were against them. Four men, all armed; his sword out of reach at the feet of a hysterical girl; and three knives tucked securely away. One on his sleeve, one in his boot, the other on his back.

"Tell the girl to stop the screaming!"

Finnikin willed her to stop. He needed to think. *Quickly.* Sword at her feet. Three knives on his person. Four men with weapons of their own.

"Stop her screaming, boy, or it's her throat first."

"Evanjalin!" he called out. "Stop!"

But the novice was too far gone, and her screams turned into piercing wails.

*Think, Finnikin, think.* Knife to the throat of the one closest to him. Other knife hurled at the man who was now standing guard at the entrance of the alleyway. Grab the sword of the one closest to him and plunge it into the third man, but that left one more and he knew that he would be dead before the second knife left his hands.

His head rang with her screams. No words, just sounds. Earsplitting.

"Evanjalin!" he called out again. And then he saw the man on watch advancing toward her.

"No!" he yelled, trying to push past the three men surrounding him. "She's simple. She doesn't understand."

He succeeded in shaking free, but he knew it would not be for long. And yet that was all it took. One moment the novice was screaming, and in the next, the moon bathed her face with light and he caught a look in her eye that spoke little of fear and more of rage. Before he knew it, Finnikin's sword was kicked toward him as she grabbed the man's sword at his hip and plunged it into his thigh.

Finnikin was stunned, but the sight of Evanjalin fighting one of the thieves was all he needed to act. One man down. Then two. The daggers silent and deadly accurate. The third he fought with Trevanion's sword, a weapon too quick for a bunch of useless thieves. From the sound made by the singing swords behind him, it was clear that Evanjalin knew how to handle a weapon. Still, when Finnikin's third man went down, he swung around to deal with her assailant, only to find himself face-to-face with her. Eyes blazing, sword held upright in both hands. Steady. Waiting to swing. At her feet the man was writhing in agony from a second wound to his ear. She dropped the sword, and they ran in the only direction open to them.

They found their way out of the maze of alleyways and back toward the main road leading out of the town, only to realize that one of the assailants, with Finnikin's dagger still embedded in his body, had managed to pursue them. The girl shoved Finnikin toward a horse tied to a nearby post. She grabbed Trevanion's sword out of the scabbard at his side and, without hesitating, held it by the blade and swung its ruby-encrusted handle between the legs of their pursuer. He heard a crack and knew it wasn't the handle that had shattered. The howl of agony was enough to wake the dead.

Finnikin mounted the horse. The girl handed him Trevanion's

sword, then planted one of her feet on the assailant's chest for balance and yanked out Finnikin's dagger. She held out her arm to Finnikin, and he swung her up until she was seated behind him, clasping his waist, with the dagger in one hand. He looked down at her hands, strong and callused and bloody, as they clung to him. He felt her face against his back, heard her ragged breath close to his ear. A sudden desire to hear her voice flashed through him.

Sir Topher stared at them in shock. Finnikin didn't know whether it was because of the presence of the horse or the half-wild state of the novice. He helped them both dismount, but his eyes were on the girl.

"She was robbed," Finnikin muttered, beckoning him away. "But she knows how to use a sword."

"I warned you to keep her away from harm, Finnikin."

"Sir Topher," Finnikin said, keeping his voice controlled, "she handled a sword and used her wits. I tell you, she's no simpleton. I don't trust her."

"Handled a sword better than you?"

"Obviously not, but she still managed to maim two men, last count. One who, in all probability, will not be fathering anyone's child for quite a while."

They both looked over to where Evanjalin stood, her nose pressed against the horse. Finnikin leaned forward to whisper. "All that silence. It's not right."

"That would be the vow, Finnikin. The novices take it very seriously."

"I saw the novices of Lagrami often as a child. My cousin was one of them. They sang; they weaved; they planted roses. They did not fight like a feral trainee in the King's Guard. They did not know the amount of damage the handle of a sword swung between a man's legs could do."

"Times have changed, and even novices have had to learn to protect themselves," Sir Topher said. "Why can't you just be happy that she used initiative?"

Finnikin was silent. He remembered how she had pushed him toward the horse while she took Trevanion's sword to fight. He realized the truth. He was not irritated that the girl had shown initiative; it was that she had taken charge.

When they woke the next morning, she was gone.

"She left the horse and her pack, which means she plans to return," Sir Topher said, agitation in his voice. "You'll have to fetch her, Finnikin. Now."

"She's gone back for the thief," Finnikin said, shaking his head in disbelief. "He took her ring, no doubt, and she's gone back for it."

One of Sir Topher's rules was to never indulge in sentimentality, never return for what was left behind. Finnikin's eyes strayed toward the road that would lead them to Charyn. From there, with the girl, they would have traveled south to Sorel. On their own, Finnikin knew they would spend time in Osteria, where peace reigned. It was where the Lumateran ambassador now lived, working as the minister for Osterian trade.

Regardless of how annoying Finnikin found their former ambassador, he pictured the extensive palace library with its well-stocked fireplace and never-ending supply of hot tea and sweet breads.

"No, Finnikin," Sir Topher said quietly, as if he had read Finnikin's thoughts. "We will not leave her behind."

So Finnikin returned to Sprie, praying that he would not be the target of four maimed men and a peasant searching for his horse. He knew it would be difficult to go unnoticed. His hair was the ridiculous color of berries and gold, and he was lankier than the Sarnaks, slighter in build. He stood out easily in the daylight. As would the novice with her bare head and ugly gray shift.

He found her almost straight away, sitting huddled on a stone bench beside a stall, watching the activity around her with those strange dark eyes. Next to her, a desperate seller and a choosy buyer haggled over a small decorative dagger. At the far end of the square, Finnikin recognized the slave traders from Sorel. These were men who preyed on the plight of a people forced to sell one child to feed another. He had heard stories about how these children and women were used, and it sickened him to think that men were capable of such evil.

When he approached Evanjalin, she stared up at him, as if questioning the time it had taken him to join her. He squatted beside her, refusing to give in to his anger. Living with Sir Topher had taught him how to harness his feelings.

"Who is in charge here?" he asked quietly.

Without speech, she had only her eyes to communicate, but she used them well.

"This hand," he said, pointing to his left, "if I am. Or this hand," he said, pointing to his right, "if you are." He held them out to her, and she tapped his left hand gently.

He pulled her to her feet. "Good," he said, pleased with her choice.

Suddenly her body tensed. She looked over his shoulder, and then she was pushing past him. He had no choice but to follow. He could see the young thief disappearing into the maze of alleyways beyond the square.

She was fast; that he knew from the night before. Although she was hindered by her shift, Finnikin struggled to keep up with her. The chase was short, for the boy made the same mistake he had the previous night and led them into an alleyway that seemed to go nowhere.

*He's not from here,* Finnikin thought.

Evanjalin backed the boy into a corner and held out her hand. She received a backhand to her face for her effort; and she staggered from the impact. Finnikin gripped the thief by the coarse cloth of his jerkin and threw him against the stone wall, pinning him there with a hand to his throat. He went through the thief's pockets and found four pieces of silver. When he showed the girl the coins, she grabbed them, flinging them with the same rage he had glimpsed the night before.

"What did you do with the ring?" Finnikin asked the thief, shaking him.

The boy spat in Finnikin's face.

"Not the response I'm after," Finnikin said, hurling the thief away from the wall. "Now we play it this way. Back there by the spring are slave traders from Sorel. I'd recognize them anywhere. They stink of shit because that's all their victims do around them, from the fear of knowing where they are going to be taken."

The thief mocked a whimper. He spat in Finnikin's face again, this time straight in his eye. Wiping it slowly, Finnikin stared at him furiously, then dragged him out of the alleyway, with the novice trailing behind. "Get the silver, Evanjalin," he ordered.

The boy tried to escape by pulling out of his clothing.

"What you doing?"

Finnikin could hear a trace of alarm in the thief's voice. He'd used Sarnak words, clumsily spoken.

"Trading you for a horse." Finnikin took a long deliberate look at the boy. "Oh, and they do like them young."

The thief continued to struggle, but Finnikin held on tightly, almost choking him. "Peddler from Osteria," the boy wheezed. "Said it fake anyway."

The novice slapped him. Her eyes were glinting with tears. Finnikin tried not to imagine what he would do if the thief had sold Trevanion's sword.

"He's not worth it. Let's go."

But the novice would not move. She stared at the youth, eyes blazing.

The thief repeated his favorite gesture by spitting in her face. He wore a black felt cap that came down to his eyes. They were a nondescript color, strawlike perhaps, and Finnikin could see his features were beginning to display a blunt cruelty, a mouth forever in a sneer. He had the build of one who would thicken with age, evident by the size of his fists. But he was young, at least five years their junior. Finnikin wondered how many more of his kind were roaming these streets.

"They come hunting," the thief said. "Hunt you people down."

He spoke like a foreigner, and it was in that moment Finnikin realized where the boy came from. There was a glassy look in his eyes that Finnikin had not seen since he was separated briefly from Sir Topher at the age of twelve and placed in a prison in the Osterian capital. There had been Lumateran exiles with him, children whose parents had either been killed during the five days of the unspeakable or died of the fever. Some of the children did not know their own names and couldn't speak a word of any language. A shared origin meant nothing in that prison, and he could tell it meant nothing to this boy, who would have been no more than three or four when his family escaped from Lumatere.

Finnikin didn't need to ask who would be hunting them. In Sarnak there was always someone. Perhaps a pack of youths. Or bitter men, no longer able to put food on the table for their families. Finnikin was certain the thief would betray them to the first person who would listen, for any price. When the novice caught his eye, he knew what they had to do.

Sir Topher stared at the three of them with his usual aplomb. "So now our little party has a horse and a thief?"

Finnikin secured the rope around the boy's hands. "It's either him or a pack of Sarnaks he will send in our direction."

Sir Topher looked at the thief. "What's your name, boy?"

The thief spat.

"It's his favorite response," Finnikin said dryly. "We can dump him in Charyn."

"Not if we find exiles there, and I suspect we will. Perhaps Sorel."

"I think he'd like Sorel," Finnikin said. He turned to the thief. "Heard of the prison mines there?"

The boy paled, and Finnikin looked at Sir Topher, pleased. "Good. He seems familiar with them." He glanced over to where the novice was huddled under the tree, her hands covering her head. "He sold her ring."

Sir Topher sighed. "As soon as we're in Sorel, we won't have to worry anymore."

A fortnight, Finnikin calculated as Sir Topher began loading up the horse. That was all they needed before the thief from Sarnak and the novice Evanjalin were out of their lives forever.

## CHaPteR 4

I t was always their eyes that gave away their Lumateran heritage, and this time was no different. As they entered the gates of Charyn, the two guards snickered and Finnikin heard one of them mutter, "Dogs." Whether from the Rock or the River or the Flatlands, whether dark or fair, Lumaterans all had eyes that were set deep in their sockets. Finnikin had heard that the king of Charyn had once ordered his guards to measure the distance of a Lumateran prisoner's eyes from his nose, deeming them too close and therefore not human. He hated this kingdom. The one time he and Sir Topher had visited the Charyn court in the early years of their exile, he had feared for their lives. There were strange and sinister occurrences in the palace that week, bloodcurdling screams in the night and shouts of rage. Many claimed that the royal blood was tainted and that the king and his offspring were all half-mad.

The path that led to the capital was lined with stone houses. They were bare except for their doorways, which were crowned with rosebushes that had not yet bloomed. Although it would take them at least ten days, they planned to travel along one of the three rivers in Charyn that ran into Sorel. If there were exiles to be found, the river was the place to find them. Lumaterans were nothing if not sentimental, drawn to any place that resembled the physical landscape of their lost world.

Four days later, they found a camp. From where they stood at the top of a ridge, they could see a small settlement of about fifty exiles. Finnikin led the way down, clutching onto branches as he slid toward the flat narrow bank where the tents were pitched.

Two of the exiles, a man and a woman, came forward to meet them. As usual, there was a moment's distrust in their eyes. Despite the distance between camps, the exiles had heard stories of what had taken place in other kingdoms and were aware of their own vulnerability. In their travels, Finnikin and Sir Topher had often come across the same exiles year after year, but these people were unfamiliar. They had obviously kept themselves well hidden.

Sir Topher made his introductions, and the man stared at Finnikin. Then he nodded and extended his arm, bent at the elbow, fist clenched. The greeting of Lumateran River people.

"Son of Trevanion," the man acknowledged.

Finnikin raised his arm in a similar way and clasped the other man's hand.

"We lived on the river as children, when Trevanion returned to defend it," the woman explained. "My name is Emmian, and this is my husband, Cibrian."

It did not surprise Finnikin that the Lumateran River people had taken charge of the exiles here, as they had in many of the other camps. Along with the Monts, they had been the toughest of their people.

"Your mother's kin were from the Rock, Finnikin," Cibrian said.

Finnikin nodded. "I spent most of my childhood there, with my great-aunt, except when my father was on leave."

"Have you crossed their paths on your travels? I have a sister wed to the shoemaker of the Rock."

"I remember him well," Finnikin said with a smile. "But we have encountered few from the Rock Village. We think that most stayed when the elders gave the order. I doubt that any of them left the kingdom unless they were in the square that day."

"It is hard to say whether that is a blessing or a curse," Emmian said quietly.

Cibrian led them to the rest of his people, and Finnikin exchanged nods of acknowledgment with a group of exiles his own age. Seeing them made him think of Balthazar and Lucian, imagining the lads they would have grown up to be.

A sprinkle of rain began to fall, and they followed Cibrian to his dwelling. The exiles were well equipped. Their tents were made of tough horse hide; there were plenty of provisions and even a few goats. Finnikin suspected that some of the exiles had found work in the nearest village. The children seemed healthier than most camp children, and he wondered if there was a healer among them.

"We have been lucky this spring to have received the benevolence of Lord August of the Flatlands, an acquaintance of yours, I hear," Cibrian said to Sir Topher. "He requested that we look out for the son of Trevanion and the king's First Man."

Sir Topher exchanged a glance with Finnikin. "Why is it that Lord August finds himself in Charyn when he belongs to the Belegonian court?" he asked.

"Palace business. He was on his way home when he paid us a visit. He asked that you pass through the Belegonian capital if you were in these parts."

"It is our intention to travel south into Sorel," Sir Topher said.

"He was very definite in his request, sir."

Emmian and Cibrian's tent was large. Two children, no more than eight or ten, lay in the corner. They soon scampered across the space to join their parents. Finnikin watched Emmian gather them against her, her fingers lingering on their arms. These children were loved. He looked over to where the thief of Sarnak sat in a huddle of hate alongside the novice and could not help but make a comparison.

The little girl was looking at him with wide eyes. "Can you tell us the story of Lady Beatriss and Captain Trevanion?" she asked.

The adults stiffened, their expressions a mixture of alarm and guilt. Finnikin remembered how much Lumaterans enjoyed a romance. He had grown up hearing over and over again the story of the young king who went riding through the mountains and encountered a wild Mont girl who captured his heart. He had not realized that Beatriss and Trevanion's story had ignited the same interest.

"They are tired, Jenna. They don't have time for telling stories," her father said abruptly.

Finnikin watched as every adult in the tent looked away or busied themselves with the nothingness of their lives. It was as if the child's request had never been made. Even Sir Topher was focusing on the river outside, and suddenly Finnikin felt lonely for his father, a luxury he rarely allowed himself.

But Evanjalin was staring at him, refusing to look away. There was something in her expression, a question in her eyes, that made him clear his throat.

"It was a fierce love," he said gruffly. "Very fierce."

The little girl's cheeks flushed with pleasure, while the shoulders of the boy slumped with disappointment. The same way Finnikin's would whenever he had to sit through his great-aunt Celestina's ramblings about the wedding vows spoken by the king to his Mont girl. Finnikin would have much preferred to hear about the jousting and fencing entertainment provided by the King's Guard as a part of the celebrations.

"But I need to go back further, if you will let me," he said to the boy. "To the time when Trevanion of the River defended his people with just one mighty sword and forty dedicated men!"

Evanjalin bit her lip as if holding back a laugh, and he found himself grinning. The young boy sat up, a look of excitement on his face. He nodded, willing Finnikin to continue.

"My father was once a lowly foot soldier. As a young man, he watched each year as the barbarians, who lived far beyond the borders of Skuldenore, came down his beloved river with dragonships that seemed to appear from out of the sky. First they would raid Sarnak to our north, and then Lumatere. They were brutal, these foreigners, plunderers of the worst kind."

"Did they take their tents and food?" the boy asked eagerly, and for a moment Finnikin saw a glimpse of Balthazar's face in his expression. It made him numb with sadness and he failed to find the words to continue.

He heard a small sound, like the clearing of a throat, and glanced up to see Evanjalin. She had a look in her eye as if she somehow understood, and he found his voice once more.

"They took gold, of course," he said, swallowing the lump in his throat. "And silver. Lumatere had the best mines in the land and became the barbarian invaders' dream. Unfortunately the king had inherited a lazy, cowardly Guard headed by his cousin, who made it easy for the foreigners to do what they liked."

"Where was Trevanion?" the little girl asked.

"He was protecting a worthless duke on the Flatlands. But things changed in his twentieth year. The barbarians returned and decided that gold and silver were not enough. They would take the young people of the river to work as slaves in their land. The older ones who tried to stop them died in battle. That's how Trevanion lost his parents and sisters. During the same time, my mother died in childbirth, so you can imagine his fury and sadness.

"One day when the king was visiting the worthless duke, Trevanion pushed past the Guard and stood face-to-face with the leader of the kingdom. He demanded to know what the king was going to do about protecting his people. Little did he know, the king would toss and turn each night, feeling helpless in his palace while his river was plundered and his people were taken. But what could a king with a weak Guard do? He had Trevanion arrested, of course."

"Did they torture him?" the boy asked in a hushed tone.

"No. The king had a plan. Each night, while pretending to demand an apology, he would speak to Trevanion about the barbarian invaders and his lazy Guard. Trevanion made him a promise. If the king released him, he would choose forty of the best fighters in Lumatere and put an end to the annual plundering, and the king agreed.

"Trevanion was ruthless in training his men, but it was worth it. One year later, when the barbarians returned, they failed to conquer Trevanion's river. By the time he was twenty-one, he was made captain of the Guard. His men were fearless warriors, and the country stayed safe. No one dared to challenge Trevanion's Guard. Even the Monts kept quiet and out of trouble, and everyone knows how hard it is to keep the Monts under control."

"But what happened to the other captain of the Guard? The king's cousin?" the boy asked.

Finnikin heard an intake of breath, and he knew it was not right to mention the impostor king to these children. But the adults knew the rest of the story. The cousin of the king had been offered a place in the Charyn royal court, where he waited for the next ten years for a chance to take the throne of Lumatere.

"Don't you want to hear about Trevanion and Lady Beatriss?"

"Oh, yes, please," the little girl begged.

"Are you sure? Because perhaps the story about Trevanion working at the palace as the new captain will bore you." He directed his remark to the young boy, who shook his head solemnly. "This is where Lady Beatriss comes into it. From the outside, she seemed fragile. She was a novice of Lagrami, as most of the privileged girls were. They were taught to be good wives. To be accomplished. I've heard some say it was a weakness for the captain to fall in love with such an indulged child of Lumatere. But Trevanion saw more in her than most."

"She was almost as beautiful as the princesses," Emmian murmured.

"No one was as beautiful as the princesses." The voice came from one of the exiles standing outside. Finnikin saw that, despite the drizzle of rain, he had acquired an audience.

"Trevanion would disagree. But that wasn't always the case. You see, Lady Beatriss was the nursemaid of Balthazar and Isaboe, as well as being a loyal friend to the three older princesses. Now, I will be the first to admit that the royal children, and me included, did not make Beatriss's task easy. Balthazar and Isaboe were very . . . shall we say, high-spirited at times? They had little fear of anything and spent many a day hanging out of the tower of the palace, calling out, 'You, there!' to the children of the villagers, while poor Beatriss would hold them back, begging them to behave.

"But Balthazar loved the villagers. He used to call them 'the neighbors,' and as he'd make his way down to the palace village, he would call out to them one by one. 'Your rose beds are a vision, Esmine. I will have to take one for my mother.' Or 'I hope you will be sharing that wine with my father once your grapes are ripened, Mr Ward.' The queen raised her children to see no difference between themselves and the poorest villagers. Although there was many a time she boxed our ears for teaching the village boys how to shoot arrows from the roofs of their cottages.

"One day, Balthazar was hanging precariously out of the tower when the captain of the King's Guard happened to be walking across the moat, into the palace grounds. I can remember an almighty roar and Trevanion ordering us down from the tower. 'Including you!' he shouted, pointing a finger at Lady Beatriss."

The younger ones in the tent laughed, and even Sir Topher chuckled. "I remember that bellow well," Cibrian said, nodding.

"A trembling Lady Beatriss made her way down to the moat, trailed by the rest of us, to receive the biggest blasting of our lives. Poor Beatriss was sobbing, but Trevanion shouted, 'Stop your blubbering! They are the royal children! They need to be kept safe. Be functional, woman. Are you nothing but a doll with a pretty face and a powerful father?' "

There were gasps from both inside and outside the tent.

"Well, of course, he was ordered to apologize, but he refused. It was his job to protect the royal family, he told the king, and he should be able to do and say whatever it took to ensure their safety. Meanwhile Beatriss was sent back home to her father's manor until the fuss died down. The three older princesses refused to speak to the king until Trevanion apologized, and Balthazar and Isaboe were full of woe because their new nursemaid was the meanest woman in the whole of Lumatere. And that's how things stayed."

Finnikin paused, almost hypnotized by the look of anticipation in the eyes of the children and adults around him. Some from outside the tent had squeezed their way in to sit beside Cibrian and his family. Evanjalin's hands were wrapped around her knees, and she rested her head against them. There was a faraway look on her face, but her smile remained and it stirred something within him.

"Everything changed one day when my father was returning me to my mother's people in the Rock Village. Balthazar and Isaboe begged to come along, and who better to look after the royal children but the captain of the King's Guard? Even the meanest woman in the whole of Lumatere agreed.

"On the way, we stopped in the Flatlands to deliver some documents to the duke of Sennington, who was Beatriss's father. Trevanion told us to stay with our horses while he walked down the path to the manor house. We became restless after a while and wandered into a nearby paddock, not realizing that it contained one very angry bull. A huge one, glaring straight at us. As Trevanion approached and saw the danger, his first reaction was to race down the path toward the paddock. That day was one of the only times I have seen fear in my father's eyes. He was the captain of the King's Guard, the best swordsmen in the land, but what did a river boy know about bulls?"

"What do you river people know about anything?" one of the Flatlanders teased.

"More than a yokel farmer," a river exile tossed back, and there was more laughter. Finnikin could tell that teasing and laughter were new to these people.

"Then who happened to be walking by at that moment but Lady Beatriss, who was a farm girl at heart and understood animals. Before we knew it, she was waving her arms, yelling for us to run as soon as the bull turned toward her. We ran for our lives, leaping over a fence that to this day I have no idea how we got over. But we were safe. She wasn't, of course. I swear that she went flying in the air when the bull charged her. My father had no choice but to maim the animal. Then he carried her out of the paddock and laid her under a tree. Princess Isaboe was sobbing over Beatriss's body, begging her to open her eyes. Which she did after a moment or two. Seeing us safe, she breathed a sigh of relief and then looked at Trevanion and said, 'Was that functional enough for you, Captain?' Then she slapped his face, because his hand was on her thigh, and promptly fainted."

There was applause from the women and groans from the men, but the children stared at Finnikin, awestruck.

"And from that day on, my father wooed her."

Finnikin glanced up as he finished. The tent was overflowing with people, young girls with wistful smiles on their faces and young men who looked as if they were imagining themselves as Trevanion. But it was the expressions on the faces of the older ones that caught Finnikin's attention most, a mixture of joy and sadness as they remembered the world they had lost.

"Ah, Trevanion," Cibrian murmured later as they sat outside the tent where the children slept. "He should have prostrated himself at the feet of the impostor king." Cibrian had gutted five large trout and was cooking them over the fire.

"No," Finnikin said firmly. "The King's Guard lies prostrate only at the feet of their rightful leader. The impostor king had a hand in the slaughter of the royal family, and my father knew it. He was not to know they would take Lady Beatriss as they did."

"I pray to the goddess Lagrami for your father's safe return to guide us home, Finnikin," Cibrian said.

"If we convince Belegonia to give us a piece of land, will you join us with your people?" Finnikin asked.

Cibrian shook his head sadly. "If we accept a new homeland, it will mean that Lumatere is lost to us for eternity."

"Maybe it always has been."

Finnikin regretted his words instantly, but wasn't that what he had always believed? That if they accepted their loss, they could stay long enough in a place as one people and discover who they were once again?

"I will not betray these people to anyone," Cibrian said in a low voice, "but we have Lumaterans among us who have . . . abilities that weren't just limited to the Forest Dwellers. There is talk of Balthazar returning."

Beside him, Finnikin felt Evanjalin stiffen.

"Dreams and premonitions," the man continued. "Could it be that the witch Seranonna is trying to reverse the curse from beyond the grave?"

With a look, Sir Topher warned Finnikin not to react, and instead they turned their attention to eating.

After dinner, Finnikin sat in the tent he shared with his three companions and recorded the names of Cibrian's people in the *Book of Lumatere*. So far in their travels, they had located one thousand seven hundred and thirty exiles. In the census taken in Lumatere in the spring before the days of the unspeakable, the population had been six thousand and twelve.

"Can we trust Lord August?" he asked Sir Topher quietly in Belegonian, finishing his entry. "I say we go straight to Sorel."

"He is our only link to the Belegonian court. He may be ready to make an offer on the king's behalf, Finnikin."

"Then why was he in Charyn? We have never trusted the Charynites."

"And you have never trusted the Lumateran dukes who chose to work for foreign kings," Sir Topher responded.

"You chose not to rely on the comfort of a foreign court."

Finnikin moved closer. He could hear the murmur of voices of those in the tents surrounding them. The footsteps of one too restless to sleep.

"It's different for a king's First Man. But I understand the Duke's decision and even the ambassador in Osteria. Have they not worked through us many times to better conditions of the exiles?" Sir Topher sighed, settling back onto his bedroll. "You will visit him."

"Why me?"

"You're Trevanion's son. Your father worked for his."

"My father hated his father."

"You will go, Finnikin," Sir Topher said firmly. "It could be our biggest step toward obtaining land for our people." He looked over to where the novice and the thief lay. "We'll take one each. Evanjalin can accompany you. We don't want the thief causing a disruption in Lord August's home. There was talk tonight that the priest-king has been seen around these parts, and it is just as important I make contact with him."

Finnikin closed his book. "All this talk about the return of Balthazar and the need for Trevanion. It will only mean that the exiles will continue to live in the past and sit waiting for a miracle."

"It is approaching ten years," Sir Topher said with a sigh. "It is not surprising that people are thinking about it. Leave them to their dreams and superstitions while we make the progress."

CHAPTER 5

They entered Belegonia through neighboring Osteria to reach the crossroads of the north. The palaces of Osteria and Lumatere and the border of Sendecane were all a day's ride from the crossroads. As they prepared to follow the arrow south to the Belegonian capital, Finnikin stared at the arrow pointing north. The name LUMATERE had been scratched out.

For a moment he allowed his memory to take him down a road lined with vineyards and olive trees. It was one he had traveled often with his father. Each time, he would climb the ridge overlooking the Valley of Tranquillity and see the kingdom of Lumatere spread out before him. Villages of cobblestoned roads that rang with the sound of hooves, meadows lush with flowers, huts lined up along a river that snaked through the kingdom and pulsed with life. In his mind he followed the river to its port, where barges loaded with crates would depart, taking the richness of the kingdom's produce as far south as Yutlind and to the farthest reaches of Sarnak. He could see his village in the Rock, his uncle's smokehouse, where meat and fish hung from the ceiling, and the quarry where he would take Balthazar and Isaboe, who would thrill the villagers with their eagerness to join in with the digging and extracting. Lucian of the Monts had said it was unnatural to live in caves. Trogs, he called them, and although at times Finnikin felt the limits of the Rock Village, nothing could take away the view over the rest of the land, where he would see a farmer knock acorns out of an oak tree for his pigs, or families working together, cutting wheat with sickles and bringing in the harvest. And there in the distance, the king's palace, perched up high, overlooking their beloved people inside the kingdom walls and those outside in the Forest of Lumatere.

The only time Finnikin and Sir Topher had returned to the Valley of Tranquillity was in their fifth year of exile. By then the dark mist that had once stopped at the walls of the kingdom had spread to consume a third of the valley, including the Forest of Lumatere. But just as Finnikin despaired that there was nothing of their homeland to see or feel, without warning, the scar on his thigh from his pledge with Balthazar and Lucian had begun to flow with blood, leaving him with a heady sense of euphoria and his body a boneless heap. He had lost all sense of the normal world that day, but in his delirium he dreamed of a moment so perfect that to put it into words seemed futile. When he woke, Sir Topher was there, his face white with worry and fear, and Finnikin had sobbed with a joy that he knew Sir Topher could not understand. He had experienced a phenomenon beyond their world, where he felt the beat not just of his own heart but of another as well, as if some great spirit had crawled into him and planted a seed of hope. As if perhaps Balthazar was alive and one day soon the curse would lift and Lumatere would be free again.

Yet when they had descended from the ridge and tried to push through the dark mist, a great force had driven them back. Still, Finnikin would not give up. He had felt something on that ridge, and despite Sir Topher's gentle urging to walk away, he tried again and again, forcing himself against the whirlpool of malevolence spinning across the valley, needing to push through as if there was someone on the other side waiting to grasp his hand. Sometimes he swore he felt fingertips against his but always beyond his grasp, and his sobs of frustration turned into grunts of fatigue. Until day became dusk. The sun disappeared. Then darkness.

"We will not return here, Finnikin," Sir Topher had said sadly. "There is nothing left for us. For our people."

Overcome with fatigue, Finnikin had known that his mentor was right. It was foolish to think that Balthazar had lived. From that day, Finnikin had not dared to entertain the hope of a return to Lumatere, and he cursed anyone who allowed themselves to think otherwise.

Three days after their arrival in Charyn, Finnikin and Evanjalin set up camp on the outskirts of the Belegonian capital. As they had traveled toward the city, Finnikin felt his mood lift. There was a magic to this kingdom. Belegonia was a center for learning, and over the years, Sir Topher had made sure that Finnikin experienced everything it had to offer. He liked the way that just when he thought he knew every part of the city, he would find another snakelike alley. He liked how they argued in these alleys. What they argued about. Not just taxes and death, but the quality of a building, the theory of the latest philosopher, the histories according to Will the baker as opposed to Jark the butcher. Throughout the rest of the land, people worked and slept and existed. In Belegonia, as they once did in Lumatere, the people truly lived.

As they approached the city center, Finnikin heard music. A girl with pipes, a man with a drum, counting the beat one, two, three, four in a way that had Finnikin's blood pumping a rhythm of mayhem to his heart. For a moment he lost sight of Evanjalin as those around them began to dance. But then she was there before him, her eyes blazing. As drum beats rang through the street, she slowly raised her arms and clapped her hands above her left shoulder. Eyes fixed on hers, Finnikin instinctively clapped his hands above his right shoulder. Then, just as slowly, Evanjalin tapped her feet and he mirrored the movement. It was the beginning of their kingdom's Harvest Moon dance, and as the rhythm quickened and those around them stamped and twirled, every part of him belonged to this hypnotic dance with Evanjalin. But then the rhythm changed, and Finnikin came to his senses. He took her hand and gently led her away.

As they made their way toward the houses overlooking the main square, Finnikin's frustration returned. He was still annoyed that they had responded to Lord August's request. August of the Flatlands was the son of the duke Trevanion had been assigned to protect as a young foot soldier. When Trevanion left to fight the invaders, Lord August followed, wanting to prove that he was more than just a privileged man's son. Finnikin knew that what had developed over the years was a fierce friendship between his father and the nobleman. Yet he could not forget that since the five days of the unspeakable, he and Sir Topher had not encountered any of Lord August's people from the village of Sayles. He knew that most of them escaped to the Valley, but he suspected that somewhere in their journey they had been abandoned by the duke and were most likely suffering in the fever camps. Or worse.

Lord August's residence was tall and narrow, with no doors on the ground level. Finnikin assumed the family entered through one of the buildings alongside, though he had no idea why Lord August felt the need for such protection. Nobility were protected by foreign courts, despite their Lumateran heritage.

A carriage pulled up outside the house, and Finnikin watched a woman and four children step out. He recognized Lady Abian, looking every bit the duchess in her silks and jewels. She was followed by Lady Celie and her three younger brothers. He had not seen Lady Celie since they were children, and she had changed little. Always fragile, she had been a strange, quiet child who was bullied by Lucian of the Monts but much loved by the royal children.

The family paid no attention to Finnikin and Evanjalin until Lady Celie dropped a bundle of cloth. Evanjalin bent to retrieve it, and the other girl stifled a scream that made Finnikin dislike her instantly. The two girls faced each other, one dainty and refined in her dress, the other plain and coarse. He saw an emotion flash through Evanjalin's eyes before the family disappeared into the building next door.

When Lord August finally appeared through the same entrance, his face was impassive but he gripped Finnikin's shoulder tightly. He was dressed in the wealthy silks of a king's court and Finnikin dismissed him, as he did most dukes in exile, as one with a meaningless title. He led them to the courtyard of the building alongside his residence. It wasn't until they were standing in a small room, bare except for the frescoes on the walls, that Lord August stopped to look at Finnikin closely.

"You're not a boy anymore."

"How does one tell, my lord?"

"By the ache in the heart of a father who understands how Trevanion would feel if he were to see how much has been taken from him."

Finnikin looked away, then mumbled an introduction to the novice. "And Sir Topher sends his apologies. There has been talk that the priest-king is in these parts, and he is keen to see if it's true."

"I have heard such talk. But I doubt he is here. The priest-king has developed a death wish over the past ten years and spends much of his time in the fever camps."

"You promised us a meeting with the king, Lord August," Finnikin reminded him.

"No," the man said firmly. "There was never a promise. Just an invitation to discuss Lumatere."

"And what is it that you'd like to discuss, my lord? As we have mentioned each time we return here, the only hope for Lumatere is land for our exiles."

"And as I have said to Sir Topher year after year, why would the king of Belegonia be interested in carving up his land?"

"You contacted *us*," Finnikin said, not hiding the anger in his voice. "We came here because you invited us. Why waste our time, my lord? Our people are dying, and you make us travel all the way here to see you."

"Give me information I don't already have, Finnikin. Tell me that you're attempting to return home and I will ask for the king's assistance."

"We don't have a home," Finnikin snapped. "Push for land, Lord August. That is all we want. A piece of Belegonian land by the river. We will settle there and fend for ourselves, and the Belegonians need not worry."

"If we have our Guard, I will bet my life that Balthazar comes out of hiding," Lord August said in a low tone.

"The Lumateran Guard no longer exists."

"As long as Trevanion lives, it exists."

Finnikin pushed back his hair in frustration. "Are you trying to trap me, my lord? Has my father escaped from one of the land's prisons and are you trying to locate him?"

Lord August laughed with little humor. "Escape? Not for want of his Guard trying. I've told you before, I have no idea where he is. They transferred him in secrecy one night seven years ago. All I know is that they took him to Yutlind Nord, but he no longer seems to be there. I suspect the ambassador knows, but he refuses to speak of Trevanion. He says he honors the wishes of the captain."

Finnikin dug his fingernails into his palms.

"I remember the times I would visit him in the prison here," Lord August continued. "He would only ever ask one question: 'Is my boy safe?' As long as the answer was yes, he did not care what happened to him. But he could be persuaded by you, Finnikin. If Trevanion was found and freed, his Guard would come out of hiding, and then we would have the most powerful men of Lumatere to lead us home."

"Even if we had my father and the Guard and the heir, have you forgotten that we're actually missing a kingdom?" Finnikin said sharply.

"The truth lies with the heir, Finnikin. Balthazar will know how to get us inside. The gifted ones among us are speaking. They sense something. Someone."

"Let me talk to the king," Finnikin repeated.

The duke shook his head, a look of angry disappointment on his face, and suddenly Finnikin felt as if he were facing his father.

"The king will want a favor in return," Lord August said dismissively.

"They can afford to have us here, my lord. It is why we have chosen Belegonia and not Osteria. Look at all the open space in this kingdom. We traveled five days to arrive here, through the most lush and fertile land. All empty. Wasted. While our people live in overcrowded camps."

"They will say it is not their responsibility, Finnikin."

"Then whose responsibility are we?"

"They will say that they have done enough! That our people need to help themselves. To integrate. They claim they have no control over the outlaws who harrass some of the camps. No control over their own people, while ours are at the mercy of the oppressed of each land who relish the opportunity to be an oppressor."

"Is that what you believe?"

Lord August stared at him. "Do you think I don't continually ask myself if I could have done more? Do you think I don't visit the people in those camps and want to take every one of them into my home? But whom do I choose, Finnikin? The motherless child? The pregnant woman? The man who has lost his entire family?" He shook his head, and Finnikin knew he was being dismissed. "Tell the king something he might find useful, and he may come to your aid."

Finnikin stood, hopelessness rendering him speechless.

"Then tell him this."

The voice came from behind him. A strong voice, yet hoarse as if it were new to speech. She spoke in the Lumateran language, and it sent a shiver through Finnikin's body.

"Tell him the impostor king did not work alone," Evanjalin said, making her way across the room toward them. "Tell him that Lumatere was never the objective, just the means." She stood by Finnikin's side. With a voice, she looked different. Words put fire in her eyes in the same way music had.

"What better way for cunning Charyn to take control of Belegonia, its most powerful rival, than to place a puppet ruler in the kingdom between them. And when Charyn decides to plunder Belegonia, the bloodshed in Lumatere will pale in comparison."

Lord August walked toward them until he was eye to eye with

Evanjalin. Finnikin could hardly breathe. She brushed up against his arm, and he felt her tremble.

"Who are you to know such things?" the duke whispered in their mother tongue.

"When one is silent, those around speak even more, my lord."

"And what do you hope to achieve with this information?" He looked at Finnikin. "What's going on here, Finnikin?"

"You asked for something the king of Belegonia did not already know," Finnikin said, as if rehearsed. "We have given it. So what can we take away with us in return? An audience with your king, perhaps?"

Lord August's face was white with fury. He grabbed hold of Finnikin roughly. "My king," he spat, "is dead. The king of Belegonia is my employer. *Never* mistake one for the other."

The girl reached over and released Lord August's hands from Finnikin. "So if we are to return to Lumatere, you would leave all this?" she asked. "Security. Privilege. In exchange for a kingdom that could be razed to the ground at any moment? Just say your lands are no longer there, my lord? Maybe worked by another who believes that he is entitled to them over you. Would you be so eager to return to Lumatere if you had nothing to go back to?"

He stared at the two standing before him. "Led by Balthazar and his First Man?" he asked. "Protected by the King's Guard? Blessed by the priest-king? Say the words, and I will be on my knees with my hands in the soil, planting the first seed."

Neither Finnikin nor Evanjalin spoke until they were outside the duke's residence. Finnikin grabbed her arm. "Explain to me your vow of silence!" he demanded in Lumateran.

She placed a finger across his lips. "Sir Topher would be furious to know that you're speaking our mother tongue in public," she said quietly, surprising him even more by speaking Belegonian.

When they returned to the camp, the thief from Sarnak was tied to a tree. The boy let out a string of expletives, spittle flying, hatred in his eyes. Still filled with his own anger, Finnikin walked over and grabbed him by the hair.

"My mother, unlike yours, never exchanged sexual favors for a piece of silver," he said, addressing the first insult by banging the boy's head against the trunk of the tree. "And," he said with another resounding thump, "although I'm very familiar with that part of the female body, I take offense at being labeled one."

"I'm presuming by your mood that things did not go well with the duke," Sir Topher called from where he sat by the fire.

Finnikin joined him. "She spoke."

"Evanjalin?" Sir Topher was on his feet in an instant. "What did she say to you?"

"She spoke Lumateran in the presence of the Duke. And later she spoke to me in Belegonian."

Sir Topher glanced over to where Evanjalin was preparing their supper. "Finnikin, what did she tell you?" he asked urgently.

"What you have always suspected about the impostor king and the attack on Lumatere."

Sir Topher paled. "Puppet king to the Charynites?"

Finnikin nodded.

"And Lord August?"

"He will take it to the king of Belegonia, but only if we return to Lumatere with my father's Guard. More talk about Balthazar as well."

"Empaths," Sir Topher said, his eyes still on the novice as she busied herself plucking a pheasant. "It's the empaths who are sensing something."

"I thought they were all put to death."

"No, only those who belonged to the Forest Dwellers. There seem to have been others with the gift, especially among the Flatlanders and the Monts. I believe it's why Saro of the Monts keeps his people well hidden."

Sir Topher walked over to where the girl was sitting. Feathers were stuck to her fingers and parts of her shift.

"Pick a language," Finnikin said stiffly. "She seems to know a few."

The novice stood, her eyes moving from Finnikin to Sir Topher. "I only know the language of my parents and Belegonian," she said quietly in Belegonian. "And I can speak a little Sarnak."

Sir Topher's breath caught. "Is there anything else you need to tell us, Evanjalin?"

She shook her head, and her bottom lip began to quiver.

"There's no need to be afraid," Sir Topher continued gently. "Where did you hear about Charyn's plan for Belegonia?"

She leaned close, whispering into his ear, "Balthazar."

Finnikin saw confusion on Sir Topher's face.

"Please don't be angry, Sir Topher," she said. "Please take me to the Monts. They will know what to do, I promise you. On my life, I promise you."

"And you believe them to be in Sorel?"

She hesitated for a moment and then nodded.

The thief was cackling with laughter. "Crying," he mimicked. "So sad. Want someone to cut my froat open and feed it to the dogs."

The girl did not respond, and after a moment Sir Topher walked away. "Come, Finnikin. Practice."

But Finnikin stayed. "Why is it that you choose silence, Evanjalin?" he said. "Something to hide?"

Her eyes met his. "Why speak when I can respond to your whistle like a dog?"

He gave a humorless laugh. There was nothing simple about this one.

"And anyway, I was so enjoying the discussions about fragile Lady Zarah."

He and Sir Topher had discussed Lord Tascan's daughter in Osterian. Finnikin's eyes narrowed as he tried to bite back his anger. What they didn't know about this girl could fill the *Book of Lumatere.*

"Is that jealousy I hear in your voice?" he asked.

"Jealousy? Of a vacuous member of the nobility who trills like a bird, according to Sir Topher?"

"Your voice could do with a bit more of a trill," he said.

"Really? Because yours could do with a bit more refinement. For someone who's supposed to be the future king's First Man, you sound like a fishmonger."

"First," he seethed, "I belong to the future King's Guard and second, my father was the son of a fishmonger, so I would choose my insults more carefully if I were you."

"Finnikin! Practice," Sir Topher called out again.

Evanjalin returned to the task with the pheasant as if Finnikin were no longer there.

"You have a very dark heart," he accused.

"It's good of you to recognize, Finnikin," she said without looking up. "There's hope for you yet."

# CHaPteR 6

The road to Sorel from Belegonia ran through ancient caverns said to be the dwelling place of the darkest gods in the land. Travelers preferred the ocean route between the two kingdoms despite the piracy on the open seas, and Finnikin could understand why. The journey through the caverns took most of the day. He was forced to stoop for the entire time and felt hounded by the carvings of grotesque forms, half-human, half-animal, on the walls around them. Yellow painted eyes tracked him, while outstretched clawlike fingers traced an icy line along his arm whenever he brushed against the jagged rock.

There was little reprieve when they reached the capital. Sorel was a kingdom of stone and rubble, its terrain as unrelenting as Sendecane. The dryness in the air caused them to choke each time they tried to speak, and rough pieces of stone cut into Finnikin's thin leather boots. He could not help but notice the bloodied feet of the novice, and he cursed her for whatever it was that drove her on. Lately she had taken the lead, though when he thought back, he realized that she had done so since Sendecane.

Sorel had a darkness to its core, much like Charyn. But if

Charyn was a knife that could slice its victim with quick and deadly precision, justice in Sorel was a blunt blade that dug and tunneled into the flesh, leaving its victim to die a long and painful death. Sorel had been Lumatere's only competitor in the export of ore from its mines and had reveled in the catastrophe of the unspeakable, tripling export fees and bleeding the surrounding kingdoms dry. The king used the mines as a prison, and it was rumored that some inmates had not seen light of day for as long as Finnikin had been alive. Worse still were the stories of the slave children, forced to work in the mines during the day and locked up underground at night. For once Finnikin was grateful that he and Sir Topher and the thief were fair in coloring and even more grateful that the novice's hair was shorn.

"Keep your head down," he warned her at the heavily guarded border town. "They distrust those with dark eyes, and this is one place we do not want attention drawn to us."

Finnikin passed through safely; not even the quiver of arrows he wore on his back and the bow that hung from his side drew the attention of the guards. But the novice did. They grabbed her by the coarse cloth of her shift, almost choking her. Finnikin lunged toward them, but she held out her hand to stop him. He watched as one soldier forced her to her knees, checking behind her ears for any marks of the phlux, which the people of Sorel believed the exiles of Lumatere carried in their bodies and spread across the land.

The soldier showed no emotion. Unlike in Sarnak, there was no hatred caused by hunger and poverty. There was nothing but a sense of superiority taught from an early age and a strong aversion to foreigners. When the same soldier forced Evanjalin's mouth open and shoved his fingers inside, Finnikin's fury returned and he made a grab for Trevanion's sword, only to be pinned back by Sir Topher.

"You will make things worse!" his mentor hissed in his ear. "You're putting her life at risk."

The thief of Sarnak snickered with glee.

In the village, Evanjalin was sick at his feet. Finnikin suspected it came from the memory of the soldier's filthy fingers inside her mouth. Without thinking, he held her up and wiped her face with the hem of his shirt. Their eyes met, and he saw a bleakness there that made him choke. Suddenly he wanted the power to wipe such hopelessness away. That moment in front of the guards, he had allowed emotion to cloud his reason. Yet he felt no regret. He understood, with a clarity that confused him, that if anyone dared touch her again, his sword would not stay in its scabbard.

She pulled away and gestured to an inn at the edge of the main square. "I want to wash my face," she mumbled, walking toward it.

He went to follow, but Sir Topher's voice stopped him.

"Finnikin. Give her a moment."

Later, they set up camp at the base of an escarpment. While Sir Topher dozed and the thief from Sarnak swore from his shackles, Evanjalin began to climb the rock face.

"Stay here," Finnikin ordered, but if he had learned anything about the novice, it was that she did as she pleased, and so he found himself climbing after her. Though cursing her inwardly, he could not help marveling at her fearlessness and the ease with which she ascended the rock in her bare feet.

When he reached the top, she was standing on a narrow ledge of granite that protruded over the camp below. But it was the view to the west that took his breath away, a last glimpse of Belegonia in the evening light.

"It's beautiful," she said, speaking in their mother tongue.

He stood silently, struggling with the pleasure he felt as she spoke their language.

"Say something," she said as the sun began to disappear and the air chilled. "Tell me what you're thinking."

With Sir Topher he spoke of strategies and dividing land between exiles and the best crops to grow and the politics of the country they found themselves in. They trained with practice swords, dealt with disappointing dukes, and quarreled with an ambassador obsessed with protocol. But in ten years, no one had ever asked what he was thinking. And he knew that the novice Evanjalin was asking for more than just his thoughts. She wanted the part of him he fought to keep hidden. The part that held his foolish hopes and aching memories.

"I miss hearing our mother tongue," he found himself saying. "Speaking it. Sir Topher has always been strict about using only the language of the country we are in, but when I dream, it's in Lumateran. Don't you love it? The way it comes from the throat, guttural and forced. Speaks to me of hard work. So different from the romance of the Belegonian and Osterian tongues."

There was a soft smile on her face and for a moment he forgot they were on this cliff, staring across at the stone and rubble of Sorel. "I miss the music of the voices in the crowded marketplace in my Rock Village, or in the king's court, where everyone talked over the top of one another. I can't tell you how many times I heard the king bellow, 'Quiet! Too much talking!' And that was just at the dinner table with his wife and children."

She laughed, and the sound soothed him.

"I swear it's true. The queen, she was the loudest. 'Is it my curse to have the worst behaved children in the land? Vestie, you are to apologize to Nurse, or I will have you cleaning the privy for the rest of the week! Balthazar, you are not the ruler of this kingdom yet, and even when you are, you will eat at the table like a human being.' "

Evanjalin's laughter was infectious, and he continued with the mimicry. He had loved his life in the Rock Village, but not as much as life in the king's court. In the palace, there were Balthazar and the beautiful spirited princesses, and most of all Trevanion. His heart would burst with pride whenever he witnessed his father's importance. Sometimes, deep in the night when on watch, Trevanion would take him from his bed and they would sit on the keep and stare out at the world below. Often Lady Beatriss would join them, shivering in the night air, and Trevanion would gather them both in his embrace to keep them warm.

He could feel Evanjalin's eyes on him as the sun before them disappeared at a speed beyond reckoning. "Then I will demand that you speak Lumateran when we are alone," Evanjalin said, interrupting his thoughts.

"Will you?" he mocked. "And why is that?"

"Because without our language, we have lost ourselves. Who are we without our words?"

"Scum of the earth," he said bitterly. "In some kingdoms, they have removed all traces of Lumatere from the exiles. We are in *their* land now and will speak *their* tongue or none at all. Our punishment for the pathetic course of our lives."

"So men cease to speak," she said softly.

Men who in Lumatere had voices loud and passionate, who provided for their families and were respected in their villages. Now they sat in silence and relied on their children to translate for them as if they were helpless babes. Finnikin wondered what it did to a man who once stood proud. How could he pass on his stories without a language?

"And how Lumaterans loved to speak," Finnikin said. "Shout

from hilltops, bellow in the marketplace, sing from the barges on the river. I had a favorite place, the rock of three wonders at the crest of my village. I would climb it with Balthazar and Lucian of the Monts. You would have known him, of course, being a Mont."

She nodded. "Son of Saro."

"We had a healthy dislike for each other. He would call me 'trog boy.' Repeatedly."

"And how would you respond?" she asked with a laugh.

"By calling him 'son of an inbred.' Repeatedly. Balthazar would judge who could come up with the worst insult. I would win, of course. Monts are such easy targets."

"They are my people you're speaking of," she said, trying to sound cross.

"How was it that your family became separated from them?" Finnikin asked. "You are the first Mont we have ever met on our travels."

Evanjalin was silent for a moment, and he wondered if she knew where the Monts were hiding. "Saro moved the Monts just days after they killed his sister, the queen, and my mother and siblings and I were among them. But my father was in Sarnak, and my mother refused to leave the day Saro took our people away from the Valley. She insisted that we wait. She believed there was still hope, and that if we stayed in the Valley, my father would travel from Sarnak to find us." She looked up at him. "Do you remember those days?"

"Only too well," he said quietly. "We all waited for at least a week. After the curse, Saro sent two of his men out to access the kingdom from the other borders, but days later only one returned." Finnikin fell silent. He remembered the Mont's words to Saro. That at each border, an unseen force had held them back, until the Charyn border when his companion pushed his way into the tempest. The Mont had watched in horror as the tempest spat his kinsman back. Splintered bone by splintered bone.

"And then everyone began to leave," Finnikin continued, "needing to feed their children and to survive, arguing whether it was better to go to Charyn or Belegonia or Sarnak. I stayed close to my father's men until I was placed in the care of Sir Topher. We were the last to go."

The wind was strong on the cliff, and it whipped his hair across his face. Suddenly her hand reached out to hold it back. When he felt her fingers, he flinched; he had not been touched with such gentleness since his childhood. He was no stranger to women and had felt their hands on all parts of his body, but her touch made him feel like he belonged someplace.

"I remember the abandoned children wailing by the side of the road," she said. "Some as young as two or three. People were forced to put their own survival and their family's above anything else and left other people's children to die. It's the only reason I can feel any sympathy for the thief from Sarnak."

He nodded. "Part of me believes there is little hope for those like him, who have become as base as the men they associate with. But there's another part of me that will search this land high and low once we are settled in our second homeland and bring them back to us, where they belong."

He felt her stare but did not turn and look. Did not want those eyes reaching into him.

"So you are destined to spend the rest of your life scouring this land? Who are you, to deserve such a curse?" she asked.

*One who has an evil lurking inside of me,* he wanted to say. An evil that Seranonna of the Forest Dwellers recognized that day in the forest as he played alongside Isaboe.

*Her blood will be shed for you to be king.*

"What is it you want, Finnikin?" Evanjalin persisted.

"I want to be left alone to do what we've always done," he said vehemently. *I want to go searching for my father,* he longed to shout.

"And what is that? Wandering the empire? Collecting names of the dead? Where would you like me to leave you, Finnikin?"

*In the numb peace we lived with before you came into our lives.*

He stared at her, and she held his gaze. "I took great comfort in your vow of silence," he said at last.

After a moment her mouth twitched. "Really? I do believe you're lying."

"It's true. I miss it terribly."

"I think you're dying to tell me what you shouted from your rock. With the inbred and the heir."

He laughed in spite of himself. "We were convinced of the existence of the silver wolf. Legend had it that only a true warrior could kill it, and we'd build traps in the forest and play out its capture. Balthazar was the warrior, and I was his guard; Lucian the wolf, Isaboe the bait. Then we would travel to the rock and practice our sacrifice of it to the gods, shouting our intentions and faith. We'd pledge our honor to each other. We even vowed to save Lumatere." He shook his head, thinking of the last pledge they had made together, mixed with the blood of all three.

"I would love such a rock," she said. "It would loosen my tongue and give me the courage to say all the things I've never dared say."

"And what would you say, Evanjalin? Would you damn the impostor, curse those who placed him on the throne?"

She shook her head. "I would speak my name out loud. Evanjalin of the Monts!" Her voice echoed and its volume took him by surprise. He walked to the rock's edge, wanting to listen to it until the last echo disappeared, wanting to capture it in his hands.

"Finnikin of the Rock!" he roared, and then turned back to where she stood, her eyes blazing with excitement. "Son of Trevanion of the Lumateran River people and Bartolina of the Rock!" He beat his chest dramatically.

She laughed and stepped closer to him. "Mortal enemy of the bastard impostor!" she yelled.

He thought for a moment, then gave a nod of approval. "Trusted servant of the king's First Man, Sir Topher of the royal court of Lumatere!"

"Follower of our beloved Balthazar!"

"Son of a man who once loved Lady Beatriss of the Lumateran Flatlands!"

"Daughter of those slaughtered in innocence!"

"Brother of one taken away before she drew her first breath!"

"Sister to those who loved her with all their heart!"

She had moved too close to the edge of the rock, and with a sharp intake of breath, he grabbed her around the waist, the strong band of his arm pressing her back into his chest. "Foolish girl," he said almost gently, his lips close to her ear. "You could have gone over the side."

A shudder passed through her, and then she pulled away. "We should go," she murmured.

"Trust me, Evanjalin," he said, holding out his hand. Trembling, she took it, and they made their way down the rock face in silence. But already he missed her voice, and when he helped her over the last of the stones, he found his finger tracing the bruise around her mouth.

*"Finnikin!"*

Within the hollow rock he could see the anxious figure of Sir Topher.

"We're here, sir."

"Don't wander too far. You know how strange a place this is."

At supper, Finnikin and Evanjalin ate their bread and cheese in silence while Sir Topher watched them carefully. Even the thief seemed subdued. Later, as Finnikin wrote in the *Book of Lumatere,* he glanced over to where she stood, distanced from them, her hands clenched at her sides. He tucked the book under his arm and walked toward her, suddenly feeling awkward, his pulse beating at an erratic speed.

"Join us," he said quietly. "Sir Topher is telling stories of his journeys with the king."

There was a hint of a smile on her face.

"What?" he asked defensively.

"When you speak Lumateran, your accent sings like those of the River."

"It was either that, or *rrrumbling* like those from the Rock."

She laughed, but it turned into a sob and she covered her mouth. He stepped forward and lifted her chin with his finger.

"Bend to their will, Finnikin," she whispered. "And keep yourself alive."

"Whose will?" he murmured, leaning his head toward her.

*"Finnikin!"*

The anxiousness in Sir Topher's voice snapped him out of his trance at the same time as he heard the horses' hooves. He turned toward the camp and saw five Sorelian soldiers riding toward them, flame sticks in their hands.

"Where is the traitor who claims to be the dead prince of Lumatere?" the one in the lead asked, dismounting.

Finnikin was stunned. Sir Topher turned to him in confusion, and in the dancing firelight Finnikin saw a trace of fear on the older man's face. The thief from Sarnak had paled. Thieves across the land knew to keep out of the mines of Sorel.

Finnikin's first inclination was to protect the girl, and he was relieved that the soldiers were looking for an impostor of Balthazar rather than someone who knew where the heir was.

"There is no impostor among us," Sir Topher said pleasantly. "We are Belegonian merchants eager to trade in a kingdom so rich in bounty."

"Why accuse us of such a thing?" Finnikin asked, but the soldiers looked straight past him to where Evanjalin stood.

"Is this the one?" the soldier asked.

"She is no one," Finnikin said firmly, blocking his path.

Then the soldier nodded and Finnikin turned, bewildered, his blood running cold.

For the novice Evanjalin had lifted her hand and was pointing a finger.

Straight in his direction.

## CHAPTER 7

D eep in the bowels of the mines of Sorel, the prisoner lay facing the rusted steel bars of the cave he crawled into each night. His bulky frame curled to fit the confines of the space, his body almost folded in half. He despised this witching hour, when he was at the mercy of his thoughts. Sometimes they stirred him into a madness of grief. Most times they made him want to beat his head to a pulp against the stone and end his life once and for all.

At his eye level, he watched feet being dragged along the narrow corridor outside his cage. There were fifty other cages spanning both sides of this stretch of cave. One was the holding cell for newly arrested prisoners, where they spent a week while the Sorelian authorities decided to which prison they would be sent. Most of the time, if they were young, they did not live beyond the third day.

He tried to ignore the fervor that accompanied the arrival of a new prisoner. He could tell this one was young by the heightened excitement of both prisoners and guards. New prisoners broke the monotony and delivered opportunities for the most base of men. If he allowed himself to, he would feel a sick kind of sorrow for the boy. But the prisoner had made a point to do anything but feel.

"They say he's a fighter. Are you going to join in the play?"

The ugly face of the night guard filled his vision as the man peered into his cage. There was a tradition in the mines, where new prisoners were fought over and conquered, owned like some kind of prize, by men who had ceased to be men. Despite his massive bulk, the prisoner had not escaped the degradation of the prison mines' traditions when he first arrived.

Another guard appeared. "You have a visitor."

He responded with silence. It was well known among the other inmates that this prisoner did not speak. He ate. He worked. He emptied his bowels. He fought like a demon if anyone chose to make him an enemy, but he never spoke.

"Did you hear, scum from the bottom of a pit of shit? You have a visitor."

He heard the clatter of keys, and then he was dragged out of his cage by the wild knot of hair that half-shrouded his face. At the end of the tunnel, he was thrown into a larger cell and shoved up against its damp stone wall. But still he refused to react. If there was one weapon he had against these savages, it was not acknowledging their existence.

He heard the clatter of keys again and was hauled around to see a figure enter. The lad was young, that was evident. Hair shorn to the scalp, large dark eyes. And then he realized he was not looking at a boy, but a girl dressed in the dull gray shift worn by the Lagrami novices.

The guard looked at both of them, an ugly smile plastered on his face. The girl waited for him to leave before she spoke.

"I did the minister a favor, and he offered me one in return," she said quietly. "I told him I had a perverse interest in infamous traitors."

It was not her words that made him flinch, but the sound of his mother tongue. It had been some years since he had heard it spoken. Not since the ambassador of Lumatere had visited him during his early days in this prison.

"They say you are the most unguarded inmate in the mines, sir. That there is no more ideal a prisoner than one who is locked up in his own prison."

He had heard it said about him before and had marveled with bitterness at how little they knew this place. Within the caves, the thick rock and endless tunnels made it impossible to escape. If he worked outside, he was chained to at least six other inmates, usually hostile foreigners who barely understood each other.

"When they next place you on work outside the mines, you will escape and travel east until you reach the shrine to Sagrami past the last cave before the mountains. In the ravine below, you will see horses tethered."

More silence.

"From there you take the road toward Osteria, where there are two paths, one to the town of Lannon and one to Hopetoun. Take neither. You will see a tiny lane through the woods that will lead you to a stable beside an abandoned cottage. This is where you will find us. Then we move north."

He knew what north meant. So now they were sending the young. Was it a group of exiles? Why didn't they tell their children that there was nothing north but the promise of death, even after all these years?

He walked over to where she stood leaning against the cage and raised his arm. She flinched. He stared down at her, then grabbed the bars above her head and rattled them to summon the guard.

"Humor me," she said, ducking under his arms. "From here I can see the prisoner they just dragged in." She crouched on the ground, straining to see to the end of the dark, stench-filled corridor.

The prisoner stayed where he was.

"I've heard a rumor," she said quietly. "Actually, I lie. Not a rumor." She beckoned him closer, and when he refused, she stood on her toes to whisper in his ear. "They say he's the son of Trevanion, captain of the Lumateran Guard."

He slammed her against the bars before either of them could take their next breath, holding her by the throat with a hand that had frequently snuffed out life. He heard a growl, low and primeval, and realized it was coming from him. Tightening his hold, he watched as her face began to change color and both her hands snaked up, trying to free herself. She shoved a knee against him, and when he stumbled back for a moment, she kicked him away from her, falling to her knees, gasping for air.

"Just the reaction I was hoping for, Captain," she whispered fiercely, looking up. "If you fail to protect him, if you fail to set him free, I will return and cut out your tongue and *then* you will have a reason for silence." She struggled to her feet. "Guard! Guard!"

"What have you done?" he asked hoarsely.

The look she gave him was pure anguish.

"What needs to be done!"


He woke the next morning having dreamed of peppermint and the wiry arms of a child wrapped around him like a monkey, refusing to let go. They would have to peel the boy off him at times, and how he would cry, this sensitive child who had not come from a line of sensitive people.

"I want to fight the boy."

The two guards stared at him in surprise. Fighting for a new inmate was a tradition the dark-eyed Trevanion had never engaged in.

*"You?"*

The guards exchanged sneers, their expressions ugly. "Heard you had a visitor last night."

The shorter of the guards leaned forward, a look of sick hunger on his face. "Did she awake in you a taste for young flesh?"

He avoided their eyes so they would misinterpret his rage for shame.

"Will you share, Trevanion?" the other asked. "The boy seems feisty enough for seconds." The guards laughed, and for the first time since his exile from Lumatere, Trevanion's rage pounded a rush of blood to his head.

*What needs to be done,* the girl had said.

This he knew. The piece of filth standing before him would be the first to die.

Then it would be her turn.


He watched the boy closely throughout the day. He was all arms and legs like his mother's people and seemed unaccustomed to a body that had grown too fast. Although skittish, he was coiled for action, not once buckling under the weight of the coal. But Trevanion read despair in the boy's eyes, and it chilled him to the marrow.

Later, in one of the larger caves, the inmates lined walls trickling with water that soon would be mixed with blood. Trevanion's only satisfaction was that he would pound senseless those who dared to want this boy. And he would do it easily. The Lumaterans of the River were the largest men in the land, and he towered over the rest of the inmates. In his early days they would come for him in packs until they realized the danger of encountering him alone.

There was an air of nervousness in the cave, and he watched an exchange between a guard and one of the Sorelian prisoners.

"They fear that your intention is to maim, Trevanion."

"Not interested in maiming." He spoke quietly, and the stare he directed at his potential opponents was enough to change the minds of half of those who had stepped forward.

The boy looked frightened, and Trevanion would have given anything to be able to send him some silent message of reassurance. But first he had this scum to fight, and then it would be the boy.

He fought five men that night. Blood was shed, and the sound of bones cracking and fists thumping bounced off the cave walls. The bets were low, the outcome too predictable. And then it was time for the boy. Trevanion allowed himself a moment to work out how to use his fists in a way that would not damage one so young and inexperienced. But they let the boy off the leash and he lunged for Trevanion, his fists flying. Trevanion felt the bones in his nose shatter, but before he could recover, there was another blow to his face and another to the stomach. He let himself fall, hoping to reveal himself to the boy, but then something hard connected with his chin. The kick sent him flying, and he knew that whether he wanted to or not, he was going to have to beat this pup into submission.

He returned to his feet, his fist connecting with the boy's cheekbone. He heard the goading of those surrounding them, both prisoners and guards. He knew he could not lose, for to do so meant that someone else would fight the boy for the right to own him in a way that made Trevanion feel sick to his stomach. And so he pounded into the boy's flesh, fighting for both their lives with an intensity that had the crowd roaring with approval. They had waited a long time to see what Trevanion of Lumatere was capable of, and they saw it this night. Yet the boy refused to yield, and Trevanion prayed to his goddess that he could hold him for a moment and let him understand.

*What needs to be done.*

He felt an elbow to his face and heard the crunch of bone, and the fires of hell danced a death march inside his head. He reached for the boy's neck and pulled him toward him, both heads colliding, blood spraying from his mouth. He tasted it on his tongue mingled with the boy's, and the taste made him roar.

But the boy would not give up. What he lacked in strength he made up for in skill and endurance. Finally Trevanion had him on the ground, a hand to his throat, his face an inch away so he could see the white fear in the boy's eyes. So he could whisper a word he had trained himself never to say again, for the sound of it brought hope and an ache so intense it could kill a man. And every lowlife who had ever entered this godsforsaken prison knew that hope had no place in the mines of Sorel.

"Finnikin."

The boy stared in shock. He was half blinded by sweat and grime and blood, but for a moment he caught a good look at his enemy. Hair knotted, the stench of the rot that lived within it, potent. A face blackened by the dirt of the earth beneath them.

"Trust me."

And with that Trevanion's fist came down on his son.

When Finnikin woke, a foul odor filled his nose and he gagged, his body heaving. He started in shock when he saw the bear of a man standing over him, and suddenly everything from the night before flooded back.

The last time he had seen his father, Trevanion had been standing on a makeshift judging post in the main square of Lumatere. He had watched as the impostor's Guard forced his father to his knees. He remembered how Trevanion's men bit their fists with rage and how it took ten of them to hold back Perri the Savage.

Then they cried out the punishment for Beatriss and Trevanion: "Death for the traitor! Banishment for the accomplice!"

In that moment, his father looked up and found him in the crowd, the bleakness in his expression so great that it became the blanket Finnikin placed over his face for years to come. Even as he knelt, Trevanion of the River had looked like a giant. His hair, black and cropped to his skull, his skin the color of bronzed oil, every bone in his face perfectly placed.

The man before him now was a total stranger. Hair covered his face, dark and tangled in knots, spliced with gray. Trevanion's eyes had no light or warmth. Finnikin had to remind himself that this was the same man who had carried him as a child, high and safe, on his broad shoulders. The same man who had lain beside Lady Beatriss, gently kneading her tired fingers, whispering words in her ear that softened her face.

"Father?" It felt strange to speak the word.

Trevanion nodded. "Can you stand?"

Their prison cell was a cave, cold and damp. There was little room for one body, let alone two.

"Tell me about the girl," Trevanion said.

"The girl?"

"Spawn of the devil."

The cell was dark and the flickering torch outside gave only minimal light. Finnikin moved closer to Trevanion. "How do you know about her?"

"Visited the night you arrived." There was urgency in the way Trevanion spoke, as if wary of the sudden appearance of a guard.

"Here?" Finnikin said. "In the prison?"

"Is she friend or foe?" Trevanion asked.

"Who can tell? We inherited her from the cloister of Lagrami in Sendecane."

"You went to the end of the earth," his father muttered.

"She claims to walk through the sleep of those inside."

"Lumatere?"

Finnikin nodded. "And that she has made contact with the heir. With Balthazar."

"Sweet goddess," Trevanion said. "What wickedness is she planning with such a lie?"

"And you say she visited?"

"She has horses waiting for us in a ravine beyond the shrine of Sagrami."

"Horses!" Finnikin snorted, and Trevanion quickly covered Finnikin's mouth with his hand.

"*Quiet!*"

"We have *one* horse," Finnikin hissed. "What does she think we will do? Walk out of here with the blessing of the prison guards?"

"I need to get you out of here. I can't look after us both."

Finnikin was already shaking his head as his father spoke. "We both need to get out of here, and I don't need looking after."

"In here you do!" Trevanion snapped.

"Don't expect me to go without you."

Trevanion did not respond.

"It's either both of us, or I stay here and you—"

Trevanion grabbed him by the cloth of his prison garb, his expression furious. "*You do what I tell you to do.* You never question me again, do you hear?"

Finnikin pulled away, shaking his head emphatically. "I go nowhere without you, sir."

Trevanion sucked in air. "I've seen them drag out the dead bodies of boys your age, and you do not want to hear what they've done to them."

Finnikin wanted something more from his father than this.

More for the ten years of longing. He stared at this stranger, his father, straight in the eye. "I. Go. Nowhere. Without. You."

Then he turned and curled up as far away as possible, understanding with bitterness that he had walked straight into Evanjalin's plan.

From the window of the stable loft, Sir Topher watched. The novice stood at the gate outside the dilapidated cottage. He knew she would stay there until the moon rose, as she had done each day since Finnikin's imprisonment.

"They will come," she said firmly when he joined her.

"And if they don't?" he asked. "I understand what you are trying to do, but your methods could get him killed."

"The captain will not let any harm come to his son."

"Sometimes fathers can't protect their children, Evanjalin. Did yours save you from harm?" Sir Topher asked, knowing the question was cruel.

"No," she responded fiercely. "But my father would warn, 'Be prepared for the worst, my love, for it lives next door to the best.' And for that I thank him each day of my life."

Finnikin spent his first days in prison adjusting to his surroundings. He knew that to survive, he had to think rather than just react. The inmates stared in the same way they had the day he arrived, but they kept their distance and he understood why. Trevanion was like an unleashed animal, and those around him, including the guards, feared the consequences of coming too close.

"You work outside this week," the guard told Trevanion as they were taken back to their cage. Trevanion grabbed Finnikin and pushed him in front of the guard's nose.

"He stays behind," the guard said flatly. He was the least sadistic of the guards, which made him one-quarter human.

But Trevanion refused to move or to relax his grip on his son. He shook him in front of the guard again, and Finnikin felt like a rag doll, like some kind of toy at the mercy of everyone around him.

"Not taking the chance," the guard spat. "The Osterian prisoner cut out the throat of the Belegonian translator. No interpreter. Can't afford surprises."

"I speak five tongues," Finnikin said calmly in Sorelian, though he felt anything but calm. "I can be your translator." Trevanion pulled him away, but Finnikin broke free, his face an inch away from the guard. "I speak five tongues," he said, and then repeated the statement. Five times in five different languages.

The guard stared from him to Trevanion and then pushed them along. "Make sure you keep him on a leash," he warned through gritted teeth.

When they were alone in their cell, Trevanion looked at him questioningly. "Five languages?"

Finnikin shrugged, cracking his knuckles. "I lied. It's seven. If you count the grunting of the common Yut and those ridiculous sounds made by the Sendecanese."

"Who taught you?" Trevanion asked.

"Sir Topher insisted I learn about the culture of each kingdom we visited. He said it was the only way they would begin to accept us and offer us assistance."

"What else did he teach you?"

Finnikin was confused by the force of the question. "You have nothing to fear," he assured his father. "Sir Topher made sure he always honored your profession. I have trained with the royal Guard of almost every kingdom in the land."

"No one in my Guard speaks seven languages."

Finnikin did not respond.

"Do you know where the priest-king is?" Trevanion asked after a moment.

Finnikin shook his head. "He does not want to be found, but rumor has it that he's on this side of the land."

"The dukes?"

"Five are in exile. Two we believe were left behind. Three are dead."

Trevanion stiffened. "Is Lord Augie . . ."

"Alive. Still works for Belegonia. Has some ridiculous obsession with breaking you out of prison so you can lead us back to Lumatere. Why didn't Ambassador Corden tell him you were here?"

"Probably because he knew that Augie had some ridiculous obsession with breaking me out," Trevanion said dryly. "And if anything frightens Corden, it's not following correct protocol."

"Sir Topher calls him the monster of propriety," Finnikin said. "I call him a painful boil on the arse. But he does fund our journeys sometimes. Convinces the king of Osteria we can be of use if we are traveling around the land unnoticed. I trained with their Guard in exchange for information."

"You are spies?"

"We collect information." Finnikin propped himself on his elbow, facing his father. "Do you get much news from outside? From your Guard or the ambassador?"

Trevanion shook his head. "Not in the past seven years. My decision, not theirs."

"What is your theory about the impostor king?" Finnikin asked.

"Puppet to Charyn," Trevanion replied.

"Good."

He caught a hint of a smile on Trevanion's face.

"I'm glad I have your approval."

"It's just that we've always suspected it," Finnikin said, all of a sudden wanting to talk. "But it's only been lately that we've heard it spoken aloud."

He went on to explain to Trevanion their plans for the second Lumatere. He tried to convey the extent of the suffering experienced by the exiles, but could not quite find the words. The slaughter in Sarnak was the hardest to explain. It had been the biggest of the river camps. They suspected that two hundred of their people had died.

"Do you ever wonder if they're better off inside Lumatere?" Finnikin asked.

Trevanion shook his head. "When I first chose to challenge the king about his Guard and the dragonships, it wasn't only because of the former captain's weakness, Finnikin. It was because of his baseness. I'd heard stories of what he allowed to happen in the palace prison. What he instigated himself."

And then there was silence. Finnikin studied the hard outlines of his father's face.

"What of the Monts?" Trevanion asked.

"We've seen no trace, but we have a strong suspicion Evanjalin knows where they are."

"Evanjalin?" his father asked.

"Spawn of the devil," Finnikin reminded him.

Trevanion grunted. "When did you last see the Monts?"

"In the Valley of Tranquillity," Finnikin said quietly. "Saro moved his people out there in the days before the curse. Almost the moment they heard the queen was dead."

He thought of the horror of that day. Of the grief of the queen's mother, the *yata* of the Mont people, wailing, "My pretty babies. Where are my pretty babies?" Many had walked away or pressed their hands against their ears to block out the sound of her anguish, but Lucian had not left his grandmother's side. And from a distance, Finnikin had kept his vigil with the Mont.

Trevanion spoke only once more that night.

"The girl," he said.

"Evanjalin?"

"She has my mother's name."

CHAPTER 8

A week after his arrest, Finnikin spent his first day in the outside world. It was a relief to be able to breathe, despite the fact that he was shackled to five of the most vicious humans he had ever encountered. The guards saw to it that every inmate who worked outside the mines was a foreigner. If escape became a reality, the guards knew the prisoners would be at the mercy of a kingdom that despised outsiders and would soon find themselves back in the mines. Or, worse still, hanging from a tree.

When the head guard gave Finnikin an instruction to pass on to the others, he was instantly confronted with snarls and bared teeth.

"They despise with a passion those who interpret," Trevanion murmured. "They consider them spies for the guards."

And so Finnikin endured one of the longest days of his life. The menacing prisoners attached to him took every opportunity to tug the chain around his neck, causing it to chafe his skin. Or to drop rocks of considerable weight on his feet. Or yank his foot shackles so he found himself flat on his face on cold hard stone. When he picked himself up for the tenth time, he was shaking with rage.

The moment they reached the caves and his shackles were removed, Finnikin launched himself at the Osterian prisoner until both had blood pouring from their noses. The three hundred pounds of pure ugliness and fury held Finnikin's head under his arm, while the guards stood by and watched. If there was one thing they enjoyed, it was the sight of the inmates trying to tear each other apart. Then Trevanion become involved and suddenly blood flew in every direction.

"I can handle this," Finnikin hissed, jumping onto the Osterian and pressing the side of the man's face into the wall as hard as he could. When the Osterian looked like he was ready to pound a fist into Finnikin's temple, Finnikin remembered how Trevanion had bitterly recounted Evanjalin's words. *What needs to be done.*

"We're going to break out," he whispered into the man's ear in Osterian, before he bit part of it off and spat it out. "Interested in joining us?"

By the time the guards dragged the inmates off each other, Finnikin had also recruited the Yut, the Sarnak, the Belegonian, and the Charynite. Although there was no honor among these men, there was a hierarchy of hate, and they despised the Sorelians first and foremost.

"You're making my hair turn white," Trevanion muttered later, when they were alone in their cage.

"That would be your old age," Finnikin replied, trying to stretch out the aches and pains in every joint in his body.

"You fight well. Like the Yuts."

"We lived in the grasslands for a year when I was fourteen."

"And you needed to fight?"

"They mocked my accent. And of course you can't have

hair my color and not learn how to fight in any kingdom."

"Your mother had that hair. Would take my breath away every time I saw her."

Finnikin was surprised to hear Trevanion speak of a memory so painful. He wondered about a man having lost not just one but two women in his life. Both having died giving birth to his children.

"You'd be best to tie a kerchief around your head and keep your hair hidden. It draws attention."

Finnikin's hair had not been cut for months and was beginning to snag and knot in wild tangles around his shoulders.

Later, as they lay in the dark, he could feel his father's eyes on him and he wondered if he was just as much a stranger to his father as Trevanion was to him.

"So are your new friends all in?" Trevanion asked dryly.

"They seem to be. But I can't promise they won't snap our necks the moment they're free."

"Tell them this. You will pick a fight with me to bring the guards as close as possible. If we are lucky, there will be five, like most days. Then I go for the guard with the keys, and at the same time you take on the second guard. The first few moments are crucial, so we need to be quick. Two swords, five seconds. The Yut at the end uses his hand chains—grabs hold of his guard's sword and makes himself useful. Do not trust the Charynite or the Sarnak with the keys or a sword. If worse comes to worst, use them as a shield."

"The Charynite and the Sarnak? Human shields?"

"They would do the same to us in the blink of an eye."

"But you never use your own side as human shields."

"This won't be a war, Finnikin," his father said coldly. "It will be an execution."

Sir Topher woke with a start. A muffled sound came from the corner of the loft. He listened for a moment, and when he was satisfied it was only Evanjalin tossing restlessly in her sleep, he closed his eyes with the same heaviness of heart he had felt these past four nights. Until he heard a scream, hoarse, as if the girl was fighting for air. He twisted out of his bedroll, and in the half dark he saw the thief from Sarnak astride the novice as she struggled under his weight. Stumbling toward them, he heard the sickening sound of a blow, but before a second could land, he had the thief by the neck and hurled him across the loft.

"Sweet goddess," he muttered when he saw the girl's face.

Clutching what was left of her shift, she gasped for breath as he placed a blanket around her shoulders. When he made an attempt to hold her, she crawled away, shuddering against the timber beams of their shelter.

He heard a noise behind him and turned to where the thief was, on his feet, pulling up his trousers, a look of hatred in his eyes.

*"What are you?"*

"I just wanted a poke," the thief spat.

Sir Topher pushed the thief hard, and the boy staggered again. It had been his decision to have the thief untied these past two nights, and for that he would not forgive himself.

He grabbed the thief and tied him tightly with the ropes attached to the beams, catching a blow to his temple that almost sent him reeling. When he returned to the girl, he crouched at her feet and slowly reached over to lift her chin, startling her. She pressed herself farther into the wall, covering her head with shaking hands. He looked from one corner of the loft to the other. The thief was hurling abuse, spitting with fury and tugging madly at his ropes. Here was Lumatere's future, Sir Topher thought despairingly. Two wild animals with nothing but rage and hate.

"Did he . . ." He could not bring himself to say the words,

and after a moment she shook her head and looked up, her face stained with tears.

"My shift is torn," she whispered. "I cannot wear it."

Across her cheek was a purple bruise where the thief's fist had connected, and her lips were swollen and bleeding.

"He knows no other way but ugliness," Sir Topher said quietly. "He was taught no other lessons but those of force. His teachers have been scum who live by their own rules. No one has ever taught him otherwise."

"Am I to forgive him?" she said, her voice shaking with anger.

"No," he said sadly. "Pity him. Or give him new rules. Or put him down like a wild animal before he becomes a monster who destroys everything he encounters."

When he went to move away, she grabbed his sleeve.

"I think they are all dead."

A chill went through him. "Finnikin?"

"No. All the young girls," she said in a small broken voice. "Inside Lumatere."

"What are you saying, Evanjalin?"

"Tonight I walked through the sleep of one who mourned the death of a neighbor's daughter, cursing an ailment that seems to be taking the young girls of his village these past five years. I remember another sleep six months back when a young tanner grieved for a girl who could have one day been his sweetheart."

"You are not yourself, and your sleep was troubled."

She shook her head. "No, Sir Topher. We need to return to Lumatere. Our lifeblood is dying, and we need to set them free."

The next day, they traveled on foot to the closest village, hoping to secure a second horse. They took the thief from Sarnak with them, his hands bound by a rope attached to Sir Topher's waist. The moment they stepped into the crowded marketplace, Sir Topher heard the novice gasp in anger and then she was pointing to where *their* horse stood among four others.

"Are you sure?" he asked.

"Of course, I'm sure. They must have come across it in the ravine where we left it for Finnikin and the captain."

"Evanjalin, they are the slave traders," Sir Topher warned as she hurried toward them.

But Evanjalin could not be stopped, and Sir Topher followed, dragging the thief with him.

"That's our horse!" she shouted to one of the men. When he ignored her, she poked him and repeated, "That's our horse."

"Do you have papers?" he asked pleasantly.

"We need that horse," she said, her voice shaking with emotion.

"Then you may have it," the man said, twisting his lips into a sneer. "For ten pieces of silver."

Evanjalin swung around to stare at Sir Topher, gripping her head in anguish. They both knew that without the horse, Finnikin and Trevanion would be caught as quickly as they escaped.

"We have five pieces," Sir Topher said.

"Then I would suggest you find yourself a peddler and buy this girl a pretty dress," he said, looking down at Evanjalin, who was dressed in Finnikin's trousers and jerkin.

Then the man's expression changed. He stepped closer to Evanjalin and grabbed her face. "She would make a fair exchange. Even with the bruises. The traders of Sorel have a great need for sturdy young things."

"She's not for sale," Sir Topher said quickly.

Evanjalin shook free, a shudder passing through her body. She pushed the thief from Sarnak in front of the trader. "But how much would you give us for him?" she asked.

With each day of his imprisonment, Finnikin's frustration grew. Fearing that their work outside the mines would come to an end and all hope would be lost, he challenged his father constantly. But it rained for days, and Trevanion argued that to escape in such conditions would hinder them the moment they were free.

"Why not now?" Finnikin whispered to his father on their first day without rain for a week. "Today's guards are a lazy lot."

"Keep silent and do not question me," Trevanion said sharply.

So yet another day passed, and that night in their cell when Trevanion transferred his rations to Finnikin's bowl, Finnikin felt his rage and frustration boil over.

"Do not treat me like a child to be fed and kept alive," he hissed, shoving the food back into Trevanion's bowl.

"Then do not act like one. Eat!" Trevanion ordered. "We will have only one attempt at this, Finnikin. If it fails, you will grow old alongside me in this cell, and at this moment I have two desires. One is to see my son free, and the other is to choke the life out of the witch who put him here. But we are at the mercy of patience, luck, and timing, and today is not the day for all three."

"And what if you are wrong?" The moment the words escaped Finnikin's mouth, he regretted them.

"On the third day of the first week of each month," Trevanion continued as if Finnikin had not spoken, "the Sorelian palace guards make their journey to the mine. If we had escaped, they would have passed us on the road to land's end."

Finnikin could not meet Trevanion's eyes. "I will never question you again, sir."

When he looked up, he saw the slightest twitch play on his father's lips.

"I'm sure you will," Trevanion said. "I'm counting on it."

The more time Finnikin spent with his father, the more he became accustomed to the long periods of silence between them. Sometimes they lasted for hours, and then he would hear Trevanion's voice deep in the night.

"I will ask you this once and then I never want it spoken of again," his father said quietly at one such time.

Finnikin knew what his father was going to ask and waited for the question. When it didn't come, Finnikin turned to face him. "It was a girl child. Tiny, they said, no bigger than my palm. Seranonna delivered the child and went to the stake with your child's blood on her hands, mingled with Isaboe's. They said it was a blessing that Lady Beatriss and the babe died together."

But Finnikin did not speak about the post where they had tied up the midwife and the healer and the young girl with smiling eyes who had once given him a tonic. Nor did he say that he would never forget their deaths for as long as he lived. The smell of burning flesh, the screams of agony that seemed to go on forever. Then the silence. He could not tell his father the truth about that day. How in the village square at the age of nine he had his first kill. He had used a dagger, its point heavy for a quick, clean, long-distance lunge. The type of dagger that would fly better, sink deeper. Kill with precision.

By the time Sir Topher and Evanjalin returned the horse to the ravine, it was late in the day. They continued down the path to the ruined cottage, where Evanjalin immediately took up her post at the gate, her body slumping with exhaustion. Nothing Sir Topher said could convince her to move. Sometimes her faith disarmed him and he truly believed that Finnikin and his father would come walking down the path toward them. Other times, he would lose his temper with her.

"The captain of the King's Guard was the mightiest warrior in our kingdom," he told her sharply when she would not return to the loft for sleep that night. "If he could not escape from the mines of Sorel, what makes you think he will be able to set both of them free?"

"Because the mightiest warrior of our kingdom has been missing one major incentive to escape, sir. Necessity," she said firmly. "It is a powerful motivator, and no one in this land will be more desperate than Trevanion to have his son free. But most important, he has a weapon now, more powerful than these," she said, clenching her fists. "A sharp mind, full of knowledge and skill. Do not underestimate the value of what Finnikin has learned from you, Sir Topher. He is not merely the son of the captain of the King's Guard. He is the ward of the king's First Man, who many say is the smartest man in Lumatere."

That night, Sir Topher prayed to his goddess for a sign, but in the morning there was still no Finnikin and Trevanion. But there was the novice Evanjalin. Waiting at the broken gate in the same place Sir Topher had left her the night before.

And this time when he reached her side, he stayed and waited.

In the middle of the second week, they took their chance. The sun was high overhead when Trevanion gave the signal.

"Why now?" Finnikin asked. "They'll have the daylight to track us down. Should we not wait until later?"

"We won't be leaving anyone behind to search for us," Trevanion said in a low voice. "And by the time the party fails to return at the end of the day, we will hopefully be on horseback."

Finnikin threw the first punch, taking Trevanion by surprise.

"You enjoyed doing that, didn't you?" Trevanion muttered from the ground, rubbing his jaw as the rest of the men chained to them joined the tussle. "Squeamish?" he asked Finnikin as the guards approached.

"No. Why?" Finnikin asked.

The first guard was dead before he hit the ground. Trevanion grabbed the guard's sword and threw it to Finnikin before tossing the keys over the heads of the others to the Yut. The Yut was vicious in his attack, and the guard standing closest to him did not stand a chance. Finnikin understood why they were considered the savages of the land.

Finnikin felt weighed down fighting with one hand while chained, but thankfully the guards were not soldiers and knew little of swordplay. He watched Trevanion work the sword in his hand as if it had been a part of his body all his life. Trevanion's speed and endurance had always put him a class above everyone else, and ten years in prison had not changed that.

"Lead with the point of your sword, Finn," his father shouted above the clashing of swords and the bellows and grunts. "And you bend your elbow at an awkward angle."

"Because it's half-broken," Finnikin shouted back, irritated, ducking as the blade of the guard's sword swung across his head.

"You're throwing your whole body in," Trevanion said critically as he plunged the sword into the third guard's gut.

"Stop watching me!" Finnikin yelled.

"You're fighting like a Charynite!"

Finnikin hissed in reaction to the insult. Charynites fought with no skill and pure adrenaline, and Trevanion had always been scathing about their methods when he taught Finnikin as a child. Finnikin thrust the sword to the hilt into his guard, muttering furiously. It wasn't his fault that his education in swordsmanship had been conducted in at least five different royal courts.

"Why aren't these chains unlocked?" Trevanion shouted, pummeling the last guard in the head.

"*Yut!*" Finnikin yelled, looking over to the man whose chains were wrapped around a guard's head. "Dead is when their heads are half off and their eyes are wide open, so let go, you halfwit. He's dead!"

The Yut let go of the mangled body and unlocked the leg shackles of the six men before leaping over the dead guards and disappearing beyond the quarry. One by one the others followed him. There would be no bond among the prisoners, and Finnikin wondered how they would fare without horses or language, but the moment his father was free, the fate of the foreigners was swiftly forgotten.

"Take the chain," Trevanion instructed as he dislodged a pickax from the ground.

"Won't swords be enough?" Finnikin protested.

"Not for what we want to do."

Finnikin stared at the bodies of the guards that littered the road. Hardly recognizable. Despite everything he'd witnessed, he felt sick to know that so much damage could be done with swords and a chain.

"Let's go."

There were two paths open to them, one that led to Bateaux and the other west to the coast. Trevanion took neither, but instead pointed back toward the mine caves. Finnikin bit his tongue to stop himself from asking what in the goddess's name Trevanion was thinking. Surely his father knew that all the caves were connected and they'd end up back in the prison mines.

"The road to Bateaux will be the obvious route taken by the others," Trevanion said as they raced toward the caves. "The soldiers and prison guards will search there first."

"But to go through the mines?"

"Not through." Trevanion pointed up. "Over. We climb, and then walk over the caves. The shrine to Sagrami is past the last cave before the mountains. We climb back down again into the ravine and there we find the horse."

The rock face before them looked almost impossible to climb. Its surface was smooth, with no jagged ruts to provide footholds. Trevanion took a step back, then grabbed the chain from Finnikin. He secured the pickax to the chain, once, twice, three times, and then swung the pickax over his head and launched it toward the top of the cave with a grunt. It missed, and they both jumped back as it landed with a clunk at their feet. Trevanion tried again, but his throw had less power this time and he yanked the pickax back before it became lodged too low. Finnikin tried, but each time, the pickax would flatten against the rock and come clanking down.

Suddenly they heard a sound from the direction of the town of Bateaux, one that chilled them. Dogs barking. Someone had raised the alarm.

"So soon," Finnikin cursed.

"Probably the brainless Charynite," Trevanion muttered.

"We can take one of the river caves," Finnikin said. "Our scent will end where the water begins."

But Trevanion was shaking his head. "I would be leading you to your tomb, Finn. It's too soon after the rains."

The hounds were closer, their barks growing louder and more ferocious. Trevanion turned toward the sound and then back to Finnikin. There was sorrow and resolution in his eyes.

"*No.* Absolutely not," Finnikin said.

"Listen to me—"

"No!" Finnikin shouted. "If you use yourself as bait, I will follow you and both of us will end up torn to pieces or back in that cesspit."

"Finn, listen!" Trevanion said, his voice raw. "I prayed to see you one more time. It's all I prayed for. Nothing more. And my prayers were answered. Go east, I'll lead them west."

"We have a dilemma, then," Finnikin said fiercely. "Because I prayed that you would grow old and hold my children in your arms as you held me. My prayers have not been answered yet, Trevanion. So whose prayer is more worthy? Yours or mine?"

Trevanion stared at him with frustration and then grabbed the pickax and swung again. It took three more attempts, but finally its sharp tip lodged in the stone. With a tug on the chain to check it was secure, he pushed Finnikin forward to begin the climb. Finnikin scrambled up the cave wall, his eyes on the pickax above him, willing it to stay in place. He felt the moment Trevanion began to climb behind him, the chain becoming taut and painful to hold.

At the top, he extended a hand to Trevanion and pulled with all his might. He felt pain shoot up from his elbow, but he gritted his teeth and ignored it. They grabbed at the chain and hauled it up to hide it from their pursuers.

"Stay down!" Trevanion said, struggling for air.

For a long while they did not move, pressing themselves flat against the rock as the dogs barked and the guards called out to one another below. Finnikin watched his father, waiting for a sign. It wasn't until the air was silent and Trevanion seemed satisfied they would not be seen from afar that he pointed out a path to the east over the caves.

"But to get to the shrine—" Finnikin began.

Trevanion silenced him.

"All you do is follow," he said.

Later, when Finnikin felt there was no more strength in his body, when the sun caused the world to double in his eyes and Trevanion half carried him down the rock face toward the ravine, he thought he heard the sound of rain. Suddenly Trevanion stopped and Finnikin stumbled to his knees. Before them, from the mountain above, a stream of water showered from the rocks in sprays of silver. And behind the waterfall, like an apparition, was the shrine of the goddess Sagrami.

Without thinking, Finnikin staggered to his feet and pulled off his shirt and trousers to stand naked under the coolness. When he looked back at Trevanion, his father was staring at the water with an expression of wonder. Then he removed his clothing and stood alongside Finnikin, lifting his face to the sky and extending his arms. Slowly he turned and placed his hands on either side of Finnikin's head, before pressing his lips to his son's forehead like a man giving thanks to his goddess for all things blessed. And for the first time since Trevanion's arrest in Lumatere, Finnikin allowed the tears to fall under the shower from the rocks, mingling them with the blood and grime and rot that he knew would never be truly washed from his father's memory.

In the ravine below was the horse from Sarnak. Trevanion leaped on and grabbed Finnikin's injured arm, almost pulling it out of its socket. Sharp threads of pain shot through him, but he held on as his father turned the horse toward the east. When they reached the fork in the road, following the novice's instructions, they found the path of stones that took them into the woods.

Trevanion rode the horse hard, and it took all of Finnikin's strength not to lose his grip. As he stared into the distance, he began to doubt that the cottage in the woods even existed. Until there it was, and standing at the gate that marked its entrance was Sir Topher . . . and Evanjalin.

Trevanion was off the horse in an instant and went straight for the girl's throat, lifting her from the ground. It took Sir Topher and Finnikin's combined strength to pull him away.

"Let her go, Trevanion," Sir Topher said. "She's more good to us alive than dead."

After a moment Trevanion released her and she stumbled. She looked to Finnikin, but he would not meet her gaze.

Trevanion took Sir Topher's hand and gripped it hard. "I am your servant until my last day on this earth," he said quietly as the two men embraced.

Finnikin winced as Sir Topher put a hand on his shoulder.

"You are in pain?"

"I'm fine." He watched as Evanjalin disappeared into the trees beyond the cottage.

"You were lucky she only sent you to prison. She sold the thief to the traders of Sorel."

"Mercy," Finnikin said, amazed that her actions still had the power to surprise him. But he had seen the bruises on her face, and he looked at the older man closely. "What did he do to her?"

"Enough to deserve what he got."

That night, as Finnikin lay in the loft nursing his arm, Evanjalin crouched beside him. He smelled leaves of rosemary and eucalyptus and watched as she stirred a substance into a paste and then administered the balm to his bruised and swollen face.

"Did I not tell you to bend to their will?" she reprimanded him.

"Have I ever given you reason to believe that I would bend to another's will?" he replied sharply. When the balm stung his face, he gripped her wrist with a firmness he knew caused pain.

"Why are you so angry?" she asked, pulling away.

"You betrayed me! Am I supposed to be grateful? Am I supposed to thank you?"

"You have your father. Lumatere has the captain of its Guard."

"Lumatere doesn't exist!"

"That is your belief, Finnikin!" she said. "I can tell by reading your *Book of Lumatere.*"

"You have no right to touch that book," he said angrily.

"You dropped it when the soldiers took you away."

"Don't you mean I dropped it when you betrayed me?"

She studied his face for a moment. "You list the dead. You tell the stories of the past. You write about the catastrophes and the massacres. What about the living, Finnikin? Who honors them?"

"You think you're worthy of the task?" he asked bitterly. "After what you've done? Go to bed, Evanjalin. Lumaterans sleep easier without your help."

He heard her sigh as she leaned toward him. "Only someone who has the comfort of two fathers sleeping close by could make such a statement."

She lifted his arm and he winced. "I'm going to have to dislocate your shoulder," she said. "I know exactly what to do, so you need not fear anything. Do you want a signal, or would you like to signal me?"

"What kind of a signal?" he said, alarmed. "Can I trust you?"

She looked hurt. "Of course you can. Maybe a count."

"As in one, two—"

His cry of pain echoed across the stable, and within seconds Trevanion was in the loft with Sir Topher at his heels.

"What have you done?" Trevanion bellowed, grabbing her by the arm and shaking her.

Finnikin was spluttering, his eyes rolling and watering from the waves of pain that paralyzed his arm.

"I know how to administer to cuts and injuries," she said in a small voice.

"Is that what you do? Administer suffering?" Trevanion snarled.

"Let her go, Trevanion," Sir Topher said. "She has suffered herself. She was with the exiles in Sarnak."

"And you believe her?" Trevanion asked coldly.

Evanjalin looked down, unable to meet his stare.

"Tell us who they were. What part of Lumatere did they come from?" Trevanion asked.

"Go on, Evanjalin," Sir Topher said gently.

But she would not respond, and despite the pain, Finnikin clenched his fist with fury.

"You lied to the High Priestess about Sarnak?" he accused.

"No, I didn't." Eyes still downcast, she handed Sir Topher the herbs. "On the arm, just below the joint," she said as she climbed out of the loft.

Trevanion's expression was hard. "We rid ourselves of her the first moment we get."

## CHapteR 9

L eaving Sorel became their only priority, and despite Trevanion's objections to anything Evanjalin suggested, they agreed with her that the lawless town at land's end was their best bet for survival. Speranza was a place that had been conquered, reconquered, and relinquished so many times that no one seemed to remember who governed it. In such a place, the presence of two escaped prisoners, even one who looked as if he had stepped out of the depths of hell, would go largely unnoticed.

At midday they entered the courtyard of the tavern in town. From the balconies, women beckoned to them with gestures that needed no interpreting. As they pointed and purred, Finnikin heard Evanjalin give a snort beside him before going off to tether their horse.

Inside, the women had descended into the main room. Finnikin watched as Trevanion quickly became the center of attention. He remembered how the ladies of Lumatere would fawn over the captain of the King's Guard. The brutal years in the mines of

Sorel had not altered the striking features of his face. With his knotted hair tied back and his dark beard cropped, he still had a presence that attracted the opposite sex, despite the unhealthy pallor of his skin.

Sir Topher returned, holding a key. "Come, Evanjalin, I have booked us a room. Perhaps a rest?" he suggested, all too aware of what was on offer for the others.

Finnikin stole a glance at her, but then the women with wicked laughter in their eyes were upon them and he allowed one to take his hand.

Later, he stepped onto the tiny balcony beside the bed and watched the vendors pack away their stalls. The tavern girl playfully pulled him back toward her. He had enjoyed their time together. She had required nothing from him but pleasure. No intelligent banter, no request to save a kingdom or sacrifice a part of himself. But he resisted the temptation to stay and pulled on his clothes before grabbing his pack.

In the courtyard, he sat at a table and retrieved the *Book of Lumatere.* He thought of Evanjalin lying in the room above and remembered their conversation from the night of his arrest. He had trusted her, and she had deceived him. He flicked through the book, his fingers running over all the names he had recorded over the years. But then he turned to a page of unfamiliar hand-writing, and his breath caught. There, in a small neat hand, was page after page of names, some written with self-assurance, others with a tremble.

He stood, about to make his way into the tavern to find her when he realized the horse post was empty.

"The horse?" he called out to the stable boy. "Who took our horse?"

"You brought no horse," the boy said.

"The novice did."

"Who?"

"Girl. Blue woolen cap. Dressed like a boy."

Recognition registered on the boy's face. "She came back for it."

"Where did she go?" Finnikin asked uneasily. The boy ignored him, and Finnikin walked away, trying to decide whether to call Trevanion and Sir Topher. Instead, he turned back to the boy. "If I were to continue down the road to the south, what would I see?"

"Not another village for at least a day."

"Nothing?"

"Nothing," he repeated.

"And how far to the closest village going east?"

"I tell you there is nothing," the boy said as Finnikin began to walk away again. "Except for the camp."

Finnikin's heart slammed in his chest. "Camp?"

"Of the filthy exiles. Should round them up and—"

Finnikin did not stay to hear the boy's suggestion. He took the road out of town and headed east.

He smelled the camp before he saw it. But nothing had prepared him for the sight. It was spread over more land than the town he had left behind, but never in his travels with Sir Topher had he seen a camp more damned. Those standing at the edges watched him with empty eyes. *This is not life,* Finnikin thought, *just day-to-day survival.* He heard the heart-wrenching wails of babies crying from hunger.

When he saw no sign of the horse, he was torn between relief that Evanjalin might not be there and a fear of where else she could be.

"I'm looking for a girl. Bare head, dark eyes," he said to anyone who looked in his direction.

When no one responded, he began to make his way through the rows of makeshift tents. Children with bloated stomachs stared at him with the vacant expressions they had inherited from their parents. Flies hovered over their faces and fed from their open sores.

A hand reached out and gripped his arm. It was a man, little older than Finnikin, his skin stretched taut over prominent cheekbones. "You are heading toward the fever camp," the man said. "You had best be on your way, for it catches you fast."

Finnikin looked past him. Excrement lined the path to the next camp, and he could hardly breathe from the stench of vomit and shit and death and sickness. He stumbled to the side and emptied his stomach of the mutton soup and ale he had consumed at the tavern. As he stayed bent, he stared with horror at the body of a woman in front of him, eyes wide open, flies feeding.

He felt a hand on his shoulder. It was the man again, compassion on his face. *Somehow compassion survives,* Finnikin thought in wonder. He stood up, ashamed, and wiped his mouth with his sleeve.

"Are you looking for the priest-king?" the man asked.

Finnikin was stunned. "The priest-king? Our blessed Barakah is here?"

The man nodded. "In the fever camp."

Finnikin walked away, covering his mouth with his hand.

"Come back for us," the man begged. "Whoever you are, do not forget us."

Beyond the tents, Finnikin saw a stretch of land that marked where the exile camp ended and the fever camp began. The fever camp was an assortment of the most basic living quarters, made up of sheets and blankets tied to posts. Bodies littered the space beneath them. Those who were bent over the sick looked like living dead themselves.

But worse was beyond the sick huts. A lad with a corpse slung over his shoulder walked by, and Finnikin followed him to a pit dug deep into the earth. Men. Women. Children. Those his age who would never lie with a woman as he had that afternoon. He saw girls, their hair the color of spun gold, or waves dark and thick. The beautiful girls of Lumatere. Dead. Piled on top of one another. Layers of wasted skin and bones. The lad passed him twice, each time carrying a dead body that he proceeded to throw into the pit of the dead. Finnikin noticed the boy's strong hands. Craftsman's hands. Made for rebuilding.

But there was no place for rebuilding here. Just burying.

He sensed her before he saw her. She was walking toward him from one of the blanket hovels, holding a baby in her arms. A baby so still, Finnikin knew it no longer breathed. Evanjalin looked up and their eyes met across the pit of the dead.

*Look away,* he told himself. Do not let yourself get lost in those eyes.

When she reached him, he watched her search for something, desperation in her movements.

"What are you looking for, Evanjalin?" he asked.

"His mother," she said in a broken voice. "She died earlier with the baby still attached to her breast."

He wanted to walk away. Go back to the sleepy girl in the tavern who asked nothing of him but three copper coins. Who made him forget for a moment, when he was deep inside of her, this girl with large pools of night-sky for eyes.

Evanjalin continued to search among the bodies, and then he saw where her gaze ended. At a woman sprawled in a pit, arms outstretched. Evanjalin looked at the babe she held and crouched down. He could see that she planned to slip into the grave. And before he knew what he was doing, Finnikin climbed into the pit and she handed him the baby. Stepping around the bodies, he made his way to where the mother lay and placed the child on her breast, wrapping the dead woman's arms around her boy.

He felt dry sobs rising inside him, carving up his throat, and when Evanjalin held out her hand and pulled him out of the pit, he knew she could read it all on his face.

"Do not cry," she said fiercely, but her own tears flowed. "Do not cry, Finnikin. For if we begin, our tears will never end."

He held her face in his hands, her tears catching in his fingers, his forehead against hers. Cursed land, Sir Topher had said. Cursed people.

The priest-king had altered so much since the old days of Lumatere that Finnikin hardly recognized him. Finnikin had been in awe of the holy man as a child. Even Lucian believed he was some kind of god in his elaborate robe trimmed with gold, each finger adorned with rings. Today he wore a grubby brown mantle and hood; his beard was long, his feet sandaled. A toe or two seemed to be missing, and the marks of age stained his hands. The only reminders of the man he used to be were the deep laugh lines around his eyes. The priest-king had always loved to laugh.

"You're still here," the holy man muttered when he saw Evanjalin. "I told you. This is no place for one so young and healthy."

"This is no place for anyone," she corrected softly. "You are the priest-king. You need to lead these people home."

The man shook his head. "A title that means nothing outside the kingdom."

"When we return to Lumatere—"

"If you want her to live, take her away," the priest-king said.

Finnikin knew they were being dismissed. He turned to Evanjalin. "There will be no return," he said quietly.

She glared at him. "Look at them. Do you believe that a strip of land in someone else's kingdom will be any better than this?"

"How can you even ask that, Evanjalin?"

"What did they do to a newborn in your rock village, Finnikin?" she said, taking his hand and clenching it into a fist. "Wrapped their little hands around stone from the village, binding it tightly for days. As they did with those from the Flatlands. Earth from the fields clenched in their fists. Silt from the river clenched in their fists. Grass from the mountains. Leaves from the forest. Joining them to the land." She blinked back tears. "We don't want a second Lumatere. We want to go home. Take us home, Finnikin."

She turned to the priest-king. "Blessed Barakah, if you return with us, people will follow. Those who are well. We will return to Lumatere where healers—"

"The healers are all dead, Evanjalin," Finnikin said, his anger rising. "The Forest Dwellers, the novices of Sagrami, any of them who had the skill and gift to heal are all dead. I was there. I heard their screams as they burnt at the stake. Even if we were able to get inside Lumatere, there is nothing to go back to. Can you not understand that? The only hope for our people is a second homeland in Belegonia."

"Why do you fear returning, Finnikin? Were you not the one who swore an oath with Balthazar to save Lumatere?"

"Prince Balthazar?" the priest-king asked.

"No," she said, shaking her head. "For if he lives, he is now King Balthazar."

"And does he live?"

"Evanjalin dreams he does," Finnikin mocked. "Do you have a plan, Evanjalin?" he demanded. "Do you believe you will belong to him? A commoner to marry a king?"

Fury flashed in her eyes. "Remember this," she seethed. "Our queen was a commoner. From the Mountains of Lumatere. Do not dare scorn such a match."

"Quiet!" the priest-king said. He waited for their silence. "So you dream of King Balthazar and believe that this is enough to convince me to follow you across this godsforsaken land in search of a country cursed?"

"No, blessed Barakah. I believe you've been told many times that Balthazar lives, and each time has proved to be false. But I can give you another name," she said, staring at Finnikin.

"I have work to do," the older man said, getting to his feet. "Names mean nothing to me."

"Not even Captain Trevanion?"

He stopped and turned, stunned. Then he looked at Finnikin as the truth dawned on him. "Finnikin of the Rock? Son of Trevanion of the River?"

"The very same," she said.

"I can answer for myself," Finnikin snapped.

"He has escaped?" the priest-king asked.

Evanjalin nodded.

"Is he with his Guard?"

"No. With a whore," she explained.

"Evanjalin!"

She looked at Finnikin with disbelief. "Oh, so now we are bashful?" But then she turned her attention back to the priest-king. "If we bring him here with the king's First Man, will you be willing to convince these people to go north, blessed Barakah?"

"Bring them to me and we will speak."

Despite everything they had seen, Evanjalin looked pleased with herself as they set off back to town. Instead of taking the main road, she crossed into the woods. "A much more pleasant track for walking," she said. "The river runs by here."

Finnikin stopped suddenly. "The horse? Where's the horse?"

She shrugged. "I don't have my horse anymore."

"*Your* horse? The horse was mine."

"Don't be ridiculous." Evanjalin continued walking up the track. "You would never have stolen the horse in Sarnak if I didn't encourage you. So I consider it mine."

"But I officially stole it," he argued.

"Fine. But the horse you officially stole was actually re-stolen and we had to trade the thief from Sarnak for it, so really the horse could be considered his," she said over her shoulder.

Finnikin tried to control his anger as he caught up to her. "So why don't you have *his* horse anymore?"

"Well, a wonderful thing happened while you were off whoring. I discovered that the thief spoke the truth and had sold the ring to a peddler from Osteria who happened to be traveling in these parts." Evanjalin dug into the pockets of her trousers and held out the the ruby ring. "Isn't it beautiful?" she asked, a smile of pure delight on her face.

"Dazzling," he muttered, bristling at the way she'd said "whoring."

"You'll like this route. The river will look lovely at this time of day," she said.

But there was nothing lovely about the river as far as Finnikin could see. Just the ugliness of the slave traders of Sorel, their young prey, male and female, trapped in cages set upon barges. The females looked no more than children and made up most of the cargo.

There was little room along the bank, yet greedy buyers were pressed against one another, bidding for humans as if they were livestock. Sorel was the only kingdom with no laws against slavery, and Finnikin had heard rumors that children were branded like animals. As always, he willed the voice inside of him to take over. The one that told him he did not know these people and could easily forget them the moment they were out of his sight. And then he saw, between the shoulders of the two buyers in front of him, the thief from Sarnak. Tied to a timber horse post, naked and shivering.

Finnikin knew the thief had seen him. He saw surprise in the boy's face, then something else. A pleading. The boy began to mouth something, his lips moving desperately.

Finnikin pushed his way through the crowd of buyers. The thief kept his gaze on him, his mouth moving even as they untied him. When one of the traders noticed him speaking, the back of his fist caught the boy across the face and the thief staggered to his knees. But still he lifted his head and his mouth continued to move.

And then Finnikin realized with horror what the boy was saying.

"Kill me," Evanjalin said beside him. "That's what he's asking you to do."

*Kill me. Kill me.*

Finnikin found himself reaching for the dagger in the scabbard on his back. He dared not look at Evanjalin. "We didn't take this route because it was a pleasant walk, did we?" he said angrily.

"I thought you loved the river," she said.

"You meant for this to happen. You knew he was here, and you want to save him."

"Don't be ridiculous, Finnikin," she snapped. "Why would I want to save a worthless thief who tried to rape me while I slept?"

When Finnikin didn't respond, she shrugged. "But then I thought of your pledge. The one from the rock in Sorel where you said you'd search the land for the orphans of Lumatere and bring them back, and I believe *you'll* want to save him. If you get the boy now, you won't have to come back for him when you're nice and settled with some lord's sweet, fragile daughter."

"You are evil," he seethed.

"Oh, the way that word is thrown around!" she said. "Everything is evil that humans can't control or conquer."

"What do you expect me to do?" he argued. "Fight the traders for the thief? You're the one who sold him."

"Because I needed a horse for your escape," she replied calmly.

"Which I would not have needed if you hadn't betrayed me. Then you go and sell the horse for the ring. So now we have no horse," he continued, "and a ruby ring that I'm presuming you're going to trade for a useless thief."

"What a ridiculous suggestion," she said. "He stole the ring in the first place!"

Finnikin held the dagger tightly, a splinter from the wooden handle digging into his palm. He looked up at the thief and saw bleak relief pass over the boy's face.

"I will do the right thing and put him out of his misery." He wondered when the horror of the day would end.

"And if you miss?"

"I never miss." There was no boasting in his tone, just sadness. Finnikin turned the dagger and held the blade between his thumb and finger. He stared at his target, bile rising in his throat. But before he could take aim, Evanjalin placed a hand on his arm and took the dagger from him.

"We are not going to buy the thief, Evanjalin," he said wearily.

"Of course not," she said, leaning to whisper in his ear. "We'll just steal him."

"And what are we supposed to do? Storm the barge? I don't have my father's sword, and I can't see myself succeeding against ten traders and these feral buyers whose type I recognize from the mines. Remember the mines where you put me? For which I will never forgive you."

"And I will never forgive you for the whore!" There was anger in her eyes. "We wait until someone buys the thief and then we ambush the buyer. Which means, Sir No Sword and Three Knives, our chances of success are high, because I'm presuming there will only be one buyer to fight."

"And what makes you think I carry three knives?"

She clutched his forearm where the smallest knife was hidden, then placed her arms around him and embraced him, patting his back to feel the second scabbard of the dagger she held in her hand.

"And the third?" he asked.

There was another flash of anger in her eyes. "Do you expect me to get on my knees before you? Like your whore? The third is at your ankle."

Fury rose inside him. "I *curse* the day I climbed that rock in Sendecane," he spat.

She looked at him sadly. "That's where we differ, Finnikin. For I believe that was when it all began."

They watched in silence as the traders unlocked the boy's shackles and bound his hands. Finnikin suspected that the buyer would take the thief along the river and wait for morning to travel down the waterway to the mines.

"If we do this . . ." he said, turning to Evanjalin.

But she was gone. He pushed through the crowd, searching, calling her name. He leaped onto the back of a man close by to get a clear view of the area and was thrown aside. There were grunts of hostility and elbows thrust into his face as he pushed his way to the river's edge, where the barges floated. Evanjalin had taken to wearing his brown woolen trousers and blue cap, but the colors were too dull to stand out in the waning light. He hoped she had enough sense to find her way back to the tavern. The thought of her being lost to them as he had once wished suddenly sent a shiver through him.

Farther down the bank, he caught sight of the thief being dragged away. Had the owner clothed the boy, Finnikin might have left things as they were. But in the fever camp, he had stumbled over the naked body of a boy the same age as the thief. In Lumatere, boys that age had been robust and full of mischief, teasing the girls they had grown up with, not knowing whether they wanted to follow their fathers or cling to their mothers. There was something unnatural about a boy of fourteen lying dead, and Finnikin had seen it too often. *Enough,* he thought. *Enough.*

Finnikin followed the thief and his owner down a trail deep into the woods. He knew if he did not succeed in setting the thief free that night, he would at least put him out of his misery. It would be simple, he told himself. He would race farther ahead and cut them off, taking the slave owner by surprise. But then he lost sight of them through the thick foliage and decided to scale the pine tree closest to him. When he reached a height that gave him a better view of his surroundings, his heart sank. From where he was balanced, he could see the thief and his owner walking toward a clearing. And in the clearing was another man setting up camp. Evanjalin had been wrong. The buyer was not alone.

He knew he had to move quickly. But just as he was about to climb down, he saw her. She leaped out of the trees at the edge of the trail and threw herself on the back of the thief's owner with Finnikin's dagger in her hand.

Finnikin hit the ground running. Between the trees he could

see she had the advantage, slicing the man across the chest, her arm around his neck, her legs wrapped around his waist. But it was too late. The buyer's companion had reached them. He pulled Evanjalin by the jerkin and threw her face forward against a tree, twisting her arm to make her let go of the dagger.

Finnikin ran harder. *Don't let him find out she's a girl. Please, don't let him find out she's a girl.*

But the man's hands prodded and poked, crawling up her torso.

"Evanjalin!"

One dagger caught the first man in the back, and the second knife landed an inch above Evanjalin's fingers on the tree. In a split second she had yanked it out and thrust it backward, catching her attacker unaware. When the man stumbled away, she plunged the knife twice more into his thigh, crippling him for a moment.

*"Run!"* Finnikin yelled as he tossed his cloak to the boy. He fought off the second man as Evanjalin grabbed the thief and they bolted into the woods. With a punch that left the man reeling, Finnikin raced after them.

"Keep running," he yelled. Ahead he could see the thief, whose leaps and lunges warned him of the unevenness of the ground. And then he was beside Evanjalin, realizing, as the blood pumped into his heart and the pulse at his neck threatened to burst, that his need to distance himself from their pursuers was less important than his need to take the lead from her.

They reached the end of the trail and burst into the open valley, where the sun was just beginning to disappear. As he inched closer, he could tell by her sideways glance and the glint in her eye that she was not going to let him pass. But she was tiring, and when she pointed up ahead to the road that led to Speranza, she held her hand in front of him, barring him, keeping him back. He shoved her hand aside, pushing her in the process, and when she stumbled, he took the lead, following the thief as he leaped over the timber fence that boarded a meadow. By then there were no sounds of heavy feet behind them, just his breathing and Evanjalin's.

When the thief stopped and fell to his knees to catch his breath, Finnikin collapsed onto the grass and Evanjalin fell down beside him. He rolled onto his back, holding his side in an attempt to reduce the pain, and when he looked across at her, he thought he caught a glimpse of a smile on her face.

The thief stared at them. There was no humility or gratitude in his expression. And little else either.

"I own you," Evanjalin said bluntly as she sat up. "Never forget that, boy."

Trevanion and Sir Topher were waiting for them outside the tavern. Sir Topher's eyes widened with disbelief when he recognized the thief, but before he could say a word, Evanjalin rushed up to him.

"Sir Topher," she said breathlessly, "I got it back!" She clutched the ruby ring in her hand. Finnikin watched Sir Topher look down at her with tender affection before reaching over and folding the ring into her palm.

"It's best you keep it hidden, Evanjalin."

"We need to move. Quickly," Finnikin said.

"The horse?" Sir Topher asked.

"No horse."

"Who—"

"Later," Finnikin stressed, pushing them toward the tavern entrance.

Trevanion was staring at the thief, who looked like he was about to spit at him.

"You won't survive the consequences," Finnikin warned.

"His name is Froi," Evanjalin said.

The thief grunted.

"It's *boy*," Finnikin argued. "It's just that his lip is split and it sounded like Froi."

"Everyone has a name, Finnikin. You can't just be called *boy*. His name is Froi." The thief from Sarnak opened his mouth to speak, but Evanjalin raised a finger to silence him. "I can sell you as easily as I bought you," she said icily.

"You didn't buy him. You stole him," Finnikin pointed out.

"I've worked out his bond rules," she said to Sir Topher, ignoring the others. "Like you said once. A new set of them."

Whatever Sir Topher had suggested, Finnikin could tell he was already regretting it.

"There's something else," Finnikin said, looking at Trevanion, who had not said a word.

"Of course there is," Sir Topher muttered. "Can we take another surprise?"

"I think you can take this one. Evanjalin has found the priest-king."

## CHAPTER 10

A s they entered the exile camp the following day, Sir Topher was speechless. But it was the look on his father's face that stayed in Finnikin's mind for days to come. He knew Trevanion had never seen a camp before, had never imagined the way their people lived these past years, so nothing could prepare him for such desolation. His father understood punishment, imprisonment, and retribution. But this? What crime against the gods had these people committed to condemn them to this life?

"It is worse farther on," Finnikin warned. The cramped conditions, pools of mud, and stinking puddles made movement through the camp slow. Yet unlike the previous day, there was a slight buzz around them as whispers began to fill the air. And then Finnikin saw it for the first time in the eyes of the man closest to them: a glimmer of hope.

"It's Trevanion of the River," he heard a woman say. "And the king's First Man."

As they went deeper into the camp, more and more exiles emerged from their makeshift homes. By the time they reached the divide between the tent city and the fever camp, they were squeezing their way through crowds of people, children watching hopefully from the shoulders of their fathers, the hunger in their eyes haunting.

A man, his hair white and his eyes the color of milk and sky, pushed his way to the front, searching Sir Topher's face for recognition.

"Kristopher of the Flatlands?"

Sir Topher's body shook as he embraced his kinsman. It now seemed as if every man, woman, and child had left their shelter to jostle around them.

"This is Micah, a farmer from the village of Sennington," Sir Topher said.

Finnikin looked at his father. Sennington was Lady Beatriss's village.

"Who is in charge here?" Trevanion said.

"We have no one in charge," the old man replied.

"Then appoint someone and bring them to us."

In the stretch of land between the tent city and the fever camp was the priest-king's shanty. As they approached, a woman clutching her child came from the direction of the fever camp and pushed the boy into Evanjalin's arms. Finnikin pulled Evanjalin toward him and away from the woman, who looked riddled with fever.

"There's nothing you can do," he said firmly.

Evanjalin shook free of him. "It's against the rules of humanity to believe there is nothing we can do, Finnikin," she said, walking away with the mother and child.

Inside the priest-king's tent, Finnikin watched as Trevanion and Sir Topher solemnly bent and kissed the holy man's hand, an action that seemed to embarrass him. The old farmer from the Flatlands entered hesitantly with two men and a woman, their eyes moving between the priest-king and Finnikin's party.

"You need to separate these people from the fever camp," Trevanion told them firmly, "and I do not mean a tiny strip of earth in between. You take the healthy away from here. *Now.*"

"Take them where?" the woman asked. "There are too many of us, and each time we have attempted to move, we have been threatened with swords. At least in this corner of hell they do not bother us."

"To cross the land, we need the protection of the King's Guard," the older man said boldly.

"Can you provide that?" the youngest asked.

Finnikin looked at his father. He had not spoken of his men, but Finnikin knew that finding them was never far from Trevanion's mind.

Trevanion shook his head. "Not for the moment. But you leave all the same. You keep to the river along the Charyn and then the Osterian border until you reach Belegonia. There, we will call on the patronage of Lord August of the Flatlands."

"We can't—"

"There is no hope for you here!" Trevanion said. "You travel to Belegonia and you will be provided for. That is my pledge."

He and Sir Topher stepped outside with the four exiles, and Finnikin found himself alone with the priest-king.

"Do not underestimate the girl," the priest-king said quietly.

Finnikin gave a humorless laugh. "I am with the king's First Man, the captain of the King's Guard, and the priest-king of Lumatere. The most powerful men in our kingdom, apart from the king himself. All brought together by her. At what point have I led you to believe that I have underestimated her?"

"You contemplate a different path from hers," the priest-king pointed out.

"And you?" Finnikin asked.

"That is not important."

"You are the priest-king," Finnikin said. "Chosen to guide."

"You have expectations of me?" the holy man said bitterly. "When I gave a blessing to that impostor as he walked through our gates, knowing that his hands were soaked with the blood of our beloveds? Do you know where I was when they burned the five Forest Dwellers at the stake? Safe in the Valley of Tranquillity, knowing that I could have given them protection in my home. I had the power of sanction, but I was ruled by my fear."

"Lord August said you had a death wish and it was for this reason that you travel from fever camp to fever camp," Finnikin said. "But the goddess has cursed you, blessed Barakah, and refuses to allow you to die."

"So the answer to your earlier question is that I take these people north to Lumatere," the priest-king responded. "With the girl. While you go west, to Belegonia. In search of a second homeland. Or has your course altered, Finnikin?"

Finnikin did not respond.

"What is it you fear?" the priest-king asked.

"What makes you think I fear anything?"

The old man sighed. "When I was a young man, I was chosen to be the spiritual advisor of our kingdom. They do not choose you to be Barakah, Finnikin, just because you can sing the Song of Lumatere at the right pitch."

"Then you have the power to sense things? Is it Balthazar?" Finnikin asked.

"I do not know, but whoever I sense is powerful. 'Dark will lead the light, and our *resurdus* will rise.' Are they not the words of the prophecy?"

"Most would call it a curse, blessed Barakah."

"Most would not have deciphered the words," the priest-king replied.

Finnikin's breath caught in his throat. "Do you know the rest?" he asked.

"'And he will hold two hands of the one he pledged to save.'"

"'And then the gate will fall, but his pain shall never cease,'" Finnikin continued.

"'His seed will issue kings, but he will never reign,'" they ended together.

After a moment the priest-king smiled. "It has taken me ten years to translate it. Please do not tell me it took you less."

Finnikin smiled ruefully. "I spent my fifteenth year in the palace library of Osteria," he confessed. "Not much else to do but listen to excruciating lectures from our ambassador and train with the Osterian Guard." He felt a strange mixture of emotions under the priest-king's gaze.

"What is it you fear, Finnikin?" the holy man repeated.

"I was the childhood companion of Prince Balthazar," he found himself saying. "And many times he said to me, 'Finnikin, when I am king, you'll be captain of my Guard. Just as your father is captain of my father's Guard. But then some days we will swap so you can be king and I can be Captain Trevanion.'"

"Child's talk."

Finnikin shook his head. "Each time Balthazar spoke those words, a fire would burn inside of me. I wanted to be king, and I began to envy Balthazar for it."

"Then your desires were small, Finnikin."

Finnikin made a sound of disbelief.

"When I was eight years old," the priest-king confessed, "I wanted to be a god." The holy man looked around the ragged tent. "Perhaps this is my punishment, but between you and me, I do not believe that the desires of young boys cause catastrophic events. The actions of humans do."

But Finnikin knew there was more. *Her blood will be shed for you to be king.*

"Take Evanjalin north to our king, Finnikin," the priest-king said. "But know that if we follow her, we take a path to salvation paved with blood."

"There is nothing for us north," Trevanion said firmly from the entrance. He was standing alongside Sir Topher. "Isn't that right, Finnikin?"

Finnikin could not reply. He could feel his father's fierce stare, but his eyes were on Sir Topher. His mentor had been respectfully distant since Trevanion's return, but Finnikin needed his guidance now.

"She bewitches you," Trevanion said. "And she is yours for the taking. Any fool can see that. So take her and *get* whatever needs to be *gotten* out of your system."

Still Sir Topher would not meet his eyes, and Finnikin knew he would have to make this decision on his own. That perhaps he already had.

"I stood in a pit of corpses yesterday. Stepped over the body of one just my age. Do you know what went through my mind? Rebuilding Lumatere. And as I watched the lad carrying the dead, I thought the same. I imagined he would be a carpenter. I could see it in these," he said, his hands outstretched. "In a pit of death I imagined a Lumatere of years to come, rather than of years past." He was staring at his mentor. "We have never done that, Sir Topher. We collect the names of our dead, we plan our second homeland, and we construct our government, but with nothing more than parchment and ink and sighs of resignation."

Sir Topher finally looked up. "Because any hope beyond that, my boy, would be too much. I feared we would drown in it."

"Then I choose to drown," Finnikin said. "In hope. Rather than float into nothing. Maybe you are right, Trevanion," he said, turning back to his father. "But it is her hope that bewitches me, and that hope I may never get out of my system, no matter how many times she's to be *gotten*. Can you not see it burning in her eyes? Does it not make you want to look away when you have none to give in return? Her hope fills me with . . . something other than this dull weight I wake with each morning."

Trevanion's eyes bored into him. Had he found his father only to walk away from him?

"She says the young girls inside Lumatere are dying," Sir Topher said quietly.

"Why do we hear so little about these walks she takes in her sleep?" Trevanion demanded. "If she has the power, why do we know so little about Lumatere? Because she lies."

"She has a gift—" the priest-king began.

"A gift for deception, unable to bear my presence for she knows I understand the nature of her vice," Trevanion snapped. "What of her lies about Sarnak?"

"There was no lie," Finnikin said.

Trevanion made a sound of frustration. "Finnikin, she could not even tell us where those people came from, let alone what happened."

Finnikin swallowed hard, remembering the perfect handwriting in the *Book of Lumatere*. "Most were from the river village of Tressor," he said quietly.

He watched his father falter. The people of Tressor were Trevanion's people, the people he had grown up among. He had visited them each time he was on leave from the palace, sat with them at their tables, and listened to their stories with his son on his knees.

"The girl is an empath," the priest-king said. "She cannot bear your presence, Captain Trevanion, because you feel too much. Hate too much. Love too much. Suffer too much. It is why she was happiest in the cloister. The novices of the goddess Lagrami are trained to keep emotions and feelings to a minimum. There she found peace."

But Trevanion would not listen. "I travel south," he said, his voice heavy. "And I will do all I can, Finnikin, to convince you to travel with me rather than take a path that may destroy you."

"If you travel south, I am already destroyed," Finnikin said.

Sir Topher's eyes met his. "Froi!" he called out. The boy came to the entrance. "Make yourself useful and fetch Evanjalin."

"I am here," she said softly from the flap of the tent. She looked past Sir Topher to Trevanion. "What would you like to know about walking the sleep, Captain Trevanion? That I journey with a child of no more than five? We are as real to each other as you are to me. No illusion or ghosts. Flesh and blood. This child belongs to the living and she has always been the guide, but we have never been able to hear each other or converse. We do not pick and choose who we visit. We hold each other's hand through our walks; hers is soft and tiny and trusting and strong. Sometimes I sense another who walks with us. I believe they are there not for me but for the child. We see only what our sleepers see and think. They are unaware of us, and most of the time we stumble through a gray mist. Last night I dreamed of the chandler who finds it strange that it's his work to provide light, yet all he can see is darkness. The armorer despises himself, for he makes weapons for the impostor king and his men, knowing they will be used against his own people. I have walked through the sleep of the plowman and the blacksmith and the tanner and the weaver and the merchant and the nursemaid. But my favorite sleep is that of the young, for they still know how to dream and they dream of the return of their king, believing that the captain of the Guard will guide him home to Lumatere."

Trevanion shook his head and turned to go.

"Her strength, it comes from you," she said quietly.

"What?" The question was like a bark, but she did not shrink back.

"Beatriss."

There was a sharp hiss of breath, and Finnikin found himself in his father's path as Trevanion advanced toward her furiously.

"Beatriss is—"

"Do not speak her name! Do not dare taint her memory," he raged.

Evanjalin did not move. "Sometimes when people sleep they agonize about decisions made. Other times they think back on the past. She spends much time doing both. I do believe it is Beatriss who has worked through the dark magic to find me."

"You lie to taunt me!"

"Enough, Evanjalin," Sir Topher ordered. "Beatriss is dead."

Finnikin felt his father flinch at the words, but Evanjalin held Trevanion's gaze.

"Most nights she is restless. There are too many people to worry about, and she wonders how she will be able to make things right. How can she be someone other than Beatriss the Beautiful or Beatriss the Beloved? But then, just when she's about to lose hope, she remembers what you would whisper to her, Captain Trevanion. That she was Beatriss the Bold. Beatriss the Brave. To all others she was a fragile flower, but you would not let her be."

Finnikin's hand was still against Trevanion's chest; his father's heart was beating out of control.

"She remembers the nights you lay with her when she worried about something happening to you. 'What would I do without you?' she would cry. Do you remember your response, Captain Trevanion? 'What needs to be done, Beatriss.'"

Trevanion shook his head with disbelief.

"You ask why I do not talk of the sleep," Evanjalin said.

"Because most days it is dark. Their souls are sad, and our goddess is weeping with despair for her people. However, Beatriss the Beautiful has become a sower, this despite the fact that each time her crops grow, the impostor's men destroy them. But Beatriss the Bold refuses to stop planting."

No one dared break the silence until Trevanion pushed Finnikin's hand away. "You know things that only I could know."

"No, Captain. You are wrong. I know things beyond what you know. Things that even I cannot understand. But my heart tells me to go north. Every waking hour and every sleeping moment tells me that there is life within Lumatere and that they wait. For us."

Trevanion took a ragged breath and walked to the entrance of the tent. Finnikin watched, wanting to go to his father and plead with him to join them. Offer him comfort. But he had no idea how.

"There is a village of rocks in Yutlind where I've been told my Guard has settled. South," Trevanion said.

Finnikin's shoulders slumped. "Father, please . . ."

"I will not return to Lumatere without my men."

A sob of excitement escaped Evanjalin's lips. She flew into Trevanion's arms and then remembered herself and jumped back. She fell to her knees at his feet, but Sir Topher pulled her up.

"You will have no regrets," she said to them all. "I promise you. On my life."

Four days later, they began their journey alongside the priest-king and the exiles. A handful of the exiles stayed behind to tend to the fever camp, but Sir Topher and Trevanion had been firm that the priest-king would not be one of them. Their groups would separate when the road diverged. The priest-king would take his people west to Belegonia, and Finnikin and his party would travel south in search of Trevanion's men. But for a day they walked side by side.

Finnikin found himself looking at his father again and again. When Trevanion caught the look, he frowned.

"What?" he asked gruffly.

Finnikin shrugged. "Nothing. Just that I heard Evanjalin say a family of sparrows has petitioned the king of Sorel to be freed from your hair."

The priest-king gave a snort of laughter, and after a moment Trevanion joined in and Finnikin's heart warmed at the sound of it. Trevanion wrapped his arm around his son's neck like a shepherd's hook and dragged him along playfully. When he let go, Finnikin thought he would have liked his father to hold on a moment longer.

When the road split in two, Finnikin watched the exiles go, a mixture of fear and hope on their faces.

"Until we meet again in Belegonia," the priest-king said.

"In the town of Lastaria on the coastal road," Finnikin reminded him as they embraced. He stood with Sir Topher, watching as Evanjalin led the way south with Froi and Trevanion.

"Salvation paved with blood, you say?" Sir Topher asked the holy man with a sigh.

The priest-king nodded. "But salvation all the same, Sir Topher."

# part two

*All the King's Men*

CHAPTER 11

The flooding rains of Sorel pounded the earth for days, forcing them to spend the week lodging in a barn when the road to the south became impassable. It was a painstakingly slow beginning to a search that would take them into the most war-ravaged kingdom in the land. While Sir Topher taught Froi the language of Lumatere, the others pored over their maps, searching for alternative routes to reach Trevanion's men, who he believed were hiding in one of the rock villages of Yutlind Sud. The most common route was to cross back into Belegonia, which bordered Yutlind from the north. But Trevanion was an outlaw in every kingdom of the land, and the road into Belegonia was too dangerous. If they traveled west through Sorel to its port, they risked having to pass through the mines as well as deal with a treacherous waterway, the Gulf of Skuldenore.

"Pirate ships," Finnikin said. "Tipped off by corrupt port officials who take a cut of anything plundered."

"Corruption in Sorel? Surely you jest," Sir Topher said, walking over to join them.

"Even if we manage to land in Yutlind," Finnikin continued,

"the heaviest fighting is in the north and the Yuts always attack first and ask questions later. I say we cross the mountains. To get here," he said, pointing to the independent coastal province of Sif, south of Sorel. "We pay passage on a merchant cog that travels south. There is a small port on the Yack River in Yutlind Sud. From there we travel up-country."

"The south is a mess, Finnikin," Sir Topher argued. "No one knows who is in charge or who is to blame or who is an ally or an enemy."

"So the last thing on their minds will be a party of Lumateran exiles and an escaped prisoner."

"Then we travel to Sif," Trevanion decided.

After the dark world of the mines and the fever camp and the dampness of the overcrowded barn where the stench of body odor permeated every one of his senses, Finnikin was relieved to see the snowcapped mountains in the distance. Though the mountains looked invigorating from afar, he never imagined how terrible their beauty would become as they ascended. Nights were bitterly cold, the icy wind numbing their faces, cloth swaddling their mouths and noses, where saliva and mucus feasted together.

They spoke little during the day. The wind was too severe and the trail too backbreaking to waste energy on talk. Sometimes, when his fingers ached from the stinging cold and his skin felt torn to shreds from the bluster, Finnikin imagined the life he would have had if he'd settled for a role as an advisor to a foreign king. Instead, he was trekking across the land for a Guard that may not want to be found, on his way home to a kingdom that no longer existed.

On the fourth night, they camped inside a cave, their bodies convulsing, their bedrolls packed tight against one another. They rotated every few hours to ensure that everyone would have a chance to sleep in the warmth. Finnikin dreamed that he was nestled in a womb, speaking to Beatriss's baby. When he woke, he found himself in the arms of his father and his own wrapped around Evanjalin. He knew she had been walking the sleep over the last few nights and wondered, as she twitched in his arms, if she was again. Her hair was now a thin dark cap on her scalp, and a strange kind of beauty had begun to appear in her face, despite the grime. Every feature was strong, strangely put together. Although she was thin from their journey, nothing about her seemed delicate. Yet Finnikin had seen brief moments of fragility. A look on her face as if she had just remembered something painful, her breath catching. At times it was as if she could barely raise her head from the demons that weighed her down.

"Sir Topher! Sir Topher!"

Finnikin heard her voice. He hadn't realized he had fallen asleep again.

"I think I've worked it out," she said.

Sir Topher woke with a start. "Goddess of Sorrow, Evanjalin! Can it not wait till morning?"

"Worked what out?" Trevanion demanded. Finnikin sat up, yawning. The last embers of the fire were glowing, and the dampness was back in his bones.

"They may not be dead," she said dreamily. "The baker dreamed of cherry blossoms. He lit a candle and made a sacrifice to the goddess Sagrami."

"Evanjalin, you need to sleep," Finnikin said. "You're not making sense."

But she shook her head. "No, I need to stay awake and put the pieces of all the sleeps together."

Sir Topher rubbed his eyes. "Froi, make yourself useful and get this fire going."

Froi grunted, not wanting to leave the comfort of the bedrolls, but was nudged out by Sir Topher. They wrapped themselves in every bit of clothing they had and drew their bedrolls closer to the fire, while Froi stoked the embers, muttering.

"Three nights ago I walked through the sleep of the baker, who was laughing," Evanjalin said.

"I cannot imagine any Lumateran inside or outside the gate doing such a thing," Finnikin said flatly.

"Yet the cook's apprentice mourned the death of the baker's daughter not three weeks earlier." Evanjalin's forehead was creased with lines of confusion, and Finnikin felt an urge to smooth them out.

"Evanjalin, you're not making sense."

"What kind of man would be laughing three weeks after he had laid his child to rest?" she asked.

"Get to the part where you claim to have worked something out," Trevanion said gruffly.

"I need to go back, then. About a year. When the child and I walked through the sleep of one of the impostor's men who was thinking of a girl from the Flatlands who had died that day. He did not share the grief of the mother and father, but her death was enough to make him think. He was doing his sums and he worked out that twenty young girls had died over the past four years."

"Twenty?" Sir Topher gasped.

Evanjalin nodded. "But I need to go back even further."

Finnikin made a sound of disbelief, but she held up her hand. "Listen. Eighteen years past, the queen of Osteria presented the queen of Lumatere with a cherry blossom plant. It was a peace offering after decades of mistrust between both kingdoms."

"Evanjalin, you are not making—"

"But I will. My mother told me the story often. About the queen deciding where to plant the tree."

"She searched the kingdom high and low for the perfect spot," Sir Topher said, smiling at the memory. "Drove us all insane. But she was with child. Her youngest, Isaboe. The child was never meant to be and the pregnancy was cursed with illness from the beginning. The queen was sure that if she planted the cherry blossom and made a dedication to both the goddess Lagrami and the goddess Sagrami, then the child would live."

Evanjalin nodded. "And although many Lumaterans were not happy with her decision to sacrifice to Sagrami, the queen found the perfect spot."

"A beautiful story, but I cannot see the connection," Trevanion said.

"There is only one cherry blossom tree in Lumatere. At least a day's ride from the palace, at the old cloister of Sagrami near the Sendecane border."

"But that cloister hasn't been used for centuries," Sir Topher said. "What are you suggesting, Evanjalin?"

"That during the five days of the unspeakable, the novices of Sagrami who lived at the edge of the Forest were taken to safety inside the kingdom walls through the east gate."

Sir Topher was shaking his head. "You are wrong, Evanjalin. The priestess of Sagrami was the first to be burned at the stake. She was captured along with Seranonna and three other mystics and healers."

"Then the novices would have been on their own," Finnikin said. "Surely the impostor's men would have attacked the cloister in the Forest first?"

"It would have been a slaughter," Trevanion said. "The oldest of the girls was no more than seventeen."

"And they had no one to turn to?" Finnikin asked.

Sir Topher opened his mouth to reply and then stopped.

"Sir Topher?" Finnikin asked urgently.

"There may have been one," he said in a hushed tone. "Someone who had lived in the Forest cloister as a child. Tell me about the other who walks the sleep with you, Evanjalin. The one who is there for the child."

"Whoever it is, they have a great knowledge of the dark arts. I sense their connection with the dead. With spirits."

"Only Seranonna had such knowledge," Trevanion said.

"No, there was another," Sir Topher said. "One who was under Seranonna's instruction."

Trevanion frowned and then realization dawned on his face. "Tesadora? Seranonna's daughter?"

Sir Topher nodded. "Did you know her?"

"No, but Perri did. They were mortal enemies. It was one of the few stories Perri would tell me of his childhood in the River swamp. From a young age, his father taught him to inflict as much pain as possible on those they considered inferior."

"Was Perri ashamed?"

Trevanion sighed. "It was not a confession, just a fact. I remember his words. 'How different our childhoods, Trevanion. You sailed your raft down the River and collected tadpoles and eels, and I held down the heads of Forest Dwellers in swamp water to see how long they could stay under without breathing.'

"Perri told me Tesadora once stayed under for five minutes," Trevanion continued, "and still had enough breath inside her to spit in his face when it was over. His father thrashed him for allowing a Forest Dweller to get the better of him. So next time Perri made sure she didn't have enough strength to even stand. They were both twelve at the time. On opposing sides, but both victims of hate."

"By the time Tesadora was little older than you, Finnikin, she lived the life of a hermit in the Forest," Sir Topher said. "But she spent her childhood in the cloister of Sagrami, and apart from her mother, the novices were her only contact with the world."

"Were the Sagrami novices mystics?" Finnikin asked.

"Healers," Sir Topher answered. "The best apothecaries I have ever encountered. The herbs and plants they grew in the Forest cloister were spectacular. If the priest-king had them in the fever camps, half our people would still be alive."

Evanjalin leaned closer, her eyes alight. "The novices are now inside the kingdom walls, and they are hiding the young girls of Lumatere in the old cloister. And three days ago, the baker traveled in secret to see his daughter and picked cherry blossoms along the way."

"You have no proof of that," Finnikin said. "Even if Tesadora did survive and save the novices, do you think the impostor and his men would be so ignorant as to not work it out? Would they not have found their hiding place by now?"

"Perhaps they don't need to hide. No matter what the impostor king decreed when he put the Forest Dwellers to death, he would fear the wrath of the gods if he stormed a temple of Sagrami," Evanjalin said. "Remember, the novices worship a goddess that has cursed Lumatere, and the impostor king is just as much a prisoner of the curse as everyone else inside," she argued.

"And if the novices are the apothecaries I think they are, they could easily find a way of sending the girls close to death," Sir Topher said.

"These Lumaterans you speak of — the baker, the other fathers and mothers of the girls — are they worshippers of Sagrami?" Trevanion asked.

Evanjalin shook her head. "They worship Lagrami. Yet somehow both cloisters, Lagrami and Sagrami, are working together to protect the young girls of Lumatere."

"How?"

She looked at them for a moment. "There are parts of this story . . . all of you might find . . . difficult."

Finnikin stared at her in disbelief. "Evanjalin, Trevanion has spent seven years in the mines of Sorel. Sir Topher and I have seen everything there is to see in our travels."

"But there are some things . . ."

"Evanjalin," Sir Topher said firmly. "Finnikin is right. There is nothing we cannot endure."

Evanjalin sighed. "The cook's apprentice who mourned his friend had blood on his mind the night she died. The impostor's guard dreamed of blood. Each time these girls 'die,' there are dreams or memories of blood. I believe they 'die' of the bleeding. They supposedly bleed to death. That's what the impostor's men and the rest of the kingdom think happens to the girls. Imagine. The impostor's men come to the home of a family who has just lost their daughter. They demand to see the dead child. There she lies. Still. Perhaps in the way Sir Topher has suggested, due to the cleverest apothecaries in the kingdom. The impostor's men demand to know what has taken place. They do not care for the dead girls or their families, but smell a conspiracy among the people. The women are clever. They begin to speak of the curse that visits young girls each month, for they know that the impostor and his men would pale with such talk of blood flowing from the loins of young girls like torrents of—"

Finnikin cleared his throat loudly. "I think I hear something . . . outside the cave," he mumbled, getting to his feet. But the look on Evanjalin's face stopped him from leaving.

"Blood!" Froi said, horrified. "Loins? Same loins you stick—"

"Froi!" Trevanion snapped.

"Flowing at times like a gutted pig," Evanjalin said.

"Evanjalin!"

Evanjalin looked at Sir Topher and Trevanion, who suddenly seemed very interested in the contours of the cave walls.

"Did I not say that there would be parts of this story that might cause discomfort?" she said.

"It is not right for a young woman to speak of such things in the presence of men, Evanjalin," Sir Topher said firmly. "And perhaps you are clutching at straws, making such a connection."

"Am I?" she asked. "And what if I told you that I only walk the sleep during my own . . . time?"

Despite the flush in Sir Topher's cheeks, he held her gaze and after a moment nodded for her to continue.

"Perhaps the impostor king's men are led to believe that when a young girl experiences her first bleeding, she is also struck by a curse and bleeds to death. An unnatural occurrence, of course. But maybe they've been told that Seranonna's curse is responsible. Her way of punishing the children of Lagrami. In truth, the young girls live inside the old cloister of Sagrami in the northwest of the kingdom. One of the few places the impostor king and his men will not enter for fear of Seranonna's legacy."

"Do you believe all our people know that the girls live?" Trevanion asked.

She shook her head. "I cannot be sure who knows the truth. If we go by the baker's sleep, it is clear that the parents of the girls know. But I cannot be sure of the others. The cook's apprentice certainly grieved."

"But still we cannot be sure that Tesadora survived the days of the unspeakable or the impostor's punishment," Trevanion insisted.

She stared at him. "I have walked the sleep of one of the Sagrami novices, and her thoughts were on the day when one with a crown came to hide them."

"Balthazar?"

"One with a crown is all I know."

"Could it be . . ." Trevanion began, but he stopped himself and shook his head.

"Someone smuggled Tesadora and the novices into the kingdom prior to the curse."

"Someone with a crown?" Sir Topher said. "It does not make sense."

"And a blood curse does?" Trevanion asked.

"It makes all the sense in the world that the other who walks the sleep with us, who may be able to break the curse, is a blood relative of the very person who created it," Evanjalin said. "Seranonna's daughter."

"But Tesadora? Perri used to call her the serpent's handmaiden," Trevanion said.

"Coming from Perri the Savage, that is not good," Sir Topher mused.

"Perhaps she is exactly what is needed," Finnikin argued.

"Seranonna sent her to the north of the Forest as a child to live with the novices," Sir Topher explained. "To keep her out of harm's way from the other Forest Dwellers, who feared her. The Forest Dwellers claimed Tesadora was evil because her Forest blood was mixed with a Charynite's."

"Yet you don't communicate with Tesadora?" Trevanion asked Evanjalin.

She shook her head. "Only the child. The first time was when I was twelve years old and had a strange, wondrous dream. Now I believe it was the birth of the child. Somehow when my"—she hesitated and looked at Sir Topher—"first blood began to flow, the child's heart began to beat. I felt her in my arms."

"And you never walk the sleep at . . . other times?" Finnikin asked awkwardly.

"Only once," she said, swallowing hard.

"Your blood flowed another way?" Sir Topher asked.

She nodded. "Two springs ago. And that night, I walked the sleep of Lady Beatriss and she whispered the words, 'The cloister of Sendecane.'"

"Why was your—" Then Finnikin realized and the word came out in a strangled tone. "Sarnak! Your blood was shed at the massacre of the exiles?"

She nodded.

"But how did you escape death, Evanjalin?" Sir Topher asked gently.

"Do you have a wound?" Trevanion said.

She opened up her shirt to reveal a patch of puckered tissue above her breast. It was an ugly scar, the wound poorly inflicted.

"They didn't even know how to deliver a clean kill," Finnikin muttered, unable to take his eyes off it.

"No, they were perfectionists," she said. "They were hunters. I could tell. I watched them. Their arrows went straight to the heart, their daggers in and out. Precise. Our people were on their knees, begging, and were cut down with their hands still raised and clenched together in prayer. Others ran. And got an arrow in the back. The hunters made sure that those shot in the back were turned around, and then they'd plunge a dagger into the heart."

"Yet your wound is the work of an amateur," Sir Topher said.

"Because I did not run and I did not beg. Wherever there was movement, the hunters attacked. Those were the exiles killed first. But I was a coward, you see. I couldn't turn my back. Could not bear the idea of the unknown. Of an arrow catching me by surprise. When those around me fell with an arrow to the heart,

I knew the hunters would not return to check for their breathing. They returned only for those with an arrow in their back. So when one of our own collapsed at my feet with an arrow in his heart, I knew what I had to do."

"Sweet goddess of sorrow," Sir Topher gasped.

"Did you not play that game as a child?" she asked quietly. "Pretend death? It's what you do to survive. You play the games of make-believe."

Finnikin had played those games daily with the royal children. But there had been no pretending to take an arrow and plunge it into himself an inch above his heart. And no pretending to bite his tongue to keep his cries from piercing the air that was filled only with the grunts of satisfaction and retreating footsteps of men who had forgotten what it meant to be human. There was no pretending to grip the object embedded in his flesh with both hands, to tear it out of skin that was meant for soft kisses and caresses. There was no pretending to pick his way through family, searching the place for survivors. And no playing at walking two weeks barefoot to the cloister of Lagrami in godsforsaken Sendecane because a woman in his sleep whispered the command like a prayer.

*What needs to be done.*

"I was fortunate enough to be born under the star of luck," Evanjalin said softly. "So I lived while others died."

Sir Topher was the first to turn away. Huddled in his bedroll, his shoulders shook with a sorrow that he fought hard to hide.

"Sleep, Evanjalin," Finnikin said gently. *Dream of cherry blossoms and the laughter of the young girls who you want so desperately to believe live under the protection of the goddess of night.*

When at last Finnikin heard the sounds of labored breathing, he turned in his bedroll and saw that Trevanion was still awake.

"What?" Finnikin asked. "If you discredit her story, I will be forced to challenge you," he added gruffly.

Trevanion shook his head. "The girl does not lie, Finnikin. She just omits information. It's the other part of the story, the young girls of Lumatere." Trevanion leaned closer to whisper. "What could have possibly happened to force the mothers and fathers to feign the death of their daughters? What are those monsters doing to our people?"

CHAPTER 12

The harbor town of Sif was the last port of civilization on the mainland of Skuldenore, accessed mostly by merchants, mercenaries, and reckless explorers. It was a departure point for those who wanted to disappear from the face of the earth. Trevanion's informant in the mines had told him that his Guard could be found in one of the rock villages of Yutlind Sud. To reach the territory from Sif, they would need to travel by cog down the coast and around the cape, which would take them to the mouth of the Yack River and into the war-torn kingdom.

"No one travels to Yutlind Sud," the captain of the *Myrinhall* muttered, eyeing Trevanion and Finnikin and spitting orange pips into the water below.

They were standing on the deck of the merchant cog, which boasted a crew of twenty men. It was a flat-bottomed vessel with a central mast carrying a square-rigged sail, sturdy enough to sail the open seas and compact enough to be steered down a river, ideal for navigating among the Yack's shallow reed beds.

"We have been told you travel south today," Trevanion said, "to collect produce and merchandise from Yutlind Sud."

"If we get paid enough, we collect goods from the traders on the river's edge, but we don't take passengers. Could hardly convince my men to come along today. Foreigners don't survive the Yack."

"We need to travel to the rock villages close to the north-south border."

The captain sent them a look of disbelief. "You come all the way south to travel north? You'd be better off going over the mountains and through Belegonia."

"Ye gods, really?" Finnikin said sarcastically. "Why didn't anyone tell us?"

Trevanion silenced him with a frown. "Take our silver and let us board," he said to the captain.

The merchant looked beyond Trevanion to where the others of their party were sitting on the pier, waiting. "Want advice?"

"No!" Finnikin said, only to receive another glare from his father.

"Give it to you anyway," the man said, spitting out another pip. "Leave the young and the old behind. Especially the girl."

Neither Finnikin nor his father responded.

"Won't be responsible for what my men or the Yuts want from the girl. Money up front. We leave the moment my men are on board."

The captain walked away. Finnikin saw the hint of a smile on Trevanion's face as he looked toward the horizon. He had read stories from the books in royal courts about the port town of Sif, where brave men set off for the undiscovered world beyond their land. Some believed the mythical stories of fire-breathing dragons and oceans tipping into an abyss, which kept the faint-hearted away.

"Have you ever wondered what lies beyond?" Finnikin asked his father.

"A kinder world than this, I would hope," Trevanion murmured.

"I say the merchant is right," Finnikin said, looking toward the pier. "It'll be safer if we leave them here. Yutlind's a bloodbath and if anything happens to her . . . to them . . ."

Trevanion nodded as they walked toward the others. Evanjalin was instantly on her feet, picking up her bedroll and pointing to the provisions. "Make yourself useful, Froi," they heard her order.

"You can do the honors of telling her she's staying behind, Finn," Trevanion said under his breath.

*Mercy.* Finnikin cleared his throat, trying to avoid her eyes. "We will be back in ten days," he announced.

"Back?" Evanjalin asked, confused. She gave Froi another shove. "By the time we find the Guard, it will be safer and closer to cross over the Belegonian border. Why return here?"

"For you. For all of you."

The crew of the *Myrinhall* jostled past. By the looks of them, they had been out all night. They appeared disheveled and somewhat sinister, especially when they caught sight of Evanjalin. Sir Topher glanced at them uneasily.

"It is safer for all," Finnikin said firmly.

"You are leaving us behind?" Evanjalin asked in disbelief. "To return here would be a waste," she hissed. "If we travel to the rock villages, then we are halfway to Belegonia heading north."

"Why would I not know that, Evanjalin?" Finnikin asked, trying to curb his growing frustration at her inability to take orders. "It's too dangerous. They say the spirit warriors guard the Yack River and could be a threat to foreigners."

Froi sat himself back down, but Evanjalin pulled him to his feet. "We are not staying," she said. "Sir Topher, tell him we are not staying."

"We don't know enough about these people, Evanjalin," Sir

Topher said. "The southerners may be Yuts, but they have different ways from the north and do not speak the same language. The south belongs to tribes of natives, and their king is in hiding. They are not going to take too kindly to foreigners in their land."

"This is the only way," Finnikin said. "It will be easier to hide if there are only two of us. It will be quicker. If we find Trevanion's men, they can travel farther north to Belegonia and we will return for you. On my oath, we will, Evanjalin."

Fury crossed Evanjalin's face. "You will be dead the moment one of the clans has you in its possession," she said, pointing at Finnikin. "You look like a foreigner. Like one from the north." She looked at Trevanion pleadingly. "No matter how superior you are as fighters, Captain, they will outnumber you and you will have nothing to bargain with."

"And with you, we will?" Finnikin said angrily. "Or do you suggest we sell Froi again? Personally I wouldn't mind in the slightest, except I know you'll drag me off to some godsforsaken place in order to steal him back."

"That's enough," Trevanion said.

Froi grunted. "Staying."

"It would be wrong to separate," she said, pushing past Finnikin with her bedroll. "Froi! I said to make yourself useful."

"You are not coming!" Finnikin grabbed her arm. "You stay here. Safe."

"That's enough, both of you," Trevanion said.

"Safe for who?" she shouted. "What happens when they capture you, Finnikin? Do we stay here waiting for eternity?"

"What makes you think we'll be caught?" he asked. "The only time that's ever happened to me, Evanjalin, is when you gave me up to the Sorelians."

There was silence, except for the sound of Evanjalin's breathing.

"We are wasting time," Trevanion said, grabbing the provisions from a relieved Froi.

Evanjalin shook free of Finnikin. "What is it?" she asked him coldly. "Really? What bothers you? That I found a way of getting your father out of the mines while you left him there to rot for years?"

The sound of blood rushing in his ears was almost deafening, yet Finnikin heard the sharp intake of Trevanion's breath and saw Froi's look of spiteful glee.

*"Enough!"* Sir Topher shouted. His cheeks were flushed with anger. "Vow of silence," he ordered, pointing his finger at Evanjalin. "You do not speak until you are given permission. Can you see that being a problem, Evanjalin? Because if it is, I will be the first to leave you behind at the mouth of the Yack. We stay together," he added more calmly, looking at Finnikin. "There are risks both ways, but we need to stay together."

Evanjalin pushed past Froi and walked up the plank before anyone could say another word. Finnikin caught the looks on the faces of the crew on board. Predators, like the prisoners of Sorel. But he didn't care what they did to her. His ears still rang from the brutality of her words. Is that what Trevanion thought and was not able to say? That his son was a coward who left him languishing in the bowels of hell?

The captain of the *Myrinhall* watched them as they filed on board, shaking his head. "You sign your death sentence, my friends. Indeed you do."

Finnikin sat by himself for the first half of the journey. His only consolation was that Evanjalin spent most of her time with her head over the side, emptying the contents of her stomach into the sea. After so many hours, he wondered that there was anything left inside her. He watched as she staggered to her bedroll on the deck, but each time she attempted to sit down, she would begin to retch again and rush to the side. Froi joined her for much of the time, a sight that brought Finnikin even more satisfaction.

In all his travels, he had never been on the open seas and he found it both frightening and exhilarating. If it wasn't the swelling waves that suddenly dropped in height and jolted them forward, it was the storms that churned the seawater into a mass of boiling foam. *L'essoupi*, the sailors called this stretch of ocean. The swallower.

Later, Trevanion joined him, and they sat side by side with their backs against the hull. As usual with his father, there was silence, but this time it suited him. After the scene on the pier, there was nothing to say.

They spent that night lying under a sky crowded with light, as though every star were fighting to be seen. The sea was still, and Evanjalin had at last stopped throwing up. Although he had no desire to be in her presence, Finnikin found himself keeping watch over her, fearing that a crew member would venture too close.

"Get some sleep," Trevanion murmured in the dark. "I'm watching them."

Sir Topher wiped Evanjalin's brow. She was weak from her sickness and almost sobbing from exhaustion, but he knew there was something else. He could sense her anxiety each time she raised her head to search for Finnikin.

"Your words were harsh," he said softly.

"He cannot complete this journey without me by his side."

"But still your words were harsh. No one gives anything for nothing. Not in this land. But that's what Finnikin decided we were called to do. To travel from exile camp to exile camp, kingdom to kingdom, and make sure our godsforsaken people were fed and taken care of. But Finnikin's thought every day was to secure the release of his father. I think it was a sorry day for him indeed when he realized that he was not just someone's son. That he had a responsibility to our people."

She closed her eyes. "Our people have never been godsforsaken," she corrected, "and he is the apprentice of the king's First Man. *You.* You insisted on furthering his education in the languages and politics of this land. Not just so he can feed the exiles, but because one day, as your apprentice, he may have to help lead them." She looked across to where Finnikin sat by his father's side. "He was born for greater things than belonging to the King's Guard, and his father knows it. Make sure, Sir Topher, that Finnikin accepts his role before we get to the main gate of Lumatere."

Trevanion watched Finnikin as he slept. Unlike the nights in the prison mine, he could see his sleeping son clearly under this illuminated sky and it was a luxury to stare so intently. Finnikin had his mother's face. Her coloring. "One kingdom, so many shades," Bartolina would say, holding her hand against Trevanion's. Then she was gone, and there were the numb days that followed Finnikin's birth. A motherless boy surviving in the world of men. Trevanion thought of his Guard and wondered how close they were. He had known most of them since he was Finnikin's age. When he handpicked them almost twenty years ago, he chose only those he could trust with the lives of every Lumateran. Especially his newborn son. At first his choices had been questioned, especially when it came to Perri the Savage. It was rumored that Perri had made his first kill by the time he was twelve. Poverty had bred malice. Bred the need to blame someone for the bleakness of their lives, and Perri the Savage suckled the sour milk of malice from his mother's breast. Younger than Trevanion by a year or two, he had seemed to resent the return of the river's favorite son and cared little for the cause of protecting their people. The river people had never lifted a hand to help Perri the Savage, and he owed them nothing in return.

"Join us," a twenty-year-old Trevanion had offered during a hostile encounter with Perri near the banks of his river swamp hut.

"Think I'm the one issuing orders here," Perri threatened, pressing the point of a sword to Trevanion's chest. There was a scar running from one ear to the other across his forehead. Eyes dark like Trevanion's, but skin milk-white.

"My wife is still warm in her grave," Trevanion said quietly. "Not even five days gone. If you try to stop me from getting home to my newborn son, I will kill you." And with that he walked away to where his men stood with August of the Flatlands.

"I will follow just to see where you live," Perri the Savage spat.

When they entered Trevanion's cottage farther up the river, a girl, the high-spirited daughter of a fishmonger, was caring for the baby.

"Have you taken leave of your senses, Trevanion?" she shouted, clutching the babe to her. "You bring Perri the Savage into your home when you have this precious boy to care for? His father is a drunkard! A rapist! A murderer!"

Trevanion took the child from her, holding the tiny form in his massive hands. He saw the bitterness in Perri's eyes, the defeat that came from not being able to escape his roots. Trevanion pointed to August of the Flatlands. "And his father is weak and deceitful and lazy, but I would trust him with my life."

She looked at August with disgust. *This?* A fine army you will build, Trevanion."

"Go home, Abie. Before it is dark. It is not safe for you to be traveling alone," Trevanion said wearily.

"Perhaps I could escort her," August suggested.

"You?" she scoffed. "You fit under my arm, little man." And with that, she kissed the baby and slammed out the door.

"Pity the one who ends up in her marriage bed," August muttered.

But Trevanion was staring at Perri. "You," he said. "If anything happens to me, protect my boy."

"Trevanion," August protested, "I will protect Finnikin. He will always have a place in my home."

"No," Trevanion said firmly. "You make sure my son gets whatever privilege allows the king's boy, Augie. The son of Bartolina of the Rock deserves nothing less. But you," he said, pointing to Perri, "you make sure he is protected."

"You have the wrong man," Perri snapped.

"No," Trevanion said, walking to the window to peer outside. "In you, I have the best marksman in this kingdom, and if you think that it was by chance I walked through your swamp today, think again. We rid this kingdom of those who try to invade through our waters and we rid Lumatere of a weak, corrupt Guard."

"What has the king promised you, Trevanion?" August asked.

"The highest honor for a warrior in this kingdom. And today I choose my Guard." He returned the baby to his basket. "Open the door."

Outside stood a group of young men. Not just from the River, but from the Rock and the Mountains and a few from the Flatlands. The room seemed full with their presence, and they spoke through the night, their voices hushed but strong with conviction.

"Where's Trevanion?" one of them asked later as the early light of morning began to seep under the door.

August of the Flatlands looked around. "Probably at the grave. He'd sleep there if not for the child."

One of the lads walked toward the baby's basket and pulled aside the blanket, only to find himself pinned to the wall with a dagger to his neck. He stared into the obsidian eyes of Perri the Savage, who snarled close to his ear, "Touch him again and you lose a hand."

At daybreak, they reached the mouth of the Yack River. Yutlind was a land of four rivers, lush and fertile, with woodland in the north and jungle in the south. The land mass of the north and south was the size of Lumatere and Osteria together, but they had lost more people in internal wars than the rest of the land combined. The ancient stories told that the god of Yutlind had created his people by mixing his blood with the earth of the jungle and the woods. The war over which soil was superior had been fought for thousands of years until a warlord built his palace in the north, his reign recognized by the leaders of Skuldenore who had grown tired of centuries of unrest. It was a reign the south refused to acknowledge.

There was a stillness surrounding them, a deliberate calm. The crew was edgy, apprehensive. The captain of the *Myrinhall* put a finger to his lips, signaling silence. Finnikin peered over the hull, but the jungle lining the serpentine river seemed mysterious, as if there were secrets hidden behind the dense foliage. It seemed impossible that human life could exist in such a place, and Finnikin was anxious for them to arrive at the dock farther down the river. There, the *Myrinhall* would offload her passengers and load the merchandise. Trevanion's plan was to find a guide among the traders to take them through the grasslands and into the rock villages.

Finnikin watched the captain. He used sign language with his crew, which must have seen them through similar dangerous experiences. It comforted Finnikin to know that these men had sailed this river before. He watched as the captain chuckled quietly at what one of his men had signaled, and for the first time since they had entered the Yack, Finnikin relaxed.

The first arrow struck the captain between the eyes.

He was dead by the time he hit the ground at Finnikin's feet, the shock stamped on his face for eternity. Then an onslaught of arrows flew overhead as Trevanion dived on top of Finnikin.

"Don't let them take the *Myrinhall*!" one of the crewmen shouted, and Finnikin felt the boat lurch as the oarsmen began their work. Trevanion was already on his feet as Finnikin grabbed his longbow. He heard the whistling of arrows flying past and ducked again and again before standing to take aim toward the west bank. He fired ten missiles into the thick of the jungle and then dropped to the deck. As the arrows continued to fly, he crawled to where Evanjalin was huddled on the other side of the boat, her face still sickly in the morning light. He dragged her behind the crates, securing her next to Froi in a cocoon of merchandise boxes and barrels of ale.

"Stay!" he managed to gasp. He crawled back to where Trevanion and Sir Topher were crouched against the hull, ready for the next onslaught. Trevanion stood, lobbing a round of arrows in the direction of the Yuts before diving back down again.

"The crew is turning the boat around," he said, trying to regain his breath. "You stay with them, Sir Topher. Try to make your way back to the port at Sif. Finnikin and I will swim to the bank and then travel north by foot to find my men."

Sir Topher nodded. From all corners of the *Myrinhall* they could hear moans from the injured, while the oarsmen grunted and arrows whistled overhead. The Yut natives hidden beyond the bank maintained a disciplined silence, and it was moments before Trevanion could mark them.

"Up above! In the trees!" one of the crew holding on to the mast yelled out.

Trevanion loosed another volley of arrows, then pushed Sir Topher and Finnikin farther along the side of the cog, away from the next onslaught, which hit their previous hiding spot with deadly accuracy.

"We go overboard on the other side, Finnikin," Trevanion yelled above the noise. "When it turns, we stay hidden by the *Myrinhall* until it reaches the mouth of the river again and then we make our way to land. Do you hear me?"

"Sweet goddess, they are swimming toward us," Sir Topher muttered. "This boat will not reach the mouth, Trevanion. They will take the *Myrinhall* with all of us in it!"

An oarsman was hit with an arrow from behind and slumped forward.

Trevanion stood to catch a glimpse of the Yuts approaching. "Change of plans. Get them off the boat and onto the east bank, Finn!" he ordered. "Make sure they are not seen. You too, Sir Topher. All of us."

Finnikin crawled back to the crates, grabbing Froi out first. "Can you swim?" he shouted.

"No!" The thief looked horrified.

Finnikin glanced up at the crewman working on the square sail. "You need to do this quickly before they turn the boat around. Try to keep underwater the whole way. Don't let them see you!"

"Can't swim!" Froi said, crawling back behind the crates.

Finnikin grabbed him by the hair and pulled him out to see what was happening around them. Bodies littered the cog, while those crewmen who were still alive moaned and writhed in pain.

"Would you prefer to stay?" Finnikin growled. Froi growled

back as Finnikin helped him over the side, holding the boy by the scruff of his neck before letting go. He turned his attention to Evanjalin, who looked gray, a film of perspiration covering her face.

"I can't swim," she whispered.

"Hold your breath and act as if you're pushing the water out of the way with your hands. Like this," he said, showing her. "And gently kick your feet. Don't put your head above water, Evanjalin. Don't let them see you. Once you get to the bank, keep hidden. Do you understand?"

She nodded, looking miserable.

"Just do as I say for once," he said, feeling the tremble of her hands as they touched his face. He grabbed one and pressed his mouth to her palm, and then Sir Topher was there, helping her over the side.

"Take care of them," Finnikin said as Sir Topher's head disappeared underwater.

He turned to find Trevanion, just as the crewman from the mast dropped out of the sky and landed at his feet, an arrow through his chest, blood already seeping from his mouth.

"Turn it around," the man croaked. "Climb the mast and turn it around or you'll never get them to safety."

Finnikin looked up at the mast and back in the direction of the Yuts, and then began climbing. At least half a dozen Yuts had reached the boat, and Trevanion and the crew were fighting them off. One who had managed to make it on board went flying back into the water with a kick to his head. Trevanion stood, aimed, shot, and then ducked, issuing orders, dividing the crew into three: those who rowed, those who lobbed arrows, and those who fought the Yuts in the water. From his vantage point, Finnikin could see what they had missed earlier. The skulls in the trees.

On the west bank, more Yuts descended from the foliage, their bodies large and powerful.

He kept climbing, not stopping until he reached the top, his legs straddling the pole, his fingers working quickly to loosen the sails. He could see that Evanjalin, Froi, and Sir Topher had reached the east bank of the river and were hiding among the long reeds and bracken. Trevanion and three of the crewmen finished off the last of the Yuts on board, and Finnikin watched as his father crawled to the edge of the boat and went over the side. He stood attached to the mast, feeling the arrows graze his arms as they flew past. He watched as Trevanion's head emerged from the water and he dragged himself to where the others were huddled, and for the first time since the captain dropped dead at his feet, Finnikin breathed with relief.

Trevanion spat out foul water as he held his side to ease the pain. The others were concealed by a cluster of reeds in the swamp water. They were shivering but safe, and for now that was enough. He knew he needed to keep them moving down the river, no matter how dangerous it was.

"Let's go. Now! There's no time . . . Finn?" he swung around. "Where's Finnikin?" He looked at the girl, certain that she would know. The girl and Finnikin never seemed to lose track of each other. She stared over his shoulder, her dark eyes wide, her hand shaking as she pointed up. He swung around to see the *Myrinhall* starting to turn, with its sail primed to take it back toward the mouth of the river. What was left of the crew was slinging arrows toward the Yut natives on the opposite bank. He could see two or more Yuts hovering around the hull of the boat, but then his eyes were transfixed by the image of Finnikin clinging to the mast, his red-gold hair twisted and knotted as the sun lit up its strands.

The movements of the Yuts on the other side showed that they too were transfixed by the sight, as if Finnikin were some wild sun god hanging from the heavens.

And then, to his horror, the Yuts took aim and Finnikin went falling out of the sky.

Trevanion prayed that the crew of the *Myrinhall* would grab the boy. Pull him out of the water and tend to him. But there was no movement toward where Finnikin lay facedown in the river, an arrow jutting from his side. The girl lurched forward, and Trevanion grabbed her, his hand stifling her scream as she struggled against him. When she finally broke free, Trevanion could hear her softly weeping, the sound more pitiful because she had seemed unbreakable.

"We wait until they leave," Sir Topher whispered as the *Myrinhall* inched further upstream, blocking their view of the Yuts but not of Finnikin's body.

"No," the girl said. "*Now.* They worship the sun god here. They'll take Finnikin the first opportunity they have."

Trevanion hit the water instantly, pounding it with his body, punishing it for placing a barrier between him and his son. The *Myrinhall* had just sailed past where Finnikin lay, and with any luck the vessel would block the Yuts' view of both their bodies. He knew he had little time. The moment the Yuts worked out where they were hidden, they would cross the river and come for them all.

When he reached his son, Trevanion turned the boy's body over and heard him splutter and gasp for air. There was no time for relief. No time to lessen the weight on Finnikin's body by removing his quiver and daggers. Trevanion dragged him back to the bank. Sir Topher, the girl, and the thief pulled them into the long reeds. Rather than take the chance to move farther into the jungle, they stayed crouched in the ankle-deep water, shivering as the sun disappeared behind the clouds. Trevanion placed his fist against Finnikin's mouth to hold back the boy's grunts of agony. The arrow had struck him in the side, just above the hip. It had to come out soon, but inflicting more pain on his son was unthinkable. He knew what type of barb was lodged in Finnikin's body; he had seen them scattered on the deck of the cog. Broad iron arrowheads meant for hunting animals. Difficult to extract.

The air rang with strange voices from both sides of the river. Bloodcurdling wails. Some seemed like taunts. As if the Yuts were playing cat and mouse with them. Not even in his ten years of captivity had Trevanion felt so trapped. He despised his own helplessness in not being able to move his party to safety and away from this muddy, insect-infested circle of swamp.

The thief looked away from Finnikin's shuddering body, his hands covering his ears to block out the taunts around them. "Don't you know magic?" he asked Evanjalin accusingly.

But Trevanion knew that their only hope was to wait.

"Do you think they've given up?" Sir Topher asked.

The voices had stopped, but the silence that followed was more alarming than Trevanion could have imagined. He shook his head and pointed to a copse of trees in the distance. The scraps of metal the Yut natives wore around their wrists and ankles flashed and winked in the sunlight.

"They want us to know we are surrounded," he said quietly, pointing to another group to the left and then another across the river.

"I can speak to them in Yut, Sir Topher," Finnikin murmured feverishly. "Tell them . . . we come in peace . . . acknowledge their right to Yutlind Sud . . ."

Sir Topher hushed him. "You'll tire yourself out, Finnikin."

Trevanion watched his son's labored breathing. Finnikin sat

half-upright, supported by Sir Topher. Crouching had become too painful, so they now sat in the shallow water, at the mercy of mosquitoes and water rats that bit with vicious frequency.

"These people are not speaking common Yut," Evanjalin said. She was staring at the arrow in Finnikin's side. Her eyes met Trevanion's, and he placed his hand against the stem.

"When they visited Lumatere in the past," Finnikin gasped, refusing to surrender to the pain, "for an audience with the king . . . you said . . . you said he promised to recognize . . ."

"But these were not the people who visited us, Finnikin," Sir Topher said. "These men are spirit warriors. They speak the old language of the first inhabitants."

"They belong to one of the tribes that guard the entrance into the kingdom from the south," Evanjalin acknowledged. Her face was chalk-white and strained. "They have done so since the time of the gods. Their customs and language are different, but they consider themselves kin to Yutlind Sud and mortal enemies of those in the north. They have lost many of their tribe to the merchant ships that enter the river and capture their people, selling them as slaves up north in Sorel."

"What do . . . they want from us?" Finnikin croaked.

Trevanion stared at her, shaking his head in case she dared reveal the answer to the question. What they wanted was his boy, with hair the color of the sun as it set.

"Do you trust me?" she whispered.

Finnikin's eyes rolled back. Trevanion had no idea whether it was from the pain of the arrow or the nausea from the filthy water he had swallowed. The girl placed her arms around Finnikin as her eyes issued a silent order to Trevanion.

"Talk to me," Finnikin slurred. "Don't let me sleep, Evanjalin."

"Perhaps I should tell you a story. So you can record it in the *Book of Lumatere* when you recover from your theatrics."

He chuckled, and Trevanion chose that moment to wrench the arrow out of his son's body.

Finnikin bit so hard into Evanjalin's flesh that he tasted her blood on his lips. And for a while the flames of fever chased him into dreams and memories. Where he saw the stake. Wood piled around its base. Set alight. And he was nine years old again, watching with horror the executions of the Forest Dwellers. Children of Sagrami. Around him people were sobbing. They had already taken his father, but he needed to be here for Beatriss. So that he, the son of her beloved, would be the last thing she saw. But Seranonna was there instead, her hands drenched with blood, flames crawling up her body as she cursed. And then he was in the tree. The one he had sat in with Balthazar and Lucian and made plans to trap the silver wolf. The tree of his childhood. That day, hidden in its branches, he pulled out his dagger. He aimed as his father had taught him.

And caught Seranonna in the heart.

CHapteR 13

Trevanion watched the tremors wrack Finnikin's body as he slept. It was dark now, but he still felt the presence of the Yuts. Voices rang through the night sky sporadically, and he could hear the girl muttering as if in prayer.

"Sir Topher," he said quietly. "Take them."

Sir Topher leaned forward. "Is he . . ." He could not bring himself to finish the question.

"Take them," Trevanion repeated. "Continue on the east bank and head toward the grasslands. Hopefully, they will not follow, for you have nothing they want. You know where to find my men. Tell Perri that his captain has passed on the greatest honor a guard of Lumatere can be given."

"Trevanion—"

"Tell him the girl will lead you to our king and our people." Trevanion looked at Evanjalin but could not read her expression. "If my boy dies, I die protecting him."

There was silence for a long moment.

"It's not right," Sir Topher said. "That it happens in this order. That a man should outlive his—" Sir Topher's breath caught in his throat. "Don't let them take him alive. Promise me that."

"Why do the men of Lumatere always speak of dying for the kingdom and for each other?" Evanjalin asked, irritated.

In the dim light of the moon, Trevanion could see her face. Her body had taken a battering on the boat, and she looked weak from fatigue. Yet there was still a glint in her eyes. She tried to rise, but he pulled her back down. "Where are you going?"

"I cannot promise that I will make sense to them, but I know enough of their language to get by."

"You have nothing to offer them," he said. "They will kill you the moment you step out in the open."

She shrugged free of him. "Never underestimate the value of knowing another's language. It can be far more powerful than swords and arrows, Captain. I've listened to them long enough to understand a little. Among them is their leader and his son. One has been on this side of the river, one on the other. And do you know what the father has promised the son? The honor of lighting the pyre to sacrifice Finnikin."

"There is nothing you can do," Sir Topher said. "You will only put your life in danger."

She looked at him sadly. "Sir Topher, do you honestly believe we are not all marked for death anyway? We entered their land illegally on a cog that has taken away their people in the past. But I may know how to convince them to trust us."

"How?"

"When the slave traders steal the young in Yutlind Sud, they sell them to the mines of Sorel." Her eyes met Trevanion's. "I knew a slave girl there who told me stories of her people."

Trevanion held her stare. He had heard about what happened to the children forced to work in the mines, tales so gut-wrenching that even the most hardened prisoners would shudder at hearing them. If Evanjalin had been in the mines, it would explain why she knew the terrain of Sorel so well, although he suspected that she was not telling them the full truth.

"When I heard their voices over our heads, it was clear to me, Captain. The chieftain is a father. There was such love and pride in his voice when he called out to his son."

"I didn't hear that love in the voices taunting us, Evanjalin," Trevanion said harshly.

"Because you don't understand the nuances of their language. We hear the grunts and the guttural sounds, and we believe them to be something worse than hate," she said.

Finnikin stirred beside them. Trevanion watched as his son reached out and gripped the girl's hand, trying to stop her from leaving. The girl gently untangled her hand and crawled away, but Finnikin grabbed the cloth of her shirt, pulling her back against him.

"Take me with you," Finnikin whispered, his breathing shallow. "We can do this together."

"Your wound is infected. You should rest rather than fight it." She turned to Trevanion. "What a stubborn nature the mixing of blood from our rock and our river produces, Captain." It was almost an accusation.

She managed to pull free of Finnikin, but this time Trevanion gripped her. "You risk his life by holding me back, Captain!" She said. "I know how to rid him of the poisons in his blood, but only if you let me convince them to allow us to remove him from this swamp." She looked to Sir Topher, her eyes pleading. "You are the king's First Man, Sir Topher. Order your captain to let me go."

Sir Topher looked torn. He knew that sending her out to the clearing meant she could be dead from hundreds of arrows before she spoke her first word.

"Let her go, Trevanion," he said at last.

His words were met with silence.

"Promise them that Lumatere will acknowledge the south's rightful claim to the throne of Yutlind Sud, but not of Yutlind Nord," Sir Topher said quietly. "It may help. Our king made no secret of the fact that he believed the claim on Yutlind Sud was illegal, and in time he would have made this view public. It may not be enough to keep them from attacking, but it's something."

Trevanion stood and pulled Evanjalin to her feet, holding her close to his side. "You don't step away me from me," he ordered. "Is that clear?"

"Captain, you don't understand. I know their language—"

Trevanion cut her off.

"All I need to understand is the unwritten law of warriors," he said firmly. "And women and children are never sent to do our work without our protection." He pointed to the trees, emphatically. "That's the language I share with them."

As Evanjalin and Trevanion walked into the clearing, Finnikin heard her shout out a word, loud and clear. In their filthy hiding place, he tried to sit up, watching her flinch as if she expected an arrow to come flying toward her at any moment. His father's eyes were like a hawk's as they searched the trees around them.

After a brief pause she stood facing east. Each time Trevanion tried to protect her body, she stepped around him, and when finally he gave up and stood by her side, she began to speak.

Sometimes her lone voice in the jungle suggested she was retelling a story, a history that seemed to have no end. Other times there was vehemence in her tone, husky in its broken delivery of an epistle to those who had guarded the entrance of this land for so long. But she continued speaking through the night until Finnikin heard her voice slur from fatigue and watched her body slump against Trevanion's.

Evanjalin was hardly recognizable in the morning light. Mud caked her shirt, and her face was swollen from the mosquitoes that had feasted on her during the long hours squatting in the river. She had scratched some of the bites to their bloody core, and even her scalp looked raw from the ordeal. Then Finnikin saw her body stiffen, her eyes on the figures that began to appear through the trees. They were like ghosts: their eyes pale and their faces and torsos so white that at first he thought they were painted. They came from every direction of the jungle. Too many to count.

The chieftain stared at Evanjalin, his face expressionless. The two men who stood before her were indeed father and son, yet unlike Finnikin and Trevanion, they were almost replicas of each other. When the chieftain gripped Evanjalin's arm, Trevanion made a move forward but she gently held him back. And then the chieftain spoke, the words blunt and almost hostile, but Finnikin knew enough about the rhythms of language to understand that she was not in danger.

The chieftain barked out an instruction, and Finnikin watched as two of the warriors walked toward their hiding place in the reeds. They pushed past Froi and Sir Topher and grabbed Finnikin's face. While one of the warriors forced open his mouth, the other brought a flask to his lips. He drank the water in great gulps, almost choking with relief, his head rolling back. And then the warriors picked him up and carried him away.

"Evanjalin?" he heard Sir Topher ask in alarm.

Suddenly Finnikin was in his father's arms. Trevanion placed him gently on the ground. Evanjalin's face appeared above him, and then the chieftain's.

"They mean you no harm," she said quietly.

One of the warriors handed her the flask of water. The chieftain continued to watch them all, though his gaze kept returning to Trevanion and Finnikin.

"The slave girl told me the southern Yuts have always been criticized by the northerners for their weakness," Evanjalin said. "You see, the northerners would kidnap the warriors' sons and keep them as hostages, and instead of defending the kingdom and fighting for the crown, the southerners always went searching for their sons. Some see it as a weakness to give up the security of your kingdom and throne for the sake of your child. I told them the story of the captain of the King's Guard who confessed to treason and was imprisoned in the mines of Sorel to save his son, who ten years later freed him."

"You said a word over and over again. 'Majorontai'." Finnikin gasped as she cooled his brow with some of the water.

"The slave girl," she responded quietly.

"She belonged to them?" Trevanion said.

"No. Perhaps another tribe," Evanjalin replied. "But she was from these parts and was stolen by the merchant ships and taken to Sorel by the traders."

The chieftain spoke, and Evanjalin nodded. "They want us to follow them and get some rest," she said.

"Can we trust him?" Trevanion asked.

"If they wanted to kill us, they would have done so by now."

"What did you tell them, Evanjalin?" Finnikin asked.

"I told them the truth," she said quietly, turning to Sir Topher. "Make sure we honor Lumatere's recognition of autonomy in the south, sir."

"But who's in charge in the south?" Sir Topher asked.

"I have a feeling we will find out soon," she said.

Finnikin fought hard to keep his eyes open. The face of a young spirit warrior appeared above him, beside Evanjalin. The warrior spoke and handed her another flask, and she nodded before turning her eyes away from Finnikin's.

"Hold him down. Don't let him go," he heard her say quietly.

He couldn't keep count of how many hands held him down as Evanjalin poured a thick substance into his mouth. It gurgled as his body thrashed and convulsed, wanting to reject it. Then one of the warriors reached over and pressed his fingers hard into the wound at his side until finally he slipped into unconsciousness.

When he woke, it was dark. Finnikin knew he was no longer lying in the clearing. He could hear the sounds of the nocturnal world combined with the spirits of the past as they screeched and moaned and possessed the night. They were not the familiar noises of the woods of the north. This was old country. Finnikin felt the icy breath of its ancestors on his face.

"Evanjalin," he whispered, his lips dry. He heard a rustle, and then she held a flask of water to his mouth.

"Are you in pain?" she asked.

"More nauseous than anything," he murmured. "How long have I slept?"

"All day and half of this night. Sir Topher and Froi are sleeping."

"My father?"

"Pacing."

"And the spirit warriors?"

"Watching you. This is their settlement. Their women and children are upriver."

Finnikin raised himself and saw the faint glow of hundreds of pale bodies surrounding them.

"They guard you until your body has rid itself of the evil spirits you consumed in the river."

"So the evil didn't come from the arrow in my side?" he asked dryly.

"Your wound is superficial. The infection, however, would have killed you within a day."

She wiped his brow, and he found himself fighting the urge to slip back into sleep. "Tell me about the slave girl," he said drowsily.

Evanjalin was silent, and for a moment he thought she was not going to repond.

"When I was ten," she said finally, "I was separated from my people and spent more than a year shackled to her under the floorboards of a house. We were the slaves of a rich merchant who bought and sold people as if they were grain or trinkets. By day we worked in the mines, and at night we were returned to him. But she kept me safe. 'Little sister of the light earth,' she called me. It was as if goddess had sent her to protect me. At night she taught me her language and I taught her mine. Her skin was strangely pale, like these people, and so were her eyes. It's why they are fascinated by the red-gold of your hair, Finnikin.

"She told me about many of the Yut traditions. That when one died away from Yutlind Sud, the person's name was to be taken back to the kingdom by the last person to hear the deceased's voice. To be shouted out for the ghosts to capture in their mouths and blow back into the land. Their spirit would never truly rest until that happened. We knew we would never see our homes again, so the Yut girl decided that if we could not plan for life, we would plan for death."

In the silence he heard her breath catch.

"One day Majorontai placed a flower in my hand. It was so rare to see something of beauty in that place that it brought a tear to my eye. But it was a highly poisonous plant, procured by one of the household guards in exchange for things she would not discuss with me. 'Tonight we see our kingdoms, little sister,' she said. 'Promise me you will put it to use this night, for I cannot leave you behind in such a place. *Promise.'* And so I did."

"And last night you returned her name to her kingdom for the ghosts to capture?" he asked.

She nodded, and they fell silent for a while.

"I'm relieved that you didn't honor your promise to take the poison," he said quietly, "but did you ever feel guilty?"

"I have no guilt to reckon with," she said, and he could hear the steel in her voice. "I honored my promise. Oh, I made sure the poison was taken, Finnikin. By someone who deserved it."

# CHAPTER 14

When Trevanion shook Finnikin awake, it was morning and the spirit warriors were gone, all except one.

"When did they go?" he croaked, holding a hand to his eyes to block out the blinding sunlight.

"Two days ago."

"*Two days?* I slept for two days?"

"And you look no better for it," Trevanion said. "But we need to move on."

Finnikin stumbled to his feet, but the quick movement caused a shooting pain through his side and then Evanjalin was there holding out a hand to him. Although he felt weak, he ignored the gesture, watching as her hand dropped to her side.

"It's best you eat something, Finnikin," Sir Topher said, filling Froi's pack with berries and salted fish.

Finnikin caught the spirit warrior staring at him. "Are we his prisoners?" he said.

"You'll have to ask Evanjalin."

But he could not look at her. In the harsh light of day he had seen the strain on her face and the way exhaustion had bruised her eyes. All from risking her life for him.

"The spirit warrior stays with us as far as the first sentinel beyond the grasslands," she said quietly. "As our guide." She walked over to where Froi was lazing against a tree, eating berries from one of the packs at his feet.

Trevanion handed Finnikin a bowl of cold stew, and he wolfed it down hungrily, watching as his father gathered up his pack. "We are three days' walk from the first rock village. The guide will take us through the grasslands rather than up the river. Too many rebel tribes to contend with otherwise."

Three days' walk from Trevanion's men. Finnikin wondered how he would feel if he were only days away from seeing Balthazar or Lucian. Most times he couldn't remember what his friends looked like, but he heard their voices now more than ever. Snatches of their conversations haunted his sleep.

He tried to take his pack from his father, who refused to hand it over. "I can carry it," Finnikin argued.

Trevanion sighed. "She was right about the stubbornness of one whose blood is a mix from the River and the Rock."

Finnikin glanced over to where Evanjalin was reprimanding Froi by the tree. "No Mont has the right to accuse anyone of bullheadedness."

They made their way out of the jungle, sweat causing their clothes to cling to their bodies in the humidity. Finnikin could hear the rasping breath of Sir Topher behind him. Tiny insects mingled with the perspiration pouring down Finnikin's face as he tried to keep up with their guide, a young man covered in decorations made from human teeth. The spirit warrior had promised them they would reach the Yut leader's rock village by the next afternoon.

"The leader of Yutlind Sud, you say?" Sir Topher asked, stopping to catch his breath.

"I believe we are being taken to the southern king's troglodyte fort," Evanjalin explained, tipping water from her flask into her hands and patting Sir Topher's face. She had not spoken to Finnikin since his rejection that morning. Each time he looked at her, he could only see her standing in the clearing at the mercy of the spirit warriors. Begging for his life.

"He says there are only four rock villages in Yutlind Sud. All are fighting posts. The captain's men could be working for the south's cause," she continued.

"Excellent idea to involve ourselves in a ten-thousand-year-old war that makes no sense even to those fighting it," Trevanion muttered.

Their exit from the thick vegetation provided little relief. Beyond the jungle the vast expanse of grassland, which would take them to the center of Yutlind Sud, was empty of any trees or shade. Finnikin remembered little of the journey except for the blinding heat and the fever that came and went and came again, until he feared that whatever infection had crawled inside him would never leave.

Late in the afternoon they stopped at a village of nomads. Finnikin couldn't help but think how different this tent city was from those built by the Lumateran exiles. Perfectly rounded canvases dyed the colors of the rainbow were scattered across the grassland. Women sat sewing pieces of horsehide together and cast shy glances at their visitors.

Trevanion walked toward the men of the village, who circled the settlement on horseback. Their horses were fine specimens, powerful and beautiful. Trevanion's admiration was clear, and after a moment, one of the patriarchs issued an order to a younger man, who dismounted and handed Trevanion the reins. The patriarch hit the flanks of his horse, and it took off at great speed, with Trevanion's mount close behind.

In the evening, they were fed yak milk and maize cake. As they ate, a young girl with a bronzed face and eyes the color of honey cooed at the sunburn appearing on Finnikin's skin. She touched his hair, running it between her fingers, speaking to him in the guttural language of the southern Yuts.

"What is she saying?" he asked Evanjalin.

"That real men don't have hair your color," she said, walking toward Froi. She snatched a cake out of the thief's hand and gave it back to Sir Topher.

When Trevanion returned, he helped Finnikin to his feet. "They have allowed us the use of one tent, Finn. It's no use traveling farther if you are still weak and in pain."

Finnikin did not argue. It was a relief to lie on a woven mat out of the glare of the sun. The tent was tiny, and when Sir Topher and his father entered, they were forced to crouch down beside him.

"Try to get some sleep," Trevanion said, checking the cloth around Finnikin's wound. "We'll see what we can do for the pain. It's the fever that weakens you."

"Evanjalin will know what to do," Finnikin said in a low voice.

"She is resting, but was kind enough to make up this paste for your aches and pains," Sir Topher said cheerfully, crouching beside him. "Can you sit up?"

Finnikin found it impossible to rest, with the steady flow of visitors to his tent. If it wasn't his father or Sir Topher, it was their guide, the spirit warrior, who insisted on speaking to Finnikin in a language he could not understand. Everyone but Evanjalin. The Yut girl came to administer oil to his sunburned skin. Her fingers were gentle and her smile warm.

When Froi entered, Finnikin knew that the thief had only volunteered to bring him food so he could enjoy a reprieve from the sun. "Make yourself useful and bring Evanjalin to me," Finnikin said firmly.

"Not moving," Froi muttered.

"Who's in charge here?" Finnikin asked. "Me or you?"

There was a sneer on the thief's face as he made himself comfortable. "I fink she is."

Finnikin dozed and awoke to see Evanjalin kneeling beside him, unwrapping the gauze from around his wound. There was an unbearable stench from the secretion, but she worked quietly. He could feel the warmth of her hand as she pressed the balm into his side, and although it stung, it was the type of pain he felt he could endure for as long as he had to.

But still there was not a word from her.

She spread the oil on his burned skin, but this time did so roughly, unlike the gentle Yut girl. Finnikin tried not to flinch, but inwardly he cursed her. When she went to stand, he gripped her wrist and pulled her back to him.

Her eyes met his for the first time since she had entered the tent, and he saw her fury. "Let go of my arm!"

"Why are you angry?" he asked. "It is not my fault that I'm wounded."

"I'm angry because you are stupid."

"Stupid?"

"Do you not understand the word?" she asked, and then repeated it in Sendecanese, Sarnak, Charyn, Osterian,

Belegonian, Yut, and Sorelian, with a few dialects thrown in.

Now he was furious. "Be careful who you call stupid. I wasn't the one who stood out in that clearing and put my life at risk! And by the way, you speak Sendecanese like an amateur. Everyone knows that the *c* is pronounced with a *th* sound."

"*Stupid,*" she seethed slowly in Sendecanese, "is when you climb the mast of a worthless cog when your father has told you to swim to the bank." She pulled her arm away. "It's not heroics we need, Finnikin. It's courage."

"Stay," he insisted.

"Perhaps the Yut girl can keep you company," she said coldly. "Sir Topher is eager for me to play the game of kings with him tonight, and I do not want to keep him waiting."

"Sir Topher has always conceded that when it comes to the game of kings, there is no one better than me," Finnikin boasted.

She stood, her expression haughty. "I suggest you ask him if he feels the same way tomorrow."

The next day, they continued their travels across the grasslands toward the first of the rock villages. Once or twice Evanjalin checked Finnikin's wound, and despite her aloofness, he found himself telling her stories of his own rock village. Although she said nothing, she stayed by his side, and a few times he caught her smiling. The Rock people were the most eccentric of Lumatere, and their close proximity to each other meant there were no secrets among them, although inside their homes, they hissed and muttered about their neighbors. When he relayed the story of his great-aunt Celestina's feud with the pig man over a recipe for pork pie, Evanjalin laughed openly. She, however, told no stories.

"Have you forgotten your childhood in Lumatere?" Finnikin asked quietly when the guide signaled they were close to the fort.

"No," she said. "I remember every single moment and will until the day I die."

They entered the village early that evening. The fort had been built high on a rock face in an attempt to protect it from northern invasion. It was linked to four other villages that stretched for twenty miles along the Skuldenore River.

From the foot of the rock, between two village huts, a stone stairway ascended to the fort. They climbed until they reached a retractable bridge that led to the entrance, a large iron gate. As they walked single file along the bridge, Finnikin took in the lookout post above them, where two men stood, their bows trained on the group. Directly in front of him, he could see arrows protruding from rectangular slits in the gate. If they had been the enemy, he knew they would have been shot down before the first arrow was pulled from their quivers.

Their guide spoke, and the iron gate opened. They walked through the entrance and were led up more stairs of stone. Flies, thick and large, buzzed around their heads.

When they were face-to-face with the true king of Yutlind Sud and his son, Jehr, Finnikin was surprised by how ordinary they looked. There was always such worthless pomp and ceremony in the royal courts of other foreign kingdoms. The Belegonians and Osterians were the worst for pageantry. The boy smiled at him, his teeth startlingly white. Finnikin felt a sudden kinship and returned the smile. Jehr beckoned him to follow and Finnikin held out his hand to Evanjalin.

From the lookout post, Finnikin could see a cave at the far end of the rock face on the other side of the valley. Jehr began to speak.

"From that cave a watchman with a horn can hear the other watchman stationed in a lookout farther downstream,"

Evanjalin translated. "It's how they warn each other of danger."

Jehr pointed to Finnikin's bow and arrow and then pointed to his own. He grunted something, and Finnikin looked at Evanjalin for an explanation.

"He wants to compete."

Jehr muttered something else to her, and she rolled her eyes. "Who can cast ten arrows first," she said. "Remember your wound, Finnikin."

Finnikin nodded at Jehr, and despite his injury, they spent the rest of the evening competing, almost equal in their speed and skill. It came to an end when their fathers arrived and the king bellowed and knocked their heads together for wasting ammunition.

Finnikin and Jehr continued their rivalry by comparing the scars on their bodies.

"Turn the other way," Finnikin said to Evanjalin, showing Jehr and Froi the scar on his thigh from his pledge with Balthazar and Lucian.

Evanjalin spent the rest of the evening refusing to translate.

Talk of rebels farther down the river forced them to stay in the rock village for a few nights. Throughout the day, Finnikin watched his father pace like a caged animal, prowling around the parameters of the village as if he were unable to get enough air. Finnikin spent his time with Jehr, Froi, and Evanjalin, perched on a flat wedge of rock jutting out over the river. Jehr taught Froi how to shoot an arrow, and among them all they chose a mark to see who could hit it first.

"I'll be king one day," Evanjalin translated for Jehr. "Of Yutlind Sud. I'll live down in that castle and your king will come to visit."

Jehr looked at Finnikin and said something to Evanjalin, but she shook her head.

"What did he want to know?" Finnikin asked.

"If you were the heir. He thinks you are and that we're keeping it from them."

The boy spoke again, and this time her face turned pink and she looked down and shook her head, again with no explanation.

"What did he say?" Finnikin asked.

"It is not important."

Finnikin looked at Jehr, who was staring at her, watchful interest in his eyes.

"Did you tell him you belong to our king?" Finnikin snapped.

"I belong to no one!"

The anger simmered between them as Jehr glanced from one to the other.

"Ahh," the boy said, nodding as if he had worked something out.

Evanjalin yelled a few words to the boy's father, who was leaning over the parapet nearby. Jehr groaned and failed to duck as the king grabbed both his head and Finnikin's and knocked them together. Jehr muttered something to Finnikin, and, whatever it was, Finnikin glared at Evanjalin and agreed wholeheartedly.

"Teach me their language," he asked later as they lay in the dark cave alongside the others except Trevanion, who slept outside on the rock face. Finnikin could smell the mixture of cow dung and dirt that covered the ground near their heads.

She started with a few simple words and phrases, and he repeated them. Sometimes she laughed at his pronunciation and he made sure he did not make the same mistake again.

"How come you're so smart?" he asked quietly.

"Because I had to be," she said. Sir Topher began to snore in harmony with Froi. Finnikin feigned his own exaggerated snore, and she shook with laugher against him.

"Jehr has never been off this rock," she said after a long moment of silence. "They won't allow it. They need to keep him safe."

"It's not a way to live," Finnikin murmured. "Should we be worried that our heir hasn't seen enough of the world? That Balthazar's locked up for protection somewhere?"

She stared at him gravely. "Have you ever wondered . . . if he'll survive?"

"Balthazar? Being king?"

"No. Actually entering Lumatere."

He was stunned. "Why would you say such a thing when you've always been so certain?"

"We do not know what will happen in the Valley of Tranquillity. There's never been a promise that the heir will survive. Just that he is needed at the main gate to break the curse."

Finnikin swallowed hard. He had just gotten used to the hope of Balthazar being alive. She had given him that hope.

"What are you thinking?" she asked quietly.

"I was envious of him as a child, you know."

"Balthazar?"

"Every day he would go off with Sir Topher to learn the languages of the land and be instructed on the politics of the surrounding kingdoms. I used to spend afternoons having to play with the youngest princess. Balthazar learned the secrets of our royal courts, and I learned the names of each of Isaboe's dolls."

She searched his face carefully. "And here you are, having learned the languages of the land and been taught the politics of the surrounding kingdoms by Sir Topher." She stared at him intently. "Is that what you fear?" she pressed. "That you've stolen his life?"

"You don't understand," he said. "I would make vows every night when I was a child. That if I were king, I'd change the plight of the Forest Dwellers. If I were king, I wouldn't be so soft on our Charynite neighbors. And Sagrami heard my dark desires."

"Sweet goddess," she cursed. "You think you were responsible for what happened to Lumatere!"

"Go to sleep," he snapped, turning away from her.

"If the heir does not survive what takes place at the main gate, the kingdom must be run by a civilian for the first time in the history of our kingdom," she went on.

"Balthazar will survive," he said flatly.

"All I'm saying, Finnikin, is prepare yourself for the inevitable. The king left the crown to his wife and children and their children's children, but if they were to die, the king's First Man would take the throne. Sir Topher is the king's First Man and you are his apprentice. Jehr may be right. Has it ever occurred to you that one day you could be king?"

He swung back to face her. "Never say those words again," he hissed. *"Never!"*

She covered his mouth with her hand, but he pushed her away. "Quiet!" she said. "Is that why you've been reluctant to return?"

"Sleep," he repeated. "And pray that the son of our king will lead us to salvation."

That night, he dreamed of Balthazar and Lucian and the silver wolf. The Forest of Lumatere turned into the Field of Celebration as the people danced alongside the king and queen and the priest-king sang the Song of Lumatere. But the words were wrong and Finnikin tried to tell everyone around him, yet no one would listen. Except for Seranonna, who beckoned him with a finger. And Finnikin was back in the Forest of Lumatere, where the matriarch stood gripping Isaboe's face with one hand and Finnikin's with another, her ice-cold breath on his cheeks as she forced him to look at the giggling princess.

*Her blood will be shed for you to be king.*

Finnikin woke, perspiration drenching his face. He saw the dark shape of his father keeping watch on the rock face and went to join him. For the rest of the night, they sat mostly in silence.

"Do you think they're out there?" Finnikin asked as the sun began to rise.

"They have to be, Finn. This isn't just about what I want anymore. This is about Lumatere, and I can't make things right without my Guard."

In the half-light Finnikin saw the anguish on his father's face.

"I owe it to our people, Finn. The five days of the unspeakable happened under my watch as captain of the Guard. I owe it to our people."

For the next few days, they traveled along the river, searching the rock villages for any trace of Trevanion's men. Each attempt ended in failure. Finnikin knew they would soon reach the border of Yutlind Nord, where their search would become futile. Trevanion's informant, a Sorelian thief imprisoned for a time in the mines of Sorel, had claimed that the Lumateran Guard was in hiding in Yutlind Sud. They had taken refuge there after an incident in Osteria five years ago that cost the lives of three of their men. An ambush, the thief had said.

"Perhaps the Sorelian thief lied?" Sir Topher said as they left the last of the rock villages.

"What would be his motive?" Trevanion asked. "Perri pays him to commit a minor crime and get himself arrested so he can pass on to me the location of the Guard. He collects the other half of his money when he is released. Where is the profit in lying?"

"There's not much left between here and the border," Evanjalin said. The landscape was beginning to look like the forested region of the north, and Finnikin felt Trevanion's frustration and despair.

"Perhaps they were forced to move on and had no means of getting the information to you," Sir Topher suggested.

Trevanion nodded. Ahead was a sign for the border town of Stophe, and one for the town of Pietrodore, which was perched high above them. They knew little about either. Pietrodore was a neutral town, visited by few travelers. The border town would be their best option for a meal and lodgings. Finnikin had been so sure they would find Trevanion's men and make plans to travel to the Valley outside the main gate of Lumatere. Now all they seemed to be doing was walking aimlessly north. Eleven days in Yutlind, he thought bitterly, and all they had to show for it was an arrow wound in his side and an ache in Trevanion's heart.

They continued soberly along the forest road. Evanjalin lagged behind, her brow creased in concentration. Sir Topher and Trevanion were silent.

"Captain Trevanion!" Evanjalin called out. "Captain! Stop!"

The four of them turned to see Evanjalin pointing up, a smile lighting her face.

"Pietrodore?" Finnikin asked.

"Did you have a dream that told you to take us there?" Sir Topher said.

She shook her head in amusement. "How could I have possibly had a dream while I've been awake and walking, Sir Topher?"

"Magic?" Froi asked, frowning.

This time she was annoyed. "I don't know any magic. I've told you that!"

"It is a long way up, girl," Trevanion said with a sigh. "Too long to waste on chance. They are not here."

Finnikin met her eyes, wanting desperately to make sense of her request. Why Pietrodore? But in a moment the realization hit, and he smiled in wonder.

"It's not chance, Trevanion," he said, kicking the golden carpet of leaves at his feet. He ran back toward her, sliding part of the way until he could grab her by the waist and swing her around. "You are a goddess, Evanjalin of the Monts."

Evanjalin was grinning from ear to ear as she tried to break free. She faced the others, who stood watching, confused. "Pietrodore. It's the common Yut word for 'rock village.'"

## CHapteR 15

The track leading up to the town of Pietrodore was bordered by dense forest on one side and a perilous drop plunging all the way to the road below on the other. The stones underfoot became more hazardous the higher they climbed. It was clear Pietrodore was a town that did not want to be reached with ease, and despite their earlier excitement Finnikin could not shake the possibility of failure. He tried to shut out Froi's endless whining about being hungry and the heavy breathing that signaled Sir Topher's fatigue. Instead he found himself drawn to Trevanion's hope; it was as if his father was willing his men to be at this last post before the border. Despite his love for Finnikin and Beatriss, Trevanion was never complete without his Guard, and Finnikin knew his father would not be fully at ease until he was among them again.

Like many places they had seen in Yutlind, the town was heavily guarded. Yet Pietrodore was aligned to neither the north nor the south and was hostile to foreigners and Yuts alike. It had been free of war for decades, due to its location and lack of strategic worth.

Finnikin could hear the soldiers at the gate speaking common Yut, and he welcomed the sound of the language with relief. After his helplessness with the spirit warriors and those in the rock village, it returned to him a small measure of pride.

But the two soldiers standing guard refused to let them enter. Their hostility was palpable and their decision final. Finnikin stepped forward to try reasoning with them, but their hands went instantly to their swords. He dared not ask about the Lumateran Guard and realized with a sinking feeling that they had wasted their journey. Then he felt Evanjalin by his side.

"This is my love," she told the stony-faced soldiers. "We are to be joined."

There was no response.

"By our spiritual guide," Evanjalin continued, gesturing to Sir Topher. "My betrothed's younger brother and father are to be our witnesses."

One of the soldiers looked over to Froi, Trevanion, and Sir Topher, who all nodded, despite having no idea what was being said.

"We have been persecuted for our union in all other regions of this kingdom." Evanjalin turned to Finnikin and gently lifted his shirt, pointing out the red wound on his side. The soldiers stared at the wound, their expressions unchanged. She looked at Finnikin with such sadness that he almost believed her pitiful tale.

"We'll find a way," he said gently.

"We come to you for refuge," she continued, turning back to the men. "For we have heard that no one in this town would call me the scum of the land." She revealed her right shoulder. "Or brand me like an animal."

Finnikin fought to hide his shock. The branding was indeed one found on cattle, numbers burnt into her skin. He saw Trevanion flinch and tears of rage well up in Sir Topher's eyes. *Oh, Evanjalin, what else have you kept from us?*

"We have been told that no other town can equal Pietrodore in its purity and integrity," Finnikin continued. "Any other is tainted by blood and sorrow, but for the love of this woman I would travel the land . . . nay, the earth, to find a place where she will never be marked again."

Evanjalin knelt at the foot of the largest soldier, who shifted uncomfortably. Finnikin did not know the history of these people. Perhaps they had endured thousands of years of persecution for their position on a war-ravaged border. Perhaps these soldiers had inherited the grief of their ancestors. But kneeling at their feet was someone who had been branded as a slave, and no other kingdom had lost as many of their children to slavery as Yutlind. The burly man extended his hand to cover Evanjalin's shoulder, and then helped her to her feet. With a flick of his head in the direction of the town, he allowed them to enter.

They passed through the gates solemnly. Finnikin stared at Evanjalin as she walked ahead of him between Sir Topher and Froi. When she stumbled, Trevanion's hand reached out to steady her, gently cradling the back of her head in his palm for a moment before letting go.

The main street was wide enough for a horse and cart, and lined with stores full of boots and armor and with colorful guilds. Tiny lanes to the left and right led to cottages decorated with flowers. From every direction, Finnikin caught glimpses of the low stone wall that surrounded the town and of the sweeping views of Yutlind beyond.

At the end of the street, they reached the town square. Here, the sandstone walls of houses were covered with climbing rose-bushes overflowing with color and fragrance. Finnikin watched as

Evanjalin stopped and stared at the roses in awe. He had become used to the plainness of her dress and appearance. That she would marvel at the color around them surprised him, and he wondered about the girl she had once been. Would she have dreamed of placing flowers in her hair or scenting her skin with the delicate fragrance of honeysuckle?

They continued on to the town's highest point, from where they could see the four rock villages of Yutlind Sud. Directly below was the river encircling the flatlands, and in the distance another rock village. The landscape was lush: ten different shades of green, some the color of rich moss, others the color of leaves in sunlight, all contrasting with the dark soil of the plowed earth.

"They are here," Trevanion murmured. "I know it."

"Because it is almost a replica of Lumatere?" Sir Topher asked.

"As close to it." There was a hint of a smile on Trevanion's face. "They were a sentimental lot, my Guard. I never pictured them in a tent city."

"Maybe we should secure this town for our exiles," Finnikin joked. "Add more color to the war in this kingdom."

Trevanion took one more look at the little Lumatere in the distance below.

"Your plan?" Sir Topher asked.

"Finnikin and I will secure rooms for the night," Trevanion said. "Evanjalin, go with Sir Topher to find food and provisions. Speak Yut, not Lumateran. Froi, stay here and keep out of trouble. We will return soon."

"I pray to Lagrami for good news of your men, Trevanion," Sir Topher said.

Finnikin followed his father into the inn. The few men who sat around drinking stared at them long and hard. From the kitchen,

Finnikin could smell roasting meat, and his stomach responded hungrily.

"We are looking for friends of ours who have settled here," Finnikin said in Yut, watching the innkeeper polish glasses behind the bar. "Foreigners."

"Not here," the man said without an upward glance.

Finnikin exchanged a look with Trevanion, who did not seem to need a translation.

"Then perhaps a place to rest," Finnikin continued. "We have traveled far."

One of the cardplayers from the back tables made his way to the bar, standing so close to Finnikin that he received a glowering stare from Trevanion.

"We are full," the innkeeper said.

"Full, you say?" Finnikin looked around the mostly empty room and then back at the innkeeper. "We are not a threat to you," he said quietly.

The innkeeper leaned over the counter, his face a hair's breadth from Finnikin's. There was something unpleasant in his smile, and as he spoke, he poked Finnikin for effect. "And we are still full."

In an instant, Trevanion had the man by the collar and slammed his face against the counter between them. His murderous stare remained until Finnikin placed a hand on his arm to restrain him. The cardplayer who had joined them inched away as Trevanion shoved the innkeeper back behind the bar.

Outside, Evanjalin and Sir Topher were waiting for them in the waning afternoon sun. There was anticipation on Evanjalin's face and disappointment on Sir Topher's.

"The shutters came down the moment we approached," Sir Topher complained. "Any success on your part?"

Trevanion didn't speak as they walked toward the edge of the square.

"No," Finnikin muttered, exchanging a glance with Evanjalin. "I think I need to do this with my betrothed and not my father," he mumbled to her in Yut.

Trevanion sent him a furious look. "We speak Lumateran among ourselves!" he said. "What you have to say to Evanjalin, you say to all of us."

"Most unfair, Finnikin," Sir Topher said.

Finnikin shook his head in frustration. "Sometimes it's easier for me to stick to one language," he lied.

Froi was on his feet the moment they approached, searching to see what they had brought. "Where food?" he demanded.

"It's lovely to know that you are picking up the language, Froi," Evanjalin sniped. "But I do not recall the authority to command being part of your bond."

"Hungry," Froi muttered.

"And we're not?" Finnikin snapped back.

"He's a boy," Sir Topher admonished, "who needs to eat. You were the same at his age, Finnikin."

"No, I was not."

Sir Topher snorted with disbelief.

"All of you stay here," Finnikin ordered. "I will get us food." He pointed a finger at his father. "No fighting with the locals!"

Trevanion was scowling. "Take my sword and the girl."

As they walked away he heard Sir Topher say, "There were times I thought he'd eat me in my sleep, I tell you."

Finnikin strode ahead of Evanjalin until she placed a hand on his arm. She pointed down one of the wider alleys to a courtyard where an outdoor spring was built into the town wall. "Let's at least fill up our water flasks," she said.

As they walked toward the courtyard, the cooking aromas from nearby cottages caused Finnikin's stomach to rumble loudly again, and he clutched at it.

"I think that was actually my stomach," Evanjalin said with a laugh. "Tonight they dine on roast pork. I would give my right arm for roast pork."

But Finnikin did not want to think of Evanjalin's right arm, branding her a slave. "Then tonight you will eat roast pork," he announced.

The courtyard was a smaller version of the main square, with houses facing the west. It stood empty, and Finnikin suspected that the town had a curfew, which meant they had little time to organize food and lodgings. He filled up both their flasks and then splashed cold water on his face.

"Of course, we'll have to steal it," he said, still thinking about their dinner.

"You're asking me to commit a crime?" she said in mock horror.

He laughed. "Not a good way to start our married life, but roast pork is my gift to you."

"And what would you like in return?"

"A goose would be nice," he said. "But then again, I don't care if it's pottage. Even stale bread would work for me. Anything to shut Froi up." He was about to put his head under the spring to wash away the grime, when the cold touch of a sword on his neck stopped him from moving. Evanjalin stiffened beside him.

"Turn around," the assailant said. The sound was more like a rumble than a voice.

He saw Evanjalin's sideways glance, but before he could speak, the assailant pushed her away and she fell.

"Let this fight be between us!" Finnikin said, swinging around.

*Mercy.* He was facing a giant of a man. Massive in height and bulky in width, the giant had dark hair and a beard that were cropped close to his skin. He clutched two swords. His fists were thick, double the size even of Trevanion's, and he defended Finnikin's first blow with great skill.

Evanjalin was back on her feet, hurling her water flask at the giant, but it made little impact against him as his sword clashed with Finnikin's.

"I'm playing with him," the giant said, his tone unkind. "Do that again, little girl, and I'll kill him."

"Push her, threaten her, or even look at her again, and I'll kill you!" Finnikin said, sending the man into momentary retreat.

"I'll make this easier for you." The giant dropped the sword he was holding in his left hand and held up his right hand, indicating who was in charge.

Finnikin caught his first clear look at the man and fought to suppress a grin. "Go get my father, Evanjalin," he said, blowing hair out of his face. He heard her retreating footsteps as she broke into a run.

"She's going to get your father," the giant scorned. "Should I be scared?"

"Probably. Lumateran, aren't you?" Finnikin asked in Yut, trying to sound as if he had the breath to fight and talk.

A dark look crossed the man's face. "You ask too many questions, skinny boy."

"*Skinny boy?* That's the best you can do?"

The giant's eyes narrowed, and his fighting pace quickened until Finnikin's arm began to ache and his legs buckled.

"You look like you're from the River," Finnikin taunted. "Second to those of the Lumateran Rock, I hear."

The giant clenched his teeth, and Finnikin wanted to laugh at how easily he was provoked.

Moss of the River.

The Guard had always mocked him because of his name. He was the biggest scoundrel among the king's men, but Balthazar and Isaboe had adored him and he in turn loved the royal children as if they were his own. His anguish at the discovery of Isaboe's blood-soaked hair and clothing in the Forest that morning had been so great that Trevanion had to hold him down to prevent him from pounding his own body with stones.

"You talk too much," Moss snapped. "And from what I know about Lumatere, the River men come first."

"Do they?" With a grunt, Finnikin shoved him back and then threw his own weapon to the side.

Moss of the River stared at him in confusion, the sword still clasped in his hands.

Finnikin held up one finger at a time. "Rock. River. Monts. Flatlands. Forest. In order of strength," he goaded.

"You have a death wish, my friend. My father would say that anyone fool enough to think they can better a Lumateran River man does not deserve to live."

"And my father would say that very few men look good with a broken nose."

With that, Finnikin twisted around and sent a flying kick to Moss's face. The big man stumbled back in shock, and then a glint of some kind of satisfaction appeared in his eyes. Throwing his sword to the side, he lunged toward Finnikin.

"Hand to hand," he said, nodding with approval. "Try not to scream like a girl."

Trevanion sprinted into the courtyard, trailed by Sir Topher, Evanjalin, and Froi. They were just in time to see Finnikin trapped in a headlock by a man who was twice his size.

"What are they doing?" Sir Topher asked in alarm.

"They're proving their manhood," Evanjalin said in a bored voice. "One of yours, I presume, Captain Trevanion?"

Evanjalin and Sir Topher turned to look at him, and Trevanion could not hold back his joy. He felt his lips twitch into a smile. "Yes," he said. "Both mine."

Finnikin came flying through the air and landed at their feet with a groan.

"Moss has a weak left," Trevanion managed to tell him before Finnikin was back on his feet.

"Sweet goddess, it's Moss of the River," Sir Topher said, hitting Trevanion on the shoulder with glee. "He's a lot bigger than Finnikin," he added. "He could hurt him."

"He says he's only playing with Finnikin," Evanjalin advised them, as some of the villagers came out to their balconies to watch the fighting below.

Finnikin danced and ducked around the giant, throwing punches at any opportunity he could take. "My father says you have a weak left," he said, his head aching from the constant movement.

Moss led with his left, and Finnikin ducked again and then leaped onto the big man's back, yanking at his ears. "And my father would know." Out of the corner of his eye, he saw Evanjalin approach. "Stand back, Evanjalin. You'll get hurt!"

"How long is this going to take, Finnikin? Ask him if they have food. You promised me roast pork."

Finnikin rolled his eyes as Moss swung from side to side, trying to dislodge him from his back. "Woman, I'm trying to fight here! Or has that escaped your attention?"

Moss reached over his shoulder, grabbed Finnikin by his jerkin, and swung him over his head. But then he stopped suddenly, sliding Finnikin back onto the ground, staring at him.

"*Finnikin?* Did she say *Finnikin?*"

Finnikin felt dizzy, the world spinning out of control.

"Finn?" Moss asked again, and then something else seemed

to occur to him. "Did you tell her to go get your . . ." He swung around to where the others stood.

"Blessed day," he murmured. "Oh, blessed day." He stepped toward Trevanion, a look of wonder on his face, and then gave a huge roar of laughter. If Finnikin's left ear hadn't already been ringing from a blow, it would have been deafened by the volume. Moss grabbed Trevanion and lifted him from the ground, both of them laughing with a joy that had their balcony spectators clapping.

"The innkeeper said there were foreigners asking after us. We thought you might be Charynite spies." Moss wiped tears from his eyes. "Never imagined this." He looked at Sir Topher and caught him in a bear hug. "A day blessed by Lagrami, Sir Topher."

Finnikin staggered to his feet beside them. Moss clapped him on the back with his huge hand before looking at Evanjalin. "Food you say, my beauty?"

Evanjalin's face beamed at the compliment.

"Tonight we feast, my friends."


The King's Guard of Lumatere was lodged in an inn at the far end of town. It had been their home for the past five years. They spent their days training Pietrodore soldiers and working out battle tactics for a strike on the palace if they were ever able to enter Lumatere. Each year, Perri and Moss had returned to the the Valley of Tranquillity to see if there was any change.

"Too dark to describe," Moss said quietly as he led the way up a flight of crumbling stone steps to the inn's flat roof. "The mist of malevolence surrounds the whole kingdom, as well as the Forest of Lumatere."

From the rooftop, Finnikin could see down into a large internal courtyard surrounded by high walls.

"It's where we train the lads of Pietrodore," Moss explained as he unlocked the rooftop door. They went down a set of narrow wooden steps until they reached a large rectangular hall, three floors down. Despite the dimness of the light, there was a great deal of activity in the room. It was full of the former King's Guard, fierce men who looked much the same to Finnikin as they had in the days when they defended Lumatere. They wore their hair cropped short, and their body language spoke of readiness. Some played cards, while others sat with their heads bent together.

Moss grinned at Finnikin. "Gentlemen," he called out, "and I hear there are some ladies present too, Aldron."

The men laughed without looking up.

"Last lady I saw was your woman as I left her this morning, Moss," the man Finnikin presumed was Aldron said from the back of the hall.

"We have guests."

Several of the men stopped what they were doing and gave Moss their attention. They squinted in the half-light, and Finnikin realized that, like the town of Pietrodore, visitors rarely entered this domain.

"Courtesy of a foreign King's Guard," Moss continued.

This time, every man in the room came to his feet. They pulled their swords from their scabbards in unison.

"Moss, where is the humor in this?" one man asked, making his way toward them.

Finnikin recognized him instantly. Perri. Trevanion's second-in-charge. The man who had placed him in Sir Topher's care during the nightmare days after the unspeakable, the man who had given him Trevanion's sword.

Perri stopped in front of them. He was lean and lacked the height of Moss and Trevanion, but there was no weakness in his body. As he had often done as a child, Finnikin trembled at the sight of men so powerful.

Finnikin saw the recognition flash in Perri's eyes. He stood before his captain, their faces twitching with suppressed emotion. They clasped each other's arms, their fists straining from the strength of their feelings. Curious, others in the room stepped forward and suddenly a roar of men's voices shouted Trevanion's name.

"Crying?" Froi scorned.

For a moment the room was silent. Finnikin watched the men turn and stare at Froi as if he were a gnat they could crush in a moment. Froi, at least, had the good sense to look frightened.

"Did he just mock us?" one of the younger guards asked.

Trevanion grabbed hold of another guard, clapping him on the shoulder. "You were half the size when I saw you last, Aldron."

"I was fifteen, Captain," Aldron protested. "And you swore you would never allow a guard so young. But you said I had the heart of a lion."

"As does your little pup." Moss grinned, looking at Finnikin.

Finnikin felt Perri's dark stare. But the look was one of pride.

"Little Finch," Perri murmured. Suddenly he grabbed Finnikin in a headlock as the others cheered. "And where is Sir Topher?" Perri asked, swinging around.

"Feeling like the shortest man in the kingdom," Sir Topher said with a laugh, lost in the middle of the group. There were three cheers for the king's First Man.

After the initial excitement, the Guard seemed overcome. Finnikin could see it in their expressions, as if they had no idea how to comprehend who had just walked into their hall. There were questions in their eyes. Trevanion sensed it and held up his hand for silence. He took in the face of every person in the room and then his gaze settled on Froi and Evanjalin, who looked overwhelmed by all the celebration. Gently, Trevanion drew them toward him and turned them to face his men, brushing the back of his hands across their faces.

"Gentlemen," he said quietly, "I present to you the future of our kingdom. The lifeblood. We take back Lumatere. For them."

The guards hoisted the two into the air, and Finnikin saw joy and fear on Evanjalin's face.

But Froi looked around with wonder.

As if he had never seen the world from up so high before.

CHAPTER 16

There was little rest to be had in the week that followed. Trevanion wasted no time in preparing his men, yet there was a spirit and energy among the Guard that not even the most backbreaking training could crush. These were men of wisdom and experience, but no one could deny the need for youth and stamina, especially if the battle to reclaim Lumatere was a long one. In the courtyard of the inn, Trevanion and Perri barked out instructions, pushing the men to the limits of their endurance, and at times their tempers.

"Protect your wrist, Callum!"

"Your feet are your first line of defense, Finnikin!"

"If he had an ax, you'd be standing on stumps by now, Aldron!"

"Oi! Froi! Make yourself useful and get some bindings!"

Finnikin fought hard for their approval, something he had not needed to work for during the past ten years. Sir Topher's admiration had always been quick, from his wonder at Finnikin's ability to remember every detail of a conversation to praise for his pupil's hunger for learning. But now Finnikin felt the need to convince the Guard that he was worthy to be part of them. He longed for their acceptance, not just because his father was captain but because they saw him as a warrior in his own right.

And so he trained long before the others arrived at dawn, his fingers bleeding from the constant use of his bow and arrow. During the day, he rarely stopped to eat or drink, his practice sword always ready for the next opponent, despite the pain in his joints. He worked hardest and longest with the glaive, knowing it was his weakness, ignoring his opponents as they winced each time the pole connected. He listened intently to every criticism and afterward worked twice as hard to make sure he did not repeat his mistakes.

By the end of the first week, his whole body ached and he wanted nothing more than to collapse onto his bedroll and sleep. Beside him, Froi picked up the practice swords, grumbling with every movement. "Make yourself useful, Froi!" he mimicked. "Fetch, Froi! Slave!"

Finnikin was beginning to regret the boy's language lessons, which now included every curse under the sun, courtesy of the Guard. He looked up to where Evanjalin sat on the balcony, her legs folded under her, head on the rails.

"Use more than the weapon to fight," Trevanion ordered. "Fight from the heart, lads."

"Train your body to do the moving," Perri shouted.

"Finnikin, too tight," Moss said. "Hold the sword like you'd want a woman holding your—"

Finnikin heard one of the men clearing his throat as he indicated toward the balcony with his head.

"Sorry, Evanjalin," Moss said meekly, waving up to her.

She spent most days watching, not permitted to participate. Despite the resourcefulness she had displayed over the last few months, Sir Topher had ordered that she keep out of harm's way.

At times Finnikin felt Sir Topher treated her as if she were some prized possession and not just Evanjalin who could take care of herself. He had noticed that whenever she watched from the balcony, the aggression of the men intensified and the competition became more fierce, especially among the younger guards. Finnikin had received great satisfaction that morning beating Aldron of the River in front of her, catching him across the ears with the buckler. When the fourth serious injury of the day occurred, Trevanion intervened.

"Froi, go make yourself useful and tell Evanjalin that Sir Topher would like her to join him for a walk. A very long one."

But she was back again that evening after the rest of the Guard had left. Finnikin felt her eyes on him and caught her look of displeasure. Exasperated, he finally dropped the practice sword in his hand and leaped up to the trellis, climbing his way toward the balcony, where she sat under the light of the moon. When he reached the railing, the sight of her robbed him of breath; her golden skin glowed in the pale light.

With his feet balanced on the trellis, he propped both arms on the timber rail. "What?" he asked.

"I beg your pardon?"

"Beg all you like. Just tell me what the problem is."

She stared at him and sighed. "What do you want me to say, Finnikin? You are as good as them. Perhaps in time you will be the best fighter in Lumatere. But you are not meant to be in the King's Guard. You are meant to be in the king's court."

He shook his head. "You are wrong. When we were children, Balthazar always dreamed of the same future. He would be king and I would be captain of the Guard. Like our fathers before us."

She looked at him sadly. She was only inches away from him, and he fought the urge to take her face in his hands.

"But that was a time when Balthazar thought he would live forever," she said. "Before they slayed his parents and sisters. When he still believed silver wolves and unicorns existed in the Forest of Lumatere and there was no difference between him and a peasant. But there was. Just like there is a difference between a great warrior and a great king's First Man. And your father is one, Finnikin, and you are the other."

"You think I can't be a great warrior?" he asked.

"Today this courtyard was filled with great warriors. What is one more? But it was not filled with great men who have the heart to rule a kingdom. Any man can kill, Finnikin. It is a stroke, an action with one's hand. But not every man knows how to lead. For that you need what's here," she said, pointing to his head, "and what's here." She laid a hand on his chest. He heard a door open below them.

"Finnikin!" Trevanion strode into the courtyard. "Where are you? We're off to the bathhouse. Are you with us?"

Finnikin's gaze was locked on Evanjalin's.

"Are you with them?" she asked softly.

"Always."

"Then go." She sniffed dramatically. "Leave me in my gilded cage."

He grinned. "You are just put out because we're treating you like a girl."

"I *am* a girl. And if I am put out, it is because a bunch of men who don't care for keeping clean are afforded the luxury of a bathhouse, and those who crave it are stuck with ten layers of grime on their face."

He reached out his hand and traced the backs of his fingers across her face. "You lie. I can only feel eight."

"Finnikin!" his father called again.

"Off you go, Little Finch," she mocked. "To the bathhouse,

where you can all sit around and compare the skills and attributes of the warrior class."

Finnikin watched Aldron of the River strut around the bathhouse before making himself comfortable next to Trevanion. The young guard reminded Finnikin too much of Lucian. Unlike Finnikin's pale, lean frame, Aldron had the coloring of the River people and had lost his leanness years before. Finnikin tried hard not to compare himself with any of the Guard in their nakedness.

"I hear we are to split up to travel to Lumatere, Captain Trevanion," Aldron said.

Trevanion nodded. "We have exiles to collect from other kingdoms," he explained. "I will speak of it tonight."

"And, of course, Aldron will be the first to volunteer to escort our younger visitors," one of the older guards joked.

Finnikin turned to Aldron. "Evanjalin and the boy travel with me," he said coldly. "It's best to keep things simple."

"Simplicity would have you traveling with Perri and Moss, and a few of the older men who can teach you a thing or two about defense, Finnikin," Aldron said.

"It takes great character to handle Evanjalin and Froi," Finnikin went on. "You would have much to fear."

"What is the worst that can happen?" Aldron scoffed.

"She could have you imprisoned in the mines. Or sell you to the slave traders of Sorel," Finnikin said with a shrug.

"You are trying to scare me off. Does she belong to you, Finnikin? If she does, say the word and I will bite my tongue and look the other way."

The men turned toward Finnikin, waiting for a response.

Did Evanjalin belong to him? No, he wanted to say, she belonged to their future king, his boyhood companion whom he had loved like a brother. But there were moments, as he lay beside her deep in the night, when he hated beloved Balthazar. When he wished to covet it all.

"I think you need to find yourselves wives," Finnikin said.

The men chuckled.

"Well, here is our dilemma," Moss began. "There are those who refuse to betray their bonding vows and consider themselves still joined to their women in Lumatere, and those who are free to come and go as they please. Except the first rule of Pietrodore is that their young women are off-limits."

"Tomas and I are bonded to each other," Bosco said from a lower step.

"Which we are forced to be reminded of each night."

"While the rest of us go with nothing," Aldron sulked.

"You're most welcome to join us any time, Aldron," Tomas joked.

The others laughed.

"Anyway, each month we enjoy a day or two in Bilson," Moss said with a grin. His face instantly reddened when he found Sir Topher's gaze on him.

"And what is it you do there, Moss?" Sir Topher asked politely.

Finnikin exchanged a look with his mentor, who was trying to hide a smile.

"Ah, of course," Sir Topher said, as if a thought had just occurred to him. "With such diverse places of worship and the tastiest delicacies, it would be hard to keep away."

"Not to mention the reading rooms," Finnikin said, catching Sir Topher's grin. "I once spent a whole week there reading about the sixth-century fighting techniques of the Leticians. I can understand what drew you to the town, Moss."

Aldron snorted. "What an exciting life you lead, Finnikin."

"Thank you, Aldron. I do enjoy the philosophical discussions

I have with Evanjalin. Reading and languages are her passion. Yours?"

"Oh yes, Aldron and Moss are great readers," Perri said dryly. "And as for languages, I do believe they know how to curse in at least six."

After dinner that evening, they sat hunched over maps of Skuldenore, combining their knowledge of the past ten years. Perri pointed to a landmass on his map in Yutlind Nord near the Sendecane border. "Exile camp. Forty-seven men, women, and children. Mostly from the Flatlands."

Sir Topher shook his head. "We thought we knew them all."

"They stayed hidden in the north. If there is one kingdom where they do not care if you're Lumateran, it's Yutlind. The Yuts have enough of their own misery."

"How do our exiles survive in these parts?" Finnikin asked.

"We send a guard each week. Lexor is with them at the moment. But we struggle to keep them fed. Thankfully some have found work on the land over the years, yet they refuse to become part of the village, which would have made life easier for them. They are firm in their belief that if they stray too far from the other Lumaterans, they will be left behind."

"A problem with most Lumateran exiles," Sir Topher said softly.

Finnikin finished the work on his own map, and the men whistled in surprise when they saw the markings.

"So many camps," Perri said with regret.

"Have you seen my father and mother in your travels, Sir Topher?" Ced of the Flatlands asked. There was a hopeful look on his face. "They escaped up the River to Sarnak during the five days of the unspeakable, but I have not come across them since or met anyone who has."

Trevanion did not speak. Finnikin knew his father had recruited the young Ced from his own river town. There was no doubt about the fate of his parents.

"I fear they may have perished in Sarnak or the fever camps," Ced continued in a quiet voice. "We have seen many die from famine over the years."

Trevanion's eyes were downcast.

"As have we," Sir Topher said, clearing his throat. "Finnikin's *Book of Lumatere* is full of the names of the dead."

"Yet we could do little," Perri said. "Each time we made our presence known, lo and behold, there was an attack on our inn or camp."

"Charynites?" Trevanion asked.

Perri nodded. "It is what you have always suspected, Trevanion."

Finnikin looked from one to the other in confusion. "How do you know of my father's suspicions, Perri?"

"We spoke about them during the early days of my imprisonment in Belegonia," Trevanion said.

"You were there?" Sir Topher asked Perri in surprise.

Perri looked quickly at Trevanion, who nodded.

"For the first three years of my captivity in Belegonia, they managed to get themselves arrested at different intervals to join me," Trevanion said flatly.

"You would have done the same. You would never have left any of us to rot in a foreign prison," Perri muttered.

"We almost broke him out once or twice," Moss said.

Trevanion looked at them, his expression softening. "It did help," he admitted. "During those early days, nothing except your news that my son was being taken care of by one of the noblest men in our kingdom made things bearable."

Sir Topher smiled humbly.

"In Belegonia we received a warning that Trevanion was to be transferred and we followed him south and then six months later to the mines," Perri said.

"Did any of you manage to get yourselves arrested in Sorel?" Finnikin asked.

The men fell silent.

"We thought it would be as easy as Belegonia," Perri said finally, a pained look on his face. "Disorderly behavior. Sent to the mines. Released within a week. Except we underestimated the prison mines and lost two men in the first two weeks. Then Trevanion forbade it. Made us promise. The hardest decision I have ever made was to honor that promise. Your father must have stopped breathing from fear when he saw you there, Finnikin."

"Who were the men?" Finnikin asked quietly. "The two you lost?"

No one spoke for a moment.

"Angas and Dorling," Kintosh of the Rock answered.

Finnikin paled. The brothers from the Rock Village. The two lads had been inseparable. They were among the youngest of the Guard, and the girls of the Rock would swoon when speaking of them. Some even said that the princesses blushed in their presence. They would have been only a few years older than Finnikin now. So similar to him in coloring. As children, when they were not pretending to be king and captain of the Guard, he and Balthazar would pretend to be Angas and Dorling of the Rock.

"We were talking about the Charynites," Perri said quietly.

Finnikin nodded, needing a moment to find his voice again. "The impostor king is weak, has always been weak, especially in his capacity as captain of the King's Guard before my father. There was no possible way that he could mastermind such a well-executed plan as the takeover of Lumatere. Just deliver it."

"But that was all we knew until Evanjalin," Sir Topher said.

"Is she friend or foe?" Moss asked. "Because she is a beast at cards, and at times I feel as if the power of the mightiest of gods is in her eyes."

"Or the darkest of spirits," Perri said.

Finnikin glanced at him. Perri knew darkness. "Evanjalin is a survivor of the Sarnak massacre."

"Sweet precious child," Moss sighed.

"And she can walk through the sleep of those trapped inside Lumatere," Finnikin added.

"And that of our heir," Sir Topher said.

Moss whistled, and Aldron squeezed in next to them, a look of disbelief on his face. "She's a mystic? A Forest Dweller?"

Trevanion shook his head. "A Mont."

"She was with me when I visited Lord August in Belegonia," Finnikin said. "And she confirmed our theory that the Charynites were involved in the deaths of our beloveds. But she had an explanation. Lumatere was just a way for the Charynites to invade Belegonia."

"She claims to have known this through Balthazar," Trevanion said.

"And you believe her?" Perri asked incredulously.

Trevanion sighed. "I think I do."

"It makes sense," Sir Topher said. "Place a puppet king in Lumatere and you get a clear path into Belegonia, the most powerful kingdom in the land."

"They could have used Osteria for that," Aldron said.

"Osteria has Sorel as an ally. Not even the Charynites would be that stupid."

"I'm not questioning her theory," Perri said. "I'm questioning her delusion that she can walk through the sleep of our heir."

"Then let's focus on her theory and not her delusion,"

Trevanion said. "The Charynites fear us. If we free Lumatere, we will have the impostor king and his men as political prisoners, weak bastards who can easily be broken to reveal the truth behind the palace murders, which will implicate the king of Charyn. The Belegonians will be eager for the evidence."

"And instigate a war between two of the most powerful nations of Skuldenore?" Sir Topher said bleakly. "A war that could affect every kingdom surrounding Lumatere?"

There was an uneasy silence.

"A war of the land?"

The men swung around to where Evanjalin stood.

"Is that what we achieve by returning? The annihilation of the whole land of Skuldenore?"

Most of the Guard seemed suddenly wary of her. Finnikin made room on the bench, and she squeezed in beside him.

"We've just been told the most fascinating story, Evanjalin," Perri said, his tone cool.

"Do you believe in the gods, sir?" she asked.

"I believe in him," he said, pointing to Trevanion. "And where he goes, the Guard follows. Don't ask me to believe in anything else."

She stared at him for a moment, understanding in her eyes. "Your family lived close to some of the Forest Dwellers, did they not?" she asked.

Finnikin could tell Perri was surprised by her knowledge, but he revealed little.

"I prefer not to refer to them as family."

"But you witnessed the gifts of some of the Forest Dwellers?"

His stare was cold. "I knew little of their mystic practices. Whatever contact I had with the Forest Dwellers had less to do with sharing our skills than with shedding blood. Theirs."

"Then it will be hard for me to explain what I can do in the sleep," she said.

"Try," Trevanion urged, giving Evanjalin a quick nod of encouragement.

"It's a blood spell," Finnikin said.

"Ah, I see. Now everything makes sense." Perri's tone was dry.

"And Seranonna's spell was a blood curse," Sir Topher continued.

"And the young girls of Lumatere are protected because the impostor's men think they have a blood disease," Trevanion added.

"Can you explain the blood spell that has given you this . . . gift, Evanjalin?" Moss asked.

Evanjalin looked at Sir Topher, as if seeking his permission.

"Maybe without so much detail, Evanjalin," he said, a flush in his cheeks. "I will explain the rest later if necessary."

She nodded. "I was twelve years old. I remember it clearly because a wondrous feeling came over me. As if I was melting into the souls of others, and I felt a wave of such peace that I truly believed I was in the heavens with our goddess. That night, I walked my first sleep with a bundle in my arms. A baby."

"The baby spoke to you?" one of the men asked.

Evanjalin looked confused. "How can a baby speak?"

"The same way someone can walk through another's sleep. With very little credibility," Perri said.

"I would have preferred if the goddess had given me a more credible gift, sir. Perhaps the ability to heal or talk to the animals or hold a sword the way a man would like his sword to be held, but alas I am stuck with walking through the sleep of others."

Perri had the good grace to look apologetic, and Finnikin heard a few chuckles around them. By now every member of the Guard had surrounded their table.

"Do you walk through the child's sleep?" Moss asked.

Evanjalin shook her head. "Yet I know every single time when we walk through the sleep of the child's mother, although we never walk the sleep of the other who sometimes joins us."

"The other?" Perri asked.

"How do you know where to go?" This came from Ced.

"I don't know. It is as if we are both lost in this dreamscape together and then suddenly we are in someone's sleep thoughts. At times it is wonderful, and other times . . . I cannot begin to tell you of the demons that visit humans as they sleep. Guilt is the greatest monster. Remorse, a killer. But the worst are the memories. Yet sometimes, they are the only things that keep our people alive."

"You must dread sleep," Aldron said.

"Not at all. When the sleep first began, it was beautiful. I felt pure joy. I think I was experiencing the euphoria of a woman of great courage holding her newborn." She looked meaningfully at Trevanion. "A woman whose sleep I had walked before."

"It was Beatriss?" he asked quietly. "Beatriss gave birth to a child five years ago?"

"*Beatriss?*" There were murmurs around them. "Trevanion, what are you saying?" Moss asked. "That Lady Beatriss is . . . she's . . ."

"Perhaps alive. Perhaps helping those responsible for the weakening of Seranonna's spell," Trevanion said firmly.

"Who would that be?" one of the older guards asked. "Very few of those who worshipped the goddess Sagrami were spared during the five days of the unspeakable."

"The cloister of Sagrami," Perri said quietly. "It can only be the novices."

"The novices would have been put to death with the rest," Moss insisted.

Evanjalin's gaze returned to Perri. "The other who walks the sleep with us is very strong in her power. The child is drawn to her as she is drawn to her own mother. I believe she has both light and dark in her."

"Tesadora," Perri said under his breath.

"You seem certain that Tesadora and the novices lived, sir," Evanjalin said.

Perri did not respond.

"Is that good or bad?" another of the guards asked. "That this Tesadora takes charge within Lumatere?"

"Her mother was Seranonna," Trevanion said.

Finnikin saw the looks pass among the guards at the mention of Seranonna's name.

"Tesadora was as mistrusted among her own people as she was by the rest of Lumatere, so let's just say that she was not raised in the bosom of her people. She is cunning and has a very dark soul," Perri said.

"Just the person we need to break the very dark spell cast by her mother," Evanjalin said.

"But you must be wrong about Lady Beatriss aiding her," Perri argued. "One would have been a novice of Lagrami, the other Sagrami. There is no way that Tesadora of the Forest Dwellers and Beatriss of the Flatlands would be acquainted. No possible way that Beatriss would trust her child with someone so dark of spirit. Do not underestimate Tesadora's hatred of the world."

"You trust your children with those who have the power to protect them," Trevanion said.

"The other . . . I mean, Tesadora walks the sleep with us only sometimes," Evanjalin said. "But I do not sense her evil. Just a forceful will. I know she is there for the child. It is when the sleep is dark and fearful that she is there. Last night we walked the sleep and there was much grief, but Tesadora's powers ensure the child sees or hears nothing that will damage her. The child has been kept innocent. I cannot begin to think of the effect that has on Tesadora."

"And you?" Finnikin asked. "Who protects you?"

"Faith in my goddess, of course."

There was a mixture of intrigue and skepticism on the faces of the guards around her.

Perri turned to Trevanion. "So what is our plan?"

"We split up, each group traveling to a different kingdom to collect our exiles. We meet in the Valley of Tranquillity as soon as possible. Moss and Aldron, I want you to leave for Lastaria tonight. The priest-king is there."

There was an intake of breath from the guards. "Blessed Barakah?" one said in a hushed tone.

Trevanion nodded. "He travels with a large number of exiles. Take them to the Valley of Tranquillity. The rest of you will travel in groups of four or five. If you come across any exiles, do your best to convince them to join you, but under no circumstances do you stay with them in their camps or tent cities. Too many of them are plagued by fever or fear. The moment you reach the Valley, I want every strong man and woman trained to use a longbow. The attack on the impostor and his men needs to be fast and accurate, or else we will never take the palace."

There were murmurs among the Guard.

"How many of them do you believe there are?"

"The impostor king rode into Lumatere with six hundred men. Our own people could have been recruited as part of his army. Who can say?"

"But how do we get in?" one of the guards asked. They were all looking at Evanjalin.

"We need to find the Monts," Trevanion said. "They may hold the key."

Perri shook his head. "Not a sighting in ten years. I return to the Valley with Moss each year at the time of the harvest moon, and we have not seen hide nor hair of them."

Evanjalin stood, and the men instantly rose with her. She acknowledged them with a nod. "Our king will get us through the main gate," she said. "That has been promised in the curse."

And then she left and all Finnikin could hear was the name Balthazar whispered around the room.

CHAPTER 17

Three days later, the King's Guard separated for the first time in ten years. Trevanion ordered that along with Perri the original party would stay together until Belegonia. They had acquired more horses, which would ensure that the journey along the coastal road was swift. As he mounted his horse, Finnikin sensed the mood of excitement and uncertainty among the Guard. He saw the look of hope on their faces. And doubt. But they had enough faith in their captain to trust his decision. And his decision was to allow this strange girl to lead them home to Lumatere.

They rode for the better part of the day, until they reached the coastal road, where the gulf divided Belegonia from Sorel. As the ill-fated captain of the *Myrinhall* had suggested, it would have been the quicker route between Sorel and Yutlind. Yet piracy in the Gulf of Skuldenore had claimed many lives, and despite their perilous journey up the Yack, Finnikin knew they had taken the right course.

Late in the afternoon, they rested their horses and sat on the dunes, watching the ocean. Nothing reminded Finnikin so much of the insignificance of humans as when he stood before the ocean's pounding waves. For a moment, he caught his father's eye. They both knew there was no turning back from the path they were about to take. Although they were gathering their fragmented people together, Finnikin could not help thinking they were also leading them to war. Taking back Lumatere would not be easy. And if they succeeded, they had no idea to what they would return. Would their land of five peoples become a kingdom split in two: those who were exiled and those trapped inside? Suddenly he missed the life they had left behind in Pietrodore. There, he had everyone he wanted in one place. Going back to Lumatere could mean the loss of them all.

Back on the road, Finnikin swung onto his horse and then turned to help Evanjalin up behind him. But Perri was already there, his hands cupped to assist her. Evanjalin leaned over and traced the scar on Perri's face, and he flinched at her touch.

"It was you," she said in wonder. "You wear a permanent crown. She placed it there." Evanjalin kept her fingers on Perri's forehead. "She doesn't regret what she did to you that day when you were children, Perri. The savagery your kin showed toward her will never be forgotten. But regardless of what you believe, I think Tesadora is forever grateful that you kept Sagrami's novices hidden that night."

Perri looked stunned. His eyes met Finnikin's, and Finnikin saw a myriad of emotions on the guard's face. But only for an instant. What had his father's second-in-command done during the five days of the unspeakable to make him feel such love and pride, but also shame? How many stories were missing from Finnikin's *Book of Lumatere*?

---

Early that evening they came to a signpost for Lastaria, a half-day's ride from the capital of Belegonia. Moss was sitting there astride his horse, waiting for them.

"We have a problem," he said soberly as his mount danced around Trevanion's.

"The priest-king?" Evanjalin asked.

"He is safe," Moss assured them. "But the journey was harrowing and they lost at least ten people to fever along the way."

Finnikin felt Evanjalin shudder as she held on to his waist.

"It gets worse. When they arrived here last week, they came across a small camp of exiles."

"How could we not have known?" Sir Topher said.

"They did not want to be found. There are at least thirty of them, and they refuse to journey with us to the Valley."

"Then we go without them," Trevanion said bluntly.

"That's where we have our problem. The priest-king will not leave them."

"And the rest?" Evanjalin asked. "The exiles from Sorel?"

"With Aldron, on their way to the Valley."

Trevanion cursed and exchanged looks with Perri. The sun was beginning to set and Finnikin knew their plan was to reach the capital before midnight.

"We cannot leave him behind, Captain," Evanjalin argued.

Trevanion turned his horse around reluctantly. "No, but we will have to convince him to leave the others."

They rode into Lastaria under the light of a half moon. Moss paid a stable boy a piece of silver to take care of their horses, with the promise of another when they returned. Then he led them down sloping, cobbled streets toward the town center. Finnikin could hear the sounds of the night bazaar before they saw it. The air was full of raised voices and music, the streets strung with lanterns.

Lastaria seemed to lack the intellect and culture of the Belegonian capital, but there was an unleashed gaiety about the town that assaulted their senses.

In the square, the minstrels played their fiddles and pipes, delighting the audience, who danced with abandon. Lovers embraced. A vendor juggled fruit. But there was heaviness in Finnikin's heart as they followed Moss to a paddock beyond the square, at the edge of town. On the way, they passed a cluster of tents selling decorated daggers and swords. Froi's eyes lit up at the sight of them, but he was pulled along by Perri.

The camp was made up of three large carts. At least thirty men, women, and children stood by a campfire. Finnikin could see the distress in the faces of the exiles at the sight of Trevanion and his party, but his eyes searched for the priest-king. The holy man looked thinner and frailer than when they had last seen him. Perri knelt before him, and the priest-king's hands trembled as he held a thumb to Perri's forehead.

"I can't leave them behind," he whispered when the blessings were complete. "They have no goddess, no kingdom, no people but their own."

"Perhaps that is enough for them," Finnikin said.

The priest-king shook his head. "Have you seen their eyes?" He looked past Finnikin to Evanjalin. "There is nothing there."

"Blessed Barakah, our people are waiting for us in the Valley," Evanjalin argued. "Waiting for you to lead them with the captain and Sir Topher and Prince Balthazar."

"What are their reasons for staying?" Finnikin asked.

The priest-king followed his gaze to where the exiles stood. "They once lived in the village of Ignatoe, close to the east gate of Lumatere. During the five days of the unspeakable, when the Forest Dwellers began to pour into their village, the people of Ignatoe turned them away, forcing them back outside the kingdom walls." The priest-king sighed. "These people listened as the Forest Dwellers burned to death in their cottages. It's their guilt that holds them back, and no amount of pleading will move them."

Finnikin stayed with Evanjalin as she walked toward the fire, where a young girl stood holding a skillet, her expression frozen with fear. Finnikin guessed she would have been no older than five when the days of the unspeakable took place. As Evanjalin approached, her path was blocked by an older man and woman, a child clutching the woman's skirt. Up close they looked younger than Finnikin had first thought, and he realized that life rather than years had aged these people.

Evanjalin stooped to hold out her hand to the child. She looked about two or three, with brown skin and pale blond hair. "What's your name, little one?" Evanjalin asked, her voice husky. She spoke in Lumateran, but the child stared back at her blankly. She was as vacant as the children they had seen in the fever camp, yet there was no hint of malnutrition or illness. Evanjalin tried to take the little girl into her arms, but she was pushed away by the man, causing her to stumble.

Finnikin drew his sword as a warning. He was not quick enough to stop Froi from spitting in the man's face, but Perri stepped forward and dragged the thief back by his hair. In the next instant the man grabbed the child and Finnikin found himself holding his weapon an inch away from the little girl's face. Evanjalin reached out and gently lowered the sword in his hand.

"We mean no harm," Finnikin said quietly in Lumateran. He watched the exiles flinch at the sound of their mother tongue.

Evanjalin took a step toward the campfire and then another. When she stood before the young girl with the skillet, she extended a hand.

"May I?" she asked, reaching over to take one of the small pieces of meat that sat on the skillet. Before the girl could respond, Evanjalin put the meat in her mouth as if it were the most natural thing, grunting with approval as she swallowed. The girl seemed to soften slightly.

"What is your name?" Evanjalin asked.

The girl looked past them to where her father stood, then looked down again. "My name doesn't matter," she said, speaking in broken Belegonian.

"Oh, but it does," Evanjalin said quietly.

Finnikin saw the girl tremble. After a life of exile with these people, the hope shining from Evanjalin's eyes must have been mesmerizing.

"We're on our way home," Finnikin said, looking around at the rest of the group. "To Lumatere. Hoping that all our people will return with us."

There was no response.

"All we suggest is that you travel with us to the Valley of Tranquillity. With the King's Guard. The captain. Our blessed Barakah. The king's First Man," Finnikin continued.

"And what will you offer us if we return?" the man asked. "A prison cell? A life of persecution?"

"There will be no arrests," Trevanion called out. "Have we not all suffered enough?"

"We offer what is owed to your children. Our kingdom," Finnikin said.

"This is enough for them," the man said bitterly.

"This is a stretch of muddy grass," Finnikin snapped. "That," he said, pointing to one of the carts, "was built to transport cattle and horses, not to shelter humans."

"We will do what we always do," the woman said. "Send your Guard away, we beg of you."

"They are your Guard," Finnikin corrected. "There to protect you and your children."

"Our children are protected," she said. "We keep them fed."

Finnikin saw the rage in the eyes of some of the younger men. Where would it all go? he wondered. The man took a threatening step toward him.

"Turn around and don't look back," he said, his voice ugly. "I suggest you take care of your own and leave us to take care of ours, or there will be a reckoning."

"You have many suggestions, sir." Evanjalin's voice rang out through the night air. "Well, here are mine. I *suggest* you give your people words, not silence. I suggest you all turn to your wife, to your husband, to your children, and you speak of those days. Of the little you did when your neighbors were taken from their houses and slaughtered. Of the sorrow you have felt all these years. And I suggest you forgive yourself. But more than anything, I suggest you beg the one true goddess to forgive the legacy that you have passed on to your children. For they wear your coat of dissatisfaction and grief tightly over their bodies, and this bloodless patch of grass you have chosen to live on will be where they die with nothing but rage in their hearts. I *suggest*, sir, that you find no joy in being an exile. Do not make it a badge to wear with honor."

She turned and walked toward the priest-king. "You belong with us, blessed Barakah," she said firmly. "You must travel with us to your people. Now."

The holy man began to shed tears. Finnikin could not help wondering what felt worse for him. Watching his people die, or feeling as if he had abandoned them? But when Evanjalin held out her hand, the priest-king did not hesitate to take it.

They walked away, and the tiny kingdom of three carts and nameless children was swallowed by the sounds of the night bazaar. Finnikin watched Evanjalin turn back once. Twice. Three times.

Later, as they traveled along the coastal road in the dead of night, the priest-king riding ahead with Trevanion, Finnikin thought he heard Evanjalin whisper the same words over and over again.

*"Take me home, Finnikin. I beg of you, take me home."*

## CHAPTER 18

C an I trust you, Lord August?"

Lord August of the Lumateran Flatlands woke to find a hand covering his mouth and a dagger to his throat. The face that appeared above him looked half-wild, with none of the softness that once gave Finnikin of the Rock a youthful innocence. With regret, he knew that if Trevanion's son dared lay a finger on his family, he would kill him in an instant. But then he realized he wasn't just at the mercy of Finnikin's dagger. In the pale moonlight that shone into the adjoining chamber, he could distinguish the outline of at least three more men. Beside him, his wife slept, unaware.

"Ah, Finnikin," he muttered. "What have you done?"

"Nothing yet. Answer my question."

Lord August grabbed Finnikin by the knotted wildness of his hair, forcing him close. "You bring these animals into my house," he said through clenched teeth, "and place a dagger at my throat as I lie beside my wife, while my beloved children sleep in the next room, and you ask me to trust you?"

"Can I take that as a yes?" Finnikin asked, shrugging free.

Lord August climbed out of bed, trying to keep an eye on the men in the adjoining chamber. "I curse myself for failing your father and not taking you into my own home. If the captain were to see you now, it would be a blunt dagger carving him up."

Lord August was a small man, but he did not let that get in his way. He would take these men down, any way he could. Images raced through his mind of what they would do to his family if he were to die first. He had always believed that if harm came to them, it would be from the Charynites or Belegonians. Not from a son of Lumatere.

"What have you done to Sir Topher?" he asked, seeing new scars and an older spirit in the boy's gray eyes.

"Aged him slightly," Finnikin murmured, walking to the window and peering out into the night. "We need a place to stay for a night or two. And food. That means you'll have to send your servants and people away. When we leave, we'll need more horses, and, if we could be so bold, a few silver coins would not go astray."

"Anything else?" Lord August said, glancing again at the three men in the next chamber. "My firstborn?"

There was a noise outside, and then a hand appeared over the rail of the balcony. Lord August watched as Finnikin stepped outside and came to the fourth man's assistance. As soon as he saw the man's face, Lord August relaxed.

"Good evening, Lord Augie," Sir Topher wheezed, looking up for a moment before doubling over with pain. Finnikin kept a hand on the older man's shoulder until he recovered. "Did you ask him about weapons?" Sir Topher managed between gasps.

"No. He offered me his firstborn and it distracted me slightly," Finnikin said. "Now that you have seen that Sir Topher is safe, can we trust you? We need to be sure. Be honest and send us away if you cannot help us."

"Is my family's life in danger?" the duke asked, with another sideways glance at the giants in the next chamber.

Finnikin stepped in front of him, blocking his vision. Lord August saw a look of vague apology on the lad's face, as if he considered using his height a sign of disrespect.

"If they are, Finnikin, I will kill you."

"Stop threatening my son, Augie," he heard a voice behind Finnikin say, as one of the men stepped out from the shadows. "Or I will have to kill you, and Lumatere cannot afford to have any more fatherless children."

"Sweet Lagrami," August swore under his breath. His eyes moved from Trevanion to Perri and Moss, who had also stepped forward, and back to Trevanion. Astounded, he burst into quiet laughter. He grabbed Trevanion in a bear hug, pounding his back and steering them all into the adjoining chamber. He pointed to Finnikin, grinning. "I knew you would listen to reason last time we spoke."

"Try not to take credit for it," Finnikin replied.

"There will be hell to pay when it is discovered that a political prisoner of the land is missing."

"Are we safe here, sir?" Finnikin asked.

"The last thing we want to do is place you and your family's lives in danger," Trevanion said quietly.

"The fewer people who know, the better it will be," Sir Topher advised.

"Augie?"

The five men swung around. Lady Abian stood at the door, clutching her night shawl, a look of terror on her face. When she saw Trevanion, she swallowed a scream, the next moment throwing herself into his arms.

"Abie," her husband chided gently. "Remember your place. You're going to make a cuckold out of me."

When she saw Finnikin, she burst into tears, covering her mouth with her hand.

"Do I look that frightening?" he asked.

She shook her head, overwhelmed by her emotion, and then she took him into her arms. "Apart from my own, I never held a prettier babe."

"A flattering compliment for any man," Trevanion said with a laugh.

"Where are you all bound for?" she asked. No one responded, and Lady Abian looked from Trevanion to her husband. "We're going home," she whispered. "Oh sweet goddess, we're going home."

"Lady Abian, there may be nothing to go back to," Finnikin said gently.

A scream, high and piercing, echoed through the house, and Lord August sped to the door, followed closely by the others. They ran down the stairs and into what at first appeared to be a closet, but instead was a tiny bedroom. Finnikin saw Evanjalin instantly. At her side Lady Celie screamed again, the sight of Trevanion and Perri causing her fear this time. In the small confines of the room, she pushed Evanjalin behind her.

Lady Abian was last in the room, and she took her daughter in her arms, her body growing still when she saw Evanjalin. "Augie," she ordered quietly, "go wake the rest of the children and our people, if they aren't already awake, and take everyone down to the parlor."

She stepped forward and cupped Evanjalin's face in the palm of her hand, as if mesmerized by the filth and scruffiness that stood before her. "Celie, go wake Sebastina and ask her to run a bath."

"Abie," Trevanion said, "we cannot have your Belegonian servants knowing we're here."

"Sebastina's one of ours. Everyone in this compound belongs to Lumatere."

Finnikin's eyes were on Evanjalin, remembering Lady Celie's reaction to her when they had first visited the house. But Evanjalin's gaze was fixed on both mother and daughter. Outside of the exile camps, he had rarely seen her in the presence of women, and at this moment he knew she would not have cared if he and the other men disappeared forever.

Lord August was staring at the two who stood half-concealed in the corner. "Blessed Barakah?" he asked, stunned, walking toward him, then kneeling on one knee.

Lady Abian seemed mortified and sent the men a scathing look. "How could you leave the priest-king to climb the trellis outside our home?" She kissed the holy man. "Blessings later," she said gently. "You look well worn and I want you all comfortable. Everyone down in the parlor, please. I will take care of the girls."

As they walked down the stairs, Lord August hammered on every door he passed. They reached the parlor, and the duke motioned for them to sit down. A few moments later, Lord August's sister and family and at least fifty others entered, filling the room to capacity. Finnikin stared around in shock. Suddenly he understood why Lady Celie's bedroom was so tiny. It was indeed a closet, as he had first thought. Every room in the house, including the storerooms, cellars, and even the pantry, must have to be used as living quarters to accommodate so many people.

"Who are these people?" Finnikin asked.

"Why, it's my village of Sayles, Finnikin," Lord August replied. "A duke is afforded the wealth of a city, and his home the right of sanctuary."

Finnikin's eyes met the duke's. It shamed him to think of all the times he had expressed his disdain for the luxuries enjoyed by the Lumateran nobility in exile, especially Lord August.

Fear and excitement lit the faces of those around him. There was a hushed celebration when the people of Sayles recognized the newcomers, the women sobbing, the men brushing quick tears from their eyes and muffling their emotions in handshakes that trembled.

When Lady Abian and the girls joined them, Evanjalin was scrubbed clean and dressed in a crisp white gown identical to Lady Celie's. Finnikin could smell sandalwood, and Evanjalin's olive complexion was as smooth and clear as honey. There was little room in the parlor, and Lady Abian sat on her husband's lap.

"Abian," her sister-in-law chided, "remember your place!"

"I am a fishmonger's daughter," Lady Abian said. "What do you expect?"

There was much joy that night. Finnikin loved watching them all. Here was a generation of men and women who had suffered greatly; the loss of their world had happened in the prime of their lives.

In the corner, Froi sat with the younger boys engaged in a competition of knuckle thumping. He who drew blood first was declared the winner. Finnikin noticed the viciousness of Froi's play and saw the younger boys wince even as they tried not to react. He reached over and boxed Froi's ears as a warning.

They spent the night arguing passionately about all things Lumateran, opinions flying, voices hushed and angry, others wavering with emotion.

"Could it have been avoided? Should the king have forbidden anyone entering Lumatere? Should he have cut off ties with the Charynites?"

"No one knew such a thing would happen, Matin," Trevanion said firmly. "No one could predict that the assassins would enter the palace. Every entrance was guarded."

"Then it was one of the Guard. A traitor working for Charyn," Lord August said.

Finnikin watched for the reaction. He had waited all week for one of Trevanion's men to make such a suggestion.

"Never," Perri said flatly. *"Never."*

"Then how?" Lord August pressed.

"The men guarding the palace drawbridge were attacked from behind. We could tell by the location of the wounds on their bodies. There had to be another entrance that not even the king knew about," Trevanion said.

"How could there be an entrance the assassins knew about when the king did not?" Lord August's brother-in-law asked.

"Perhaps because the impostor king was the former captain of the Guard and cousin to the king. He may have found it," Finnikin suggested.

His father shook his head. "I knew every inch of that palace. Unless a tunnel was built from inside, I would have known."

The most bitter arguments centered around the circumstances leading up to the slaughter of the Forest Dwellers.

"The king should have provided more protection for the worshippers of Sagrami. They were a minority," Lady Abian said firmly.

"Abie!" a chorus of voices reprimanded her. "It is wrong to speak ill of the dead."

"I loved our king as much as the rest of you, but he used poor judgment when it came to the Forest Dwellers. If the king had been more open in his approval of the ways and practices of those who worshipped Sagrami, our part in the days of the unspeakable would never have occurred."

"The king was not to know his people would turn on the Forest Dwellers the moment he died. As far as he was concerned, Lumaterans were living in peace," one of the women said.

"It's what the king wanted to believe. What we all wanted to believe," Lady Abian maintained.

They were silent for a moment.

"There is no proof it was the Charynites," Lord August's brother-in-law said, speaking to an earlier argument.

"Of course it was the Charynites," Finnikin argued. "And the king should have treated Charyn as a threat. Instead he signed treaties with their king and cocooned himself in domestic life." He looked at Sir Topher. He knew his mentor agreed with him but would never voice his opinions aloud.

"I should have protected the worshippers of Sagrami," the priest-king said sadly. "Instead I allowed myself to be flattered by the importance of my title. I blame my hubris for not seeing what was unfolding in front of me."

"They should not have been so secretive about their ways," one of the women said.

"And that gave us the permission to turn them out of their homes and persecute them?" Lady Abian protested.

"In other kingdoms they worship more than one god or goddess with few issues about which divine being has superiority," Finnikin said.

"It is wrong," Lady Celie blurted out, her face flushed. It was the first time she had spoken that evening. Perhaps the first time she had ever raised her voice in the company of adults.

"What is, my sweet?" her father asked.

"That we persist in speaking about the goddess as if she were two. The fault lies with the men of the ancients."

"And not the women? Must men be blamed for all, my sweet?" her father asked gently. "Celie has a great love of history," he added with pride. "She has taken to recording the stories of our village."

"The men are to blame," Lady Celie continued, her voice

232

wavering, "because they wrote the books. They were frightened by the power of our goddess complete."

There was an awkward silence.

"So they split her in two," Evanjalin spoke up, placing a hand on Lady Celie's shoulder. "The goddess Lagrami and the goddess Sagrami: light and dark. But all that did was cause division and a belief that one people was better than the other."

"Those who worshipped Sagrami practiced dark magic," Lord August's sister argued. "They were instrumental in our exile."

"Yet it is the work of those inside the cloisters of Sagrami and Lagrami that will ensure us entry back into our kingdom," Evanjalin said.

"Evanjalin can walk through the sleep of our people trapped inside Lumatere," Lady Celie said boldly.

At his daughter's comment, Lord August looked at Evanjalin for the first time since she had spoken to him about the Charynites. He could not forget her voice as she stood beside Finnikin that day. He had described to his wife with wonder the power he felt in the two young people. The voice of Lumatere had come from the sun and the moon, he said. Abie called him a dreamer. "See them together and you will feel a force that will take your breath away," he had responded.

"When we return, I would love nothing more than to be part of the cloister," the duke's niece said. She was a pretty girl, more confident than her cousin Celie.

"The cloister of Lagrami?" Lady Abian asked. "Why? All they teach you to be is a rich man's dutiful wife and a blind worshipper of half a goddess."

"Oh, the idea of a dutiful wife," Lord August said with a sigh. "Why did no one point me in the direction of the cloister?"

Lady Abian raised her eyebrow. "You were lucky I was not taught by the priestess of Lagrami to bore you to tears, Augie, or by the priestess of Sagrami to poison my husband with the proper herbs. Instead, I prayed to the goddess complete to send me a man who would accept me whole and not as two halves, as men have treated our goddess for the past thousand years."

"I was a novice of Lagrami," Lord August's sister sniffed. "Do I bore people to tears?"

"Of course not, my dear," her husband responded, patting her hand. "Nor are you a dutiful wife."

The others laughed.

"You are harsh on the cloisters of both sides, Abie," Trevanion said solemnly. "Lady Beatriss was a novice of Lagrami, and she had much strength to offer."

"That I know, Trevanion," she said gently. "But the cloister of Lagrami is there for the daughters of those with wealth, like our Celie and Beatriss the Beloved. But what of the daughters of our dear friends here?"

"Privilege does not necessarily lead to freedom for our noble young women," Sir Topher said. "The princesses were always going to be sacrificed for the kingdom. The older girls had already been promised to foreign princes and dukes. Sooner or later, Isaboe would have been sacrificed in the same manner."

"Sacrificed?" Finnikin asked.

"Of course," one of the women said. "To be taken away from your family, your homeland. To be a foreigner for the rest of your life, with no true right over your children. Did it not happen to the dead king's aunt? Given to a lesser prince in Charyn, whose seed produced the monster who rules our kingdom?"

"Regardless, we must concern ourselves with what takes place inside Lumatere now. If the novices have united, as we believe they have, then those of Sagrami will teach us to be healers. Physicians," Evanjalin said. "And those of Lagrami will teach us the ways of the ancients and the beauty of goodwill. Perhaps because of the most dire of situations, daughters of peasants are secure in one of the old cloisters in Lumatere as we speak."

"When will we return to Lumatere?" one of her younger boys asked. "When Balthazar is found?"

Sir Topher nodded, but Finnikin recognized the look of uncertainty that always crossed his mentor's face whenever the heir's name was mentioned.

"How do we know that for sure?" the boy piped up.

"Because Seranonna decreed it," Lord August said.

"I fort she damned the kingdom," Froi said.

The others looked at him, uncomfortable.

"We do not consider the kingdom damned," Lord August said politely. "We prefer not to use that word."

"What would you call it, Lord August?" Finnikin asked. "A little magic? A slight curse? A bit of bad luck?"

"Finn," his father warned in a low tone.

"For the sake of the children—" Lord August's brother-in-law began.

"Only a chosen few have been privileged enough to have a childhood," Finnikin interrupted. "There have been few children since the days of the unspeakable. Were you ever a child, Evanjalin? Or Froi? Or half the orphans of Lumatere? Or even me? Was I ever a child, Sir Topher?"

"I applaud any of you who have been able to preserve innocence for your children," Evanjalin said, turning to the younger ones. "But our kingdom was cursed. Damned. Taken away from us, because good people stood by while evil took place. Let that be our lesson."

"Has it been revealed?" Lady Abian asked. "What was said that day? When Seranonna . . . cursed us?"

Sir Topher nodded. "It was difficult to decipher, for we heard the words spoken only once, in an ancient language, and there are many interpretations of each word. At every camp, we searched for those who had been in the square the day of Seranonna's death and we gathered more words, poring over the books of the ancients, until four years ago Finnikin made sense of it."

Everyone's attention was directed at Finnikin. Opposite him, he watched Evanjalin take a breath, as if in anticipation.

"Finn?" his father urged.

Finnikin's eyes met the priest-king's. " 'Dark will lead the light and our *resurdus* will rise. And he will hold two hands of the one he pledged to save. And then the gate will fall, but his pain shall never cease. His seed will issue kings, but he will never reign.' "

"Balthazar," Lord August confirmed.

" 'Our *resurdus*,' " Finnikin said, nodding. "King."

"I think the exact words were 'her *resurdus* will rise,' " Sir Topher said.

The priest-king nodded. " 'Her' being our kingdom of Lumatere."

"I don't understand the two hands," Perri said.

"And you believe Balthazar can . . . survive such an entrance of damnation? 'Pain shall never cease'?" Lady Abian said. "And 'he will never reign'?"

"Regardless of whether he lives or dies," the priest-king said, "the main gate of the kingdom will open."

There was silence until Lord August stood. "Then we must make a decree. Here. This night. In the presence of the priest-king and Trevanion, Captain of the King's Guard, and myself, Lord August, Duke of Sayles." He turned to the king's First Man. "That Sir Kristopher of the Flatlands, as regent of our dead king, is to rule if our beloved heir does not survive."

He took in the faces of all present. "We enter Lumatere with a king," he continued forcefully. "We will never allow the leaders of other kingdoms to crown a king for Lumatere again."

Finnikin felt the weight of his father's stare. He shifted his gaze to Sir Topher, and saw that the king's First Man was looking at him with the same intensity. He was a son blessed by two fathers, one a warrior, the other a leader.

"We enter Lumatere with a king," Trevanion acknowledged.

"Sir Topher?" the priest-king said.

Sir Topher stood, looking from Finnikin to the priest-king. "I pray to the goddess . . . the goddess complete, that our heir will live to see the new day in Lumatere, but if that is not to be, our kingdom will have a leader and that leader will have a First Man." His eyes rested on Finnikin. "I accept."

There was a cheer in the room as people began to chant Balthazar's name. Finnikin felt as if his breath had been wrenched from his body.

*Her blood will be shed for you to be king.*

He had not prayed since that day in the Valley of Tranquillity, but as the others celebrated, he began his mantra. *Be alive, Balthazar. Live forever, Sir Topher.* He looked over to where his father was speaking to one of Lord August's men, Matin. The steward was showing Trevanion something he had retrieved from his pocket, and Trevanion, in a rare show of emotion, drew the man toward him in an embrace.

On shaking legs, Finnikin made his way across the room to where Evanjalin stood, tears in her eyes.

"*Resurdus,*" she whispered to him. Her lips trembled and she held his face between her hands. Suddenly Sir Topher stood between them.

"Evanjalin is tired, Finnikin," he said firmly. "She needs to sleep. Let Lady Abian take her."

Later, the sounds of Lord August making love to his wife echoed through the house. Their cries were earthy and raw, and the paper-thin walls ensured that their guests heard each murmur and groan.

"What is it with the nobility?" Sir Topher muttered, putting a pillow over his face. "The queen and king were always at it like rabbits."

Moss groaned. "If they do this every night, I'd rather give myself up to the king's prison."

Froi shuffled where he lay under the window.

"Froi, if I hear one sound coming from you," Trevanion warned.

"Must I remind you that we have the priest-king of Lumatere among us?" Sir Topher said.

The priest-king chuckled. "I'm used to hearing people dying, Sir Topher. Why would I be threatened by the sounds of people living?"

But all Finnikin could think of was the scent of sandalwood soap and a golden face scrubbed clean, and with every thrust he heard, he imagined himself inside her until his body ached for release. And the evil within him that wished for the death of Balthazar, and the realization of the prophecy spoken to him in the forest alongside a doomed princess, rejoiced that if he were to be king, he would make her his queen.

## CHapteR 19

Sometimes Froi of the Exiles thought he dreamed it, what happened at the crossroads. That it seemed like forever, not just a few days, and that the difference between left and right and north and west meant everything and nothing.

It began with tears when they left the home of the duke. His daughter was the worst, sobbing like a baby as she held on to Evanjalin, as if they had known each other forever rather than just two nights. She cried even more when Finnikin gave her the *Book of Lumatere* to keep safe. They were stupid like that, these Lumaterans. Not that he minded the duke's house. The fireplace always seemed to be working, and there was lots of food. But too much touching and kissing. Sometimes the duke's wife hugged Froi and he would try hard not to growl and shove her away, because when her arms were around him and her chuckles were in his ear, he felt calm. As if his blood wasn't beating hard all the time, urging him to fight.

Then they left and traveled north. To the crossroads. Nobody grumbled, because soon they would reach the valley outside the kingdom of Lumatere, which meant nothing to him really, because they still said, "Froi, make yourself useful!" and Evanjalin still made him practice his words with that look on her face that said she was in charge. Sometimes he would dare to look at the captain and his face didn't seem angry or hard like it usually did. It looked the way it did when he was looking at Finnikin, and it always made Froi feel strange in the stomach when he saw the captain look at Finnikin. It made him wonder if anyone had ever looked at him that way.

But things changed when they found one of the exile camps they were searching for and met one of the Guard who had been traveling with Ced. He was waiting for them, and he wasn't smiling like they had smiled when they were with the others in Pietrodore. Froi couldn't hear much about what was going on, but he saw the look on everyone's faces and he heard words like *Moss's grave,* which was strange because Moss was with them. And then he heard it again and maybe it was *mass grave,* but they were speaking too fast for him to understand. The captain, he walked away with his hands on the back of his head and he crouched by the river after that, and he kept his hands over his head for a real long time. When he stood up, there weren't tears on his face, because the captain wasn't one of the crybabies, but he looked like he wanted to kill someone, so Froi stayed out of the way and just made himself useful and looked after the priest-king. He could tell the old man wasn't traveling too well, and he was glad when Sir Topher said that they needed to find a safe place for the priest-king. Froi liked the priest-king because he treated him like he was as important as everyone else and when he taught him words in Lumatere he didn't laugh at the way he said them. He just showed him the right way.

And then they moved on, all quietlike, and reached a clearing with at least ten tracks heading in different directions, and Froi remembered looking up from the back of Perri's horse to see the

sign. He knew this was the crossroads, and Finnikin explained that
the border of Lumatere was one day's ride from here. There were
so many arrows on that one signpost and so many words and Sir
Topher read them out because they were written in Belegonian:
east to Charyn/Osterian border; south to Belegonia; west to
Sendecane; north to Lumatere, except someone had scratched
out Lumatere as if it didn't exist, but Finnikin took the stick out
of his pack and wrote the word again. The captain picked one of
the arrows to follow that didn't have any words near it and Froi
couldn't understand why he would pick an arrow to follow that
hardly had a track, but nobody ever questioned the captain.

They traveled for what seemed hours and Froi truly thought it
was night because it was so thick with trees and no light crept in.
But then he saw the shine in the distance and the forest turned into
a meadow, that was the word Sir Topher used, and the meadow
had the tallest grass with so many yellow flowers that it hurt
Froi's eyes to look at. But he didn't look away because it was
a different kind of hurt, one he hadn't felt before and he found
himself walking through the long grass and yellow flowers just to
see what they felt like against his skin. Behind the meadow, there
was a barn with shutters hanging, deadlike, from its room in the
roof. Inside it smelled of every animal that had ever been there
and it was where they put the priest-king, in the barn, and then
the captain spoke, deciding that this was a safe place for them,
that nobody would find them here. And that Froi and Evanjalin
would stay behind with the priest-king while the others traveled
to where Ced was at an inn waiting for them on the western road
to Sendecane where there was the grave that belonged to Moss or
Mass. And everyone pretended everything was all right.

They did a lot of pretending, these people.

So when Evanjalin didn't complain about being left behind,

Froi watched Finnikin pretend that he wasn't going to be both-
ered by the fact that Evanjalin looked tired and pale, and Froi
got irritated and wished that someone would tell him to make
himself useful so he didn't have to stand around through the
good-byes.

Finnikin kept on saying that all they needed was a bit of rest,
pretending there was nothing wrong with the priest-king, and Froi
tried to tell them that it looked like fever and he had seen enough
fever to know, but then Perri told him to make himself useful and
fetch water from the stream, so Froi got his wish and was almost
saved from watching Finnikin pretend he was leaning in to tell
Evanjalin something important and then forgot what it was he
had to say. Which meant that they both stood close to each other,
their heads almost touching for a long long while.

And then the others were gone and things got worse.

On the first night they lay in the barn listening to the priest-
king talk about Lumatere as if he wanted them to remember everything because he knew he was going to die soon. The priest-king
told him about the Song of Lumatere and how he would sing it
at the Harvest Moon Festival when everyone in Lumatere would
sleep out in the open and they'd dance and sing and laugh and
how it was bad luck to sing it outside the kingdom. Froi didn't
see anything wrong with the priest-king singing it now because it
wasn't as if they weren't used to bad luck. And during the night
Froi stayed awake and tried to hold the priest-king down in that
barn because his body was shuddering and jumping and Froi was
scared he'd crack one of the priest-king's ribs because the priest-
king was skinnier than him. And Evanjalin sat and watched with
her arms around her body to keep it warm and he knew by her
shivers that she would be next. And when she looked at Froi's
face she didn't pretend. She just bit her fist to keep herself from

crying and then the priest-king stopped breathing for a moment and something inside Froi hurt in a way he couldn't explain.

"I fink you should use magic."

Evanjalin's lips were dry and flaking and her skin looked a funny gray color and there was sweat all over her forehead that made it shiny. She looked almost dead, but she could still send him a look so evil that it made him flinch.

"I've told you before, Froi. I don't have magic!"

She coughed and it sounded like there was all this vomit in her throat and it made him sick to listen to it and more scared than he had ever been in his life.

"You're cursed," he said. "Him too. Survives the camps for years and years and survive everyfink else between. But it's fever you die from. Two days' ride from homeland."

And she cried. He had seen her shout with rage and had seen tears in her eyes over and over again, but he had never seen her cry properly and it made her look pathetic and helpless as she bent and put her head in her hands, all the while coughing stuff out of her mouth.

"In Lumatere, the novices of Sagrami would mix herbs found in the Forest and bring people back from near death with the fever," she told him.

"Then do somefink."

"I don't know how," she cried. And he didn't know what to say to make her feel right so he walked to the other part of the barn.

And began to pretend.

Later, they both sat by the priest-king who grabbed Froi's hand in his, all oldlike, with its veins and scratchy skin.

"I dreamed last night, Froi," he whispered through dried-up lips, "that you were holding the future of Lumatere in your hands."

"Only saying that 'cause you dying." Froi scowled.

Evanjalin elbowed him to be silent. Then the priest-king closed his eyes, and she dragged Froi away to the corner of the barn where he could smell horse shit and he knew that if the captain or Finnikin or Perri were around they'd tell him to make himself useful and clean it up.

"When people are dying, you don't tell them," she hissed angrily.

"What about the truf Finnikin always goes on about?"

"There are different types of truth, Froi. Let the priest-king tell you whatever he wants. So when he says you'll hold the future of Lumatere in your hands, nod. Agree."

"We all be dead soon."

She looked at him long and hard. Sometimes he thought he hated her the most because it was as if she could read inside his head. The others pretended that deep down he wasn't bad. That he didn't come from evil. But she knew. She saw the badness. She saw it now and she shivered. He didn't know whether it was because of the fever or because she knew what he would do, but there was an understanding in her look.

"Go," she said tiredly. "Save yourself. It's what you want to do. And if you have any heart, find Finnikin and Captain Trevanion and Sir Topher. Walk to the crossroads and wait for someone to come riding by to take you west to the inn on the main road to Sendecane. There's not much else out there, so you will find them. Tell them we have the fever." She reached into her pocket and held out the ring. "To save you the trouble of stealing it from me."

He hated her for knowing he would.

"I have a plan. But if I fail, the priest-king and I will be dead by the time you return. Make sure we are buried. By Finnikin. At an altar made to the goddess complete. With his blood sprinkled on the rocks, which will guard me in death. Do you hear me, Froi? It's all I ask of you."

She stumbled back to the priest-king and put her hand on his forehead. "Hold him up," she ordered as he moved behind the priest-king's head.

"A joy," the old man murmured. "To die in the arms of the future of Lumatere."

Froi nodded. "I agree." He looked at Evanjalin to see if he had said it right, but she just whispered to the priest-king that she had a plan and the priest-king would need to stay alive.

Later, he watched from the window as she stumbled into the woods with a dagger in her hand and then he looked back at the priest-king as he slept, the death rattling his breath.

"Fink I would have liked to hear you sing that song," he said, leaning over the old man.

Then he walked away. And as he went through that meadow where the grass grew to his armpits, he felt a strange feeling inside of him that he had never felt before. Like someone had punched him in the stomach and he was all mashed up in there.

He didn't believe in fate and destiny and gods and guides. He didn't believe in people or goodness or love or what was right. But he understood survival, and at the crossroads, where he thought he saw the sign to Belegonia he knew he could return to the towns they had passed, full of rich people careless with their coin purses and their goods. His life would go back to the way it was before he saw Evanjalin in that alley in Sarnak what seemed like a lifetime ago. But no one had ever taught Froi the difference between left and right and south and west, and later when he rode with the toothless man in his two-horse cart and realized he had taken the wrong turn, he tried to convince himself that maybe he would have made that decision to find the others along the western road. And when fate had the toothless man stopping at the inn where the captain and Finnikin and Sir Topher and Moss and Perri and three others sat, staring at one another as if they had seen things that made them dead inside, he blurted out the words. "She ask me to come fetch you. To bury them."

Perri stared at him as if he knew the badness that lurked in Froi because Perri was dark himself. But it was Finnikin he tried not to look at, except he heard something come from him that sounded like some wild animal and then Finnikin said her name and as long as Froi was alive he had never heard a word said with such pain and he knew he never would again. The captain told Moss and Sir Topher and the two other guards that they would meet in the valley where their people waited, while Perri and Finnikin and Froi traveled with him to bury the priest-king and Evanjalin. Froi liked the way the captain included him, so he did more pretending. Evanjalin said there were different types of truth, so he showed them the truth of what he could have been rather than what he was. He climbed onto Finnikin's horse and he clung on to him and sometimes he thought Finnikin would tumble off dead because it was as if he had stopped breathing for all that time. He heard Finnikin pray to the goddess that if she spared Evanjalin's life, he would always ask her for guidance. Never doubt her again. Lead Lumatere wherever she believed it had to be led. Finnikin's head was bent low over the horse and he kicked its flanks hard and Froi had never clutched the body of one who felt so much but it reminded him of the time when he had tried to take Evanjalin in the barn. Both times the touch of their bodies had burned him, but this time something entered his bloodstream.

Planted a seed.

And this is the way Froi of the Exiles remembered that moment they entered the golden meadow that hurt his eyes but made him dream of all things good. On one side of the path was a stone fence half-covered with overgrown weeds. On the other, olive groves with pomegranate and apple trees mixed. And there in the middle stood the priest-king like one of those ghosts who appear in dreams and Froi saw Evanjalin in the high grass, her face pale but not with death or fever. She wore flowers in her hair and Froi liked the way their stems fit into the bunch of hair beginning to stick out of her head. And when Finnikin grabbed her to him and buried his face in her neck and then bent down and placed his mouth on hers, the others pretended that there was something very interesting happening in the meadow. The priest-king even pointed at the nothing they were pretending to see. But Froi didn't. He just watched the way Finnikin's hands rested on Evanjalin's neck and he rubbed his thumb along her jaw and the way his tongue seemed to disappear inside her mouth as if he needed a part of her to breathe himself. And Froi wondered what Evanjalin was saying against Finnikin's lips when they stopped because whatever the words were it made them start all over again and this time their hunger for each other was so frightening to watch that it made Froi look away.

When Evanjalin almost fell down with weakness, Finnikin picked her up and carried her to the barn and he lay her down, all gentle-like, and then they listened to the soft tone of the priest-king's voice, which always made Froi feel dreamy and warm, and Evanjalin slept. Froi bit into a pomegranate and felt the juice soak his chin as the priest-king told them that one day he would sing a new Song of Lumatere. Her song. Of the one named Evanjalin who walked the sleep and took the child's hand in hers. Knowing she and the child could not hear each other speak, Evanjalin prayed that she could read as she wrote two words on the walls of the chamber they walked. *Fever cure?* But the child could not read and the words on the wall disappeared.

And so she used her nails to scratch the words on the arm of the child, who cried from the betrayal of the pain, and she waited one whole day to walk the sleep that night, praying for an answer. But for a moment she lost hope. There were no words alongside those on the child's arm and Evanjalin's heart sank because she knew it was the end. For the priest-king had already begun his walk to the land between theirs and that of the gods. But as the child turned her back, Evanjalin saw markings above the crisp nightdress and slowly she lifted it to reveal a world painted with instructions and names and drawings of plants. And one question. Three words.

*Is hope coming?*

And Evanjalin did a last cruel thing to the child who did not deserve so much pain. She scratched one more word on the child's arm.

A name that would bring hope.


Sometimes Froi thought it never happened and the way he said it was all wrong and dreamlike. But Lumaterans had enough of their curse stories so he asked Finnikin of the Rock to write it down exactly the way he remembered it.

So he could one day place it in the *Book of Lumatere.*

Far away from the pages of the dead.

# CHAPTER 20

*R* *esurdus.*

Finnikin woke in the loft of the barn with the word on his lips. Beside him, Evanjalin slept quietly, her skin paler than usual but her breathing even. He would never forget Froi's words in the inn. Never *ever* forget the sight of her standing in the meadow breathing life back into his dead heart.

He and Evanjalin slept away from the others, who tossed and snored, except for Perri, who lay with his eyes wide open, forever on the alert. Finnikin knew that if Sir Topher were there, he would have insisted that he not lie beside the girl, deemed it unacceptable in a way the priest-king didn't seem to question. Finnikin cradled her, shuddering at the confused images that came into his head. Of the mass grave he had seen the night before on the border of Sendecane. Of her body among the dead. Evanjalin pulled his arm tighter around her, holding it to stop the shaking. "It's only a nightmare," she murmured gently.

"Do you belong to the king?" he asked, his voice husky.

She gently placed his hand against the beating pulse of her

heart. Always, *always* it beat out of control, and he held his hand to it until he felt it perfectly match his.

"Yes, Finnikin," she said. "I belong to the king. I will always belong to him."

And there lay the bittersweet despair of what awaited them in the Valley.

Beloved rival. Cursed friend.

He wondered what they'd say to each other after all these years. If he would recognize him in a crowd. Balthazar looked like his father. The Flatlanders claimed the king was descended from their people. "Hair like chestnuts, eyes like the heavens," they would say. He even heard Trevanion whisper it lovingly to Beatriss. They were the queen's favorite words to her older daughters and son, although Balthazar would be mortified when she said it in the presence of Finnikin and Lucian. "And me?" Isaboe would ask, hating not to be the center of their world. "You're our precious little Mont girl," the queen would say.

He wondered if the cousins had been together all this time. A streak of envy washed through him at the thought of the prince staying with Lucian and the Monts. They had been a trio, despite the fierce competition between Lucian and Finnikin. They had fought like brothers and made pledge after pledge from the moment they could talk. He missed them both. But here in the meadow, so close to his homeland, he felt the presence of Balthazar and Lucian so strongly that he knew with certainty he would see them soon.

The next morning, Trevanion announced they would leave by midday. Finnikin and Evanjalin stole away and lay in the meadow, forehead to forehead, musing and hypothesizing.

"Do you remember the main village in Lumatere? There was a bridge that took you to the smithy, where the Flatlands began?"

Finnikin said. "My father would have his horse shod there and I'd hang over the side waiting, watching the water and following it in my mind downriver. I used to imagine going beyond the kingdom where the river would flow out to the lands beyond ours."

"Imagine if someone was standing there right now. What would they be doing?" she wondered. "At this very moment? Do they know we're so close?"

"Perhaps they are living in total tranquillity," he said. "Do you think we could have had it all wrong? Do you think they've been happy and will not care about our return?"

She shook her head. "I know they suffer," she said quietly.

"More than the exiles?"

"How does one measure it, Finnikin? Does a man who's lost his family to famine suffer less than one who's lost them to an assassin's knife? Is it worse to die of drowning than be trampled under the feet of others? If you lose your wife in childbirth, is it better than watching her burn at the stake? Death is death and loss is loss. I have sensed as much despair in the sleep of those inside as I have seen in the exiles. When I saw the words painted on the child's body, I sensed their urgency, their anguish. 'Is hope coming?' "

"They will have the question answered soon."

"If there is a future in Lumatere and you weren't called upon to be Balthazar's First Man," she asked, her mood lightening, "what would you want to do with the rest of your life?"

"First," he said, brushing a fly off her nose, "if there is a future in Lumatere, I will be in my father's Guard. And second, Sir Topher will be Balthazar's First Man."

"First, it is not your father's Guard. It belongs to the king. And secondly, Sir Topher would want you with him, advising Balthazar."

He imitated the cross expression on her face, and she giggled.

"So if I were a mere mortal in Lumatere?" He looked around the meadow, pondering. "I would put my name down for ten acres on the Flatlands. I would build a cottage there, and with my bride I would—"

"Where would you find this bride?" she interrupted.

"A novice from the cloister of Lagrami would do me fine," he said in a pompous tone. "Obedient. Biddable."

"And with the ability to bore you to tears, according to Lady Abian."

"Not a problem. I will be so tired by the end of the day that sleep will be the only thing on my mind."

She gave a snort. "You?"

He laughed at her expression. "Your meaning?"

"Last night you lay pressed against me, Finnikin. I could . . . *feel* that sleep was the last thing on your mind."

"How unladylike of you to mention such a thing," he said.

She touched the lines around his mouth. "You look lovely when you laugh."

"Lovely? Just the way a man wants to be described." He grinned. "I hope for the day that someone describes me the way they do my father."

"All right, silent dark bear with angry frown, tell me more about your land."

He settled back down, picturing it. "I would tend to our land from the moment the sun rose to when it set and then you . . . *she* would tend to me."

He laughed at her expression again. The world of exile camps and the Valley felt very far away, and he wanted to lie there forever.

"Let me tell you about your bride," she said, propping herself up on her elbows. "Both of you would cultivate the land. You would hold the plow, and she would walk alongside you with the ox, coaxing and singing it forward. A stick in her hand, of course, for she would need to keep both the ox and you in line."

"What would we . . . that is, my bride and I, grow?"

"Wheat and barley."

"And marigolds."

Her nose crinkled questioningly.

"I would pick them when they bloomed," he said. "And when she called me home for supper, I'd place them in her hair and the contrast would take my breath away."

"How would she call you? From your cottage? Would she bellow, 'Finnikin!'?"

"I'd teach her the whistle. One for day and one for night."

"Ah, the whistle, of course. I'd forgotten the whistle."

He practiced it with her, laughing at her early attempts until she could mimic it perfectly. Froi came running up to them, a frown on his face.

"Captain said to fetch you. We leave."

"Speak Lumateran, Froi. You're not from Sarnak!" Evanjalin ordered, getting to her feet. "And you haven't returned my father's ring."

He scowled. "Fort you said it was mine."

"Don't be ridiculous," she said, vexed. "Only because I thought I would die. You'll have to give it back." She ran ahead of them, jumping over the tall grass and daffodils, her legs tangling at times, causing her to stumble.

"Hope she falls," Froi muttered. "Meanest girl I ever know."

"I've met meaner," Finnikin mused. "The Lumateran girls from the Rock are quite frightening, and you never turn your back on a girl from the River. And Princess Isaboe? Used to tell everyone she could mend her cat's broken limbs, which she could, of course. But no one knew that she'd break them first."

When they reached the barn, they joined the others in preparing their horses.

"Perri? Is there something wrong?" Finnikin heard Evanjalin ask in a quiet voice.

Perri was silent, and the question seemed to be forgotten. Or so Finnikin thought until he glanced over to Evanjalin and found her eyes locked on Perri's.

"Perri?" Finnikin prompted.

Perri's stare was loaded with controlled hostility. "She lied," he said curtly.

There was confusion on Evanjalin's face.

"Perri, leave the girl alone," Trevanion murmured, grabbing the leg of his horse by the fetlock and holding the weight of its hoof on his knee.

There was no malice in Perri's face. Just cold certainty.

"She could not have walked the sleep two nights past. She spoke of walking the sleep in Pietrodore. It's not her time to bleed again."

Suddenly everyone turned in her direction. Evanjalin's face flushed with color.

"It's not important how—" she began.

"What else have you lied about?" Perri interrupted.

This time she stayed silent.

"Did you lie about Lady Beatriss?" Perri persisted. "And Tesadora? Did you lie about the young girls of Lumatere?" The priest-king and Froi looked on anxiously. Trevanion put his horse's leg to the ground and walked over.

"Answer him," Finnikin said quietly, wanting her to put an end to Perri's suspicions.

But she refused to speak, not taking her eyes off Finnikin.

"Answer him," he said more forcefully.

She shook her head sadly. "There's always doubt in your eyes,

Finnikin. How can you lead us home with so much doubt?"

"I'm not here to lead us home. Balthazar is," he replied.

The fear that ran through his body when she cast her eyes down chilled him.

"Did you lie about Balthazar, Evanjalin?" he said, his throat dry. It was strange how calmly he asked the question. But he knew that if he shouted at her, it would only mean he believed she was capable of such deception. So he waited for her to deny it, to explain the sleep to them again so he could tell Perri to shut his mouth and then convince her that there was no doubt in his eyes. Just a desperate need for answers.

But there was no denial from Evanjalin.

"Did you lie about the return of the king?" Perri asked, his tone level. Finnikin realized that he had never heard Perri shout. Never seen him lose control. Froi and the priest-king stood waiting quietly, as if willing Evanjalin to provide the right answer.

"Say no, Evanjalin," Froi blurted.

"Answer him, Evanjalin," Trevanion said.

Finnikin saw it in her eyes before she responded. He saw it because she chose to look directly at him. There was no plea for understanding.

"Balthazar is dead."

He felt his stomach revolt, his knees buckling beneath him. But still she refused to look away.

"You would never have come this far if you thought he was dead," she said calmly. "All of you. The exiles. The Guard. No one."

"You lied all this time?" He could hardly recognize his own voice.

"You wanted a king," she said quietly.

"You lied."

"I gave you a king. I gave you what you wanted."

"You. Lied."

*"Stop saying that!"* she shouted, and the others flinched at the fury in her voice. "There are worse things than a lie and there are better things than the truth!"

He stared at her in bewilderment. "Who are you?"

"Who do you want me to be, Finnikin?" There were tears in her eyes, and he wanted to tear at his own so he didn't have to see her. Didn't have to witness her deceit.

"I once asked you to trust me."

He shook his head with disbelief. "Do you belong to the Charynites?" She clenched her fists as he stepped forward. "Or are you one of Sagrami's dark worshippers, bent on more destruction?"

"If I am, then burn me at the stake, Finnikin," she cried. "As they did the last time they found out a king was dead in Lumatere. Someone had to be blamed. Someone had to die. Because that's what happens when logical men can't explain why an old woman has the blood of an innocent on her hands, or why another can walk through the sleep of our people. What you can't understand, you destroy."

Perri made a sound of disgust, and she turned to stare at him. "It's what your kin did to Tesadora and her people all those years, Perri. How your people taught you to hate. Your father made you watch. Made you take her hand and place it in that furnace and watch it burn. And you did, with tears in your eyes because you were a child and you believed what your father had to say. It's what made you a savage."

"You lied about the king!" Finnikin shouted. "What is there to understand? We have people waiting outside the kingdom. For their *king*."

Trevanion placed a hand on his arm to calm him, but Finnikin pulled away, his eyes wild. "If harm comes to those people, with the power appointed to me as Sir Topher's First Man, I will charge you with sedition," Finnikin threatened bitterly, swinging onto his horse. "Curse your existence if we've led the entire kingdom-in-exile to a mass grave in the Valley."

When they reached the crossroads, Finnikin felt Froi tremble as the thief held on to him. Perri and Trevanion drew up alongside, and he saw the grief and hopelessness on their faces. North pointed to Lumatere, the word he had rewritten not five days past. But five days past the world had been different and a prophecy promising the return of the king had been possible to fulfill.

He had sensed Evanjalin's stare for the length of their journey as she rode behind him on Trevanion's mount. He turned to look at her now, and she held his gaze as she slipped off the horse and untied her bedroll. She looked small and vulnerable where she stood, surrounded by all five of them, and then she pointed east, her hand shaking.

"Get back on the horse, Evanjalin," Trevanion said wearily.

She shook her head. "I go east," she said.

No one moved or spoke.

"We go north to the Valley," Finnikin said firmly. "And you don't have a choice. Get on the horse, Evanjalin."

She shook her head again. "If it's sedition you accuse me of, stop me with a dagger. If not, I go east. The gods whisper words to me as I sleep, telling us to take a path that makes sense only to them. But I trust it."

"Ah, the privilege of the gods whispering in your ears," he mocked. "Did you have to bleed for that, Evanjalin?"

The pain in her eyes was real. "The gods whispered to you once, Finnikin. And you listened. But they are proud and refuse to speak to those who do not believe that there is something out there mightier than the minds and intellect of mortals."

But his heart could not be moved, and he turned his back on her. He could hear the crunch of the leaves as she walked and he dared not move until the sound faded away.

Froi slipped off Finnikin's horse, quietly looking up at him and then the others before turning in the direction Evanjalin had taken. He removed his bedroll from the saddle and placed it on his shoulder.

"She and me? We the same in some fings. We live. The others, those orphan kids, they dead. Because she and me, we want to live and we do anyfing to make that happen. That's the difference between us and others. I seen them. I seen Lumaterans die, and you know what I do to live? Anyfing. Do you hear me? I do anyfing. Just like her."

Froi turned and followed Evanjalin, and this time it seemed he understood exactly which path he was taking.

One mile from their homeland, Finnikin stopped. In front of him stood the ridge. From there, it would be possible to see the Valley of Tranquillity, which had once seemed like a carpet of lushness leading to Lumatere's main gate. He imagined what it would be like to see inside the kingdom, all the way to the rock of three wonders, where once he made a pledge with his two friends, believing in their omnipotence. That they could save their world. His scar throbbed with pain as if the blood they had sacrificed ten years ago had seeped into the earth and was welcoming him home.

*Home.*

"Finn? It's just over the ridge," Trevanion said.

Finnikin swung off his horse and stared up at the last place he had ever worshipped his goddess. "Take the priest-king," he said quietly. "Our people need him in the Valley."

"And you?" Trevanion asked.

Finnikin shook his head. "I just want to sit for a while."

Trevanion walked up beside him. "I'll sit with you."

"No." He shook his head emphatically. "The people will want to see the captain of the Guard. They need that hope if they have already returned."

Finnikin turned to the priest-king, who sat astride Perri's horse. There was a look of intense sadness on the old man's face. "Blessed Barakah, what does the word *resurdus* mean in the ancient language?" he asked, already knowing the answer.

"King," the old man replied.

Finnikin nodded.

Trevanion mounted his horse again. "Climb your rock, Finn," he said firmly. "When you return, I'll be waiting here."

Finnikin walked toward the ridge, then stopped as Perri spoke.

"Warrior. Guide."

Finnikin turned and met Perri's eyes.

"I had a . . . friend once who knew the language of the ancients," he said, his face impassive. "I asked her what the word for 'warrior' was. It was the only word I cared to learn. *Resurdus.* In the time when the gods walked the earth, a king was a warrior. But in other dialects it meant guide."

Finnikin stared after them as they rode away. Then he began to climb. He had promised the goddess a sacrifice if she allowed Evanjalin to live, and there on the ridge he pierced his old wound and watched it bleed, his mind growing light.

*Dark will guide the light, and our* resurdus *will rise.*

He made a pledge to honor the prophecy that may have always been meant for him.

But there were no visions, and no sense of peace or euphoria.

The goddess was angry.

Her message was clear.

It was not enough.

It was almost dark when he climbed down from the ridge. Waiting with his father were Perri and Moss and Sir Topher. Finnikin swung onto his horse. Without speaking, he turned its head away from the Valley of Tranquillity and took the path the priest-king had said would be their salvation paved with blood.

The path to the novice Evanjalin.

And without questioning his decision, the others followed.

## CHapteR 21

They traveled through the night and by sunrise reached the tunnel that separated Belegonia from neighboring Osteria. It was a pass carved inside one of the mountains, hacked out of the granite over the centuries. Finnikin was the first to lead his horse through the low narrow entrance, placing his hands on the stone around his head to guide him. The ground was littered with fallen rocks, and his ankle twisted continuously on its awkward angles. When the light hit his eyes on the other side, the pain was intense, but he gulped the air with a hunger that came from a profound sense of relief.

The Osterian capital was the closest to Lumatere. The two kingdoms were the smallest in the land and less than a day's ride from each other. As they rode over the hills from the west, Finnikin caught sight of the turrets of the Osterian palace in the distance. The small palace lay in a valley in the center of the kingdom, encircled by sixteen hills, which served to protect it from Belegonia to its west, Sorel to its south, and Charyn to its north and east. Finnikin knew the Osterian hills were home to several ethnic communities that had enjoyed autonomy since the time of the gods. They were watched over by a number of sentinels whose job it was to keep peace within the land, but Finnikin suspected that the sentinels were also there to keep an eye on Charyn, which lay beyond a narrow river to the north.

"So where can you be, Evanjalin?" Sir Topher asked as they rested their horses in one of the valleys. Finnikin had been surprised to find his mentor waiting with Trevanion, Perri, and Moss the previous evening. As the new leader of Lumatere, he would be better protected in the Valley under the watch of the Guard. But Sir Topher had been determined to find Evanjalin and Froi, and at times during their short journey to Osteria, Finnikin had seen the censure in his mentor's eyes.

"She lied about the king," Finnikin said quietly as the other men separated to see what they could discover beyond the northern hills.

Sir Topher did not speak for a moment. So much had changed since they climbed the rock to the cloister in Sendecane months before. Too much had happened, more emotions than they had felt between them in the last ten years.

"You wanted Balthazar to be alive, Finnikin," he said gently. "He was a beloved friend, and in the mind of the child you were at the time, he seemed a mighty warrior who could conquer anything."

Finnikin felt naive and foolish. "I know it doesn't seem possible that one so young could have lived through such terrible events, Sir Topher. But Evanjalin and Froi and even I have been in situations of grave danger, and we lived. So I believed that he would too. That somehow he endured what took place in the Forest of Lumatere that night."

"Do you know what I think?" Sir Topher asked, tears in his eyes. "I think Prince Balthazar made a decision that night. I think he was a warrior of the gods. You wanted him to live for all the right reasons, my boy. But more than anything, you needed him to live because you feared the inevitable."

Finnikin was silent as Trevanion and his men returned. He could tell from the grimness of his father's expression that their surveillance from the top of the hills had provided them with more than just a scenic view of Osteria.

"Tell us good news, Trevanion," Sir Topher implored.

Trevanion shook his head, his mouth a straight line. "From our vantage point we had a clear view of the river and into Charyn. There are soldiers there. At least fifteen. Swords in hand. Exiles at their feet."

"Sweet goddess," Sir Topher said.

"I counted at least forty," Moss said.

"Why are you so sure the captives are Lumaterans?" Finnikin asked. "Might they not just be Charynites camped by the river?"

"They're exiles," Moss said firmly.

"Evanjalin? Froi?" Sir Topher asked.

Trevanion shook his head.

"Do they move freely?" Sir Topher asked. "Are you sure they are under guard?"

"They have separated the men from the women," Perri said bitterly. "Never a good sign."

"Since when have exile camps been under guard?" Sir Topher asked.

"Since the rumor of the return of a king," Trevanion said. "If there is one thing that will threaten the royal house of Charyn, it is talk of the curse on Lumatere being broken and the impostor king revealing the truth. Charyn would consider any group of exiles a threat."

"I say we cross the river. We can take them by surprise," Perri said. "They are weakened by ale and boredom. I can see it in their sluggish movements."

"Except we have a guest. Remember?" Moss said, pointing up to the peak of one of the smaller hills to the east of them. Finnikin followed his line of sight and made out a figure crouching.

"He may belong to one of the autonomous communities," Finnikin said. "It wouldn't be rare for them to be traveling the hills."

"Not a traveler, Finnikin. He is spying. On the Charynites and the exile camp. He cares little if we are aware of his location but does not want to be seen by the soldiers on the other side of the river."

Finnikin sighed, shading his eyes with his hand, trying to think. He looked at the figure again. The youth was standing now. He was almost Finnikin's height but much broader, dressed in clothing cut from the fur of animals. There was an aggression in his stance, an arrogance that instantly made Finnikin bristle. As if sensing Finnikin's anger, the youth removed an arrow from the quiver strapped to his back and cocked his longbow, holding the arrow at eye level and pointing it straight toward Finnikin.

"Provoke him, Finn," Trevanion instructed, aiming his crossbow in the direction of their intruder. "Let's see what he does."

Finnikin grabbed a blunt-tipped bolt from his quiver. "Do you want me to discharge?"

"No, leave that to us if he chooses to attack. He seems focused on you. Find another way to provoke him."

Finnikin thought for a moment and then raised his hand and made a gesture with two of his fingers twisted together, pointing them toward the bridge of his nose and then jutting them forward with force.

The others stared at him, amused. Trevanion and Perri even barked out a rare laugh.

"I think that's the River people's way of telling one to do something quite obscene with their mother," Moss mused.

"Just something I used to see you all do when I was a child," Finnikin said with a grin.

"You'll have to try another one," Perri advised. "It won't work as provocation. It's purely a Lumateran insult. Unknown to the rest of the land."

"How proud we must feel," Sir Topher said dryly.

The men laughed again, but when an arrow landed close to Finnikin's feet, they leaped back in alarm, diving for cover behind a cluster of rocks and cocking their weapons.

"Bastard!" Finnikin muttered.

With their backs against the rocks, the realization hit them all at the same time.

"He recognized the gesture."

"An exile, perhaps?"

"But armed?"

Finnikin crawled over to his saddle pack and pulled out an ochre-colored stone, then retrieved an arrow from his quiver and handed it to his father.

"Hold it still while I write."

Across the stem of the arrow he scribbled the words *Finnikin of the Rock* before stepping into the open and aiming toward the figure on the hill. He followed the arc of his shot, pleased when the youth jumped back, and he could tell by the youth's stance that he was less than happy about the close proximity of the arrow between his legs. He picked up the arrow and then stared at it before disappearing. They were disappointed when he failed to reappear.

"We go to the river," Trevanion said finally, "and ask the Charynites to kindly let the exiles cross."

"Just don't ask me to be kind for too long," Perri muttered as they began to climb the hill.

They stood on the riverbank not five steps away from where the Charynite soldiers held the exiles captive. Finnikin thought it seemed wrong not to wade across and end it all right there. The moment they arrived, the soldiers had casually made their way toward the opposite bank. Huddled behind them were the exiles, divided into three groups: women and children, grown men, and then the youths. While the males were seated, the women and children stood, clutching each other with fear. One of the mothers held a hand over the mouth of her wailing baby, her face stricken with terror at the thought of what would happen if she failed to silence the child. Finnikin knew what the guards planned to do with these people. Worse still, the exiles knew it too. He could tell that most of them came from the main village of Lumatere. The villagers were merchants and craftsmen and had a distinct personality. There was a humility and dignity to them that the queen had encouraged her children to emulate. "If you do not get what you want in life, Balthazar," Finnikin would hear her say, "take it like a villager. Hold your head up and accept the inevitable."

One of the older exiles raised his head from where it rested on his knees and saw them on the bank. Finnikin watched as his expression changed from despair to recognition to elation. He nudged his neighbor, and an excited whisper went through the group. There was no such reaction from the Lumateran lads. Unlike their fathers and uncles, they had no idea who Trevanion and Perri were. As far as they were concerned, the five men standing before them on the Osterian side of the river could easily add more woe to their situation. Death was inevitable. Finnikin could see it in their faces.

A soldier stepped closer, his boot touching the water between them. "Go back to guarding the garbage," he instructed his men. "I'll take care of this."

Finnikin felt Sir Topher stiffen beside him and was relieved that Trevanion, Moss, and Perri did not understand the Charyn language. As Perri had said, these men were bored. It was their job to guard a rarely used crossing two days' ride from the capital. Taking thirty unarmed exiles hostage and doing to them whatever they desired was a way to relieve the boredom. In the prison mines, Finnikin had asked his father how humans could treat each other in such a way. "Because they stop seeing their victims as human," Trevanion had responded quietly.

The soldier with one foot in the river was young; Finnikin smelled his ambition and saw the look of dogmatism in his eyes. He would have preferred to have been dealing with a madman full of anger than someone so blinded by self-importance. The Charyn soldier stared at them. Finnikin imagined what he was thinking. Five men, swords at their sides, longbows in their hands. They had enough bolts in their quivers to create havoc among fifteen restless guards.

"On behalf of the government of Lumatere, we order you to release our people," Sir Topher said in the Charyn language. Finnikin heard the tremble of rage in his voice.

The Charynite laughed, but with little amusement. "The government of Lumatere? Old man, if you were on this side of the river, you would be imprisoned for treason against our neighbor's king for such a statement." He spoke to them as if he were reprimanding disobedient children. Finnikin translated for Trevanion, Moss, and Perri.

"Translate for me word for word, Finnikin," his father

instructed, his eyes never leaving the Charynite. "Tell him that if we were on his side of the river, we would be the only ones standing. Tell him the present king of Lumatere is an impostor and a murderer falsely placed on the throne by the ignorant."

Finnikin relayed his father's message.

"To call the Lumateran king an impostor is an offense against every kingdom of the land," the Charynite snapped, his anger growing.

"There have been worse offenses perpetrated against Lumatere by its neighboring kingdoms," Finnikin translated for his father.

"And you are?" the Charyn soldier asked. The question was directed at Trevanion.

Finnikin translated the question, knowing the inevitable. The Charynite soldier would be assured a promotion to the Charyn palace with the capture of Trevanion, but Finnikin knew his father had no choice. The exiles would either live if Trevanion succeeded, or die if they failed. Nothing in between.

"Captain of the Lumateran King's Guard," Trevanion answered, looking the man square in the eye.

The head of every Lumateran lad shot up, their expressions astonished, and the flickers of hope that appeared in their eyes made Finnikin feel like a god. One or two of the lads extended their fists in a show of solidarity. Moss and Perri held theirs up in response, and the Charynite soldiers began to look uneasy, waiting for the translation. With great satisfaction, Finnikin watched the beads of sweat appear on their faces when he spoke.

"What is your purpose with these people?" Finnikin asked on Trevanion's behalf.

"We have in our barracks a youth who claims to be the heir to the throne of Lumatere," the Charynite said. "A throne belonging to another. Approved by our king ten years ago. Imagine what an insult it is to us when one takes it upon himself to render our king's decision null and void. It is obvious that these people were harboring the claimant, and the moment we ascertain the truth, we will let these people go, *Captain*."

"And the moment you let our people go," Trevanion said after hearing Finnikin's translation, "I will convince my men here to let you live, *squad leader*."

"*Lieutenant*," the man corrected. "You think we are frightened to cross to your side? You think the Osterians will go to war with us if we do? You think they won't turn a blind eye to anything we choose to do at the arse-end of their kingdom to a bunch of dirty Lumateran scum? There are five of you, Captain, and many more of us. You have made a mistake today."

The lieutenant grabbed one of the Lumateran lads by his hair and jerked him to his feet, holding a sword to his throat. There was a whimper from one of the women—the mother, Finnikin suspected—but his attention was drawn back to the face of the lad standing before him. All that separated them was a narrow body of water. Over the years Finnikin had seen many Lumaterans his age lying in unmarked graves or dying from fever or weighed down by the apathy of exile. But this lad was living and had a fire in his eyes, a fury.

"What needs to be done," Trevanion murmured. Then he was in the river, less than a foot away from the Charynite, his bow pointed directly between the man's eyes. Within seconds Finnikin had removed a bolt from his quiver, cocked his longbow, and was beside his father, his arrow pointed in the same spot. He could feel the breath of the Charynite and Lumateran lad before him. Around him every sword was drawn and behind him every arrow.

"Perhaps there are only five of us, Lieutenant," Finnikin acknowledged, not taking his eyes off the Charynite, "but know this. Before any of your men raise their weapons, any one of us will have released at least five bolts. You will be my first hit," he said. "Second, third, fourth, and fifth go to those guarding my peers. My father will aim for those with swords pointed at the women of Lumatere and my friends will finish off the rest with time to spare. So today you decide whether you live or die."

The Lieutenant met Finnikin's stare. Then his eyes flicked away for a brief moment, and suddenly Finnikin felt someone by his side. He did not look away from the Charynite but saw the tip of a longbow as the person beside him adopted the same stance as his and his father's.

"Are we speaking Charyn?" Finnikin heard a gruff voice ask. "Mine's a bit weak, although it is one of the rules of my father to learn the language of your neighbor. It could come in handy when you live at the arse-end of a country beside the biggest arseholes in the land."

Finnikin heard Sir Topher choke back a laugh.

"So please excuse my poor accent," the voice continued. "And may I draw your attention to the hills behind me?"

Finnikin watched the lieutenant raise his eyes and grow noticeably pale.

"May I remind you that Osterian goatherds cannot declare war on Charyn," the lieutenant said snidely.

"Certainly, and I will inform you in return that we're not Osterian," the voice continued. "We're Monts. Lucian of the Monts, if you please, and when it comes to speed and accuracy with an arrow, my father's better than his," he said, gesturing to Finnikin. "So if that is fear I read on your face, I commend you for being smart enough to recognize a threat."

Finnikin felt weak with relief. His childhood rival and friend stood beside him. He was filled with a sense of hope. If the Monts were in the hills, then Evanjalin would be among her people. But the feeling did not last. The lieutenant had begun to loosen his grip on the lad, and when he raised his left hand, Finnikin caught sight of a ruby ring on his finger.

He shuddered as he realized that the Charynite had crossed paths with Froi. He tried to recall what the soldier had said. That in their barracks they had a claimant to the throne.

"Sir Topher?" he said quietly.

"I see it, Finnikin."

"Do not react," Trevanion said.

The Charynite watched the exchange.

"Lieutenant?" one of the other soldiers called out to him, fear in his voice. "They're coming down the hill. Hundreds."

He watched as the lieutenant swallowed, his eyes still on Trevanion.

"Let our people go unharmed and we will spare you," Sir Topher said.

As more Monts appeared with their weapons raised, Trevanion lowered his longbow and moved closer to the bank, careful not to place his foot on Charyn land. He held out a hand to the women. One stepped forward with a sob, placing her two children in Trevanion's arms. Slowly the business of crossing the river took place. Finnikin stayed in position beside Lucian, their bows trained on the lieutenant, who still held on to his prisoner. It was not until half of the exiles had crossed the river that the Charynite shoved the boy forward and then retreated.

They had little time to spare, but Lucian of the Monts took a moment to size up his old childhood friend. Finnikin thought there was more than a touch of arrogance in the way the Mont swaggered about as if he had single-handedly saved the day. But he was too sick with worry to respond.

"Do you have Evanjalin?" he asked Lucian, pulling him away from where he was shamelessly charming one of the exile girls.

"Who?" Lucian asked.

"She's a Mont," Finnikin pressed.

"We have no Monts named Evanjalin," he said dismissively.

Finnikin gave up on Lucian and went searching for Saro, the leader of the Monts and Lucian's father. The man embraced him. Older than Trevanion by at least ten years, his build was intimidating but he had a gentle smile. "How proud your father must be, Finnikin."

"Thank you, sir. But we're looking for a friend who has been traveling with us. A Mont girl named Evanjalin. Has she made contact with you these past two days?"

Saro shook his head, a look of confusion on his face. "You can't possibly have traveled with a Mont, Finnikin. We have all our people. We accounted for every single one in the Valley that terrible day."

"Her name is Evanjalin," Finnikin repeated. "She claims to be a Mont. She was entrusted to us by the High Priestess at the cloister of Lagrami in Sendecane. Somehow she has led us here . . . with the belief that Balthazar was among you."

"*Balthazar?*" Saro whispered. "My beloved nephew?"

"Balthazar's dead," Lucian said sharply. He stood behind his father, glaring at Finnikin. "It was fool's talk that said he lived. And fool's talk that these men claim to have him."

"But they do have at least one of ours," Finnikin insisted, searching the area for his father. There was a sea of faces around him but no one familiar. "We have been traveling with two young Lumaterans, a youth named Froi and a girl called Evanjalin. A Mont," he said firmly, looking at Saro. "We separated two days ago and held great hope that Evanjalin made her way to you. She claims she walks through the sleep of those inside Lumatere, accompanied by a child," he added.

Lucian and Saro looked shocked, and Finnikin felt frustrated that he would have to explain the sleep yet again.

"So far away?" Saro asked.

"What do you mean, 'so far away'?" Finnikin asked.

"Some of our women have the gift of the walk," Saro explained. "But they can only walk the sleep of those in our community. In close proximity. Here on the hill, or on the mountain when we lived back home. We have never had anyone who is able to walk through the sleep of those so far away."

"Your women walk through people's sleep?" Finnikin asked.

"Some of our gifted ones," Saro replied.

"It's called the 'gift of the walk,'" Lucian said, glowering at Finnikin. "I feel you disrespect it."

"Lucian," his father instructed, "take Finnikin up to your *yata*. She will want to know about this girl. I need to organize these people. Trevanion and Sir Topher want them taken to the Valley of Tranquillity at first light."

Lucian grabbed hold of Finnikin but he pulled away. He needed Trevanion and Perri. They would have to cross the river to find Evanjalin and Froi, and they could not afford to waste a moment. Finnikin walked over to the lad who had been the Charynite's prisoner.

"Sefton," the lad introduced himself, clasping Finnikin's arm.

"Tell me what they said about the claimant, Sefton," Finnikin said.

"I understood nothing of their language," Sefton said, "but my aunt worked in the village and speaks some Charyn. Esta!" he called out to one of the women. "Esta! Finnikin needs your help." He turned back to Finnikin. "Let me come along. I am fast with a longbow."

Finnikin smiled at the lad's eagerness. "Then they'll need you in the Valley, Sefton. The Guard is training there. Tell them I sent you."

A woman Trevanion's age held a hand to Finnikin's face. "Ask of us anything, lad."

"The claimant in their barracks?"

She nodded. "I heard the Charynites speak. They arrested a boy in the woods and believed him to belong to our community. Whatever it was about this boy, he was the reason they came to arrest us."

"Did they mention a girl? Evanjalin?" Finnikin asked.

She shook her head. "Just the boy."

He squeezed her hand in thanks and stood in the middle of the chaos. Some of the exiles were still close to tears. Moss dealt with them calmly as Saro instructed his people. The decision was made to rest for the night under the guard of the Monts in the foothills, then go to the Valley of Tranquillity at dawn. Finnikin tried to breathe normally, but breathing made his chest ache, and the sight of Lucian approaching with Sir Topher, an expression of superiority on the Mont's face, made him want to lunge at his childhood nemesis.

"Where's my father, Sir Topher?"

"Go with the Monts, Finnikin," Sir Topher said evenly. "Saro wants you to speak with Yata, who will be keen to hear of Evanjalin."

*Yata.* Balthazar and Lucian's grandmother, matriarch of the Monts, mother of the dead queen.

"We need to find them," Finnikin insisted. "We need to cross the river. Don't ask me to stand here and do nothing."

"You've done enough, Finnikin. Your father and Perri will take care of locating Evanjalin and Froi. Rest. In the next few days, you are going to need everything inside of you. Everything."

Lucian of the Monts stood by, arms folded, waiting. He pointed up the hill, and when Finnikin didn't move, he grabbed him by the shoulder and shoved him along.

They said little to each other as they walked through the trees and began to climb. The day had turned cold and blustery, and Finnikin envied Lucian his long fleeced coat. He pulled his own coat tighter around him as they traveled up the hillside toward where he imagined the rest of the Monts were hidden.

"Sheep shit," Lucian warned a second after Finnikin stepped in it.

The Mont sauntered ahead. Finnikin followed him, muttering. The path had become narrow and steep. When they passed a water trough on the track, Finnikin smelled the sheep instantly. Although the valley behind them was bathed in sunlight, there was little protection from the elements up on the hill. But the Monts had never been interested in creature comforts. In the mountains they had been sentinels for the Charyn border. Mont children were born to defend from the moment they could walk. It was what Balthazar had adored and envied about his cousin. Although Balthazar was the prince, more often Lucian was their leader. The better hunter. The better fighter. The fiercest and most loyal of allies. He had once carried Finnikin all day on his back when Finnikin was bitten by a snake. He had sucked the venom out himself and held Finnikin until help came. Like he would a brother.

"But they can't control their emotions," Balthazar would whisper to Finnikin, who had no idea, like the prince, what that meant.

Until he witnessed the grieving of the Monts on the first day of exile. Unabashed, unashamed. Sometimes he envied it, wanted to rage at the world, bite his knuckles, gnash his teeth. Spray the air with his fury. But Finnikin belonged to the Rock people, contained, like those of the Flatlands.

"Sheep shit."

*Bastard.*

Finally they reached a wide summit. Scattered across the grass was an assortment of tents, beautifully colored, each one bordered with flowers and pebbles. Children ran among the tents, and women sat in circles, their heads close, their fingers busily sewing. Goats, cows, horses, donkeys, pigs, chickens, and perfectly aligned vegetable gardens dotted the hill settlement. The Monts had found their little corner of the world, one day's ride from their homeland.

"Tents?" Finnikin scoffed. "You've been here ten years and you've never built homes?"

"So?" Lucian asked.

"Well, wouldn't this be a home to settle in?"

"These are hills, fool. We're mountain people. This is nothing like home."

"Balthazar always said—"

Lucian shoved him. "And here we don't talk about Balthazar or the princesses or the queen or the king. Do you understand?"

Finnikin shook his head in disgust. "You live in tents; you don't talk about the past. You exiles are all alike," he said. "Pretending it didn't happen."

"We are no exiles!"

Lucian's fist connected with Finnikin's cheek. The blow unleashed something in Finnikin, a need to cause as much pain as possible, to destroy. He pounded into Lucian with the full force of the rage that had built up inside of him. Each punch he delivered to the Mont's face or body lessened the numbness he had felt since Perri's revelation in the meadow. But Finnikin knew that something more than rage was driving him. He sensed the same emotion from Lucian, who now had him trapped with an elbow to the throat and a knee on the thigh, exactly where his pledge-wound lay.

"We've been with our people from the very beginning," Lucian spat, "so we're exiled from *no one*. And our *yata* lost five grandchildren and her daughter that night. It's heartbreak, trog boy. Not pretense."

And then both of them were at it again, hammering fists into each other until at last they exhausted their anger and, clutching on to each other, collapsed onto the ground.

Finnikin had no idea how long they lay on their backs, staring up at the sky, side by side yet refusing to acknowledge each other's presence.

"Come," Lucian said finally, his voice husky. He got to his feet and extended a hand to Finnikin. "We need to clean up. My *yata* will skin me alive if she sees us this way."

## chapteR 22

At the entrance of Yata's tent, Lucian gave Finnikin a shove and a look of reprimand. "Don't mention my cousins," he said gruffly. "She may seem strong, but she will never recover from losing them."

Finnikin nodded, and when Lucian called out a greeting, they entered the large tent. Candles burned brightly and flowers scented the air. The matriarch of the Monts sat weaving, her hair in long curls of gray, her eyes dark and probing. She was the symbolic *yata* to all the Monts, but the grandmother of Lucian and his cousins. She smiled up at her grandson and then at Finnikin. He could still see the handsome woman she had been when he was a child. In those days, her hair had been mostly black and there was more flesh on her frame, but the strength in her eyes had not diminished.

"Finnikin of the Rock," she said, her voice husky. *What is it with these Mont women?* he thought. Sixty-five years old and he was still blushing at the sound of her voice.

He bent to kiss her cheek three times, following the Mont custom. One for the recipient, one for the giver, and one for the goddess, who was part of their union. "My father and his men and Sir Topher travel with me."

"So finally we return home?" she asked, breaking a thread with her teeth and putting her work aside. She beckoned them toward her, and they sat on a fleeced blanket, where she poured them cold tea and fed them sweet bread.

"We return to the Valley of Tranquillity first," Finnikin acknowledged.

"They have found another Mont, Yata," Lucian said. "Her name is Evanjalin and she walks the sleep of those inside Lumatere. Finnikin has led her to us."

"No, she has led me," Finnikin corrected.

Yata's dark eyes widened with surprise. "Inside Lumatere? Such power," she said, shaking her head.

"I believe so," Finnikin said. "She swears that Lady Beatriss of the Flatlands lives, as do the novices of the cloister of Sagrami and Tesadora of the Forest Dwellers."

Yata placed a trembling hand to her lips. "How were the novices saved? And Lady Beatriss? Her babe?"

"She is certain that my father and Lady Beatriss's child died," Finnikin said sadly. "As for the novices of Sagrami, they were hidden during the five days of the unspeakable. I suspect by Perri the Savage." He watched as Yata shivered, despite the warmth in the tent. "Can you tell me more about walking the sleep?"

"It began with Seranonna of the Forest Dwellers," she said in a soft voice. "I was giving birth to my fifth child. Seranonna lived far away from the Monts, but she swore she heard my cries of pain and so she made a journey through the Forest, into the village, across the Flatlands, over the River, and into the Mountains. She delivered my daughter, a beautiful girl who would grow up to be queen." She sighed, and Finnikin saw Lucian sit forward, ready to leap up if she needed him.

"I was ill for a long time after I gave birth, so Seranonna stayed. She had just given birth to a child who had lived only a week and her breasts were full of milk, so my babe suckled from the breast of one who worshipped Lagrami and one who worshipped Sagrami. Every child Seranonna delivered thereafter during her time with us had the gift of walking the sleep."

"Perhaps Evanjalin and the child in Lumatere she walks alongside were delivered by Seranonna as well," Lucian said.

"Not possible," Finnikin replied. "The child was born after Seranonna's death."

"Evanjalin travels with another?" Yata asked, intrigued.

"Is that rare?" Finnikin said.

She nodded. "Most of our women who have the gift walk alone. Although sometimes I would walk the sleep with my daughter, the queen. Perhaps there is a strong bloodline between Evanjalin and the child."

She pointed to the jug when she noticed that his cup was empty. "And do not be shy with the sweet bread. Lucian certainly isn't."

Finnikin glanced at Lucian, whose mouth was full but whose dark eyes were alert with interest. "What is she like? Evanjalin of the Monts?" he asked.

Finnikin thought for a moment. "Strong. In here," he said, thumping his chest twice. "Humbling. Ruthless. Cunning. She can love people with a fierceness that I have not seen before." He smiled when he realized he was talking too much. "And she looks like a Mont woman, so of course she's very beautiful."

"Does she belong to you, Finnikin?" Yata asked, her eyes piercing.

"No," he said after a moment. "But she belongs to my heart. I feel her absence strongly and it brings me . . . sorrow." He looked across at Lucian, who made a pretense of wiping a tear from his eye. Knowing he had said enough, Finnikin stood to politely excuse himself.

"My grandson has missed you all these years," Yata said.

"Balthazar?"

Lucian sent him a scathing look, and Finnikin instantly regretted his stupidity.

"I'm sorry . . ."

"No." She chuckled, holding out a hand to her grandson to help her to her feet. "Lucian has missed you."

"I have not!" Lucian looked horrified.

She tugged his ear. "I walk your sleep, silly boy. Not a place your *yata* wants to be most of the time, but there are some moments that bring me joy."

Lucian turned red. She kissed them both, and Finnikin found comfort in the feel of her hands on his face. Lucian had lost his mother young but had always had his *yata* close by. It was what Finnikin missed about his great-aunt Celestina and even Lady Beatriss.

The matriarch of the Monts studied Finnikin's face carefully, as if she saw the things written on his mind and soul. "How you warm my heart, Finnikin of the Rock," she said. "Bring your Evanjalin to us. If she guided you here, she wants to be with her people."

That night, after he heard Sir Topher's heavy snores and the world of the Monts seemed to be asleep, Finnikin crept out of the tent. He wrapped his arms around himself, his teeth chattering uncontrollably as he made his way toward Lucian's tent. He knew what he had to do. He also knew he could not do it alone and that Lucian was his only choice. Although it annoyed him to have to ask the Mont for help, his desire to find Evanjalin was greater.

"Lucian!" he hissed. "*Inbred.* Get dressed. Get your sword and your bow. You're coming with me. No arguing."

"Already dressed. Sword in hand. You're late, trog boy."

Finnikin hid his surprise as Lucian joined him. The Mont wore a cap over his head, his bulky frame layered with a wool jerkin and trousers of animal hide. He threw Finnikin a fleece coat, and they crouched behind his tent, watching the three Monts on guard. The moon hung low in the sky, and it seemed to Finnikin that he could almost reach out and touch it.

"Are we finding your woman first or saving the boy?"

"She's not my woman, Lucian, and only inbred Monts go around saying 'your woman.'"

"Not your woman? Good. By the sounds of things, I could be very interested in this Mont girl. So now that you've given me permission . . . Finnikin? Did you just jab me in the back? If not, and that was something else pressing into me . . . really, I'm not interested in trog boys. But I can introduce you to my kinsman, Torin."

"You talk too much, Mont! So shut your mouth and don't ever think of her as yours."

From where they crouched, Finnikin could see the camp fires of the exiles under the guard of Saro and his men in the foothills below. He wondered how they would sleep after a day that had begun in captivity and ended in the comfort and protection of their people.

Lucian took the lead as they half stumbled toward the woods that lead to the river. Finnikin knew the Mont would be familiar with every inch of these hills. After watching Lucian carousing with his cousins earlier that day, he suspected that they spent many a night getting up to no good, far from the watchful eyes of their elders.

---

They waded through the river, holding their weapons high above their heads. The only noise to break the silence was their breathing and the sound of the lapping water. When they reached the Charyn riverbank, Finnikin indicated for Lucian to follow the trail the soldiers had taken deep into woods. The foliage was so dense that little moonlight penetrated and at times they held on to each other for fear of being separated. Branches scratched their faces and raised tree roots caused them to trip and stumble. Then Lucian seemed to vanish into thin air, and it was only the thud of his body hitting hard earth that stopped Finnikin in his tracks. He knelt and patted the ground before him, feeling the place where the earth fell away to nothing.

"Lucian!" he whispered. "Are you down there?"

"Where else would I be?" Lucian hissed back.

"Shh! What can you see?" Finnikin could barely make out Lucian's form crawling around in the darkness.

"There's nothing down here," Lucian said. "Just a big empty hole. Freshly dug, by the smell of things. Can you see me waving my hand to you?"

Finnikin heard the snap of a twig close by. *"Don't speak!"* he hissed. He lay facedown, holding his breath, staying alert to the sounds around them.

"Talk," Lucian finally said into the silence. "I'll follow your voice and try to climb up."

Finnikin moved closer to the edge, extending his arm and half his body into the hole for Lucian to grip on to, when suddenly a hand grabbed his leg. He swiveled around, kicking the intruder in the gut with as much force as he could muster. He heard a grunt of surprise and he scrambled for his dagger, only to have it jerked out of his hand. In the next second, he was thrust against the trunk of a tree with a fist at his throat.

"Finn?" his father said.

He shrugged free, shoving Trevanion away, furious that his father would plan the rescue without him. Perri was on his feet beside Trevanion, winded from the kick to his stomach.

"Lucian's down the hole," Finnikin muttered. He moved away and lay flat on the ground again, extending his arm into the empty space. His father held him by the feet, and when they could see Lucian's head, Perri reached over and hauled him out by the scruff of his neck.

There was a moment of tense silence.

"You had no right to leave me behind," Finnikin said tersely.

Trevanion grabbed him. "What do you think we are out here to do, Finn?" he said. "Have a chat with these animals? Do you think I want to drag you along to see what I excel in? Not languages, Finnikin. Killing. That's what I do best, and if we ever want to see the boy again that's what we'll be doing."

"And Evanjalin?"

There was no response. Trevanion motioned for Perri to lead the way, and they followed him to the edge of the woods. In the near distance, they could see flame sticks at the four corners of the soldiers" barracks.

"We wait here," Trevanion said in a low voice, guiding them to the hollow trunk of a tree. They sat huddled together in the small space. An owl hooted, and slowly the sounds of the night creatures, some shuffling and measured, others with scuttling speed, resumed around them.

"If she's—" Finnikin began.

Perri put a finger to his lips. He pointed toward the barracks and then pointed up, indicating that the Charynites may have soldiers posted in the trees close by. Finnikin watched as Perri took out his dagger and put out a hand to stop him.

"If she's out here and not locked up in the barracks, I'll know," he said. He took a deep breath and whistled.

"You share a whistle?" Trevanion said in disbelief.

"Do you have a problem with that?" Finnikin asked.

"I have a few whistles," Lucian murmured. "Very confusing sometimes."

"Whistles are meant for combat," Trevanion said. "Not wooing women. Women do not understand whistles."

"Shh! Shh!" Finnikin jabbed his father with his elbow. "Did you hear that?"

Finnikin whistled again and held up a hand for silence. Even the night creatures seemed to obey. They waited. Nothing.

And then they heard it, faintly but coming toward them, and Finnikin felt as if he could breathe again. He grinned. "Is she not the smartest girl in the land?"

"And the biggest liar and the most unpredictable," Perri muttered. Finnikin crawled out from the tree, but Perri was already on his feet. "Let me do the honors," he said, disappearing.

Finnikin waited, thinking of all the things he had to tell her. That perhaps he was the *resurdus* of Seranonna's prophecy, the one to break the spell at the main gate. And that she, Evanjalin, was the light of his sometimes very dark heart who would lead him.

Then he heard the crunch of footsteps and she was there and he opened his coat and wrapped her inside, holding her tight until the beat of their hearts slowed to the same pace and her lips were against the base of his throat. When he stepped back, he could see that she was wild-eyed and exhausted.

"Back to the tree," Perri ordered.

Lucian made room for them as they squashed in together. The Mont took off his cap and gently placed it on Evanjalin's head.

She stared at him for a moment, and Finnikin saw her shudder. He sat her in the crook of his body, keeping her warm.

"I watched the barracks from a distance last night and through today and tonight," she whispered. "There's a courtyard with three men guarding it. One dog tied up. High walls. The rest of the men are sleeping inside the barracks. I believe that's where they are keeping Froi."

"What happened, Evanjalin? How was he caught?" Trevanion asked.

"We both were," she said, her voice small. "We'd just arrived, and were walking through the woods early yesterday evening. We crossed the river to catch some food, and the Charynites found us. It was clear that they were going to kill us, for no other reason than we were Lumateran. I heard them say so, but I didn't let on." She stared up at them, shaking her head with anguish. "I told Froi I would make up some lie to create a diversion, and in the confusion, he was to run and not stop running. I ordered him. His bond was to me. To listen to every word I said." She began to shiver again, and Finnikin held her closer to him.

"And he looked at me and told me . . . told me that people with magic need to live. He told me he was dispensable. He speaks our language like an idiot," she spat out through her tears, "yet he knows the word *dispensable*. He still had my ruby ring, and before I could stop him, he was shouting out that he was the heir, Balthazar."

"But they would have known he was too young," Perri said.

"Everything happened too quickly. Froi waved the ruby ring in the air and yelled, 'Run! Run!' and then, 'Balthazar, Balthazar, Balthazar,' repeating that he was Balthazar, heir to the throne of Lumatere."

Finnikin felt Lucian flinch each time his dead cousin's name was spoken.

"So I ran and hid in a ditch until it was safe to climb a tree. And I watched them. Today the soldiers went out, and when they returned, they threw punches at each other and kicked the poor dog. Repeatedly."

"That's why they rounded up the exiles," Lucian murmured. "They would have known the boy was lying and probably suspected that the true heir was with the exiles on the river."

Evanjalin turned at the sound of Lucian's voice. "I told you the Monts were here," she said to Finnikin.

"No, you didn't," Finnikin accused gently. "You just pointed and said, 'I'm going east.'"

Lucian stared at her. "Definitely a Mont. Yata and my father will be distraught that we did leave one behind."

Evanjalin reached over and took Lucian's hand in hers. "Yata," she said in a trembling voice.

Finnikin watched as Lucian kept ahold of her hand, and then the Mont's fingers traveled up her arm and Finnikin saw him shudder. "Lucian!" he warned gruffly.

Lucian sighed, not letting go. "My father and Yata will be very angry when they see what you have done, Evanjalin. To have cut yourself to bleed and walk the sleep."

Finnikin could not make out his father's and Perri's reactions, but he felt deep shame as he reached over to reveal the horrific scars that not even the pale light of the moon could hide.

"You humble me, Evanjalin," Perri muttered, and then he was on his feet. "Let's go get our boy."

They made their way to the tree where Evanjalin had spent the night and day hiding.

"Stay," Perri said, disappearing up into its branches.

Trevanion took charge. "Perri and I go over the wall. Finn and Lucian, you climb the tree and cover us. The moment you see that Froi is safe, shoot anything that moves. The moment he's outside the walls of the courtyard, you run at the speed of the gods. Evanjalin, you stay here on the ground." She opened her mouth to speak, but he stopped her. "You stay here on the ground."

Perri dropped quietly in front of them.

"Three guards and one dog tied up?" Trevanion asked.

Perri shook his head. "It's not a dog," he said flatly, and then he and Trevanion were gone.

"Stay," Finnikin repeated to Evanjalin before he scrambled up the tree with Lucian and straddled a branch that gave him a good vantage point and room to move with his bow. He watched Perri and Trevanion scale the wall of the barracks, glance down for a moment, and then disappear over the side. The courtyard was lit with oil lamps, which made it easy to see what was taking place within. Finnikin realized why Trevanion wanted Evanjalin to stay on the ground as soon as he saw the quick movement of a blade against the throat of the first soldier. So effortless. So cold in its execution. Soldiers kill, he reminded himself. It's what they are trained to do. He wondered what was going through his father's and Perri's minds. Was it satisfaction? Did it soothe their blood or make them sick to the stomach?

"Three down. Too easy," Lucian whispered. "Perri is untying the boy she mistook for a dog. Why is your father going inside the barracks?"

Because his father was a soldier, Finnikin thought, and his blood ran hot with the need to avenge every one of their exiles who had died by the sword.

"Don't ask questions. The moment Perri's out with Froi, jump and take Evanjalin. I'll cover the barracks until Trevanion's out."

"That's not what they said," Lucian hissed. "The moment Perri's out with the boy, we both run. I don't go without you."

Finnikin kept his aim on the entrance of the barracks. "Would you follow their orders if Saro was in there?"

Lucian muttered a curse, and they watched as Perri lifted Froi in his arms and raced to the gates.

"They're out!" Lucian began scrambling down the tree. With relief, Finnikin saw his father emerge from the entrance. Whatever Trevanion had done, it had been silent, for nobody followed.

Finnikin waited for his father to leave the courtyard. Waited . . . waited . . . waited . . . and then Trevanion was out and Finnikin climbed down, leaping from the last branch to the ground, and fell at Evanjalin's feet. The three of them grabbed at each other and sprinted through the woods. They were barely aware of Perri's approach, and then Trevanion was upon them and they ran, their boots pounding the earth, their blood pounding in their brains, needing to breathe, needing to get to the river with Froi in their arms and Evanjalin between them. To take them home.

When they had crossed to the Osterian side of the river, they stopped for a moment.

"*Sagrami*," Perri cursed, dropping to his knees with Froi still in his arms. Finnikin watched Lucian flinch when he saw what the soldiers had done to Froi's face.

"My father has alerted the Osterian soldiers, so I doubt the Charynites will cross, but I know a place to stop and rest before we get to the foothills," Lucian said.

They followed the Mont through the cluster of trees. As Finnikin had suspected, he knew his territory and navigated easily through the wooded gully. Before long, he stopped at an overhanging rock and they crawled underneath it.

"Froi, speak," Evanjalin said firmly.

He seemed to croak. His face was a mass of bruises, and blood was caked around his nose and mouth and ears.

"You *never* do anything stupid like that again," she whispered with fury. "You could have been killed, you idiot boy. It's part of your bond that *I* give instructions, not you."

Froi mumbled, and Perri leaned closer to listen. "That's very rude, Froi. And quite impossible for her to do with a bond."

Finnikin and Lucian laughed in relief. Trevanion reached out to Evanjalin and pressed something into her hand. She stared at it for a long while before looking up at him. The ring.

"I lied about it, you know," she said quietly.

"Why, Evanjalin, I can't believe you would ever tell a lie," Trevanion said, almost smiling.

She smiled for him. "It was in the exile camp, more than two years ago. I was watching a card game. There was a thief there, full of remorse now that the king was dead. He had stolen the ring one day while the king and queen and their children traveled from the Mountains to the Flatlands, years before the days of the unspeakable. But despite the remorse, there was a boast in his voice. So I challenged him to a game of cards. The winner kept the ring. I was fifteen years old and a girl, so nobody took me seriously and they let me join."

"What did you have to offer?" Finnikin asked.

"I had been there for almost a year, and each night I would watch one of the women bury twenty silver pieces in a pouch near the trunk of a tree. So I borrowed it for the night."

They heard Froi snort. "And I'm s'pposed to be the feef."

"Wouldn't you have felt guilty if you lost?" Lucian asked.

"I knew I would win," she said pragmatically.

"But—"

"Lucian," Finnikin warned. "Trust me. Her gambles pay off."

"But you did return the twenty silver pieces?" Lucian pushed.

"No," she said, shaking her head.

Lucian looked disappointed. Monts weren't thieves. It was the worst thing to be accused of.

"I didn't have time," she said quietly. "The next morning, a group of Sarnak hunters surrounded our camp."

Lucian swallowed. "*Sarnak?* My father and a few of his men traveled there, once we heard. To see if there was anyone left alive."

"That night, I walked through the sleep of Lady Beatriss," Evanjalin continued. "She dreamed of the cloister of Lagrami in Sendecane, and I knew it was a sign that I should go there. That after eight years I should stop traveling from one kingdom to another. I was tired and sick at heart, and for the first time since I was eight, I lost hope. But in the cloister of Lagrami, Finnikin came searching for me."

"Because the priestess sent a messenger," Finnikin said. "The messenger woke me and whispered Balthazar's name."

She shook her head. "There was no messenger, Finnikin. Someone whispered your name to me in my sleep. Telling me you would come. I told the High Priestess, 'Finnikin of the Rock will come for me.' To guide me." Evanjalin smiled, and it was a look of pure joy. "To my people."

"Let's keep moving," Perri said.

Finnikin grabbed his father's arm as the others ran ahead. "She's wrong. It was a messenger," he said forcefully. "I know it was. I remember it well. I remember because I was dreaming of Beatriss and I was angry to be woken from such a dream."

"What were you dreaming?" Trevanion asked.

"That you placed your babe in Beatriss's arms and she held her to the breast, feeding her with so much love, and that . . .

that . . ." Finnikin felt stunned, remembering things he had long forgotten.

Trevanion stopped, gripping his wrist. "Tell me more." It was almost a plea.

"Beatriss had the child to her breast," Finnikin went on, "and you were teasing her about the cloister of Lagrami, and Beatriss said, 'Little Finch, what say you? Will we give her to the cloister of Lagrami to keep her safe? As you pledged? As you pledged?' She kept repeating it." Finnikin shook his head, trying to make sense of his thoughts. "And now it seems that Evanjalin or Beatriss or someone else called me to the cloister of Lagrami in Sendecane that night."

Trevanion was silent for a moment. "Did she . . . seem happy?" he asked quietly. "In the dream?"

Finnikin knew he was speaking of Beatriss. "As happy as she always was when you were by her side," he said honestly. "So happy that it made me travel to the end of the earth without questioning where it would lead me."

When they stumbled into the foothills where the exiles slept, Trevanion called out an acknowledgment to the Monts who stood guard.

"Stay awhile," he told Finnikin and Lucian. "Sleep first, and then in the morning take Evanjalin and Froi up to your people, Lucian. Perri and I need to return to the Valley tonight. Saro will know to follow soon."

Lucian nodded, and Finnikin waited as Trevanion and Perri mounted their horses.

"Rest, Finn," his father said. "I fear there will be much for you to do when you reach the Valley of Tranquillity."

And with one last look at Finnikin, Trevanion and Perri headed west, where their exiled people waited.

At the edge of the camp, Finnikin and Lucian lay near one of the fires to dry their damp clothing. Evanjalin and Froi were already asleep, and Finnikin covered them with the fleece-lined coats.

"He was my hero. Balthazar," Lucian said quietly, looking at Finnikin over the small blaze.

"I think you were his," Finnikin acknowledged.

"No. I think half of him wanted to be Trevanion of the River and the other half Finnikin of the Rock." Lucian laughed. "I, of course, wanted to be Perri the Savage, although after tonight I'm not sure I have the stomach for it."

"There's more to our Perri."

Lucian leaned forward. "Anyway, I'm not sure Balthazar would have made the finest of kings."

"Why do you say such a thing?" Finnikin asked.

"Perhaps better than his father, but not like his mother. My family says the queen married beneath herself."

Finnikin snorted, careful not to wake Froi and Evanjalin. "Only you mountain goats would believe you're better than royalty."

"It's not conceit," Lucian said. "She had grit. She had a thirst for knowledge and a ruthlessness, passed on to her daughters, that any Mont would envy. The oldest princess, Cousin Vestie, would have been a great leader. Yata always said she had strength much like her mother, the queen. The king was . . . soft, especially with his cousin. So it was no shock to us that that scum beneath our boots found his way back into Lumatere as the impostor king."

"The impostor king was a pawn who was placed there by the king of Charyn in an attempt to use Lumatere as a road to invade Belegonia."

Lucian shrugged. "The king was weak with Charyn. He should have sent in the army the moment Charyn first stopped the goods wagons from the north."

He looked over at Froi and Evanjalin. "Do you know why I was certain Balthazar had died that night?" he asked.

Finnikin sighed, wanting to sleep. "Perhaps because you think you know everything?"

Lucian was in no mood for humor. "Does your wound weep? The one from the pledge?"

Finnikin nodded.

"So does mine, and that's how I know he's dead and has been from that night."

Finnikin said nothing.

"The wound lives because the pledge was real. It worked."

"Lucian . . ."

"What did we pledge that day on the rock of three wonders, Finnikin?" he whispered urgently.

Still Finnikin didn't respond. There was something about Lucian's tone that was causing his heart to hammer against his chest.

"Balthazar pledged to die protecting the royal house of Lumatere," Lucian said. "You pledged to be their guide. I pledged to be their beacon. And ten years later we are all here."

"Not all of us."

Lucian moved closer toward him. "Balthazar's pledge was that he would die protecting the royal house of Lumatere," he repeated, tears in his eyes. "Three witnesses saw him running through the Forest that night." Lucian shook his head in disbelief. "Not possible. Balthazar would *never* have allowed himself to live that night if Isaboe died. That's the difference between the king's son and the queen's daughters. The king's first priority was the survival of his wife and children. But the queen's? Survival of the people. Because the people were Lumatere."

"What are you saying?" Finnikin asked.

"Balthazar took from his father," Lucian said with force. "We all honored our pledge. And Seranonna of the Forest Dwellers and two others, who had no reason to lie, claimed to have seen a child running from the Forest that night. The child who stamped bloody handprints on the kingdom walls. I saw those handprints. All the Monts saw them that week we stayed in the Valley of Tranquillity. My father and his brothers had to drag my *yata* away from them."

Finnikin could hardly form words. Lucian looked slightly crazed as he pointed at the figure lying beside Finnikin.

"*Balthazar* protected her. *You* were her guide. You brought her here because she sensed her people. *I* was the beacon."

"*Isaboe*?" Finnikin said, his voice hoarse with shock. He stared at her sleeping figure as Lucian stood and drew his sword from its scabbard. Instantly the Mont was on guard, but Finnikin could not move. *Isaboe.* Why would he not have known? How could he not have recognized her? Worse still, he wondered with hurt and rage, why had she not trusted him? After all this time, when they had walked side by side? Yet he leaped to his feet beside Lucian. To do what he was born to do. Protect the royal house of their kingdom.

"You started this when you forced us to cut flesh from our bodies, Finnikin," Lucian whispered. "But I would do it a thousand times over to see our queen lead us back home to Lumatere."

## chapteR 23

When the sun appeared in the sky, Finnikin woke her with shaking hands. The exiles had left for the Valley with Saro's men at dawn. Still exhausted, Froi and Evanjalin begged for more sleep, but Finnikin shook his head. There was desperation in him, in Lucian too. To take her to Yata.

"It's only a short walk," he said quietly.

A few feet away, Saro of the Monts was talking with some of his men. He seemed surprised to see Lucian and Finnikin in the foothills and approached them with a questioning look on his face. Until he saw her.

"This is where it begins," Lucian whispered.

A look of intense shock crossed Saro's face. Sensing him, Evanjalin looked up from where she was crouched, tying her boots, then stood and walked toward him. When she reached him, she bent to kneel in respect for the Mont leader. Horrified, Saro pulled her to her feet in the same way Sir Topher had once reacted when Evanjalin tried to kneel at Trevanion's feet. Sir Topher knew, Finnikin realized, had always known. A queen never bent to her people.

Saro of the Monts held his hand out to her, and she took it calmly. Finnikin watched as she walked alongside her uncle. The higher they climbed, the more hurried her footsteps, her fingers clenching and unclenching by her side. Saro looked down at her, and the Mont leader's shoulders shook, overcome with the strength of his feelings.

But when they reached the settlement, she stopped and turned, and her eyes found Finnikin's. He wanted desperately to protect her. To hide her. To take her away to a place where he could pretend she was a novice named Evanjalin. And there they both stood for a moment. Until she turned and walked toward Yata, who stood in the distance laughing at something with Sir Topher as they went about their morning chores. And then the queen of Lumatere broke free of her uncle's hand, a sob escaping her throat as she sprang toward her grandmother, who stared like she'd seen an apparition.

"*Yata!*" Isaboe's cry of anguish rang through the hills. Her body pressed against her *yata,* collapsing under the weight of her memories and grief as the names poured out of her mouth. Names of her sisters and brother, mother and father, echoing with a sorrow that seemed as if it would never end.

Yata's tent, where the queen stayed, was heavily guarded that night. Out of respect for the family and a need to be alone, Finnikin had kept his distance. But his desire to see her was strong. The need to lie by her side and gather her to him was so fierce that it made him weak.

As he went to enter the tent, four of the queen's cousins stepped in front of him, swords in their hands.

"I'm with the queen," he said firmly.

The Mont who seemed to be in charge shook his head. "She's with her family and the queen's First Man," he was told. "Who are you to her?"

Who was he to the queen of Lumatere?

Lucian appeared before he could answer. "He's with us, lads," he said, stepping back to allow Finnikin to enter.

He could not see her from where he stood. Saro and his brothers and wives and their children were clustered around the middle of the tent. He could see Sir Topher, his head bent close to Saro as the two men spoke.

"They trapped the silver wolf," Lucian whispered as they sat at the edge of the tent. "In the hole we dug and covered with foliage."

"Who?"

"Balthazar and Isaboe. That night. And when the assassin gave chase, Balthazar hid Isaboe in a burrow and led him to the trap."

Finnikin stared, horrified.

"Isaboe later returned to the main gate," Lucian continued, watching the scene around Yata's bed, "but the bodies of the royal family had already been discovered and the gate was closed. She knew something terrible must have happened in the palace as it had in the forest. So she returned to the Forest and went searching for Seranonna and led her to where . . . Balthazar"—Lucian shuddered—"lay dead alongside the assassin in the dugout. Torn to pieces. The wolf still lived."

"They buried the wolf alive with Balthazar and the assassin?" Finnikin asked hoarsely.

Lucian shook his head. "Isaboe would not allow her brother to be buried beside the assassin. She was afraid it would keep the gods from taking Balthazar to his rightful place in the afterlife. She killed the wolf with Balthazar's crossbow. She said Finnikin of the Rock had taught her how to shoot as a child. Seranonna retrieved the bodies of both the animal and Balthazar and buried them together. Then the death bells from the palace began to sound. Seranonna knew that Isaboe might be the only surviving member of the royal family. She made sure that whoever the assassins were, they would be led to believe that Isaboe had died, not Balthazar. So they would never search for a girl child."

"The clothes . . . hair . . ." Finnikin swallowed, not able to continue.

"Belonged to Isaboe. But the fingers . . . ears . . ."

"Mercy."

The queen was sleeping, her head resting on Yata's lap, as if the ten years of journeying had finally exhausted her. Yata caught Finnikin's eye among the crowds of people, and she beckoned him with her hand.

"She asks for you each time she wakes," she said, smiling as he approached.

*Who are you to her?*

He knelt beside the bed, wanting to reach out and touch the smooth flushed skin. "All this time she wanted to get home to you," he said quietly.

Yata shook her head. "No. She is mine for these few precious moments, Finnikin, and I will be selfish and take every opportunity to hold her to me. But all this time she needed to get home to her people of Lumatere." She took his hand and placed it alongside the queen's cheek. "Is she not the image of my precious girl?" she asked, tears in her eyes. "My other sweet lovelies were the image of their good father, the king, who treated my daughter like a queen from the moment he first saw her. But this one? This one was our little Mont girl."

Finnikin looked up at Saro. "If I could be so bold, Saro. Please send your people ahead to the Valley tonight and allow us to keep our traveling party small. It will be dangerous to draw attention to ourselves this close to Lumatere, and the protection of the queen is paramount. We must inform Trevanion that Queen Isaboe is returning to the Valley to take her people home."

Saro nodded. "We will send word through my brothers."

"We leave at first light," Finnikin said.

They left the hills of Osteria the next morning with the last of the Monts. The queen rode in the middle of the group with Finnikin. At times he felt her tears against his back, and he knew they were for him as much as for her. What was about to take place in the Valley outside the kingdom was a mystery to them all, and he sensed her fear as her hands clutched him tight. Strong hands, he had once observed when they stole the horse in Sarnak. They would need to be to lead a kingdom. Heal a people. On either side of them rode Saro and Lucian, and in front Yata, Sir Topher, and Froi. They were quiet. They knew too much not to be. The entry into Lumatere would cost the Monts dearly, if not through the loss of their queen then through the loss of their men. After ten years of keeping their people safe from harm, Saro and his men would be the first to enter the gate after the Guard.

Before they reached the Valley, Finnikin stopped. They were traveling along a narrow path between wheat fields that shimmered on either side.

"I need you to come with me," he said quietly to Lucian. "Saro, can you take care of the queen? We will not be long."

She gripped his hand. "Let me come, Finnikin."

"You'll be safer here," he said gently.

Lucian followed him to a place among the crops, and Finnikin wasted no time in speaking. "I need you to pledge," he told the Mont when he was sure no one could hear them.

"Definitely *not* from my upper thigh."

"We don't have time to argue. Just bleed and pledge to the goddess."

"Lagrami or Sagrami?"

"Goddess complete." Finnikin held out his dagger, and Lucian stared at it for a moment before taking it and making an incision across his arm. He handed the dagger back to Finnikin and waited for him to repeat the action, but Finnikin shook his head.

"Just you."

"Whatever it is, we pledge together, Finnikin," Lucian said firmly.

"Pledge that you will kill me—"

Lucian stepped away from him in fury. "You go too far."

Finnikin grabbed the Mont by his shirt. "Pledge that you will kill me if I am ever a threat to the queen."

Lucian shrugged free. "I will kill anyone who is a threat to my queen," he said through gritted teeth.

"Pledge, Lucian. *Please.*"

"A blind man can see what she feels for you and you for her. Your souls are not merely entwined; they are fused. There is your threat, Finnikin. Why can't you just tell her you love her and pretend you live normal lives like the rest of us damned mortals?"

"Pledge it! I beg you as my blood brother."

Lucian traced a line across Finnikin's arm with his dagger. "Balthazar's pledge," he said forcefully. "That I protect the royal house of Lumatere. The queen." He looked at Finnikin. "And the one she chooses to be her king."

Froi leaned his head on Finnikin's horse beside where the queen sat, desperate to see the captain and Perri and Moss. Then everyone would start scowling and yelling orders again and he would know that things were back to normal. The night before, he had overheard the Mont lads talking about Finnikin and the queen. He hated the way they called Evanjalin the queen, as if she wasn't a person anymore. The Mont lads were whispering about the force needed to break the curse at the main gate and one of them called

Finnikin a skinny trog and Froi wanted to tell them that he had seen Finnikin fight and that he was better than all of them. Then the other Mont lad whispered that Finnikin or the queen would probably die at the gate because the curse was so strong, and it would probably be Finnikin because he wasn't used to the darkness. Froi knew the captain wouldn't let Finnikin or Evanjalin do anything that would cause them harm, so he was glad when Finnikin and Lucian returned so they could get down to the Valley and the captain could take charge and forbid Finnikin from doing anything that could end in his death.

He watched as Finnikin swung onto the horse, his sleeve stained with blood. Froi liked the way Finnikin reached behind him and took Evanjalin's hand, placing it around his waist. It made everything seem normal because Finnikin always wanted to touch her.

"Let's go," Finnikin said quietly, and like each time he had spoken on this day, everyone listened and followed.

## CHAPTER 24

Whi hen they reached the hill overlooking the Valley of Tranquillity, Finnikin saw the tempest. It was impossible to approach the Valley and not see the dark clouds shrouding the kingdom beyond. But it was what lay just ahead of them that took his breath away. Not a valley, but a sea. Of people. Tens of hundreds of them waiting to go home. Finnikin heard the queen's sob behind him.

"I want to walk," she said urgently, slipping off the horse. He followed, trailing her, his hand resting on the handle of his sword, ready for anything that might go wrong. There were too many people, any one of them a threat to her. He was used to small camps of exiles, but not half the kingdom.

As they reached the edge of the crowd, he became aware of the energy around them. At the other end of the settlement was a training camp where weapons were being made and men were taking target practice. In other areas, people stood in clusters talking and arguing, and he recognized Lord August and Lady Abian with those from the Flatlands, distributing food among their group.

Finnikin caught a glimpse of Trevanion and the Guard patrolling the boundaries on horseback, and for the first time in days he felt relief. As if Trevanion sensed them, he turned to face the slope where Finnikin and Evanjalin stood. He exchanged a word with his men, and then the Guard was making its way toward them and Finnikin was nine years old again, his chest bursting with pride because he would never see anything as grand as his father astride a horse leading his men.

Trevanion dismounted, his hand coming out to grip Finnikin's shoulder. Finnikin knew this was not just a greeting. It was an acknowledgment of what would take place in the next few days beyond the main gate. Trevanion's men dismounted, and all around them groups of exiles stopped to see what was taking place.

And then the captain of the Guard reached the queen. He knelt and then lay prostrate on the path before her, his men following his lead as a hush came over the settlement.

Finnikin saw the tears in her eyes as she stared down at her men. She looked small and vulnerable and he feared for her, but then he remembered that Isaboe, the youngest daughter of the king and queen of Lumatere, had walked thousands of miles over ten years to get to this place. And it was this, he knew, that caused his father to bow down to her more than her royal bloodline. The Lumateran royal family truly came from the gods. Never had Finnikin believed it more than in this moment watching his father lie before their queen.

After some time, Trevanion stood. Finnikin held out his hand to her. Quietly, hesitantly, she walked the path among the exiles. There was silence, but Finnikin knew that these people were stunned. A hand snaked out toward the queen, and in an instant Finnikin had stepped in front of her, sword in hand. But she gently touched his arm and moved around him. Despite Finnikin's hold on her, she was swallowed by the crowd, yet she pushed through them, becoming a part of them.

"Don't let go of her, Finnikin," he heard Trevanion say.

They were jostled from side to side, hands reaching out, wanting to touch the queen, to see if she was real, to convince themselves they were truly going home. Yet the queen seemed to take it in her stride, as if she had been born for this. Born to it. And at last Finnikin understood why he had felt so sorrowful and silent these last few days.

He knew how to be Finnikin of the Rock to Evanjalin of the Monts. But he had no idea who to be to Queen Isaboe.

Finnikin watched Lord August and his family come toward them, and then the queen was engulfed by the women. Behind Lord August, he could see Ambassador Corden and his entourage approaching, looking flustered. Instinctively, Finnikin pulled the queen toward him.

"Everyone must step back," Ambassador Corden said, full of self-importance. "Finnikin, is that you behind all that hair? It is not right to touch the queen. Step away! Lady Celie, would you be kind enough to find some proper attire for Her Majesty?"

Lord August looked unimpressed. He fell in step beside Finnikin as they followed the entourage to the main tent.

"I'm presuming you knew about this the whole time as well," Finnikin said, watching the ease with which the women conversed.

"Of course I didn't," the duke snapped, irritated. "Because I'm not married to an obedient novice of Lagrami, am I? I'm married to one who chose to tell me about the queen only as we entered this valley."

"Do you suppose the queen told them while we were in your home last month?"

Lord August nodded. "Abie saw it instantly. She knew our previous queen well. And Evanjalin confirmed who she was to my wife and daughter."

As they approached the main tent, a party of nobles dressed in silks came toward them.

"Lord Castian and his mob. Try not to fall asleep as he speaks," Lord August muttered.

Long days of waiting followed. Two thousand and twelve exiles had returned, and more trickled in each day. Finnikin could not help but think of the Valley as it had been ten years ago on the day of the curse, back when they had no idea what lay ahead but the clearest memory of what they had left behind. Now the years had numbed their people into silence, as again they waited for the unknown, too frightened to hope for anything more than a queen in their midst. But there was no news of when they would attempt to access the main gate and little was seen of her.

Finnikin spent his time with his father and the Guard as they drew up plans for the attack.

"When we get past the main gate," Trevanion informed his men, squeezed into an overcrowded tent, "we attack them on ground with as many as one thousand missiles in the first minute. I want the impostor king and his men decimated with the sheer volume of our arrows, and I want our body count close to nothing. Then the Guard takes the palace, along with the best of the archers and swordsmen among the exiles."

"But how do we get past the main gate?" one of the guards asked.

"The queen will know what to do," Trevanion said firmly, daring anyone to challenge him. He looked over to Saro, who had joined them with Lucian and a number of the Monts. "The moment the bastards know we're in, they'll ride to the mountains and attempt to cross the border to Charyn. The Charynites may be waiting there to invade once they see the curse has lifted. They will want the impostor king dead almost as much as we do, for no other reason than to stop him from talking. Saro, you ride to your Mountains the moment we enter. Take all your warriors." Trevanion turned back to his Guard. "Make sure those of you working with a team of exiles explain to them their role before the fighting begins."

"When will we enter the kingdom?" Saro asked.

Trevanion's eyes met Finnikin's across the crowded tent. "It is the queen's decision," he said. "She is waiting for a sign."

Finnikin trained Sefton and the village lads who had been part of the group of exiles taken hostage by the Charynites. They were Finnikin's age, strong and sturdy young men. They had recognized Finnikin when he entered the Valley and trailed around after him, keen to play a part in the upcoming battle. Froi was usually close by. The thief spent his time being a messenger, racing from one end of the Valley to the other, ensuring that communication between the Guard, the nobility, the queen's First Man, the queen and the priest-king stayed open. Not once did the boy utter a word of complaint, and Finnikin felt a fierce protectiveness toward him. He came from strong stock, that was evident. But it was all they would ever know. There were no telltale signs of lineage. No memories of anything Lumateran before his days in Sarnak. Froi was one of the orphans of their land whose life as a Lumateran would begin at the age he was now.

On the fifth afternoon, while handpicking the swiftest archers from a group of exiles, Finnikin found himself being watched by Sir Topher and the priest-king. He had kept his distance from his mentor since the day they entered the Valley. The knowledge that Sir Topher had been aware of Evanjalin's identity stung Finnikin like a betrayal.

"Sir," Finnikin said politely. "Blessed Barakah." He felt the sharp gaze of the priest-king on him.

"I'll answer your question, Finnikin," Sir Topher said.

"I haven't asked one," Finnikin said gruffly.

"But you've wanted to," Sir Topher said gently, "from the moment it was revealed to you who she was."

Finnikin sighed. He gazed around the Valley, where many of the exiles were reacquainting themselves with their neighbors as they had their names recorded in the *Book of Lumatere*.

"Sefton, can you take over?" he called out. He led Sir Topher and the priest-king away from the training ground, toward the camp.

"Did she tell you, or did you work it out yourself?" he asked bluntly as they approached the secured area where the queen was staying.

"She suspected I knew," Sir Topher said truthfully, "but I never imagined that the youngest child of the king and queen would survive. That the tiny creature overshadowed by such brilliant and fearless siblings would be the one to live. Who would have thought?"

"Was it the ring?"

Sir Topher shook his head. "No. The ring was stolen in Lumatere years before the unspeakable. At first I thought her father must have been the thief. Trevanion explained the story she told about winning it back in Sarnak." He paused. "I began to suspect from the moment I truly looked at her face in Sprie. I was there, you see, when the king brought home the queen as a young woman, and each day for the next twenty years I looked

across at both their very dear faces. I knew the queen's manner-
isms, the king's expressions, the other children's traits. But then
in Sorel, when you were imprisoned, she said something to me
that I'd heard the king say more than once to each of his children.
'Be prepared for the worst, my love, for it lives next door to the
best.'"

"You never questioned me about the messenger who directed
us to the cloister in Sendecane," Finnikin said.

"Because there was such conviction in your voice. I trusted
you, and look where that trust has brought our people. We have
achieved what we always wanted, Finnikin. Our exiles together
on a piece of land. That itself is enough to give thanks for."

"But you didn't trust me enough to tell me what you suspected." Finnikin could not keep the hurt and anger out of his
voice.

"Because I needed you to choose our path, Finnikin, and I was
certain that the moment you knew that one of our beloveds lived,
guilt would force you into retreat. A childhood delusion makes
you believe that somehow your ambition and desires caused their
slaughter. Whereas I always believed you were born with the heart
of a king. A warrior. The true *resurdus*."

Finnikin shook his head.

"But I do doubt you," Sir Topher went on. "Because you doubt
yourself. Isaboe isn't just a queen, Finnikin. She is a valuable
asset. A tool to use, and she knows that more than anyone in this
kingdom. She was born with the knowledge, as were her sisters.
If you choose not to be her king, then we will need to make the
throne secure through alliances with Osteria or Belegonia."

Finnikin clenched his fist, and the arrow in his hand snapped
in half. Sir Topher looked at him with such concern that it made
Finnikin's eyes sting with tears.

"While you've been fighting the possibility of wearing the crown, perhaps others have been preparing you for it," the priest-king spoke up.

"A stolen crown, blessed Barakah. A dead boy's crown," Finnikin said fiercely. "Is it beyond my control? And hers? Have I meant nothing more to her all this time than the fulfillment of a prophecy?" He shook his head bitterly. "The gods make playthings of us, but I would like to have some control over the events of my life."

"Have you not done things according to your own free will, Finnikin?" the priest-king asked. "Because I heard a tale today. Of a twelve-year-old boy, who on a visit to Osteria, as a guest of our ambassador, came across his first exile camp. Nothing ever prepares you for that, does it, lad? You notice the strangest things. You see children whose thickest part of their body is their knees. I could never understand what kept them standing. This boy turned to his mentor that day and said, 'Tell me how to say, *Feed these people.*' But our ambassador and the boy's mentor would not respond. They were guests of the king of Osteria, and although they felt sorrow for the plight of their people they were unable to make it right. How many times had these grown men said to themselves, 'There is nothing I can do.' But the boy would not give up. So he learned the words from one of the Osterian servants, and that day he made his way up to the king of Osteria as he sat on his horse and shouted the words over and over again, 'Feed these people.' He even threw a rock at the king to get his attention. The King's Guard dragged the boy away, of course, and it took our ambassador thirty days to secure his release. Thirty days shackled to a stone wall in the palace dungeon. The punishment for humiliating a king."

Finnikin cast his eyes down.

"Look at me, lad," the priest-king said firmly. "Those people were fed, weren't they, Finnikin? Because grown men, including a king, were shamed by a twelve-year-old boy. And from that day on, the king's First Man taught his apprentice to speak the language of almost every kingdom in the land. True?"

Finnikin nodded reluctantly.

"The gods do make playthings of us," the priest-king acknowledged. "But it is we mortals who provide them with the tools."

As Finnikin approached the queen's tent, he saw Aldron standing guard.

"I need to see her," he said coldly.

"You're not on my list of people who are allowed in," Aldron said.

"Then may I ask where this list is?"

Aldron tapped his head. "It's up here."

"It's good to know that something is."

Aldron smiled in spite of himself. "I will notify her of your presence and ask if she is interested in seeing you." He turned his back for a moment and Finnikin swung him round, his face an inch from Aldron's, anger in every muscle of his body.

"Don't you *ever* turn your back on one who could be a threat to the queen," he snarled. "Don't you *ever* put her in that kind of danger again."

Suddenly Lord August and Sir Topher were there, pulling him away. "What is going on here?" Lord August demanded.

Aldron stared at Finnikin, shrugging his clothing back into place while the others waited for a response. He nodded to Finnikin as if in acknowledgment.

"Nothing," Aldron said quietly. "My mistake."

Inside the tent, Evanjalin stood in a corner, her body tense. A wife of one of the dukes, a self-appointed chaperone, stared at Finnikin with a stony countenance. Evanjalin was dressed in the same plain calico gown her *yata* had sewn for her, and there was almost a hungry relief on her face to see him, to see anyone familiar.

"I will find a way," he said, his voice husky, "to go through the main gate without your having to risk—"

"Finnikin, stop," she said quietly.

*Her blood will be shed for you to be king.*

"I will find a way," he said angrily, gripping her arms. "To keep you safe."

"This is what I always feared," she said. "That you would put me in an ivory tower and keep me hidden. Thank the goddess I didn't reveal the truth six months ago, Finnikin. I would still be in the cloister of Sendecane, or in some boring foreign court being protected."

"It's not right for you to be in here, young man," the duchess called out. "To be touching the queen in such a way!"

Finnikin ignored the woman and kept his eyes on Evanjalin. She was an asset. An article for trade. A commodity to sacrifice. He remembered Sir Topher's words in Lord August's home. *The princesses were always going to be sacrificed for the kingdom.*

"Lady Milla, would you be so kind as to leave us, please," Evanjalin said.

She knew how to be strong as well as polite. It was an order, and with a sniff and a last glare at Finnikin, the woman was gone.

"I have said this before, Finnikin. You cannot complete this journey without me by your side. Seranonna prophesied it. You will hold the two hands of the one you pledged to save. My hands," she said.

He recalled their conversation that night in the rock village in Yutlind Sud. When she had questioned the possibility of Balthazar surviving the reentry into Lumatere. All this time she had been frightened of dying at the main gate, yet nothing had stopped her. Her courage and fear tore up his insides.

It seemed a lifetime before he found his voice again. "Who is the dark and who is the light?" he asked.

"Perhaps we are both one and the other."

"And the pain that 'shall never cease'?"

Tears welled in her eyes. "That you should experience any pain because of me is an ache I can't bear."

"But what is the pain the curse speaks of?" he repeated gently.

For a moment she didn't respond. "Mine, Finnikin. And that of the whole of Lumatere."

"Then I'll share that burden with you. Now. This very moment."

She shuddered as if she had held her breath for far too long. It was there on her face. The acceptance of her fate.

"Do you need to speak to the Guard?" he asked. "To give them any instructions before I take you to the main gate?"

She nodded.

"We do this now, Evanjalin."

"Isaboe. My name is Isaboe."

Just before dawn they gathered in her tent. The queen, the queen's First Man, the priest-king, the captain of the Guard, the ambassador, five dukes and duchesses, Saro of the Monts, and Finnikin of the Rock.

There was no room for ceremony in such a small space, and the queen sat on the hard ground with the rest of them. Sir Topher nodded for her to begin, but it took a while before she spoke.

"This is my bequest," she said finally, "witnessed by the court of Lumatere in exile in the presence of the goddess complete."

There was a muttering from Lord Freychinat at the mention

of the goddess complete. The same Lord who had left his people behind in Lumatere without a second thought all these years, Finnikin thought bitterly.

"If the goddess wills that I am to enter the kingdom of the gods and not Lumatere this day, I appoint Sir Kristopher of the Flatlands as my successor to lead my people. In turn, Sir Topher, you are to appoint a leader for each province. My uncle is to govern the Mont people, and Lord August, the Flatlands. But those who are to govern the Rock and the Forest and the River will be chosen with the consideration of our people who have lived within the walls of Lumatere these past ten years."

More muttering and this time Finnikin glared at the perpetrators.

"Sir Ambassador, upon our taking back Lumatere, you will send word to the king and queen of every kingdom of Skuldenore. Tell them that the impostor rules no more and that any nation who chooses not to recognize Lumatere as a sovereignty led by either myself or my successor will be our enemy.

"You are to ensure Sarnak is notified that no access will be given to our river if they do not bring to justice those responsible for the slaughter of our people on their southern border two years ago. Advise them that I am witness to the massacre that took place. Also ensure it is made clear to the rest of the land that the kingdom of Lumatere recognizes the original inhabitants of Yutlind Sud, and honors the southern king's right to the throne in the south and the current king's right to the throne in the north." She turned to the priest-king. "Blessed Barakah, in time, and with the collaboration of both the worshippers of Lagrami and Sagrami, the goddess is to be worshipped complete."

There was silence when she finished speaking, and Finnikin saw her look to Sir Topher for approval. The queen's First Man stood and held out his hand to help her to her feet.

"May the blessing of the one goddess be with you all," she said quietly, before turning to Finnikin. "I am ready."

"Should the queen not be dressed . . . more appropriately?" Lady Milla sniffed.

Isaboe looked down at the shift given to her by her *yata*.

"At her coronation, the queen will be dressed appropriately," Finnikin bit out. "Today, we might approach things from a more practical point of view, Lady Milla. Unless you would like to take her place at the gate and the queen can dress in silks and relax in her tent?"

There were more mutterings between the dukes and duchesses about "impudence." Lady Abian gave them a withering look, but Lord Artor spoke up.

"If the queen enters Lumatere dressed—"

"The queen enters Lumatere dressed as she is!" Sir Topher said firmly. "There will be no more discussion about the queen's dress."

Isaboe gripped Finnikin's hand as they left the tent. "Do I not look like a queen?" she asked in a distressed whisper. "Is that what people are saying?"

He leaned forward to whisper in her ear. "They are saying you look like a goddess."

"It's time," Trevanion said.

Moss and Perri waited outside. "We've only got as far as the moat. A fierce force holds us back. As it always has," Moss informed them.

"All the way around?" Trevanion asked.

"At every border," Perri said.

Trevanion looked toward the tempest and then at Finnikin. "I will see you on the other side of the main gate," he said. "Do what you have to do, and I will see you within the walls where you will fight by my side. Do you hear me?"

Finnikin nodded, still gripping the queen's hand. Her face was pale, and her fear so potent that he felt nausea rise up in his throat.

"Perri will accompany you as far as he can," Trevanion said, gently cupping Isaboe's chin. There was a tsking sound from one of the duchesses, and Finnikin bit his tongue to not lash out at her.

"Tell them to move away, Sir Topher," Finnikin said. "They're upsetting the queen."

Accompanied by the Guard, Finnikin and the queen walked toward the tempest, where Lucian and Froi stood waiting. The queen quickly hugged her cousin and then stared at Froi. Finnikin could see the tears of anger in the boy's eyes.

"He had the better plan," Froi said, pointing at Finnikin. "Second Lumatere. No blood curses or spells or not knowing whever you live or die. We can stay here. People like it in the Valley. I heard them say. They just want you here wif them."

"Half her people are inside, Froi," Lucian said quietly. "And this is not a way to live."

Froi turned to Trevanion and Perri. "I'll never do anover evil fing if we stay here. Never. I will do anyfing you want. How can you let them do this, Captain? It's Finnikin and Evanjalin. I fort you loved him more than anyfing."

Trevanion did not respond. His face was pinched and unreadable.

The queen took Froi's hand and slipped something into it. He stared down before slowly opening his fingers. The ruby ring.

"It's worth everything, Froi. Priceless. Whether I return or not, it belongs to you for the rest of your life. Not because you deserve it, for I do not know how to measure the worth of one so young and I will never forget what you tried to do to me in that loft in Sorel. But when I look at it, I think of how loved I was by the owner of this ring, and by my mother and my precious sisters and my beloved brother. You asked me once what my magic was. That is my magic."

Froi held the ring miserably in his hand, clutching his body as if in pain.

Finnikin looked at his father one last time. Then he took the queen's hand and walked up to the main gate accompanied by Perri, until the guard was stopped by a force that pushed him back. He watched the queen turn around. The Guard sat on their horses, swords ready. Behind them an army of exiles held bows trained toward the kingdom walls. In the distance he saw Sir Topher and the queen's *yata*.

They took a step together, and suddenly Finnikin felt the path to the main gate beneath his feet.

On the grassy knoll, Trevanion stood with his men, holding his breath. And then the queen and Finnikin disappeared beyond the tempest and suddenly there was a gasp in unison across the Valley of Tranquillity.

"*Sagrami*," Perri said in wonder. "We're going home."

Finnikin stared at the gate in front of them. At the intricate beauty of the inscriptions around the edges, written in the language of the ancients. When he turned, the queen took a step back, trembling.

"I should be brave like the gods," she said quietly.

He held out his hand. "Each time the gods have whispered your name to me, their voices have trembled."

Her eyes were fixed on the gate. "We would sneak out each night because I wanted to see the unicorn."

Finnikin remembered the lies they would tell Isaboe, of the unicorn in the forest that would appear only to a princess.

"How did you get past my father's guard at this gate?"

"One morning Balthazar and I were playing in the garden, along that narrow stretch where the walls of the kingdom and the outer walls of the palace merge into one. Balthazar decided we would scrape our names on one of the stones of the wall so that one day another young prince or princess might know that Balthazar and Isaboe had lived there. As we carved our names, we found that a stone in the wall had become dislodged. Perhaps it happened during the tremor of years before. For months after, deep in the night, we would sneak out of the palace through the cook's chamber and crawl through the wall into the forest." She looked at him with sorrow. "Because I wanted to see the unicorn. And all that time the enemy was watching us and that's how they came into my home and slaughtered my family. Because I wanted to see the unicorn."

"No," he said gently. "Balthazar wanted to trap the silver wolf. It's all we spoke about."

He held both hands out to her, to fulfill the words of the curse. She took his hands and he heaved against the gate, hoping it might miraculously fall open. Nothing.

"The blood on your hands that night? Do you remember where it came from?" he asked.

"Here and here," she said, touching her knuckles and palms. "From knocking at the . . ."

They both realized at the same moment and he took one of her hands and led her along the wall, his fingers tracing any mark. And then he saw them. So tiny and faded with years. The bloody imprint of Isaboe's hand.

She slowly reached out and measured her hand over the imprint, her palm against the cold stone. With shaking hands he removed his knife from its scabbard.

"I'm going to have to cut you here," he said, kissing her palm gently. "Did the blood come from any other wound?"

She shook her head. "I had little blood on me until I returned to bury Balthazar. What kind of a person leaves behind their beloved brother to be mauled by an animal?"

"A smart one, my queen."

She took his face in her hands. "Do you know what Balthazar's last words were? Find Finnikin of the Rock. He'll know what to do. But I couldn't find you, Finnikin. For so long I couldn't find you."

He wiped her tears tenderly. "When it begins, don't look away from me. Keep your eyes fixed on mine. Remember my face when you lie between neither here nor there. Let it be your guide to come back from wherever the goddess chooses to take us."

She nodded. "Let me hear you say my name," she said softly.

"Isaboe." He whispered it, his mouth close to hers. "Isaboe."

"Do not despair in the darkness, Finnikin. It will be my despair you sense, but I have never allowed it to overtake me, so do not let yourself be consumed."

As gently as he could, he pressed the tip of his dagger across both her palms and then his.

"Tell me about the farm," she pleaded as drops of blood began to appear on her hands.

"The farm?"

"The farm that Finnikin the peasant would have lived on with his bride."

"Evanjalin. That was her name. Did I mention that?"

She laughed through a sob. "No, you didn't."

"They would plant rows upon rows of wheat and barley, and

each night they would sit under the stars to admire what they owned. Oh, and they would argue. She believes the money made would be better spent on a horse, and he believes they need a new barn. But then later they would forget all their anger and he would hold her fiercely and never let her go."

"And he'd place marigolds in her hair?" she asked.

He clasped her hands against his and watched her blood seep through the lines of his skin. "And he would love her until the day he died," he said. He placed his other bloody hand against those imprinted for eternity on the kingdom walls.

They had never spoken about what would happen at this point. Whether the gate would open and Lumatere would be revealed. If the darkness would disappear in front of their eyes and the bluest of skies welcome them home. But Finnikin only had a moment for such imaginings before the ground began to shake beneath their feet, and the tempest became one with him, its murky cloud entering his body. Polluting him. And so he heard every cry of those who had lost their lives during the five days of the unspeakable and those slaughtered in Sarnak and those who died in the camps. And he walked every one of the sleeps the novice Evanjalin had taken. Not just of the innocent, but of their enemies within the gates: the assassins, the rapists, and the torturers. Until her memories shattered the fragments of his mind, filled it with rage, and when he thought he could bear it no longer, she was there. He felt her. Inside him. Soaking up his darkness until it consumed her and she fell at his feet.

And then the earth stopped moving and the gate lay open and he heard the war cries from the Guard as their horses pounded past him. But Lumatere was already awash with flames. The silence Finnikin had imagined from within was a roar that blasted his senses as he stumbled with her in his arms into a blazing hell.

## CHapteR 25

Finnikin staggered away from the road that led to the palace, carrying the queen toward the bridge that would take them to a meadow in the Flatlands. He needed to lay her down so he could breathe life back into her. He needed to rid himself of the murky images of horror that were now part of his own memory. But like the rest of Lumatere, the meadow was ablaze.

Falling to his knees, he clutched her, covering her body with his own. The thick smoke smothered and blinded him, and he sobbed with fury at the futility of dying in this meadow in their homeland. If he could have found words, he would have opened his mouth and roared his anger to the gods. His only consolation was that Isaboe was unable to see the ruins of her beloved kingdom, a kingdom that had soaked up too much of her family's blood. Cursed land, Sir Topher had once said. Cursed people.

His head spun as everything turned to white, and the emptiness was so soul-chilling that he almost prayed for the rot inside him to return. If this was death, where was the light he had been promised? Where was his mother, Bartolina of the Rock? From the moment he could understand words he had been promised by Trevanion that his mother would be there at his death. And where was Balthazar, the mightiest of warriors, who hid beloved Isaboe in a burrow and leaped into the mouth of a wolf to save their future queen?

He closed his eyes, wanting to see something that made sense. But he knew Isaboe would have scolded him for doing such a thing, so he stopped waiting for what made sense and instead turned to what brought hope. He staggered to his feet with the queen in his arms and walked forward blindly.

He heard it before he saw it, and prayed it did not belong to the impostor king and his men. And then it was before him, a horse and cart, steered by a white-haired creature. Ghost or witch?

"Lay the queen on the ground and step back!" she screeched, jumping from the cart, holding a double-edged sword above her head.

She was a tiny woman, but there was wildness in her eyes. Up close, he saw a face the age of Lady Abian, yet the woman's hair was prematurely white. Slowly his senses returned and he heard men roar and the sound of arrows flying in the distance, but he refused to let go of the queen, a snarl escaping his lips when the witch stepped closer.

"Lay the queen on the ground I say!"

"You risk your life if you take another step!" he shouted above the noise. He looked over and saw three young novices crouched in the cart, terror on their faces as they looked from him to the woman. The creature came toward him with the sword in her hands.

"Step back or you die," he hissed.

"You cannot hold the queen and kill me at the same time, boy," she jeered, pressing the sword to his throat. "Lay her on the ground."

"She stays with me."

He wanted to hurt this creature. The feeling was so intense that it took everything inside of him to fight against it. He stepped forward with Isaboe in his arms and felt the witch's sword press into the flesh of his throat. But still their eyes stayed locked.

"*Stop!*"

The word was accompanied by screams from the novices. Perri stood at the rear of the cart. His sword was already stained with blood, and Finnikin could see the battle rage in his eyes as he stared at the strange creature between them. Two of the young girls in the cart scuttled to its corners, while the third stared at Finnikin and Perri. "*Demons,*" she hissed.

"Step away from the cart!" the white-haired woman said. The vehemence in her voice was directed at Perri, but Finnikin saw the sword in her hand tremble.

Perri took a step back, and Finnikin read more in the guard's face than he had ever seen before. "Give Tesadora the queen, Finnikin," he said.

Tesadora of the Forest Dwellers directed her gaze back to Finnikin, slowly lowering her sword. "The boy from the rock with the pledge in his heart. I expected someone mightier in build."

"Your father needs you by his side, Finn," Perri said.

Finnikin refused to move, looking down at Isaboe. She felt cold in his arms, and he shook his head fervently.

"Finnikin, if you lay her in the cart, they will do all they can to help. Tesadora may be the only one who can save her."

There was something in Perri's voice that made him surrender the queen; he knew Perri trusted no one but the Guard and Trevanion. Perri moved toward Finnikin to help him lay her on the cart, but Tesadora hissed and the young novices cried out in fear.

"Not a step closer," Tesadora threatened. "Put her on the ground and move away."

"We will not touch your girls, Tesadora," Perri said impatiently. "Let us place her on the cart."

The novices stared at Finnikin as he settled Isaboe on the cart beside them. Stared as if he was some sort of fiend. Had he turned into one? Could they see the darkness in his eyes? Slowly he bent and placed his lips against Isaboe's cold skin, and then the cart jolted away.

"Do not let the darkness consume you, Finnikin of the Rock." With the reins firmly in her hands, Tesadora disappeared beyond the dark clouds of smoke with Isaboe safely nestled in the arms of the novices.

As Finnikin followed Perri into battle, the lust for killing consumed him. Each time he stared into the eyes of his enemy, he saw a madman responsible for the pain of every one of their people who had burned at the stake, died by the sword, swung from a rope, shuddered with the fever, ached with hunger. Worse, he felt the grief of their loved ones who had stood and watched helplessly. This was the agony that had made the novice Evanjalin stumble after she walked the sleep, her face pinched, her heart black with despair. He could save her from an enemy with a sword, but how could he shield her from her people's suffering?

One thousand arrows had found their target within the first minute. As the enemy began to fall, Trevanion's men and the Monts unleashed a wrath borne of ten years of exile. Axes broke bones. Blades sliced flesh. Men who once were farmers cut down the enemy like crops of wheat.

By early evening they had breached the palace gate and entered the grounds where half the impostor king's men had retreated. Finnikin watched as the area that had been his playground as a child became a slaughterhouse. But there were reports that a mightier battle was raging farther in the kingdom. According to one of the Guard, Saro and the Monts were fighting an enemy group that included the impostor king, at the foot of the mountains. Leaving Perri in charge, Trevanion and Finnikin leaped onto their mounts. As they rode through the kingdom, Finnikin took in the inferno around them. Every Flatland village was on fire. He prayed that the villagers had escaped their burning homes. He could not endure the thought of having to search these cottages for the charred remains of their people in the days to come.

When they reached the foot of the mountains, they were confronted by the sight of a hundred men in fierce combat. The Monts were savage in their attack, and Finnikin knew that no Mont would allow the impostor's men to reach the summit of their mountain. He caught glimpses of Lucian and saw what set him apart from the other lads. Not just sheer bulk, but a perfect symmetry in the swing of his ax, an ability to achieve in seconds what took others minutes. Lucian did not hesitate as he fought alongside his father. It was as if he had waited a lifetime to avenge his cousins, and this was the day of reckoning. But Finnikin wondered when his own need for revenge would be satisfied, whether thrusting his sword into enemy flesh and watching the blank open stare of death could make up for what had been lost these ten years. He had never seen anything as brutal as the battle to reclaim Lumatere. He fought close to his father, at times almost sobbing with fatigue, wanting to beg for a sword to be plunged into his body to end it all. But each time he sensed Trevanion by his side. "Stay with me, Finn. Don't let me bury a son this day."

They had always known they would lose some of their own, and as night descended, Finnikin saw Saro of the Monts fall, a sword through his throat. Where he fought, Lucian stopped for the first time in hours, his face registering the anguish.

*"Fa! Fa!"*

The Mont stumbled away from his opponent, and Finnikin watched with horror as the impostor's soldier raised his weapon. Finnikin threw his dagger and caught the man between the eyes. "Lucian! Lucian! Protect yourself!"

Then Finnikin was running toward Lucian with his bow. Aiming, shooting, running. Aiming, shooting, running. But the Mont could only think of getting to Saro. He fell at his father's side and gathered him into his arms, his hoarse cry mingling with the clash of steel against steel. Until Finnikin could hear no more sound from Lucian but saw the pure sorrow. And on a day he believed he could feel nothing more, his heart seemed to shatter as he flew onto the Mont's body to shield him.

When he looked up, Finnikin saw the angel of death above him, an ax raised over his head. He knew he would die. The jagged blade would split his head like a watermelon. And in those seconds before death, he kept his eyes on his father fighting less than ten feet away. He wanted his last thoughts to be of this man. And of her.

But the ax, and the hand attached to it, went flying through the air, and the enemy crashed to the ground in front of him. Finnikin stumbled to his feet and stared into the face of the exile from Lastaria. The man held out a hand to him and pulled him to his feet, and then he was gone.

Without hesitation, Finnikin turned back to Lucian and stood guard, lobbing arrows toward anyone who dared to enter the Mont's circle of grief.

Later, those who had lived the horror inside the kingdom for ten long years spoke of vindictive retribution. As if the bastard king, as they called him, had sensed that Lumatere was about to be reclaimed and set their world alight. Those of the Flatlands and the River hid with those of the Rock and watched as their kingdom was razed to the ground, watched from up high as their lost ones entered the gate and fought the bastard king and his men on the path leading up to the palace.

Some said it was the end of days and planned to climb to the highest point of the rock of three wonders, where they would plunge to their deaths.

But a sliver of hope stopped them. Hope created by a promise scratched into the arm of a child.

The promise that Finnikin of the Rock would return with their queen.

## CHAPTER 26

When it was finally over and Trevanion stared into the face of the impostor, he wondered how such a pitiful human being had created such despair in all their lives. It had been his order to keep the impostor and nine of his men alive, but he fought hard against the urge to plunge his sword into this man's heart.

"Trevanion," Finnikin said quietly as one of the guards threw the prisoners into the back of a cart, their mouths gagged, their hands and feet chained. Trevanion knew that every member of his Guard itched to snuff the life out of these bastards.

"Don't worry, Finn. They'll get there alive," he said soberly. "Perhaps just not in one piece."

When he returned to the palace village, the dead and dying had been dragged into the main square. Villagers tended the wounded, and Trevanion suspected they had emerged from their cottages in the darkest part of the night, when the battle had raged at its worst. Now the world was silent, but for the sounds from those who lay dying. This was no place for triumph or celebration.

"Captain, you wounded," Froi said, following Trevanion as he weaved his way toward Perri.

"How many lost?" Trevanion asked Perri.

"Too many," Perri muttered. "The impostor king?"

"Imprisoned in the palace with the rest of his scum," Trevanion said, looking at the wretchedness around him. When he asked about the queen, he could sense Froi's anxiety, almost as if the boy had stopped breathing.

"With those from the cloister of Sagrami," Perri said quietly.

"We need to count them," Trevanion said, gesturing to where the dead had been laid out at the edge of the square.

Froi's expression was one of acceptance. "I know. Make myself useful and count the dead."

Trevanion grabbed his arm. "A sorry task. Mine, not yours. Return to the Valley of Tranquillity and tell Sir Topher that Lumatere is free from the impostor king. Then find the priest-king and bring him home."

Trevanion looked over to where August of the Flatlands sat with his head in his hands, between the body of his sister's husband and Matin, one of Augie's men. He remembered the excitement that night in Augie's home, the bantering and the fierce friendship between these kinsmen. The key Matin had showed him. "It is the key to my house in Lumatere," he said. "I keep it in my pocket at all times as a reminder that I will return one day."

Trevanion had seen Saro fall, as well as Ced, one of the younger guards. Ced had been the first into the palace grounds and the first of his men to die. Ced, the last of a bloodline. Already Trevanion felt their absence from the earth. In the makeshift morgue, he closed the eyes of one of the men they had rescued from the Charynites on the river not even seven days past.

And then Trevanion saw her. When the sun began to appear in the blood-red sky as Lumatere continued to burn. She stood with fresh linens in her arms at the edge of the square. Between them lay rows and rows of corpses and the wounded she had come to tend.

A child was by her side, a miniature Beatriss, with eyes the color of the sky.

He thought of the child they had created together, the child who had died in the palace dungeons where the impostor king was now imprisoned. His face reflected the rage and hatred he felt toward those who had taken so much from him.

And Beatriss of the Flatlands saw the fury as he looked at her child.

Saw the hatred.

And quietly she covered the child's eyes and walked away.

Later, Trevanion returned to the foot of the mountain, where the Monts were collecting their dead. With a sickness in the pit of his stomach, he went searching for Finnikin. He found him with Lucian, sitting alongside Saro's body, their heads bent with exhaustion and grief. Both stood when he reached them, and Trevanion placed his hands on Lucian's shoulders, kissing him in the Mont tradition of respect.

"The last thing we spoke of, Saro and I, was how blessed we were as fathers, and the joy and pride we felt in our sons, Lucian."

Lucian nodded, unable to speak.

"I need to take my father home," he said finally.

"I will have the Guard take care of that, Lucian."

"No. I will carry my father home now. So I can lay his still warm body on our mountain. It's all he spoke of these past ten years. Returning to his mountain."

Finnikin crooked an elbow around Lucian's neck and pressed the Mont's forehead against his face. Then Trevanion stood by his son as they watched Lucian tenderly lift his father's body and carry him away.


"Will you come with me to the river?" Trevanion asked. Most of the Monts, except those tending the dying, had left.

Finnikin nodded listlessly. He was numb as he followed his father. In the morning light, villagers had appeared as if from nowhere. It was eerie to see so many faces, yet hear no sound. They looked different from the exiles. No better or worse, but damaged all the same. He wanted to feel a sense of home, as he had always dreamed he would. Lumaterans were connected to the land, yet he feared the dislocation for him would last forever. He had once read in a book from the ancients that one could never truly return home after years of absence. Was he cursed with such a fate?

He swung onto the back of Trevanion's horse, and they rode through their smoldering land, following the waterway that wound through the Flatlands, where the blackened stumps and leafless trees looked like skeletons, specters of death. Cottages were burned to the ground, and the barges on the river were nothing more than black pieces of timber floating on stagnant water. Finnikin sat on the banks with his father. Above them in the Rock Village, Lumaterans emerged in the hundreds.

"Tell me," Trevanion said, his face blackened with ash and streaked with blood. "At the gate with Evanjalin? What took place?"

"Isaboe," Finnikin corrected quietly. He rubbed his eyes, wondering when everything would stop looking blurred. "She lied."

There was silence before his father spoke. "The queen omits rather than lies, Finnikin. For a purpose. One that will humble us each time. I feel shame that I can hardly remember the child who grew up to be the novice Evanjalin. I remember the older princesses and Balthazar, but not the little girl."

"She omitted. Walking the sleep was not the only part of the gift. Or curse." Finnikin laughed bitterly. "Oh, to have such a gift. To sense the pain every single time a Lumateran suffers. She feels every death, every torture, every moment of grief. And when she walked the sleep of those inside, it was not just that of our helpless people." He looked at his father. "She walked the sleep of the assassins," he whispered, his voice catching. "Those of the impostor King's Guard who were Lumateran."

Trevanion cursed.

"The king died last. They made him watch, and what they did to those princesses and his queen I will never repeat as long as I live. But Isaboe knows, for she walked the sleep of a monster who was witness to it, and if I could have *one* wish in my life," he said through gritted teeth, "it would be that I could tear from her mind the memory of such depravity. Sweet goddess, that I would have such a gift. I would give my life for it." And then he was sobbing, despairing at his uselessness.

Trevanion watched Finnikin, unable to offer any hope. That men could conquer kingdoms and fight armies of such power and might, yet not be able to offer comfort to one so beloved. Where Finnikin's wish was to have the power to remove the ugliness of memory, Trevanion's was to have the gift of words needed to bring solace to his son.

"Finn, look," he said after a while. "The river's beginning to flow."

As Trevanion and Finnikin rode back into the palace village, the first exiles from the Valley entered Lumatere through the main gate. Froi was leading the priest-king, and the silence of those walking into the kingdom seemed strained.

Lumaterans stared at each other as strangers. Those who had tended the injured within the palace grounds walked to a nearby hill and watched the procession of exiles coming toward them. Finnikin and Trevanion swung off their horse and made their way between the villagers. Finnikin could hear Trevanion's name being whispered. And his. They must have looked frightening with their knotted hair and blood-soaked clothing. Beside him, he heard a sharp cry, and a moment later he was jostled out of the way by one of the women. She stood on her toes, her neck outstretched as she searched through the exiles coming their way.

"Asbrey, my brother," she said quietly. She spun around to look at the older man standing behind her. "*Fa*? It's Asbrey, your son, with a babe in his hands." Her eyes stayed on the group behind Froi and the priest-king, and then she placed a hand over her mouth as if to hold back a sob. "And my ma."

Finnikin turned to look at the man. His eyes were dull with shock, but his daughter began running, stumbling toward her family as she called out their names. Finnikin saw an expression of annoyance cross Froi's face when he sensed the commotion around him. The thief stood in front of the priest-king while the exiles behind him began to push past, trying to get to the young woman. But one of them tripped at Froi's feet, the one holding the baby, and the priest-king managed to catch the child and thrust it into Froi's hands to keep it from being smothered. So

Froi held it high above their heads as it proclaimed its freedom, the cries heard all across the village and the square beyond and the palace up above.

And it was this image that was stamped on the hearts and minds of all who were present that day.

Of Froi of the Exiles holding the future of Lumatere in his hands.

# part three

*All the Queen's Women*

## chapter 27

From where Trevanion stood, he could see nothing but burnt stumps and acrid smoke. It had been a week since they had entered Lumatere. Longer since the deposed impostor king heard the strange whispers from those inside the kingdom that spoke of the return of the heir. As a punishment, the impostor's men had set fire to the kingdom, destroying most of the cottages and the arable land of the Flatlands. In this village, only the manor house had survived. Unlike other parts of Lumatere, where plowing and rebuilding had begun, the fields here would need to be cleared before they were fit to plow, a task that seemed backbreaking. Yet each day as he rode by, resisting the urge to stop, Trevanion watched them as they worked. This village of Sennington. Beatriss's village.

He dismounted at the road and walked his horse down the long narrow path that led to the house. Several men were loading carts with rubble and bits of timber, the charred remains of a village. The workers stopped as he passed, exchanging glances and nodding in his direction.

He reached the front door and knocked. When there was no response, he entered tentatively, following the noise of chatter into the parlor. It seemed as if most of the village of Sennington was in the room. He recognized exiles among them. Some stood, but most sat around a long table, chewing on corn cobs and drinking soup. He guessed there was not much in their bowls but water and flavoring, yet their talk was cheerful.

And then they noticed him.

The room grew silent, and suddenly she was there, standing by the stove. She stared at him, pot in hand. Her hair, once long fine waves of copper, was short, framing a face darkened by the sun's rays. She was thinner than he remembered, but neither the exiles nor those trapped inside had much flesh on their bodies. He felt uncomfortable under her gaze, like an intruder.

"Lady Beatriss."

Still no one spoke and then one of the men stood. Trevanion remembered him as Beatriss's cousin, a wealthy merchant who had spent much of his time traveling the land. Except in the last ten years.

"Captain Trevanion. Welcome home." The older man bowed.

"Excuse my rudeness, Captain Trevanion," Beatriss said finally as she came forward with a hand extended. Part of him wanted to laugh at the idea of them shaking each other's hand. Strangers and acquaintances shook hands. Not a man and a woman who had created a child. Not lovers who had cried out their pleasure in unison during those early hours of the morning when the rest of the world was asleep, their bodies speaking silently of never letting go.

Her voice was the same, if stronger and firmer. But her eyes had changed. He could only remember them looking up at him with trust, or at one of the princesses and the younger children with laughter and affection. During the past week, he had seen from a distance her tenderness with her child, but her innocence and openness were gone.

The silence became uncomfortable. Trevanion desperately wished Finnikin were by his side. His son would know what to say. He would charm them all with his honesty, and impress them with his earnestness and knowledge. No one made a move to accommodate him, but Trevanion could not blame them. Lady Beatriss of the Flatlands would never have been arrested and tortured, would never have been subjected to such horror if she had not been his lover.

The child appeared at the door. Trevanion had seen her frequently during the past week, in the palace village where members of his Guard handed out provisions and instructions. Each time, the sight of this other man's child was like a blunt ax carving up his insides.

She clung to her mother, staring up at him. He was suddenly aware of his appearance. He touched his hair, clumped in knots. There had been more pressing things to attend to during the past week, although Lady Abian had ordered him to stop by that very afternoon so she could attend to his hair and beard. He felt as he had when he was back in the mines of Sorel and Finnikin had first set eyes on him. Ashamed.

"I am sorry to have disturbed you," he said quietly, and abruptly left the room.

He was halfway up the path and almost at his horse when he realized he was being trailed by the child. She said nothing, just watched him as she tried to keep up. Her tiny face was framed by thick copper curls, and she stared at him with large blue eyes.

"Vestie!"

They both turned and watched as Beatriss hurried toward them. She picked up her skirt to stop herself from tripping, and when she reached them, she took her daughter's hand. He stared at the child's arm, saw the scratches inflicted by their queen in her desperation.

"I'm sorry for her forwardness, Captain Trevanion," Beatriss said. "There are many new people passing through and it must be overwhelming for our children."

Their children. Not his.

He looked around the village, or what was left of it, for a distraction. "We would recommend that you move your people to Fenton," he said gruffly. "There is a pocket of fertile land there, the exact size of Sennington."

He watched her face pale. "Move my villagers away from their home?" she asked.

"There is nothing left here, Lady Beatriss."

She looked at the blackened earth around her. "Burning my land to the ground, Captain Trevanion, has been a constant these past ten years."

*But Beatriss the Bold refuses to stop planting.*

The child was looking from one to the other.

"In the coming week, will you welcome Sir Topher and my son, who is assisting him in the census?" he asked. "I have heard you and your villagers have kept the best records, and we need help in locating names . . . people . . . graves."

She nodded and he walked toward his horse.

Her voice stopped him. "It brings me great joy that you have been reunited with your beloved boy."

"Sadly not a boy anymore." He thought for a moment and nodded. "But a joy all the same."

"Finnikin," the child announced.

Trevanion stared down at her, and his look seemed to frighten Beatriss. But not the child. She returned the stare, an inquisitive expression on her face as if she were attempting to recognize him. And when the awkwardness and silence became too much, Trevanion climbed on his horse and rode away.

When Finnikin returned home to the Rock Village, his great-aunt Celestina wept for what seemed an eternity. Although he now felt like a stranger among his mother's people, he allowed them to fuss over him, though they did so with a certain shyness and hesitation. At first he thought it was because he was one of the few exiles from the Rock, but one night when his great-aunt kissed his forehead, he saw the sparkle in her eyes. "Is it true, Finnikin, that the queen has chosen you to be her king?"

"Do not speak of such things, Aunt Celestina," he said quietly. "When there's so much sadness in our kingdom."

Although Sir Topher had sent messengers requesting his presence, Finnikin could not bring himself to walk the road to the palace. Instead he focused on the task the queen's First Man had assigned him, to account for every one of their citizens based on the last census. It was with a heavy heart that Finnikin began his new role, yet what started as a task of asking heartbreaking questions turned into something that marked the end of years of silence for their people.

"Talk," he would suggest gently wherever he went. It had been what the novice Evanjalin had allowed him to do on the rock in Sorel. What the queen feared had happened to her people: nobody had talked these past ten years. They had whispered words to survive. Muttered curses beneath their breath. Murmured plans in the deep of the night. Even exchanged words of love. But nobody had told their stories, until Finnikin asked them to.

In the days that followed, he listened, sitting at their tables, if they were fortunate enough to have a roof over their heads, or working alongside them harnessed to a plow, baling hay, thatching roofs. He heard tales of anguish from people as fractured as the land they were rebuilding. He saw more tears in that time than he had seen in his lifetime, but he wrote with a steady hand so the lives of these Lumaterans would not be forgotten. Perhaps, he thought, these chronicles would be read in centuries to come. Perhaps they would act as a deterrent. He could not believe anyone who heard such stories of wickedness would allow it to happen again. Never had he loved his fellow Lumaterans more than in those moments when they told their stories of terror.

"If we challenged or resisted," Jorge of the Flatlands told him, "the bastard king's men would return the next day and say, 'Pick one.'" The man fought back a sob. "'Pick one you love to die. If not, you sacrifice your whole family. Your whole village.'"

"Men were on their knees begging, 'Take me. Take me instead,'" Roison of the River explained.

"We would sit and discuss our plan, Finnikin," Egbert of the Rock whispered. "We would work out, as a family, who we would choose to die alongside us if we were forced to decide. Better to make the choice as a family, rather than in moments where there would be no time for good-byes."

"So men would choose their sons?" Finnikin asked, sickened by the idea of Trevanion having to make such a decision.

The man looked at him with tears running down his face. "No," he said, shaking his head. "No father would leave his daughter behind to be raped and abused. We chose our daughters. Always our daughters."

As Finnikin and Sir Topher had expected, the royal treasury was almost intact; the curse meant that the impostor king and his men had not had opportunity to squander the gold. Horses and oxen purchased from Osteria and Belegonia provided much needed assistance to those plowing the Flatlands, and the construction of cottages became a priority. Both Osteria and Belegonia had volunteered to send workers to help with the rebuilding, but Trevanion refused to allow any foreigners into Lumatere and kept the borders heavily guarded. In the first week, the Guard brought back fruit and vegetables from Osteria and hunted the woods for game and rabbits. By the end of the second week, activity on the river had begun and the first of the barges came upstream from Belegonia. Finnikin stood with Sefton and the lads, watching his father as he supervised the goods being unloaded. Trevanion's hair and beard had been clipped in the same fashion as the rest of his Guard, which made him seem more like the Trevanion of old. Yet there was still a haunted look in his eyes, and Finnikin knew it would be a long while before songs were sung on the riverbank and laughter rang through the air once more.

That afternoon Finnikin traveled with Sir Topher to see Lady Beatriss. He had caught a glimpse of her earlier that week in the palace village but was reluctant to approach for fear of not knowing what to say. But when he stood before her in the parlor of the manor house, he realized no words were required. She took his face in her hands and kissed him gently on the forehead, then gestured for them to sit, and began to prepare the tea.

"Please do not serve me, Lady Beatriss. It humbles me to have you do so," Finnikin said.

"It should humble you to have anyone serve you, Finnikin," she said without reprimand.

On the table before them, Sir Topher laid out the pages of their records. "We have already recorded the names of all the exiles. If there is a cross marked next to the name, it means we know they died outside the kingdom," Sir Topher said. "If there are two strokes, we know they live."

She looked at him for a moment. "Exiles? We called you

'our lost ones.'" She looked at the records in front of her, her fingers brushing gently over the names. A small sound escaped her lips and she covered her mouth with her hand. "Lord Selric and his family?"

Sir Topher nodded soberly. "There was a plague in Charyn. Three years ago."

"All of them?" she asked in a hushed tone. "All those beautiful children?"

Sir Topher cleared his throat and nodded again.

She went back to the list on the table. "The family of Sym the potter?"

"Sarnak," Finnikin said flatly.

Her face paled. "Sarnak," she whispered. "The queen spoke to us about it just yesterday, when I visited the cloister of Sagrami with Lady Abian. I could tell the queen exactly when the massacre had taken place. When my Vestie was three years old, she screamed for days until she had no voice left. I could only sit by and watch over her. Tesadora gave her a tonic that would make her sleep. We had no idea what had happened, only that it must have been catastrophic for our people."

"The queen walked your sleep that night and said it was the reason for her journey to the cloister in Sendecane," Sir Topher said gently.

"I was never aware of her walking my sleep. It was a shock when the queen spoke of it. For a long time we could not question Vestie, for she began to speak late, and even then it was only a few words. But I always sensed there was something different about my child each month during those days of walking."

"Good or bad?" Finnikin asked.

"Unlike the queen's or Tesadora's experience, it was usually peaceful for Vestie. Tesadora was somehow able to keep the darkness away from her. But during the time of Vestie's unrest, which we now understand to be the time of the massacre in Sarnak, I remember praying to the goddess Lagrami to protect the queen. And so our goddess sent her to Sendecane, where she was safe and at peace for a time."

"So you knew it was the queen all along?" Finnikin asked.

She nodded. "Vestie's only word for a long time was 'Isaboe.' But you had best ask Tesadora about the connection between Vestie and the queen. There are things about the curse and magic that I will never understand." She looked up, sensing Finnikin's gaze on her.

"So you spoke to the queen?" he said quietly. "Just yesterday?" He had not seen Isaboe since he placed her on Tesadora's cart. "Yet the Guard has not been allowed inside the cloister."

"Tesadora will not allow men near the girls."

"We would never hurt them, Lady Beatriss," Sir Topher said.

"The damage is already done, Sir Topher. Boredom made monsters out of the bastard king and his men. They went for the cloister of Lagrami first. It was close to the palace, and the novices had no protection. On the night the impostor's men attacked, not one of them was left inviolate, not even the priestess. One night, they all disappeared, and although I suspected that Tesadora and the novices of Sagrami had taken them into their protection, it was many months before I knew for certain."

"Wouldn't the impostor king have known where the novices had disappeared to and attacked the Sagrami cloister?" Finnikin asked.

"Oh, he knew," she said bitterly. "But if there was one person in this kingdom the bastard king feared, it was Tesadora. Her mother had cursed the kingdom and there were stories that the daughter was even more powerful."

As he had many times in the past week, Finnikin wanted to tear someone apart with his bare hands. He wanted to be like

Trevanion and Perri and forget protocol. Yesterday his father and some of the senior guards had entered the palace dungeon to question the impostor king and his surviving men. Finnikin knew that few words had been exchanged and that the howls from the prisoners could be heard all over the palace. He remembered the look on Sir Topher's face when they later saw the blood-splattered dungeon walls. Horror, certainly. But mostly satisfaction.

"If I could make a request, Finnikin, on their behalf. Could you ask your father to remove some of the guards from around the cloister?"

Finnikin shook his head. "Not as long as the queen is within those walls," he said firmly. "Tesadora will have to let them in soon. The queen's *yata* and the Mont people will want her with them for a short while before she returns home."

"Her *yata* is with her now."

"Lady Beatriss," Finnikin said, trying not to let his frustration show, "can you not see a problem with the fact that the queen's First Man and the captain of her Guard have to obtain information about her well-being from you?"

She gave him a piercing look. "I do believe, Finnikin, that the queen would be happy to speak to you if you were to visit."

"Has she made such a request?" he asked quietly.

"Does she need to?" This time there was reprimand in her tone.

"Finnikin will speak to the queen soon," Sir Topher said. "After he follows his father's example and has his hair clipped and looks . . . presentable."

Finnikin stared at his mentor in disbelief, a stare that Sir Topher studiously ignored.

"It's what the people of Lumatere expect from the one they believe will bond with their queen," Sir Topher continued.

"What?"

Sir Topher sighed. "Finnikin, I know I can speak of such things in front of Lady Beatriss. The people of Lumatere will want the queen to choose a—"

The snarl that came from Finnikin stopped Sir Topher in his tracks. "The people of Lumatere are trying to rebuild their lives, Sir Topher. The last thing they're thinking about is who the queen chooses to bond with." Yet Finnikin knew it was a lie, for he had been asked a number of times during the past two weeks if the rumors were true.

"How wrong you are, Finnikin," Lady Beatriss chided. "The queen is everything to our people. She's the leader of our land. As a single woman she is vulnerable. When Lumatere celebrates our reunification, our people will expect her to be settled so she can carry on with running the kingdom. Ever since the word on Vestie's arm hinted a return, the talk has been of you."

"And was I ever to have a choice in the matter?" He was furious, but Beatriss did not seem fazed.

Sir Topher looked exasperated. "Finnikin, you have loved her from the moment you climbed that rock in Sendecane."

"When she was a novice, not a queen."

"Oh, I see." There was disappointment in Lady Beatriss's eyes.

"I don't think you do, Lady Beatriss."

"If you were king and she were a mere novice, would you have chosen her to be your queen?" she asked.

This time he could not lie. Not to Beatriss. "Yes," he said quietly.

"Yet the queen cannot choose you?"

Suddenly he felt as if he were eight years old and Beatriss was reprimanding him for tying Isaboe to the flagpole by her hair.

"If this is about power, then perhaps you are not the right person for our queen after all, Finnikin."

"The prince of Osteria has expressed interest," Sir Topher announced.

"I've heard he's a strapping boy," Lady Beatriss responded pleasantly as she disappeared into the other room. Finnikin kept his hooded stare on Sir Topher, who yet again chose to ignore it and turned instead to Lady Beatriss as she returned with a large book in her hands. She placed it on the table before them.

"Here are the dead," she said, opening to a page. "Marked next to each name is how they died." She turned to another page. "Here are the arrests. Here are the attacks on our property, although we stopped recording them after the first two years."

Finnikin pointed to the names marked in red ink.

She stared at him. "Informants."

"Traitors?"

She shrugged. "Whatever it is they did or said kept them free from any type of punishment. I'm ashamed to say that the nobility were the worst. We could have done with Lord Augie and Lady Abian. And I would have imagined the same noble behavior from Lord Selric."

"Your actions were beyond reproach, Lady Beatriss," Finnikin said. "Your name has often been praised these past weeks in my travels. You went beyond the duty of a citizen."

"Circumstances present themselves, and at times we have no choice. I had no choice but to work for the good of the people. Perhaps if I had been presented with different circumstances, I would have taken the path of my fellow nobles."

"How is it that you survived, Lady Beatriss, when all exiles believed you to be dead?" he asked gently.

"Perhaps Lady Beatriss would prefer not to speak of such a time, Finnikin," Sir Topher said.

Finnikin held her gaze. "My father mourned your loss for ten years."

"Finnikin," Sir Topher warned.

"The births," she said quietly, leaving Finnikin's question hanging in the air. "There are one thousand, nine hundred, and twenty-three of us, last count. It is hard to determine with the Forest Dwellers. There were some who survived, perhaps hidden by our people during those days. I have never seen them, but Tesadora has hinted of their existence in the woods beyond the cloister."

"Yet Tesadora allowed you to be part of her world with the novices," Finnikin observed.

Beatriss nodded. "But she was secretive all the same. There were so few of them in the end that they trusted no one." She leaned forward to whisper. "We were very lucky to have her hide the novices of Lagrami, and later the young girls."

Finnikin took her hand gently. "The impostor king and his men are no longer in power. You have no need to fear. So we must learn to speak with loud voices rather than in soft whispers. That, I know, is what the queen wants."

She nodded. "The crops." She turned another page. "The days of darkness." She pointed. "The days of light."

"Did that happen often?" Sir Topher asked.

She nodded. "The first five years were the worst. Some weeks there was day after day of darkness and we feared the crops would fail and we would starve. Even the surviving Sagrami worshippers had no idea how to control it or what it all meant. The answers seemed to have died with Seranonna."

She pushed the book across to Finnikin and stood to refill their cups. Sir Topher walked to the window and peered outside. "Is that Gilbere of the Flatlands, Lady Beatriss?"

"My cousin, yes."

"We studied together as children. Will you both excuse me?"

"Of course."

Sir Topher left, and Finnikin began to copy the recordings from Beatriss's book into his own.

"It's because she returned to fulfill her mother's request to save me," Lady Beatriss said after a while.

Finnikin put down his quill. "Tesadora?"

Lady Beatriss nodded. "She's very frightening when you first see her, isn't she?"

He smiled, abashed. "She's half my size, so it might be slightly humbling for me to admit that."

"Well, I will admit it for you," Beatriss responded with a laugh. Then her face grew serious. "Seranonna and I were locked in the same dungeon cell. The day before the curse, she was permitted a visitor. A novice from the cloister of Lagrami. The novice was there to give a blessing to the Sagrami worshippers so they could repent before death. I remember feeling ashamed to hear such piety coming from a novice of my order. But it was a deception. The novice was Tesadora, her hair shorn, dressed in the stolen robes of a Lagrami novice. She gave Seranonna a blessing in the language of the ancients and pressed into her mother's hand a potion concealed in a tiny vial. It was a substance that would render her mother unconscious; she would be dead to all who saw her. But Tesadora knew enough to be able to revive her."

Finnikin paled. "Seranonna gave the potion to you instead?"

Beatriss nodded. "We have never spoken of it, but I cannot imagine how Tesadora felt that day, watching the guards drag her mother into the square to be executed. When Seranonna screamed out that I was dead, Tesadora knew the words were meant for her. A message to retrieve my body and bring it back to life. I drank the potion after I gave birth, praying that I would not regain consciousness. I have no memory of what took place during the curse. All I know is that Tesadora took advantage of the confusion and came to find me. She said I was still holding your sister, Finnikin."

Tears sprang to his eyes before he could stop them.

"She lived for only a few moments, and in those moments, I said her name out loud so she would one day be able to shout it through the heavens. I knew she could not possibly survive, because she was too tiny. I had carried her for less than six months. But she knew the important things before she died. That her father's name was Trevanion, her mother's name was Beatriss, and her brother's name was Finnikin. I called her Evanjalin after Trevanion's beloved mother, and when my precious Vestie was born five years later, I swear I heard her cry out that name when she first entered this world. As if somehow the spirit of Evanjalin lived within her. You may think I sound like a mad woman for believing such a thing, but there are moments when I see qualities of your father in Vestie, Finnikin."

"I've learned to accept the unexplainable and not consider myself mad," Finnikin said.

"When Tesadora revived me in the dungeons, I begged her to let me die. I was frightened. I knew the bastard king would come for me again. But she refused to leave me there. She half carried me out of the dungeons, both of us sobbing. Hers were tears of fury, mine of fear. How strange and unnatural a day it was, Finnikin. The palace village destroyed, the streets empty except for the dead who had been crushed under cottages. I could see people wailing against the kingdom walls, pounding them with their bare hands. On the road to the Flatlands, we passed those who looked like the walking dead, muttering about curses, claiming there was no way out of the kingdom. It was Tesadora and my villagers who buried my child. Down by the river." She shook her head, lost in her thoughts. "I think I buried your father that day as well."

"But he's alive," Finnikin said bluntly.

"One day I want you to take him down there, to the grave," she said. "So he can begin to heal. I see so much hurt in his eyes."

"Why can't he heal with you?" Finnikin pushed.

"Because I am not even half the person he once loved."

"Some things don't change, Lady Beatriss. Can you ever bring yourself to love him again?"

"Oh, Finnikin," she said with great sadness. "After everything that has happened, how do any of us begin to love again?"

Later, Finnikin traveled the road to the palace with his mentor.

"Did she speak?" Sir Topher asked.

Finnikin looked at him, surprised. "You left because you believed she would?"

"No, I honestly did want to see my childhood friend," he said with a smile. "But I could tell she needed to talk, and I learned years ago, Finnikin, that people divulge things to you that they would not divulge to anyone else."

"A good skill for the apprentice of the queen's First Man?" Finnikin asked.

"Way beyond the skill of an apprentice," Sir Topher said solemnly. "Or the queen's First Man, at that." He sighed, looking around. "Where do you think our boy is?"

"Froi? Who knows? If he's left the kingdom, I don't want to be the one to tell the queen. I've sent Sefton and the village lads out to search for him."

They heard the pounding of horses' hooves behind them, and a moment later Trevanion and Moss appeared.

"Something's wrong," Finnikin muttered, his heart hammering in his chest. Trevanion and Moss pulled up beside them, their expressions grim.

"Isaboe?" Finnikin asked.

Trevanion shook his head, and Finnikin could sense his father's suppressed rage. "It's the impostor king and his men," Trevanion said bluntly. "They're dead."

## CHAPTER 28

P oisoned?"

Trevanion, Finnikin, Sir Topher, and Moss walked through the dungeons, covering their noses and mouths with cloths. The impostor king and his men had obviously suffered long and painful deaths. One had managed to batter his head to a pulp against the dungeon wall in an attempt to end the agony.

"How?" Trevanion asked, fury in his voice.

"We do not know," the prison guard said quietly. "But we arrested the baker who supplied us with the loaves for the prisoners this morning."

"He confessed?"

The guard shook his head.

"This could only be the work of one who knows their poisons, so I'm hoping we've removed the queen from Tesadora's cloister," Finnikin said.

"Perri's already on his way," Trevanion replied. "He will take the queen to the Monts until she is ready to return to the palace."

"We must treat this with care," Sir Topher said. "We cannot have a repeat of the past when it comes to those who worship Sagrami."

"Agreed," Trevanion said flatly. "But if Tesadora is responsible for what has happened here, she must be arrested."

"Surely you are not suggesting she's working with the Charynites to keep the impostor king from talking?" Sir Topher asked.

"We take no chances."

It took most of the day to ride to the cloister at the northwest tip of the kingdom. On the way, they passed the cherry blossom tree that had been planted in honor of the dead queen's youngest child, Isaboe. The cloister, where Perri had hidden Tesadora and the novices all those years ago, was one of the most ancient temples in the land. It was surrounded by woodland, where Trevanion's men were now positioned, some in the open, others concealed.

The cloister's entrance was a covered walkway, which led into circular gardens where the novices worked and meditated. Surrounding the gardens were the living quarters. Tesadora stood at the entrance, staring at the men impassively. Light played through the arched opening, and it made her look almost ghostly with her strange hair and beautiful face. Finnikin could not help wondering how such a tiny woman had managed to carry the much taller Beatriss out of the dungeons that day.

"There seem to be a lot of angry men in the vicinity, Captain," Tesadora said by way of greeting. "They are disturbing my girls."

"I'm hoping you made Perri's acquaintance this morning, Tesadora."

"The Savage and I are well acquainted, as you would know," she said coldly. "He had the queen removed from our cloister, much to the distress of both the novices and the queen."

Trevanion looked to one of his guards nearby. The guard nodded to verify her story.

"We would like permission to enter," Sir Topher said.

"I will not have my novices alarmed any further. I fear you will also have me removed from the cloister by force if I allow you to enter."

Finnikin was sure that Tesadora's only knowledge of fear was how to instill it in others. "Out of respect for the role you played in the survival of Lady Beatriss, my father will restrain himself, Tesadora," he said.

She stared at him, as if seeing him for the first time in the midst of the others. "Leave your men outside," she ordered. She turned and walked down the passageway. Trevanion, Sir Topher, and Finnikin followed.

"Do not speak for me again, Finn," his father warned in a low tone. "A poor captain I would make if all my decisions were based on how my loved ones were treated."

They walked through the gardens, aware of the stares from the novices. Those belonging to Sagrami were dressed in blue, those to Lagrami in gray. Most were young. *"Finnikin of the Rock,"* he heard one whisper to another. *"He belongs to the queen."*

They reached the main temple, where Tesadora lit a candle.

"We have the impostor king and nine of his men lying dead in the palace dungeons. Poisoned," Sir Topher said after she had finished purifying the air with the scented smoke of the candle and a prayer to her goddess.

Tesadora held his gaze. "Are you accusing me, Sir Topher?" She turned to Trevanion. "Is this an arrest, Captain Trevanion? Or are you expecting me to shed tears for these . . . What did you call them? *Men?*"

"Our only evidence that Charyn was set to invade Belegonia

through our kingdom has been destroyed," Trevanion said. "What would you do in our place, Tesadora?"

She gave a small laugh. "In your place I would declare this a day of joy for the people of Lumatere."

"Especially, perhaps, for those who worship Sagrami," Finnikin said.

"These past ten years the bastard king and his men have not discriminated between worshippers of Sagrami and those of Lagrami. All Lumaterans were victims of their reign of terror."

"The surviving Forest Dwellers?" Trevanion asked, indicating the woodlands. "Did they order the murder of the impostor king and his men, Tesadora?"

Tesadora ignored the question. "The Forest Dwellers have requested autonomy."

"No," Finnikin said firmly. "Your people belong to this kingdom. Autonomy will only make things worse for you."

"Those who worship Sagrami did not feel as if they belonged to this kingdom during the five days of the unspeakable. Is that not what you call those days?"

"The queen would never allow anything to happen to the Forest Dwellers."

"And if something happens to the queen? We were protected under our previous king and queen, yet the moment they were gone, we were hunted like animals and slaughtered. Would you like to carry out your census here, Finnikin? Before your five days of the unspeakable, there were four hundred and thirty-seven Forest Dwellers. Today there are less than forty."

"They will be protected," Sir Topher said firmly.

"Despite what happens to me?"

"Have we treated you as the enemy?" Finnikin asked. "We need what you can teach us. We need to know about the magic."

"So you can control it? Cage it?"

"Perhaps to celebrate it," Finnikin said. "So we can learn to be healers. Your young girls have skills."

"And you expect me to believe this is your reason for visiting today? When I'm here, answering your questions in an interrogation room?"

"No one is arresting you, Tesadora, and this is a temple," Sir Topher said.

"Yet your captain holds his sword, ready for attack."

"The baker stands accused of murder unless you can shed some light on what took place in the palace this morning!" Trevanion snapped.

There was no response.

"He will suffer for something you planned, Tesadora."

"And Beatriss suffered for something you did, did she not, Trevanion? The captain of the Guard who chose not to lie prostrate at the feet of the bastard king. But by our goddess," Tesadora swore, "they ensured that his lover lay prostrate at their feet. *Continually.* Dragged by her hair out of her home night after night. She was once the most envied of women in Lumatere when she was loved by the captain of the King's Guard. But nobody envied her during our years of captivity. She was their perfect weapon to keep our people in place. When they discovered she was alive and re-arrested her, the bastard king chose not to have her executed. No, he found a better use for the former lover of the captain of the King's Guard. 'See this woman,' he would taunt whenever his men dragged her broken and bruised body into the square. 'This is what will happen to your loved ones if you dare to challenge a king.' "

Sir Topher hissed with fury as Trevanion walked out of the room. Finnikin could not imagine what images had just passed through his father's head. He had been told tales of Beatriss's fate but had foolishly hoped his father would never hear.

Sir Topher stared at Tesadora. "I have a better tale to tell," he spat. "The one where the captain sensed what would happen between himself and the impostor king. So he sent a message to his trusted friend Perri the Savage, telling him to take Lady Beatriss from her manor to the Valley of Tranquillity, where Lord August and Lady Abian had taken refuge. To leave her with them so she would be protected. But Perri was nowhere to be found that day and never received the message. You see, Perri was on his way to warn a childhood nemesis. Someone he believed his family had wronged for many years. Someone he believed deserved to live. I heard the sorry tale from Perri himself, still grief-stricken after all these years that he let his captain down. Imagine, Tesadora, if Perri had received Trevanion's message. Imagine the life Beatriss would have had with Lord August and his family in Belegonia."

Tesadora's mouth twisted with bitterness, but she failed to prevent the tears from welling in her eyes.

"Yet Perri never regretted his decision to travel this far to hide you and the novices of Sagrami. And I never believed he should regret it, nor Trevanion. Until perhaps today."

Finnikin went searching for his father. He found him stooped over with his back to the cloister, one hand against a tree. When Trevanion turned, he was wiping his mouth with the back of his sleeve, his face ashen. Sir Topher stood at the cloister entrance and they walked toward him in silence.

"We have no more business here today," Sir Topher said.

Tesadora appeared in the passageway behind him. Her face was still impassive, but her eyes had softened.

"It began with Beatriss's first child," she said. "Your child, Trevanion. My mother went to the stake with the child's blood on her hands. We believe that the blood, mingled with Balthazar's and Isaboe's, got caught up in the dark magic of the curse. And became its light."

Trevanion was silent.

"Because both the royal children and the babe were pure of heart?" Sir Topher asked.

"No," she said and Finnikin flinched as her eyes met his. Despite the strangeness of her hair and the darkness of her spirit, she was probably the most beautiful woman he had ever seen.

"No," she repeated. "I believe it's because a young boy made a sacrifice to keep the princess safe. Flesh from your body, Finnikin. But it cost you more than that."

He dared not look away.

"I was there in the square the day my mother died," she said, anger in her voice. "Even through her curse, while others ran, I stayed. She watched me come into this world, delivered me herself. So I watched her leave it. The perfect balance, don't you think?"

No one spoke.

"I saw you that day," she continued, her eyes fixed on Finnikin's. "Saw what you did. I keep a dagger with your name on it, Finnikin of the Rock. My only consolation in mourning my mother is that she did not feel those flames for too long."

Finnikin heard Trevanion's and Sir Topher's intake of breath, saw the shock on their faces.

"What did Finnikin's actions have to do with making contact with Queen Isaboe outside Lumatere?" Sir Topher asked.

"I know as much as you do, Sir Topher. The dead do not send a guide or explanation. We work things out for ourselves. I met Lady Beatriss in the dungeons of the palace, where she lay clutching a dead child. After returning her to Sennington, I did not see her again for another five years. The darkest of years. And then one day, in the fifth year of our captivity, Lady Beatriss arrived on the doorstep. Just over there," she said, pointing to the entrance. "In the early hours of the morning. And she did not come alone." She turned to where a young woman knelt in the garden, planting. "Japhra?"

The girl walked toward them, and Finnikin realized she was one of the novices who had been in Tesadora's cart the day they entered Lumatere. She was short, almost stout. Her eyes were deerlike, her sable-colored hair thick and lush.

"Friends of Lady Beatriss, Japhra," Tesadora said. "Can you fetch us some tea?"

When the girl left, Tesadora walked them back inside to one of the rooms in the cloister.

"The night she came to me, Beatriss had smuggled Japhra out of the palace and they rode through the dark to find us. Japhra of the Flatlands was twelve. Taken from her family by the bastard king to do with whatever he pleased. She was almost catatonic, and even today her spirit is damaged."

Finnikin shuddered.

"I had been trying unsuccessfully to contact my mother through the magic of the goddesses and had failed repeatedly. That all changed the night I was reacquainted with Lady Beatriss. Japhra wasn't the only reason she came to see me. Let's just say it was for . . . medicinal purposes."

"She was with child?" Trevanion asked.

"I don't think I need to tell you that if this conversation ever goes beyond us—"

"You'll poison us?" Trevanion said.

She sent him a scathing look. "It would shatter Beatriss's heart if you knew why she came to see me that night, and we don't want to go around doing that, do we, Captain?"

"She wanted to rid herself of the babe inside her?" Finnikin asked.

"I don't think she knew what she wanted. But she was exhausted from the ride, so I allowed her to stay the night. The girls and I had had very little contact with the rest of the kingdom up until that point. I had twelve of the forty remaining Forest Dwellers in my care in the cloister, as well as the priestess of Lagrami and her girls. I trusted no one with their lives."

The girl returned and poured the tea with trembling hands.

"Thank you, Japhra," Trevanion said quietly.

She nodded and left them.

"That night, the spirit of my mother came calling. I felt her. As if she were holding me somehow. She spoke words to me that I could not recall the next morning, until Beatriss told me of her strange sleep. She had dreamed she held her first child in her arms. And the child had spoken to her. Delivered a message."

The three men waited.

" 'The child of Beatriss will share dreams with our heir, who will set us free.' "

She took in the looks of shock and disbelief on their faces.

"You could argue that it was the need of two grieving women, one for her mother and one for her child. But at such times, gentlemen, you grab at any sign of hope. You grab it with both hands and breathe life into it, day after day. You do *anything* to keep it alive.

"We talked about it, the priestess of Lagrami with us, all day and night, putting forward different theories. Seranonna and the child died on the same day and we believed that my mother carried Beatriss's child to the heavens to be protected by our goddess. That night in our cloister, your child came looking for her mother, Trevanion."

"What magic did you use to contact Isaboe?"

"None. It's beyond even my power or knowledge. I can heal because my mother taught me what plants and flowers to use.

It's what I teach the novices. Japhra is one of our most talented. But healing and magic are different things. One must be very powerful to make contact with another through the sleep. A spirit so strong, full of all things good and all things wicked. An ability to look into the darkness and find a light."

"Isaboe," Finnikin said.

Tesadora nodded. "She found us. *She* found Vestie, but I believe her sleep spirit was searching for Beatriss's first child, Finnikin's half sister. Somehow, blood caused a bond between Isaboe and any child that Beatriss would give birth to. All because Finnikin made a sacrifice to keep the princess safe, and I'm presuming he used the same dagger for the sacrifice as he did to end my mother's suffering."

Finnikin did not respond.

"Of course, Beatriss was petrified about the message, but she knew she had no choice. I promised her that if she gave birth to the child, I would take it and she need never be reminded of who it was or what it represented. She agreed. She had nothing left to give. Oh, but the moment she saw Vestie," Tesadora said with a sigh, "I believe that if anyone had tried removing that child from Beatriss, they would have lost their life. I think many people were strengthened by the sight of them together. Villagers would visit Beatriss, afraid to speak but not afraid to hope, and somehow Beatriss gave them that hope. 'What needs to be done,' she would tell me.

"Then one day the blacksmith of the River village of Petros came to see me. Confessed to me that he had turned a Sagrami worshipper out of his home after the deaths of our beloveds. He begged me to take his daughters for protection."

"It was good of you to agree," Trevanion conceded.

"I didn't," she said flatly. "So that night, while his family slept, he smothered his wife and three daughters and then plunged a dagger into his own heart. He couldn't bear the idea of what the bastard king and his men would do to those girls.

"Beatriss threatened that if I did not agree to come up with a plan to protect the young girls of Lumatere, she would refuse me access to her child. A child whose first word was 'Isaboe.' It was our earliest indication that the heir and Vestie had walked the sleep together. We were stunned by the knowledge that it was the princess who had lived and not the prince. When I argued that there was nothing I could do, Beatriss spoke about the potion my mother had once given her. She left me no choice but to take in the young girls. Unbeknownst to many, Beatriss of the Flatlands is quite a bully when she sets her mind to it. One can imagine who she learned that from," Tesadora said snidely, looking at Trevanion.

"You had a choice," Finnikin said. "You protected the priestess of Lagrami and her novices long before that night."

"Don't paint too sentimental a picture of me, young man," Tesadora said sharply. "It will only make you look like a fool." Her expression was hard, and Finnikin could tell that she had said as much as she was going to. She stood up to walk them to the entrance.

"We will be questioning the baker tonight," Trevanion said as they followed her.

"I doubt that very much," Tesadora said.

Sir Topher and Finnikin exchanged glances.

"The queen has already arranged for his release," she advised them.

"Is that what you convinced her to do?" Finnikin asked angrily.

Tesadora gave a humorless laugh. "I hear the queen allows only one person to convince her, Finnikin."

"Once the queen knows what took place in the dungeons —" Finnikin began.

"There is little that takes place in this kingdom that the queen does not know about," she said, a glint of victory in her eyes. "I would take her advice, Finnikin, and concern yourself less with truth and more on what is for the greater good of her people."

Finnikin shivered as he realized the truth. He saw by their expressions that Sir Topher and Trevanion had come to the same conclusion. This was no random act from vengeance-seeking Forest Dwellers. The poisoning of the impostor king and his men had come from the highest office in the kingdom.

"Where is she?" he asked, as Moss approached them. *"Where is she?"*

"Remember your place," Trevanion said firmly. "In Lumatere the queen rules, Finnikin."

"Perri has taken her to the Monts," Moss said quietly.

Finnikin was on his horse before another word was spoken.

Trevanion felt Tesadora's furious stare as Finnikin rode away.

"Remember his place?" she said angrily. "For the sake of this kingdom, gentlemen, I am hoping that you have not prepared your boy to *remember his place* among royalty, but rather to recognize it alongside the queen."

"A very hard task indeed with your mother's premonition ringing in his head since he was a child of eight," Sir Topher replied.

"The boy remembers her words the way he wants to remember them," she said, "but the man must understand them the way they were intended."

Finnikin caught up with the queen and Perri as they rested at the foot of the mountains. Isaboe was sitting next to the guard, her back against a weeping willow, her knees tucked under her chin. The ride had done nothing to quell Finnikin's rage. When Perri saw the horse's fast approach, he was on his feet in an instant, his sword ready. Isaboe stood behind him, her eyes dark and piercing. Perri returned his sword to its scabbard and she stepped past him as Finnikin dismounted.

"I hope you've come to tell me that Froi's been found," she said, anger lacing her words. She wore a violet dress, scooped at the neck with gold trimmings, falling loose to her ankles to give her the freedom to mount and ride a horse.

"What have you done?" he asked, his fury barely contained.

Her hands were clenched. "What I needed to do," she responded.

"*We* needed proof," he spat, "of what Charyn had planned. Yet you ruin any chance of bringing to justice those who were responsible by destroying the ones who could prove it."

There was so little guilt in her eyes that it fueled his rage. Over her shoulder, he could see Perri poised for action, a look of warning on the guard's face. Finnikin knew he would be flat on the ground the moment he stepped out of line.

"You feel no remorse?" he said. "Regret nothing?"

Hatred blazed in her eyes. "I regret not being able to watch them suffer. I heard it was long," she said through clenched teeth, "and my heart sang to hear just how painful."

"Belegonia has been—"

"*Wanting* a chance to invade Charyn for as long as this land has existed," she shouted. "*Waiting* for any justification."

"They have every right to know that Charyn was planning an attack on them through us."

"Belegonia will not care for those who are caught in the middle, Finnikin. They will take Charyn, not out of revenge but for what they can get from that kingdom. And they will use Lumatere as the pathway."

"So the truth stays hidden?" he asked.

"Better than a truth revealed that will lead to war involving our three kingdoms. Not to mention Sarnak and every other kingdom on our borders. Let Charyn pay, Finnikin. Let Trevanion and Perri do what they do best. Let's not pretend the captain and Perri know nothing about slipping into a palace and cutting the throat of a savage foreign king who deserves to die. But do not ask me to sacrifice my people."

"That's called assassination, isn't it, Perri?" Finnikin called out to the guard. "To do exactly what was done to our king and—"

"*Don't!*" she shouted, sobbing the word. Behind her, Perri shook his head at Finnikin in warning.

"Do *not* compare the slaughter of my family to the killing of the monster who planned it and the traitor who carried it out. We are not ordering the deaths of innocents here. We are taking revenge, while ensuring that Lumatere is not bled dry."

"Your people need to know the truth, Isaboe."

"What my people need to know is that the beast and his men who razed our kingdom to the ground are dead. That they suffered. That the beast and his men who raped their wives and children no longer exist. Do you know how they punished the men who dared to stand up to them? How they kept them from resisting? Do you know how they came for their young daughters in daylight hours? Do you know how many drowned themselves in the river rather than endure what was happening? And I felt every one," she sobbed, hitting her chest with her fist. "Every single one, Finnikin. Oh, that leaders of kingdoms should feel the pain of every one of their citizens who they send out to fight their wars. Put me out of my misery now, rather than allow me to feel the deaths of my people fighting for such a *truth* to be known."

Finnikin gripped the hand pounding her chest, and she leaned toward him, emotion strangling her voice. "If you want to help run my kingdom, you do so from by my side and not from your rock village," she said.

"What makes you presume that I have a desire to run your kingdom?" he said coldly. But she was standing too close and he wanted to rest his forehead against hers. Take everything she was offering.

"Is it not what Seranonna predicted?" she asked quietly. "In the Forest when we were children? Light and dark. And what else was it that she said, Finnikin? What is it you fear so much?"

He shuddered. "Why don't you fear *me*?" he said, his fingers digging into her arm. "Why don't you fear me shedding your blood to be king?"

He saw her wince with pain and felt Perri's arm around his neck as he was pulled away.

"You are a fool," she said, the tears spilling down her cheeks. "Do you believe you are not man enough for the task? Perhaps I should give that privilege to the prince of Osteria, who begs to come calling to strengthen ties between our kingdoms."

Finnikin bit his tongue until he tasted blood. Something savage inside him wanted to kill any man who dared touch her.

"But know this, Finnikin. I will despise you for the rest of your life if you force me to take another man to my bed as my king."

She walked away and he ached to follow, but Perri refused to let him go, his lips close to Finnikin's ear. "Speak to the queen or touch her like that again," he threatened in a quiet voice, "and you will find yourself, on your father's orders, guarding the barren border at Sendecane."

Finnikin broke free, his breath ragged. "Make sure you leave someone behind to protect her as you would, Perri. For it looks like sometime soon you're going to Charyn," he said bitterly. "To kill a king."

"If that is what my queen wants of me, Finnikin, that is what I will do."

CHAPTER 29

A week passed and then another. Cottages began to
appear, built from mud bricks and straw, their roofs
thatched and floors earthen. But the exiles had slept
in worst conditions and many of them relished the idea of having a door and space and privacy. Those who had been trapped
inside became accustomed to greeting their new neighbors. In each
village, plowing and planting continued and routines began to
be reestablished.

One morning, Trevanion stood with Perri and Moss watching
Lord August work the land alongside his young sons and the
villagers. The sun was hot, but August looked content among
the men. Their lives were beginning to return to something close
to normal, and talk of crops and planting at times erupted into
healthy arguments. Trevanion noticed the workers seemed to
enjoy the task of turning over the soil with the hand-held plow,
despite the demanding nature of the work.

"Where are the oxen?" Perri asked, holding out a hand to take
the plow from Lord August.

"We share them with the rest of the Flatlands on rotation," the

Duke said, wiping sweat from his forehead. "I think the village of Clough has them today."

"Sennington was extensively damaged, Augie," Trevanion said. "Can you not have Abie convince Lady Beatriss to move her village to Fenton? They lost most of their people in the fever camps. There are acres of fertile land with no one to work it."

Lord August gave a small humorless laugh. "Have you been in the same room as my wife and Lady Beatriss and Tesadora?" he asked. "Terrifying. The moment I tried to make such a suggestion, I was cut down. Then I displayed greater stupidity by suggesting to the viper Tesadora that since the queen had been removed from her cloister and the guards were no longer there, I could request some sort of protection for her and her girls. Just in case." He shook his head, shuddering. "I'm sure she cast a spell on me with one flick of her eyelid."

"You're scared of the women?" Trevanion asked, amused.

"I am not ashamed to say so, and you are a fool if you're not," Lord August said pointedly.

"Lucian has volunteered to send the Monts down to work on Fenton," Perri said as he returned with the plow.

"I fear the boy is too young and does not have the heart to lead the Monts," Lord August said.

Trevanion shook his head. "He carried his father's body up that mountain over his shoulder, Augie. That has less to do with physical strength and more to do with heart. Finn has spent much time with him and his people, and they are doing what Monts do best. Getting on with life."

"I'm presuming Finnikin is not there now," Lord August said disapprovingly.

"He's in Sarnak. On palace business," Trevanion replied, frowning at Lord August's tone.

"On his own?" Perri asked.

"He took some of his lads from the village. Why are you so certain that he wasn't with the Monts?" Trevanion asked.

"Because the queen is with them, and some say that Finnikin can be found wherever the queen is not."

Trevanion bristled. "Another contribution from the women? If anyone has a problem with my son's movements, Augie, I will tell them to politely mind their own business, whether it's your wife or Tesadora."

"You left out Lady Beatriss," Moss said.

"I could not imagine Lady Beatriss concerning herself with Finnikin's business, but if the question arose, I would be just as firm with her."

"Finnikin needs to bring the queen home to the palace, Trevanion," Lord August pressed. "Not her Guard. Not Sir Topher. *Finnikin.* And Lucian of the Monts will need to be looked out for. He's still a young man who will have to work hard to gain people's confidence, no matter whose son he is. Those mountains are Charyn's entrance into our kingdom."

"Why are you telling us what we already know, Augie?" Perri asked tersely.

"I have Lucian looked out for," Trevanion said. "He has his uncles and his *yata*, and the Mont lads are under constant training."

"And who is guarding the novices of Sagrami?" Lord August continued. "It's too secluded out there in the west, and if we ever have a repeat of —"

"Tesadora and the novices are protected," Perri said firmly, "whether they know it or not. Men trained by me, Augie. So anyone who decides to walk into that part of the kingdom for no good reason may find himself with the sharp edge of a dagger across his throat. Now, do you have any other questions about the protection of this kingdom?"

Lord August stared from Perri to Trevanion and Moss.

"Tell me our Perri's not sharing the viper's bed?" he asked Trevanion.

Moss chuckled. "Brave man indeed who strips himself bare in front of that one."

Trevanion saw Lady Abian walking down the path to the manor house on her return from the palace village.

"Gentlemen!" she called out with a wave.

They held up their hands in acknowledgment.

"Finnikin?" she asked. "Where is he? I have seen little of him, Trevanion."

"In Sarnak. On palace business," he called back. "I'll have him come see you as soon as he returns." He heard a snort of laughter beside him as Lady Abian shook her head in disapproval and proceeded toward the house.

"Oh, you really told her to mind her business," Perri mocked.

Later, Trevanion, Moss, and Perri traveled farther into the kingdom, as they had done each day since their return. Trevanion knew the people of Lumatere felt comforted by the presence of his men, and he made it a priority to ensure they were visible in as many villages as possible. He was careful, trying to find the fine line between authority and protection. It was Lady Abian who suggested that the Guard not wear formal uniforms. Both the exiles and those trapped inside had been victims of the violence delivered by guards across the land. Instead, they wore gray and blue, colors representing both goddesses.

In the afternoon, they reached a village at the edge of the Flatlands, where men and women worked together to prepare the soil. Before the others realized what was happening, Perri had leaped off his horse. "Froi," he said with satisfaction.

Trevanion sighed with relief. In addition to his own fondness for the boy, he had feared the queen's anguish if they had lost him.

Froi saw Perri and Moss coming toward him, and he couldn't stop the smile, couldn't stop the happiness he felt inside as he put down his tools. And then Perri was grabbing him and they both pretended it was a tussle but really it was a hug.

"Where've you been, Froi?"

"Been here. Working a strip," he told them.

"Has our boy got some crazy notion he'll earn enough to buy a small pocket himself?" Moss asked, and Froi liked the way Moss said "our boy" as if Froi belonged to them instead of belonging to no one. Sometimes, during their travels, he had imagined there was someone inside Lumatere searching for him. But there had been no mother like Lady Abian or father like Trevanion waiting. No kin who recognized him as theirs.

Perri ruffled his hair. "Moss, go see the bailiff and tell him Froi's coming with us."

Perri began to walk back to the road, and Froi followed to where he could see the captain astride his horse. But then Froi looked back to where his work lay unfinished and it made him sad because there had been something about the touch of earth in his hands that made him feel worthwhile.

"Disappear like that again, boy, and I will send you back to Sarnak, where they found you," the captain growled when Froi reached him. "Where I'm certain Finnikin is roaming the streets looking for you as we speak."

Froi felt his eyes smart, but he kept his anger and hurt inside because anger made him want to spit and that was the last thing he wanted to do to the captain.

"What have you been doing, Froi?"

"Plowing, Captain," he said quietly.

"Plowing?"

"Soon they'll begin the planting. Barley and oats and onions and cabbage. There they'll plant ten apple, five pear, and two cherry trees," he said, pointing up to the mountains. "The ones donated by Osteria."

"Get on my horse, Froi," the captain said, holding out a hand to him. "You belong with us."

And as much as Froi wanted to belong with them, he stared at the hand the captain was holding out to him but didn't take it. "To do what?" he asked.

"The Guard protects the kingdom, Froi. The people of Lumatere honor us by allowing us to protect them," Perri explained.

"But I can't," he said, and he could feel the captain and Perri staring at him and he wanted to say all the right things to them. He had tried to explain to one of the workers the other day how being with the Guard and Evanjalin and the priest-king and Finnikin and Sir Topher had made him feel, but he hadn't been able to find the words for it.

"That's respect," she told him later when she understood what he was trying to say. He had never heard that word before and although he knew what he felt for them was fierce, it didn't mean he could protect the kingdom with them.

When the captain leaned down to hoist him onto the horse, Froi tried to speak but it came out like a whisper. "How can I be part of the Guard and protect this kingdom when I feel nofing for it? Captain Trevanion, they made a mistake. Finnikin and Evanjalin and Sir Topher. I'm not from here. I can tell from the way the others watch me. It's as if they sense fings of me. Fings I don't know myself." He stared down at the ground because he didn't want the captain to see his face.

"Everyone looks at each other that way these days,

Froi. Brothers and sisters, fathers and sons. Even those who were once lovers," the captain said.

Froi looked from Perri to the captain. "How can I die for any of the Guard? It's what you're supposed to do, isn't it? If somefing happens?"

Perri nodded.

"I wouldn't," he said truthfully. "I'd protect myself first."

Moss approached them, looking happy, but the smile left his face when he saw their expressions.

"You're Lumateran, Froi. You'd fight for this kingdom," Perri said, but Froi shook his head.

"It's just a word. Lumatere. Feel nofing for it, except for this patch of land I've worked on."

"Nothing. For no one?" Moss asked.

Froi thought for a moment. "I fink I'd die for Evanjalin. Probably Finnikin too."

"She is the queen," the Captain said firmly. "She's not Evanjalin, Froi."

"Whoever she is, I fink I'd die for her and Finnikin. Because that time in Sarnak when she came searching, sometimes I fink she didn't come back for that ring. It was for me." He realized it was the first time he had ever said anything like that out loud and it made him think of saying other things in his head that were the truth. "But I wouldn't die for anyone else. Not even you free or the priest-king or Sir Topher. I'd sell you out the first moment someone convinced me."

The captain gave a short laugh of disbelief, but he seemed amused all the same, and then Perri joined in.

"He would," Perri agreed. "I believe him."

Froi felt ashamed, but Perri flicked him under the chin with his thumb. "So would have I, Froi. At your age."

"I don't understand," Moss said. "Finnikin's lads from the

village are begging us to let them train with the Guard."

"Climb up on my horse," the captain said with a sigh, his arm still extended.

Froi didn't dare disobey, and with a heavy heart he held on as they rode toward the palace. As he took in the Flatlands on both sides of the road, he realized that it scared him, all these people and all this work they had to do and the way some of the villagers who had worked around him would drop their planting tools and just cry. Men, too, not just women, and it was a different crying from what Lady Celie had done in Belegonia. It was the type of crying that gave him tears and most times he pretended there was dirt in his eyes. Deep down, Froi wanted it to go back to the time when it was just them hiding in the woods and there weren't so many people to feel sad for.

The captain slowed down at a Flatland village where everyone seemed to be working, and he could see the towers over the trees in the close distance and he knew they were almost entering the palace village.

"It's Lord August's estate," the captain explained. "Here is the deal, Froi. You can work the land, but we choose whose land. You continue your lessons with the priest-king. You make the queen happy."

Froi looked at him, not understanding.

"Perhaps you are right. You've not known this kingdom long. It takes time to love a land and a people and want to protect it, especially when those around you have eyes full of mistrust. It would be wrong for us to expect more from you now."

"But one day we will ask you again," Perri continued.

Froi stared at them. "But if I am the enemy?"

"Enemy to whom, Froi? To our queen?" Perri asked.

"*Never.* Not her."

"Then that is a start, Froi."

He thought about it for a moment and then looked at the village of Sayles. "As long as I don't have to live inside the big house with Lord Augie and Lady Abian," he said. "Because if they're going to spend every night screwing—"

"Froi!"

The captain laughed for the second time that day, and Froi liked the sound of it.

"Queen's orders that you stay close," Perri said. "Do us a favor, Froi. Do not defy the queen's orders. She is frightful these days up in those mountains."

Froi nodded. "I'll stay. But you're wrong about the queen," he said, swinging off the captain's horse, looking out at the village he was to be a part of.

"About her being frightful these days?"

"No. About her being in the mountains. I saw her. This morning, but I kept my distance. Didn't want to shame her. She was wif the Monts and everyone around me ran to the road to greet her. She was off to help in some village. Bal . . . Bal . . . ?"

"Balconio," the captain said. He cursed as he exchanged looks with the others. "I'll go," he said. "Perri, can you go back to the palace and escort Sir Topher to the village of Balconio?"

Froi looked up at the captain, confused. "Everyone wants Finnikin to bond with her and not that prince from Osteria. Why is Finnikin not wif her?"

The captain sighed. "Same reason as you, Froi."

"Because he's not worvy?"

The captain placed a hand on Froi's shoulder as they made their way down the path toward Lord August's house. Froi liked the feel of it and understood why Finnikin always puffed out his chest when his father was around.

"He is in the queen's eyes," the captain said, "and she measures worth better than anyone I know."

Trevanion saw the queen the instant he arrived. She was dressed in peasant clothing like those around her, and she was hacking at the earth with the same determination he had seen when she walked ahead of them on their journey to Lumatere. One of the villagers with her pointed to Trevanion, and she turned and watched as he dismounted and strode toward her. He saw the slump in her shoulders as if she knew the time had come. Her guards appeared beside her, and Trevanion grabbed hold of them both in anger.

"You said they weren't to let me out of their sight, Captain Trevanion, and they haven't," the queen said calmly.

"They do not need defending, Your Highness," he said, glaring at the two guards before letting them go.

She handed the hoe to the worker alongside her. "Can you continue without me, Naill?"

"Of course, my queen."

She followed Trevanion to the manor house. "There's much work to be done here," she said.

"Yes," he acknowledged, "but not by you. We still have the borders closed for fear of reprisal from those kingdoms who have not yet acknowledged your reign," he explained. "There are collaborators of the impostor king who are yet to be rounded up. The Forest Dwellers have not come out of hiding."

"If I return to the palace, you'll lock me up like you and Sir Topher did that time in Pietrodore," she accused. "Or have me surrounded by at least ten of the Guard."

"Yes," he said truthfully. "Because if something happens to you, my queen, I don't think we would survive."

"Then I must teach our people how to survive," she said. "Because they can't keep giving up every time something happens to their king or queen."

"Sir Topher's on his way," he said, and the sadness in her eyes stopped him from saying any more.

Later, when the sun began to disappear and the wind felt fierce on their skin, Sir Topher sat on the hill alongside the queen, watching the workers below.

"Next summer we will have a surplus of grain and barley and oats, and all the kingdoms around us will be keen to import our produce," she said. "The ambassador has also managed to secure interest from the Belegonians for produce from the river, and the export from the mines will please those kingdoms who no longer want to deal with the Sorelians for tin. And we have enough in the treasury to keep our people from starving until then. Within two years, Sir Topher, we will be on the road to some kind of prosperity."

"And perhaps at war," he said soberly.

"I walked through the meadow in the village of Gadros," she continued as if he had not spoken, "and I imagined that it could look like the one near the crossroads where I took ill with the priest-king. So I'm going to plant hollyhocks and wild strawberries and daffodils and daises and calendula and columbine." Despite her words, she was weeping and he forgot all protocol and placed his arm around her.

"I've crossed this kingdom many times over the last few weeks, Sir Topher," she whispered through her tears. "So many people. So many sad stories. To be responsible for so many souls. How did my father do it?"

"With the same expression on his face each day as you have now, my queen. With fear and with hope."

She wiped away her tears.

"Isaboe," he said gently. "These people do not need another

peasant to help plow their fields. They want their queen. They want her in the palace, leading them."

"And a king?" she sniffed.

"I believe you have already chosen a king," he said quietly.

She rolled her eyes. "When I'm with the Monts, he hides himself in the Rock Village, when I'm in the Rock Village, he's in the Flatlands, and when I return to the palace, he'll hide himself with the Monts. I've become accustomed to passing him by."

"While he's been . . . traveling around the kingdom, he has written the constitution of the new Lumatere, which he wants you to look over, and I think he has convinced the king of Sarnak to try those who were responsible for the massacre of our people."

"In the Sarnak royal court or here?"

"Negotiations are taking place as we speak. Last correspondence I received from Finnikin had the king of Sarnak inviting us to the palace. We will be advising you not to attend, of course. Not until we know it is perfectly safe. Finnikin is also against the visit from Osteria and he's right. It's too soon. When we allow visitors into Lumatere, we must look as if we are truly back on our feet."

She sighed and stood, looking over the village where some of the guards were helping to thatch cottage roofs.

"When he returns, Isaboe, he will have made the most important decision, not only of his life but for this kingdom. You must have patience."

"Ask me to also maintain my pride, because it slowly dwindles away each day that he does not come to see me."

"You know how he feels about you, Isaboe."

"I know nothing," she said sadly. "He gives me nothing and I cannot rule with nothing. But I know what my people want. For me to have a king. So a king I will give them, even if he's not my first choice."

Trevanion waited for them on the road to the palace with several of the Guard and the horses. "Will you mount the horse, my queen?" he asked as she approached, holding the reins out to her.

"I'd prefer to walk," she said quietly. It was the road the impostor king and his men had used to take the women and girls of Lumatere to the palace. The road where they used to hang the children of men who chose to rebel.

"It would be easier for us if you rode, my queen," Sir Topher suggested.

She stopped for a moment, shame on her face as she looked up at both men. "If the truth be told . . . I don't think I'm ready to return . . . to my home."

Trevanion was silent, remembering the first time he had re-entered the palace. It was still full of memories of the horror he had witnessed that terrible night all those years ago.

"We have prepared the eastern wing for you, Isaboe," Sir Topher said gently. "It has not been touched for the last five decades."

She nodded, relief in her expression. "If I promise to return on the next day of rest, then we can invite the people to celebrate with me. It could be a celebration of our journey back to some kind of normality." Her eyes held a plea.

"That is five days from now," Sir Topher said reluctantly.

"The priestess of Lagrami has moved her novices back to their original cloister and is keen to have me visit. The cloister is not far from the palace, so it may be the perfect place to stay until then. I can visit the people of the palace village. They were once my neighbors, and they treated my sisters and brother and me as if we belonged to them." She fought to hold back her tears.

Sir Topher caught Trevanion's eye and nodded. "I will ride ahead to the cloister and have Lady Milla organize the festivities to celebrate your return to the palace."

As they traveled on, Trevanion politely repeated his request for her to mount the horse.

"I hear you found Froi," she said, politely ignoring it. "Keep an eye on him, Captain Trevanion. Let him play peasant farmer, but remind him he belongs to the queen."

"He doesn't think he's worthy."

She stopped for a moment. "Froi? Humble?"

A hint of a smile touched Trevanion's lips. "For a moment or two."

"When I choose to call him back, he will have no right to refuse."

"Yet you haven't exercised the same right to call Finnikin back."

She stopped again. "You speak out of place, Captain, and too much conversation today has revolved around your absent son."

He nodded. "And for that I apologize."

"For what part are you apologizing?" she asked.

"For what part would you like me to apologize?"

She held his gaze, and he remembered this steadfast look of hers from the time in the prison mines. He sighed, gazing beyond her to where the Flatlands were beginning to look rich and dark, the soil in perfectly aligned mounds.

"I belong to queen and country first," he said after a while, "but I am his father, Isaboe. You will have to pardon me on this occasion for speaking bluntly, but I will always want to tear out the heart of anyone who causes him pain, and whether you're the queen or Evanjalin, you have that power. You always have. For feeling that way, I apologize."

"And you think I'd use such power?"

He didn't answer, and she continued to walk.

"When the time comes to tear out the heart of anyone who causes him pain, Captain Trevanion, know this," she said fiercely.

"I will fight you to be first in line."

After a moment, he smiled. "Will you mount the horse, my queen?"

"No," she replied, also with a smile.

They entered the village of Sennington, and the villagers ran toward the road to greet her.

"Is Lady Beatriss home, Tarah?" she asked one of the peasant women, whose cheeks flushed with pleasure at the queen using her name.

"Should be soon, my queen. She's down by the river with Vestie."

The queen smiled her thanks and took the small gifts made for her by the children. "Could you locate Lady Beatriss, Captain Trevanion?" she asked without looking up from the villagers. "I would like to rest here before I present myself to the priestess."

Trevanion knew exactly where to find Beatriss. He had watched her disappear behind the manor house and walk down to the river many times. Part of him wanted to keep his distance and call out rather than join her by that tree, but the yearning inside him was too strong and he found himself walking toward her. Yet he could not go all the way. He knew what lay before him. A grave. With more buried than their dead baby. Like most days, Beatriss was with the child, and he wondered at her ability to adore a reminder of the times her body had been savaged by the impostor and his men.

"The queen is waiting to see you, Lady Beatriss," he said from his position on the slope.

She nodded, as if it was the most natural thing for him to be there, and then walked toward him. "She is returning to the palace?" she asked.

"Yes."

The child looked at him from where she stood by the grave, and he returned her stare, this strange miniature Beatriss. But then she went back to busying herself with her seeds.

"Your silence makes things difficult, Trevanion," Beatriss said quietly. "It would be wrong to pretend we have nothing to say, so I will be the one to speak. I cannot go back to being who I was, or desire what I once felt. The thought of a man touching me, any man . . ." She swallowed, unable to finish, and he nodded, choking back something inside of him that ached to be let loose. He turned to walk away, feeling as if his insides were splintering.

Her voice stopped him. "I woke with your name on my lips every morning. Like a prayer of hope. For now, that's all I can offer."

He hesitated, remembering something Finnikin had said to him on their journey. That somehow, even in the worst of times, the tiniest fragments of good survive. It was the grip in which one held those fragments that counted.

"Then for now, my Lady Beatriss," he said, "what you have to offer is more than enough for me. I'll wait."

She sighed and shook her head. "How long will you wait, Trevanion? A man like you?"

"A man like me will wait for as long as it takes."

They stood and watched the child sprinkle seeds around the grave, humming a sweet tune to herself. When she dropped the little cup that held the seeds, Trevanion walked over to where she stood by the headstone and read the words inscribed upon it: *Evanjalin. Beloved child of Trevanion and Beatriss.*

He bent to pick up the cup, placing it into the child's hand. On the earth beside the grave was a stray seed. As he laid it on the rich mound of dirt, he felt tiny fingers press into his.

"Like this," Vestie said, patting his hand. "So the seed can take."

## cHApteR 30

That night, Finnikin of the Rock dreamed he was to sacrifice the rest of his life for the royal house of Lumatere.

The message came to him in a dream from Balthazar and his sisters as he slept in the cottage of the queen's *yata* in the mountains. Yata did not seem surprised the next morning. "They visit me often, my babies do," she said, pressing a kiss to his temple. "It's time for you to go home, Finnikin. You do not belong in these mountains. You have other places to be."

Five days past, he had returned from Sarnak and somehow found himself traveling to the Monts. He stayed, completing the census and the trade agreements with several of their neighboring kingdoms. As he left Yata's home that morning, he knew that a part of his life was complete and that whatever path he chose, he would experience the ache of unfulfilled dreams. For a moment he allowed himself to feel regret at the thought of never building a cottage by the river with Trevanion. Or living the life of a simple farmer connected to the earth. Or traveling his kingdom, satisfying the nomad he had become. To be Finnikin of the Rock and the Monts and the River and the Flatlands and the Forest. To be none of those at all.

Yet he also knew that to lose the queen to another man would be a slow torture every day for the rest of his life.

Lucian walked with him down the mountain. "I will meet with her this evening," Lucian told him, "when we celebrate her return to the palace."

Finnikin did not respond.

"She said it's cruel that everyone she loves is together while she is miserably alone. I could have told her you were turning into a miserable bastard yourself, but instead I told her how much time you've spent working on the archives, flirting with your scribe. Your sweet and passive scribe who lets you be in charge."

Finnikin shook his head, amused in spite of himself.

"I think she was jealous, you know," Lucian continued, waving to a family of Monts who had settled further down the mountain. "Said she would have me beheaded if I said another word."

"We don't behead people in Lumatere," Finnikin said dryly.

"Ah, Finnikin, in Lumatere we do whatever our queen wants."

At the base of the mountain, Lucian embraced him and handed him a package. "Yata wants you to give this to Lady Beatriss of the Flatlands. Can you find time to pass by today before the celebrations?"

*Celebrations indeed,* Finnikin thought bitterly. It would be a long time before the kingdom remembered how to celebrate.

Finnikin knocked on the front door of the manor house in Sennington, the package under his arm. When there was no response, he entered the house and walked toward the kitchen.

"Finnikin?" he heard Lady Beatriss call, her tone warm and welcoming. He reached the doorway but stopped when he saw Tesadora standing by the stove, her arms folded, an expression of disapproval and hostility on her face. Lady Abian sat with Lady Beatriss at the table.

"I'm sorry," he muttered, cursing himself for his bad timing. "But Yata of the Monts requested that I pass by this way to give you a package." He placed it on the table as the three women stared at him.

"Stay, Finnikin," Lady Beatriss said. "Drink tea with us. You must be exhausted after your travels, and you'll need to rest before tonight."

"Your appearance is a disgrace," Tesadora said sharply.

He touched his hair self-consciously. It resembled tufts of lamb's wool. Yata had managed to braid it, although she had found it difficult to separate the knotted strands. The color had dulled to a murky shade.

"I will have it taken care of tomorrow," he conceded.

"Sit," Tesadora said firmly. "You are fortunate that I have time today."

*Fortunate indeed,* he thought. He reluctantly sat, and Lady Beatriss handed Tesadora a cloth to place around his neck.

Tesadora tugged at his hair as she cut at it with a knife. It was easy to hate her. There was no gentleness in her hands, no softness in her eyes, despite the beauty of her face. He watched the thick clumps of his hair carpet the floor. Already he felt naked with half of it gone. As he went to feel the bristles of his hair, Tesadora slapped his hand away.

He stared at the package on the table and then at Lady Beatriss. He realized too late that she had expressed no interest in it. She looked at him solemnly.

"What is it that you fear, Little Finch?" she asked gently.

"I fear that the queen accuses me of running the kingdom from my rock village, yet she runs it from the hearts of you women, along with her *yata*," he said, anger in his voice. "Is this where you planned the poisoning of the impostor king?"

There was silence.

"No," Lady Abian said finally. "But if such a thing were to be spoken about, Finnikin, it would have been in my parlor. Next to the room where my three sons play. Oh, to think of a world where I would have to give them up to a futile war."

"Why is it that you keep our queen waiting?" Tesadora demanded.

Finnikin longed to leave, but Tesadora had the knife against his scalp.

"I believe I know what it is, Finnikin," Lady Beatriss said. "To be king would mean your father would one day lie prostrate at your feet."

Tesadora held him down by his remaining hair as he tried to leap to his feet. "I will never allow my father to lie prostrate at my feet!"

She kept a firm hold on his hair. "Then you are not the man for our queen. So let her go, Finnikin. Go to her now and tell her that she must choose a king. When she hears it from you, she will know there is no future between you. She will not listen to anyone else. The prince of Osteria will have no problem with your father lying prostrate at his feet and in time she will find happiness with him. I hear he's a strapping boy."

Finnikin snorted.

"Nothing will make Lumaterans happier than to know our beloved queen is being taken care of by one who loves her," she continued, pulling viciously at his hair. "Waking each day in the arms of a man who will keep her marriage bed warm and fertile."

He realized he did not hate Tesadora. He despised her. "What would a novice of Sagrami know about a bed being kept warm and fertile, Tesadora?" he sneered. "It seems to me that you hate all men."

"Never presume to know my needs or who warms my bed! And if you believe it is men I hate, you are wrong. I despise those who use force and greed as a means of control. Unfortunately for your gender, such traits are found more often in the hearts of men than women. But place me in a room with those women who aligned themselves with the bastard king and I promise there will be a bloodbath I would relish soaking in." She grabbed him by the chin. "What is it about you that stirs the blood of the strongest in our land? For she is the strongest, make no doubt of that."

"Do not underestimate her vulnerabilities," Finnikin said, fuming. "I've seen them. They can destroy her."

"Do you see my hair?" Tesadora asked, tugging at the white strands. "It is this color because I walked some of those sleeps to protect Vestie from the horror of what she would see. This is what the darkness and the terror of the human soul did to me. But the queen? It is not her youth that keeps her hair from going white at such images of horror, Finnikin. It is her strength."

He was silent for a moment. "Then why was she almost lost to me . . . to us," he corrected himself, "when we entered the kingdom?"

"Because your grief at what you saw in those moments was too much for her to bear. Your pain made her weak. Her pain made you strong. Light and dark. Dark and light." Her ice-blue eyes stared into him. "I wonder what it was that my mother saw in you that time in the forest. To look at a boy of eight and see such strength in his character. Enough strength for our beloved girl who would one day rule. Do you remember what Seranonna said to you? Because I remember clearly what she told me that very night when I was no more than your age now."

"Her blood will be shed for you to be king," he said quietly.

"No." Tesadora shook her head. "For you to be *her* king. There's more than one way for you to shed her blood, fool!"

The women stared at him, and he felt his face redden. Lady Beatriss smiled and it embarrassed him even more.

"It's why my mother cursed you with Isaboe's memories as you entered our kingdom. Not as a punishment. *'His pain shall never cease.'* How can it, Finnikin, when your empathy for her is so strong? It's so our beloved will never feel alone. Have you not seen her in those moments, Finnikin? When she disappears inside herself and almost lets the darkness consume her. I saw it in the cloister when she was with us. It chilled me to the bone. Your power lies in never allowing her to get lost in those voices."

He remembered a morning the week before, when he was passing the royal entourage on one of their visits to the River people. He watched her from a distance, the distance he had carved out between them since he had discovered her true identity. For one moment, she seemed removed from what was taking place around her. She stood completely still, her gaze fixed on a distant point. She had gone inside herself, as she'd done many times on their journey back to Lumatere. And now he knew what it was that weighed her body down. The agony of those voices he heard as they entered the main gate. The ones she had lived with for years. So he whistled from where he stood and her body stiffened with awareness and slowly she turned in his direction. He held her gaze, knowing her moment of despair had already passed.

And there it was, he thought, as he looked at the women in Beatriss's kitchen. The memory of a look that spoke to him of power. His. A look that made him want to kneel at the feet of his queen and worship her.

Because it made him feel like a king.

"I must go," he said huskily.

"Not in those clothes," Lady Abian said, unwrapping Yata's package.

He walked toward the palace, wearing perfectly cut trousers, a crisp white shirt, and a soft leather cape, his hair cropped to his crown. Many Lumaterans traveled with him, talking quietly, shyly greeting strangers whose paths they crossed on their way to the celebration. He heard them speak of their weariness, but stronger was the desire to be there for their beloved Isaboe, so she could feel the presence of a mother who loved and a father who doted and sisters who cared and a brother who teased. No one was more an orphan to the land than their queen.

He hurried past the priest-king's home, where the holy man sat with Froi, greeting those who were traveling to the palace.

"Finnikin?" the priest-king called out.

"I can't stop, blessed Barakah. Can we speak later?" He could see turrets in the near distance, and his pulse quickened.

"Do not approach her unless you have something worthwhile to say," the priest-king advised.

Finnikin returned to where the priest-king sat, and knelt before him. "And if you hear word that I have said something worthwhile, blessed Barakah, will you sing the Song of Lumatere at first light?" he asked.

The holy man broke into a grin. "On my oath to the goddess complete."

Finnikin nodded and sprang back to his feet.

"Finnikin?" Froi said.

"Yes, Froi."

"You must give her somefing." The boy's eyes were bright.

"If you offer the ruby ring, you die, my friend."

Froi laughed and shook his head. "Not offering the ruby ring to no one."

"Then I have nothing to give but myself."

He reached the outer edge of town where the bridge marked the end of the Flatlands and the beginning of the palace village. Trevanion was there with some of his men, watching one of the lads training. Finnikin knew that tonight the area around the palace and the queen would be heavily guarded, three circles of guards who would slow him down.

He was suddenly conscious of his appearance. He mumbled a greeting to his father, then called out over his shoulder, "I'll come by later." He crossed the bridge where the river flowed at great speed, as if its life force had not been extinguished for ten long years.

"Finnikin?" he heard his father say. Just his name. But the emotion in that one word made him turn and walk back to where Trevanion stood. He took his father's face in both his hands and kissed him. Like a blessing.

"Your mother walks that path with you," Trevanion said. "With such pride that as I speak . . . it fills my senses with things I can't put into words. Go," he added gruffly, "or you'll have my Guard thinking I'm soft."

Finnikin broke into a run through the village square, weaving his way among the Lumaterans before him. As the path leading up to the palace became steeper, he could see over the roofs of the cottages on either side, all the way to the land where the Rock Village stood to the west and the mountains to the north.

At least ten guards were stationed at the portcullis of the palace, and Finnikin's arrival was met with a chorus of jeers and laughter. He expected nothing less from his father's men. Kisses were blown his way, accompanied by mock whistles of appreciation. He thanked the gods that Aldron was not among them, for his ridicule would have been the loudest. There were taunts and high-pitched declarations of love as Moss grabbed Finnikin, rubbing his knuckles over Finnikin's short berry-colored hair.

In the palace grounds Finnikin heard some of the villagers call out his name in greeting, while others whispered it with feverish excitement. The courtyard on the northwest corner was set up with trestle tables, and palace staff placed huge wooden casks of wine alongside platters of roast peacocks, wood pigeons, and rabbits. Another table was covered with pastries and sweet breads. In the corner by the rosebushes, minstrels played their tunes. The beat of the drum and the twang of the lute caused those around Finnikin to begin to sway, as if their bodies had not forgotten the beauty of music.

"Finnikin?" he heard Sir Topher call out from above. He looked up to where his mentor was standing on the balconette of the first floor, adjusting the cuffs on his sleeve.

"Sir Topher, I need to do something. I promise we'll speak later this night."

Finnikin felt his anxiety take over, his desperation to get to where he knew she stood beyond the cluster of people in the courtyard. He jumped onto one of the empty trestle tables and leaped up to the latticework of the balconette. From up high he could see her in the middle of the courtyard, elevated on a makeshift platform and surrounded by Lady Celie and the young novices of both Lagrami and Sagrami. The Guard formed a circle around them, and he could see Perri allowing people to pay their respects one or two at a time. There was gaiety in the air. She was a giggler, the queen was. He remembered that about Isaboe as a child. Her giggles back then would turn into snorts and then laughter. He saw traces of it in these girls, their eyes closed, their hands covering their mouths as they laughed at what she had said. There was no restraint in their mirth, despite the clucking of the overprotective hens of the royal court, who seemed to be battling the Guard to take control of the girls. He remembered what Beatriss had said to him one afternoon. "What was it about those beloved, spirited princesses?" she had asked, tears in her eyes. "I will miss them for the rest of my life. You know how it is with Isaboe, Finnikin? The way she intoxicates you with her hope and her capacity to love."

From his vantage point he could only stare. At the one who intoxicated him. There was a suppleness to her now that showed good health, curves that were lovingly outlined by the ivory silk dress she wore, its wide sleeves pinned to her side. In her thick dark curls she wore flower buds, and on her head was her mother's crown, sparkling with rubies.

She was gracious in her attention to her people. He could tell by the gestures of those who got close that they were complimenting her, and she was accepting the compliments with a poise and charm that had them beaming. She leaned forward to hear their stories, gently asking her guard, Aldron, to move back when he held up a hand of restraint to one who dared to step too close. Beatriss's child was clinging to her sleeve, jumping up for attention. He watched the way the queen gathered the child to her, letting Vestie cling to her waist as she swung the girl from side to side.

"Do not allow her to lead the negotiations, Finnikin. You know how stubborn she is."

Finnikin looked at the queen's First Man with irritation. "This is a private matter, Sir Topher," he said, perspiring from the effort it took to grip the lattice.

Sir Topher laughed, shaking his head. "Privacy? Finnikin, climb down that trellis, and this moment between you and me will be the last private moment you will ever experience."

But Finnikin no longer cared. Amid shouts of reprimand from the palace staff, he jumped onto the trestle table and then to the ground.

*His seed will issue kings, but he will never reign.*

For she would be Queen of Lumatere.

But he would be king to her.

He saw Lucian as he approached, standing with two of the Mont lads and Sefton, leaning against the northern wall and watching the throng before them.

"They are beautiful," Sefton said with a sigh. "But very haughty."

"What are the others doing?" one asked, trying to catch a glimpse of the platform through the crowd.

"Preening," Sefton said. "Lucy, the stonemason's daughter, won't even look my way these days, and we were neighbors as children."

"Patience," Finnikin said. "And it's not haughtiness or preening. They have suffered greatly, and if any of you hurt them in any way, you will have me to reckon with."

"I have no idea what Lady Celie's problem is," Lucian muttered. "We used to play together as children, and the other day I heard her refer to me with disdain as 'the Mont cousin.'"

Finnikin stared at him. "Lucian, you sat on her head when we were children. And wouldn't move until Balthazar counted to one hundred."

Lucian shrugged arrogantly. "A Mont girl would never carry such a grudge." He took in Finnikin's appearance, his dark eyes growing serious. "Wish our boy luck, lads," he said. "When the time is right, I will stand by your side to display her kin's support and approval. It's the Mont way, Cousin."

Finnikin clasped Lucian's hand tightly. Then he turned to make his way to the queen. As he pushed past the crowds of people, he heard Balthazar's chuckles and Isaboe's giggles and Lucian's snorts. He felt the love of his mother, who had died giving life to him, and took heart in the strength his father had shown during his darkest moments in the mines of Sorel. He heard the voices that had drowned his mind as he entered the kingdom, and within all the cries of anguish, he heard the songs of hope. He sensed the first babe of Beatriss and Trevanion and the presence of Vestie, the child who had walked with the queen and whose arm bore the answer to the question, "Is hope coming?" His name.

When he reached the circle of guards, Perri gestured for him to enter, but then grabbed him by the back of his cloak.

"I must confess that I dropped you on your head once or twice as a babe," Perri said, "and if you walk out of the palace grounds tonight without a title, I'll do it again."

Finnikin shrugged free. "My father will hear about this."

Perri chuckled and swiped him affectionately across the back of the head before propelling him toward the platform.

She saw him instantly, surprise on her face at his appearance. They faced each other in silence.

"My queen."

"Finnikin."

Aldron stood between them, his expression impassive. Lady Celie and the novices looked on solemnly. The crowd behind pushed forward, and he found himself shoulder to shoulder with the young guard.

"I can take over from here, Aldron," Finnikin said.

"Not your decision, Finnikin," Aldron said arrogantly. "Nor is it the queen's. I take my orders from Trevanion or Perri."

Isaboe stared at Finnikin, waiting. But the smirking Aldron stood in the way, and anger welled up inside of Finnikin. Everything he wanted to say was stuck at the back of his throat. "If I agree to become king," he began, "you . . ."

She gasped with fury. "*If* you become king, I would prefer that you see it as something you want, rather than something you have to *agree* to."

He took a moment to regain his composure. He heard the hiss of whispering around him. "*Finnikin of the Rock is speaking to the queen.*"

"If I become king," he began again, "will you promise me no more impromptu visits throughout the kingdom until the borders are secure?"

"If you become king, perhaps I will invite you along on one of my impromptu visits," she said airily, turning toward the novices, who looked at him as only novices trained by Tesadora could.

He shoved past Aldron and took hold of her arm to swing her back to face him. The music had begun to play again, and he could hardly hear himself. "Your security is not a laughing matter, Isaboe!"

"Do you see me laughing, Finnikin?"

Aldron yanked him away and the circle of girls closed around her, but he pushed through as gently as he could. "Excuse me," he said politely to Lady Celie before moving her aside. "If I become king, do I have to ask your guards and your ladies permission each time I want to touch you in my marriage bed?"

Her eyes blazed. "When you become my king, Finnikin, you can touch me whenever you want. Wherever you want."

He had the satisfaction of watching Aldron gulp. The novices gasped. Lady Celie giggled behind her hand.

He drew as close to Isaboe as he could, but still Aldron refused to move, and he could sense every pair of eyes in the kingdom watching them. "If I become king, will you sometimes humor me and allow me to win?"

"Isn't it enough that you have won me if you become king?"

A hint of a smile appeared on his lips.

"If you become king," she said, pushing Aldron's head to the side so she could have a better view of Finnikin, "you will work on the archives without the help of a sweet Mont girl as your scribe."

Finnikin's smile broadened. "If I become king, I will continue my work on the archives *with* my scribe, who happens to be Lucian's great-aunt, on his mother's side. Lots of hair on her chin. Looks like Trevanion in those days after the mines."

She bit back her own smile as he shoved Aldron's head out of the way for a better view of her. The guard growled. "If I become king, when the prince of Osteria comes visiting, I will be the one to meet with him," he said firmly.

"Pity. I hear he's a strapping boy."

"Strapping boys are overrated. Sometime there's nothing up here," he said, pointing to Aldron's head.

"And sometimes there's too much up there," she replied.

"If I become king, we declare war on Charyn," he said soberly.

"Without involving Belegonia."

He nodded. Suddenly he seemed to have more space. The girls had stepped back, but not Aldron. He reached over the guard's shoulder. "This I like," he said, touching her hair.

"I knew myself better without it," she said honestly. "I miss yours. It made you look softer. Kinder."

"Soft and kind will happen when you get rid of this between us," he said, shoving Aldron, "and allow me to guard you. Do you think you should warn him that I'm going to kiss you?"

He loved the flush that appeared on her face, and there was an intake of breath from the girls.

"Aldron," she said, clearing her throat, "if he agrees to become king, I'm going to let him kiss me. Please don't stop him."

Aldron thought for a moment and sighed, holding up his hand. "Wait there and do not move," he ordered Finnikin, before calling out to one of the other guards who stood on the platform. "Ask Perri if he's allowed to touch her if he's agreed to be king."

Suddenly a great cheer erupted from the crowd around them, and then another and another as the news spread across the court-yard. The novices formed a circle around Isaboe and Finnikin to keep everyone out, standing with their backs to the couple. For a brief moment they were in their own private cocoon.

"This hand says you spend the rest of your life with me," he said, holding out his left hand, "and this one says I spend the rest of my life with you. Choose."

She bit her lip, tears welling in her eyes. She took both his hands in hers and he shuddered. "I will die protecting you," he said.

There was a look of dismay on her face. "Just like a man of this kingdom, Finnikin. Talking of death, yours or mine, is not a good way to begin a—"

She gave a small gasp when he leaned forward, his lips an inch away from hers. "I will die for you," he whispered.

She cupped his face with her hands. "But promise you'll live for me first, my love. Because nothing we are about to do is going to be easy and I need you by my side."

Lady Celie cleared her throat. "Hurry up and kiss her, Finnikin. The Mont cousin is coming this way with alarming speed."

"Then turn the other way, Lady Celie," Finnikin murmured before placing an arm around the queen's waist and lifting her to him, his mouth capturing hers.

Hours later, when everyone seemed to have gone home except for Trevanion and the Guard, Finnikin and Lucian sat on the roof of one of the palace cottages with Isaboe sleeping between them. They spoke of the past. And of Balthazar. About the ten years in exile. About their fathers, and the mothers they missed.

About the queen.

Finnikin heard a cry in the distance as a hint of light began to appear. He leaned down to whisper into her ear. "Wake up, Isaboe."

He helped her to her feet and wrapped his arms around her, his cloak engulfing them both. They watched the light crawl across the kingdom, illuminating their land piece by piece. Its mountain and rock, its river and flatlands, its forest, its palace. She placed his hand against the beat of her heart and he felt its steady pace.

"Listen," he whispered.

And then they heard the first words of the priest-king's song traveling across the kingdom, and they saw flickers of light appear across the landscape of their world.

"My king?"

"Yes, my queen?"

"Take me home."

# acknowLeDGments

Thanks to Laura Harris, Tegan Morrison, Christine Alesich, Marina Messiha, Clair Honeywill, Anyez Lindop, Kristin Gill, and everyone else at Penguin who has kept me monogamous for sixteen years.

Much gratitude to Elizabeth Butterfield, Anna Musarra, and Maria Boyd for letting me speak this story out loud before I wrote a single word.

For those who plowed through early drafts and still made me feel as if I had written something worthwhile: my mum, Adelina Marchetta; Jenny Barry, Patricia Cotter, Philippa Gibson, Sophie Hamley, Siobhan Hannan, Jill Grinberg, Brenda Souter, Patrick Devery, Adolfo Cruzado, Maxim Younger, Toby Younger, Sarah Darmody, Barbara Barclay, Edward Hawkins, Deborah Noyes Wayshak, and Nikki Anderson.

Thanks to Kyle Rowling and Patricia Cotter of the Sydney Stage Combat School for your lesson in medieval sword fighting techniques and dagger throwing.

And to my dad, Antonino, and the gorgeous Luca and Daniel Donovan, who make me feel like a goddess.